# Astrocity
# Sagan

(Book III in the Nelta Series)

**J.P. Osterman**

# Astrocity Sagan

## Copyright © 2014 J.P. Osterman

All rights reserved.

This book is a work of fiction. Names, characters, places and incidents are either the product of the author's imagination or are used fictitiously and any resemblance to actual persons, living or dead, business establishments, events, or locales is entirely coincidental.

**CreateSpace, Charleston SC**

Published by J.P. Osterman.com

ISBN-10: 0692326243
ISBN-13: 978-0-692-32624-4
First Edition
Date of Publication: November 2014
Printed in the United States of America

Cover Photo: © Luca Oleastri | Dreamstime.com

**Astrocity Sagan**

*His Universe is Marvelous*

# J.P. Osterman

## ACKNOWLEDGMENTS

I thank Drew, and Luca Oleastri, Bologna, Italy, creator of many 'Fantastic Fiction' works of art for the cover.

# Astrocity Sagan

## Chapter 1 – Spacefolding To Nelta

Monday, January 18, 2168, Space-Fold Time Onboard *Sagan*

January 18, 3070, Real Time on Earth

Today is almost the hundredth anniversary of our launch from Earth, and while people are packing up and celebrating, I'm getting ready for work. But it's my *last* day of work on our giant spaceship, actually an astrocity—*Sagan*—that's been spacefolding to Nelta. It's been home, to all 100,000 of us who can't *wait* to step on solid ground! But not everyone is sure they want to stay and settle among the Neltans. Some people are homesick and want to return to Earth. *If* returning is even possible!

It'll be up to the Neltans. They're millions of years more advanced than us but are currently in subterranean stasis chambers, waiting for our help. By now, their powerful Matter Stream *should* have healed Nelta and their M84 solar system. We'll find out soon. We're scheduled to arrive there in six weeks.

Our first task will be to revive Ambassador Shaesar, who in

turn will resuscitate the rest of the population using a special mix of our DNA they desperately need. That's *The Pact* we signed: Our DNA in exchange for a sample of their Matter Stream to restore our depleted ozone. If they hadn't come to *our* rescue, humanity would have experienced an extinction-level event and we'd all be dead. But there's another bad situation on Earth.

Prior to our launch, a directed energy explosion that ended the War on Terror began splitting the Moon. We need a *big* fix, and we can't contact home. Making matters worse, many of us are wondering: Can humans *really* live and thrive among those technological geniuses? Even after a hundred years of using their technology, we can't *begin* to fathom the ways they've mastered the forces in the universe. And virtual renderings of the planet and their species are just participation games! We *should* have answers to those questions soon.

# Astrocity Sagan

## Chapter 2 - Hobby

Dr. Elisa Holton took out several old digital cameras her parents left behind after they died during the terrorist attacks on June 10, 2057. Their stored images are all she has left of her parents, which she uploaded to her personal *matrix grid* so she can call on them whenever she wants to hear their voices, see their faces, or just ask for a little advice. Since then, the cameras have become a serious hobby. Many of them were broken, which has provided her with hours of fixing, updating, and learning how to work with antiquated 21st century Photoshop. In addition, she's been adding to her collection, and has thirty-five of them in all, one manufactured way back in 2013!

Clicking on one of her favorites, the 2060 iPad Concave, she began dictating: "I think it's about time I document what's happening on our astrocity and our last days before arriving at Nelta. I've been narrating events to my avatar, as she stands next to me, and directing her to pay close attention to the strange occurrences popping up around *Sagan*. They're scaring and confusing people! I wanna know what's going on, and I have the way and means to find out."

"That's me! She calls me Twin!" her avatar said into the camera.

Motioning for Twin to step back, she called on a few of the mysterious phenomena to render at the center of her room. "One is what I would call a Jekyll apparition and the other a hulking demon. Both appeared suddenly in front of a few residents, frightening 'em half to death. Then just as fast, the creatures disappeared into the walls, slurped right into them! The victims barely had time to capture photos of their backs."

Twin and the two images were appearing in *standard* holographic format, human-size, at the center of her studio Living Cube. Her LC is on the small side, but she once said, "A woman's home is her castle, and mine *is*, in a *manor* of speaking." A *medium* rendering fills the center of a room, and a *large* rendering revs up all the wall and ceiling hardware, changing an entire room into a virtual-reality zone—a computer-integrated experience with audiovisuals, multi-media exchanges, and even smells.

Terra IV's quantum-computing matrix is processing them all. Everyone calls the system, Terra, or the matrix.

Into the camera, she whispered, "As you can see, these bizarre creatures are beyond anyone's ability to examine them in detail from what victims have managed to stream to the crew. I want to start tracking them down myself, encounter them, and get proof." She held up two of her old-fashioned devices. "I don't trust what I'm receiving into my personal grid from the matrix."

Through her own grid connection, she can download, upload, and stream from her wrist device, neck processor, and Twin. If she desires, she can make any person, place, or object into a rendering, and then make the rendering available for full viewing, limited viewing, or complete participation. Terra is responsible for editing everything previously deemed by the residents as criminal, and there is also restricted access.

"*Humph!*" Twin appeared offended and her folded arms.

# Astrocity Sagan

Elisa can alter Twin into any image; however, she prefers keeping her in her *standard* form—a white-coat lab doctor, a reflection of herself, although she frequently alters Twin's clothes and hairstyles. All personal grids are voice interactive, and residents can Photoshop avatars and virtual worlds while they walk and run. Life can be like living in a graphic game, thanks to Terra who even sustains the environment. Terra is a real AI matrix that evolved to interpret human behavior and language, and then respond within programmed moral and ethical parameters. The population refers to Terra and her matrix as "her," and "she;" and because of Privacy Laws and individual buffers, we can control what she hears.

She ordered Twin, "Take me off full Matrix-mode please."

Now she can trust her avatar Twin with her secrets while trying to capture the creatures that are suddenly stalking people. Elisa treats Twin as a friend, confidant, sounding board, and social-media interface. Every resident has at least one avatar, another medium to connect with people socially, financially, and politically. Daily, people vote on pertinent issues. Prior to launching from Earth, humanity voted on and approved *Sagan* to function as an authentic democracy. Since leaving Earth, our democratic ways changed a bit. Our ten original governing leaders—The Regents—can't be voted out as they once could on any day on Earth.

Elisa turned off the malfunctioning iPad and turned on an old iPhone-10. Focusing its camera light, she motioned Twin to take a few steps back. She then began fidgeting with it to adjust the peripheral view. "Darn! I thought I fixed this thing with the part I scavenged from the old 3D printer." She took out another spare part; and as she worked to fix it, she remembered how the technology around her had evolved, and if *she'd* change one day after what had happened to her in the Press Room of the White House.

# J.P. Osterman

## Chapter 3 – Encantado's Lingering Effect

For the past hundred years, she's been living in the same unit but hasn't felt caged in because she can alter her surroundings into any rendering. She can invoke any scene from any of her personal collection, and the media material Terra absorbed, but only up to the point where we left Earth early and boarded *Sagan*. The Regents ordered a lock down, and blocked all image capturing thereafter to insure the 75,000 of us wouldn't panic and spend the voyage to Nelta fraught with worry over what might be happening to relatives, humanity, the Earth, and the moon. Ever since the lunar catastrophe, we've had our hearts set on securing Neltan technology, returning to Earth, and fixing the moon—an unheard of task without Neltan intervention! That's what we vowed to do before *Sagan* launched on November 29, 2068, eighteen months early from its scheduled June 2070 launch. All anyone on *Sagan* currently knows about Earth's status is that humanity is still in peril; and long ago, space-folding made it impossible to communicate with anyone on Earth during our voyage.

Elisa turned on her camera and continued her documentary:

# Astrocity Sagan

"We have six weeks before arriving in orbit and we have *no* idea of the planet's status. We haven't received the *Update* transmission the Neltan scientists set to transmit at about this time prior to going into their protective shelters from the destructive supernova. The Update is days late…and it's concerning every single Saganite!" Twin motioned to her in a puzzling expression. "Oh, Saganite. That's the name we decided to call ourselves after we launched from Earth's orbit on November 29, 2068 Real Time. Real Time, RT, is the current date and time on Earth which is different from Space-Fold Time, SFT, the measured date and time we spend gliding through wormholes to Nelta. When *Sagan* deactivates its fission-fusion turrets and resumes ripple-speed dynamics upon entering the Neltan solar system, time on Earth will have lapsed a thousand years, but we Saganites will have only aged one hundred years. That means a thousand years have passed on Earth, and therefore technically, everyone on board Sagan is as old as Methuselah, yet we look no different than the day we stepped on *Sagan*!"

"You don't look a thousand though," Twin whispered to her.

"Yeah, thanks to Regeneration. But that'll stop soon," she said, feeling a bit anxious. "Our first cultural change will be re-starting the normal human aging process. Everyone who decides to remain on Nelta will no longer be able to regenerate their bodies. For them…and that includes me…once *Sagan* begins orbiting Nelta, I'll start growing old. I just wonder how people are gonna handle that?"

Her camera light blinked. The battery almost exhausted. Twin touched the camera with her finger—her eyes illuminating green—as a jolt of power re-ignited the camera into action.

"Thanks," she told Twin, "and please do that again whenever you see this red light flashing." Twin nodded yes, and Elisa continued her recording. "According to our last communication with the Neltans on February 27, 2068, the day prior to the lunar tragedy, Ambassador Shaesar told us he would pre-program an Update to stream into *Sagan's* Navigation, when we passed a specific intergalactic location, which our astrocity just did. Shaesar also told us that after our special team would finally step on Neltan soil, a *Greeting* program will activate. We have one very detailed rendering of Nelta that has allowed us to virtually acclimate to the terrain. The place is a breezy tropical equatorial valley, and its lush verdant landscape is a safe harbor for various species of birds and wildlife. In the middle, a Welcome Archway is situated over one of the many subterranean stasis chamber caves and tunnels. Our landing site is called Tractum. The images we have depict a beautiful tropical terrain with pristine shorelines. It's definitely human habitable! A tropical paradise that can be compared to Oahu, only seventy times as big! That's how their architects even designed *Sagan.* Upon arriving there, our special landing team is scheduled to touchdown at the Welcome Archway where we will revive and shake hands with Ambassador Shaesar. Then they will present him with our special cargo of purified human DNA, followed by our assistance in reviving the rest of his people. That's the plan. It's *The Pact* we made with the Neltans on October 4, 2061 when Shaesar agreed to give us a sample of their Matter Stream to restore Earth's ozone in exchange for our DNA to rescue their species from extinction. Now, we're all wondering why we haven't heard a whisper from Nelta!

Could something have gone horribly *wrong* on Nelta during our thousand-year voyage? That's hard to believe! Shaesar and his people are a Kardashev Type-V civilization, billions of years more advanced than humanity. Prior to shielding themselves in stasis capsules from the onslaught of the supernova strike, they determined a 100% success rate not only in *Sagan's* intricate wormhole glide to their world, but also in their Matter Stream rejuvenating their solar system. They also helped humanity advance in consciousness and technology thousands of years—almost overnight. No one can fathom *any* of their intricate calculations failing.

Still, why haven't we heard the Update? We're only six weeks away from accomplishing our mission.

*Six weeks to Nelta!*

Every Saganite has become a clock watcher as the time ticks down the hours, minutes and seconds to our Arrival Time. On the regular digital clocks around the ship, half are now devoted to the countdown clock, now reading: 42 days, 3 hours, 39 minutes and 16 seconds, 17, 18…

Meantime, as we wait, *Sagan* continues spacefolding on its guided course via the Living Breath entity the Neltan Scientific Committee instilled inside our Navigation system. The entity's "spirit" presence is a good sign that everything quantum and technical is still progressing as planned, and that a presence beyond our awareness is alive, operating, and directing us to Nelta. So we still believe and hope."

Then, she remembered her past connection to the Living Breath. She was beginning to feel differently lately and felt compelled to explain what had happened to in the Press Room in case anything should happen to her during her hunt for creatures and she might need help. First, she had to check for a breach in her wall-and-ceiling hardware to make sure there were no eavesdropping eyes-and-ears. Panning her camera around her little apartment as its infrared detector revealed no intrusions, she continued in a whisper:

"I have a special 'charmed' connection to the Living Breath…at least I *believe* I do, although nothing real strange has happened to me since I interacted with the Neltan technology. I'm sure people have forgotten what happened to me when Daryl Coflin attacked the Press Room. I touched the Neltan nano-organic Encantado material on the quantum-communication transmission screen. The Encantado technology acted as an amplifier between Earth and Nelta. When the material touched my wrist, Neltan nano-machines transferred onto and into my skin." She turned and showed the camera her left arm and shoulder. "They multiplied rapidly and wrapped around my entire arm as they created a glowing living armband." She lifted up her sleeve, showing her camera her arm. "It looks okay…normal." She shivered, remembering how terrified she felt at the thought of possibly changing into something beyond recognition. Slowly, she touched her arm and moved her fingers over it…pale, normal, and silky smooth. She sighed in relief. "The effects of the armband are most likely dormant, and thank goodness invisible. All I know is that the armband evolved to the point where it entwined genetically with my DNA, but no one as of yet has been able to locate the residual effects in my body. They chalk it up the Heisenberg principle. The minute you try to observe anything quantum, it's changed. But my whole body and mind were affected by it!" She stopped, took a drink of cool water, and then continued. "Don't get me wrong. It was a positive thing. The armband helped save everybody. That's what scientists on *Sagan* said when they watched excerpts of what had happened to me while analyzing my blood and scanning my brain. Still, the Encantado entities in the armband—and now in me—helped us defeat one of Regent Thornton Manning's enemies."

She rubbed her arm and her face, looking to Twin to affirm her wellbeing. Twin showed her a quick result of a metabolic scan. Elisa was okay…no sign of anything foreign or poisonous bubbling up within her. She continued recording her experience:

"No one's brought up that occurrence for decades, and maybe there's a reason. We don't have the armband anymore. It unleashed off my arm when I said goodbye to a dying friend of mine, Maureen Strickler. We were the last people inside the tunnel leading out of the White House."

"Or perhaps a prototype of the armband might be on Level-9 at The Regents' Research and Development Center," Twin said, her holographic light shining brightly.

"Hmm," Elisa said, rubbing her left arm. "Could be." She felt puzzled, and thought about the terrifying entities appearing around the astrocity. If Twin was postulating the existence of an alien prototype, maybe The Regents are experimenting with a technology on their private Level-9. Could they be creating the entities? She had to turn her focus back to her recording. She didn't have much time before leaving for work. "I suppose Maureen is gone now, dead, *uh-um*," she paused, sniffling back tears until Twin suddenly showed her a rendering of Maureen. "I miss her, but when I gave her the armband, I told her I hoped she and some other scientists could develop special technology that might fix the moon. Maybe they did, maybe not…or maybe someone's managed to modify some *other* type of technology to fix the lunar breakup. We can't know until we arrive on Nelta, and then, hopefully, establish a communication link with scientists at the Decagon accelerator beyond Jupiter. Of course that assumes the accelerator is still there. Who knows what's been happening on Earth. Is Earth even there?!"

She sipped some water, took a few deep breathes, and then continued: "Well I'm running out of time and have to report to work in a little bit, so here's the rest. Getting back to what happened to me…Regent Thornton Manning had his specialists conduct all types of tests on me, but all anyone could detect was a shadowy glow in a section of my DNA, and a change in my lipoproteins. I sure hope those nano-Neltan things inside me don't begin an irreversible change in me of some type!"

Twin bent down and looked in her eye.

"See anything?"

She opened up a *standard* rendering of Elisa's body and initiated another scan. "Nothing."

"Don't link the scan with the Medical Facility though," Elisa whispered firmly. "I don't need anyone investigating me right now with all this packing up I'm doing, with today being my last official day at work."

"Okay," Twin said, "but I am showing your Body-Double vitals and organ stats as normal. That glow and protein interference are there but—"

"Well delete those stats!"

"I cannot—"

"Yes you can. I order you. Expunge the scan, now!" Elisa said.

After a pause, Twin's brown eyes flashed yellow. "All vitals and BDI stats interface immediately with the Medical Facility—"

"You're linked with the medical facility but I told you to separate from the matrix. Stop transmitting the scan!" She paused, fear exhaling in her breath. Doctors with Special Access clearances or the Regents' medical specialists could be gleaning the results. They could call her in for questioning, or order her to undergo more testing if they believed she might be a hazard. She didn't have time for that. "You *can* resolve the conflict, Twin, *please*? For me?" She gently touched Twin's holographic arm. "For old time's sake?"

Twin backed up. She had her finger to her lower lip and began pacing, looking like a bright translucent spirit walking over the floor. "Hmm."

"Think about it this way, what if you include it *only* in this documentary and with *this* camera?" Through another *hmm*, she said, "After I'm done taking a look around the astrocity with this ancient old memory chip, I'll just give it to you, and you can upstream all the data. Whataya think?"

After a pause, Twin stopped pacing and her eyes flashed green. "Done deal. That is what *you* usually say, Elisa Holton."

"Thanks, *whew*!" She plopped back down in her chair and adjusted the camera light to shine just a little over her head. "Now back to what I was saying...since I know what I'm telling you will stay between us until we disembark on Nelta, right?" Twin nodded yes. "*If* I'm different because of that Encantado armband, no one's been able to discover it. Besides, I feel fine. I've never even been sick since we launched! So most likely, people have forgotten about what happened to me and that Encantado technology." She felt a bit sentimental. "Yep, we sure had a special connection…and the feelings I had when we bonded were energizing and increased my IQ to 145!"

Activating a scroll down of all of Elisa's surveys, inventories, and IQ ratios, Twin said "I have the scores."

"Hey, that high score was one of the reasons Thornton Manning *personally* appointed me to my position—without voter approval—as Chief of a Regeneration Corridor when we boarded *Sagan*. He recognized me as being someone special." She felt suddenly filled with disappointment. "Yet, I haven't seen or heard from the guy since, but that doesn't mean he and the other Regents aren't secretly watching me, and everyone for that matter," she whispered. She opened a large packing box and took out bubble wrap.

Plastics are hard to acquire as they're not recyclable and also illegal due to their useless properties. *Sagan* is a Kardashev Type-III civilization, utilizing all the energy inside and outside its hull as the massive spaceship traverses through wormholes and amasses dark matter and dark energy from black hole event horizons. Only lately are some plastics being manufactured at the Recycling Center on Level-7, but only for packing special items, and only after signing for them.

She set her camera on the bar overlooking her little sink and continued: "Like me, the vast majority of people are packing up their belongings, and queuing up, as my British colleagues like to say, to schedule last-minute appointments at the Regeneration Corridors to undergo one last body Regeneration. The procedure is everyone's last-ditch effort to stay young for those who decide to stay on Nelta." Meanwhile, movers continue to fill the disembarkation platforms with personal possessions and scientific equipment in preparation for relocating to the planet." Then she had another thought that made her squirm.

She moved her chair closer to her camera so she could speak more secretively. "Here's another thing I've observed.

# J.P. Osterman

Whenever a wave of people voice their anxieties, concerns or complaints, their emotional messages disappear from the multi-media stream, until *another* wave of Saganites voice *another* ship-wide round of nervous questions to the Regency. Then those questions disappear. Their complaints just wash away!" She sipped more water and activated her *standard* Homepage showing the date, time, Regency Homepage, and *Sagan*'s position in space. "I've spoken to several doctors; all of them claim they haven't administered *any* type of cognitive treatments which would cause this anomaly. Something's not right but *very* wrong when you can't locate *one* complaint or concern. I'm going to get to the bottom of it as well."

"Just you?" Twin asked.

"You and I...the two of us, all right? We're *all* a team." She tapped her camera and gestured towards some other portable devices she was planning to stick on to her body before leaving for work.

"Right!" Twin said, smiling proudly.

Elisa gave her the thumbs up. "Waiting to receive the Neltan *Update* is like counting seconds underwater while holding your breath...so anxiety provoking! Hourly, the Regents have been making emergency appearances everywhere. If I had my connection to them on right now, they'd be flashing a signal, requesting I immediately answer 'em! And if I had on my wrist device or neck device, they'd be trying to shine front and center of me. Frankly they're probably here right now. I just refuse to hear another broadcast."

"They're all off," Twin said.

"Good. And make sure they stay that way until I give you the signal to turn 'em on," she laughed, and then continued her narrative recording: "The Regents are trying to assure us that Terra *will* announce the Update when Navigation receives it. Meanwhile, we all feel like we're living in suspended animation, not knowing whether they should bust out partying, go on lock down, or maybe even abandon ship! There are all sorts of opinions about what the crew should do if we don't hear something from Nelta soon." She called into the wall panel requesting a display of the long corridors leading to the nearest transport station.

Between the city of towering beehive living units are neighborhood moving sidewalks. They're made to look like replicas of old-Earth sidewalks transporting people to their destinations—mostly Maglev stations. As far as she can see, the entire domed area is crowded with early morning pedestrians rushing to work, talking to their avatars, watching renderings over their portable devices, and navigating by directional arrows while replying to messages.

She quickly closed the outside view. Her recording time is running short. "Still, almost everyone is ready to celebrate our hundred-year journey through the universe. Party settings are appearing everywhere, rendering in the smallest of corners around each of the 27 transport platforms and recreation areas. Holograph artists and musicians are performing at the celebrations. There have been concerts in the parks for the last week, outdoor festivals, and fun activities for families. I've noticed they're goodbye events. People are gathering and crying together while also trying to decide whether they're going to return to Earth or stay on Nelta. And the artists are taking advantage of the situation by seizing these last few opportunities to gather a little extra income before disembarking." A rendering of several Enforcers appeared. They were trying to direct traffic at several transport stations and break up crowds. "Yep, this is also happening. The Regents consider the party atmosphere a waste of time and a disruption as we count down for Disembarkation Day. They make known their disapproval when they send their elite Enforcer agents who hover high around our nine domes, policing every niche for even minor transgressions of *The 10 Laws*."

She recalled the time on Earth when humanity first approved The Regency political management structure, elected the first fifty Regents, and affirmed the first *Global Laws* in

# J.P. Osterman

January 2057. "A hundred years seems like an eternity. For the most part, since our quick exodus from Earth, we've remained true to those laws, but cut down on the number of managing Regents to ten—a Regent representative for every level—with Executive Regent Thornton Manning directing them. Over several decades, the Regents added addendums to our rule of law."

All the changes made her think of the anonymous quote: *In a democracy your vote counts. In feudalism your count votes.*

"Not everyone is happy with their power grab," she continued. "But the changes have worked to keep a civilized order during our long trek. *We* do our assigned tasks and jobs. And *they* observe us and assess how best to control us. That's what I think. Although they say we are in control because of privacy laws. The Regents have told us no one can break through privacy barriers. Yeah right! Although there has been no evidence to mistrust them, no one has seen *any* of the them in pubic for over 75 years, Real Time, since September 10, 2093, Lock Out Day, when they separated from us in favor of seclusion. Am I right about that date, Twin?"

"That day was Lock Out Day," Twin affirmed, showing her a visual of their announcement.

"That's when Thornton Manning, a person I believed was my friend, announce from their livings quarters behind the Navigation suite on Level-1: 'We will only communicate through augmented appearances. This is *Addendum 1* to our ten-item *Global Law.*' I guess they felt that because we left Earth, they could no longer be bound by those democratic rules. *He* instigated that first addendum without a vote. Isn't what he did a mistrustful deed, Twin?"

Twin had a pensive inspection on her face. "Evidence of mistrust? The answer to your question will take some time, Elisa."

"Never mind. I'm just talking to you as a friend."

"And you *are* my friend," Twin grinned.

She took another break from her recording when she heard a rush of footsteps outside her Living Cube. She opened the sliding door to the corridors. People were now rushing faster than before to catch the next Maglev about to dock at the platform.

Each of the astrocity's nine levels has three Maglev transport stations: one at the bow, one at the stern, and a central station. Hers home is on Level-2, near the Central Transport Station. She felt overwhelmed by a sudden thirst, drank a half-bottle of water, and then continued her record in a whisper:

"*A few brave* Saganites have been crying 'government conspiracies' for the past few weeks. I don't know how this rogue groups is doing it…but like they used to say back in the 21st century, they've 'gone viral' and are creating quite a stir! But without challenging Thornton Manning or any of the other Regents publically, their elephant-in-the-room blends in with the nine mile-high levels and mall-sized transport centers. And this radical group is somehow living off matrix. I can't believe *anyone* can exist like that at all, 'cause if they did, they'd have to be completely off Terra! No way…no way could even *one* person live like that, especially me."

"I've never heard of such people either," Twin said in a tone of disdain.

"Of course not, because Terra can't get coordinates on people who must be camouflaging themselves!" she exclaimed, gesturing at a row of her cameras sitting on a long shelf like large cryptic words in an alphabet. "That's more reason Twin, for you, me, and my *digital* cameras to take a few days traveling around this ship and snap photos and take some old-fashioned videos."

"Sounds like fun," Twin said, "and you'll have lots of time. Today is your last day at work."

"That's right, so when we're done recording here, I'll put several cameras in my backpack and Velcro a few to my clothes so I take 'em with me."

"They're almost all charged," Twin announced.

# J.P. Osterman

"*Sagan* is a small world Twin, but like I've always said: I wouldn't want to paint it, yet here I am ready to explore every nook and cranny."

She remembered another puzzling occurrence. "Oh, and here's another thing that's really hard to believe. The Regents say they've been living in complete seclusion without anyone ever once seeing them for over 75 years. Ha! I don't buy it. I know they have two special Maglevs and a direct passage to every level. I can't believe they've never once stepped out into public, do you?"

"I can step out of Private mode check," Twin replied.

"No!" she gasped, adjusting the camera to focus in on her face.

"Okay—okay," Twin said in a calming gesture.

Elisa continued: "I think The Regents are walking among us incognito, Twin. A few people maintain they've spotted several of them, but they disappear so quickly, just like the mysterious virtual creatures. No one's quick enough to capture proof."

"Yesterday, on Main Station News, a woman claimed to have spotted Regent Steven Jenkens," Twin said, calling up the woman's 10:27 a.m. appearance on the news, but keeping the show on *extra-small* rendering so as not to interfere with Elisa's zone of recording.

On the Regency's Homepage, Steven Jenkens refers to himself as Steve. He's Thornton Manning's Second-In-Command and looks like the dead comedian from the twentieth century, Jackie Gleason.

"But before the woman couldn't capture a picture of him on her wrist device," Twin said, "because he absorbed into a rendering of a movie someone was watching while waiting for a Maglev."

"That's *just one* reason more why I intend to use these old digital cameras. If I do see someone or something out of the ordinary, I'll be able to capture their presence in a different way other than today's technology." She walked to her line of small digital surveillance devices, inspecting them for battery life. "I need to make sure I fasten a couple just right around my body. You and I are going to be on the lookout for Regents too. And if we spot one, we'll have proof they're mingling among us!"

Twin pointed at two cameras: one manufactured in 2016, an ultra-thin component of the iPhone; the other a tiny 2045 trim-line Samsung/imager combination. "I suggest these, Elisa. You fixed them, and can easily manufacture parts." She gestured at Elisa's replicator in the corner—a 3D printer and food generator all in one device. "They'll never quit on you."

Elisa took the two devices off the shelf, touched them with her wrist device to synchronize them with Twin, shut them off, and then set them down gently on her eating table. "If I *do* see Thornton Manning, I'll *definitely* talk to him and remind him of how I helped."

"That was the time he nearly died and you saved him, not just helped him," Twin said.

"I wonder if he still remembers me?" she asked, reminiscing. "He never contacted me after Lock Out Day. Still, if I *could* talk to him, who knows what job he could help me secure on Nelta."

Twin closed out the newscast shows and then launched a rendering of Elisa's Living Resume. A *small* rendering of Elisa appeared in a doctor's uniform. It showed her in her current position as Chief Regeneration Specialist on Corridor-15, Station 14. Behind her doctor's persona there appeared images of her performing other jobs, and everything about her that a prospective employer could call on and observe. They're mostly renderings of the jobs she had held during her lifetime, including her university positions on Earth.

"Still, I think I'm a bit afraid of Thornton," she said.

"Why?" Twin asked.

She breathed, and her disjointed feeling of being so separated from them faded, replaced by longing. "Time always changes people, Twin, and not seeing him for so long means not knowing him. Fear. It's a *powerful* deterrent."

"But you don't have to let it rule you, like you did before," Twin said softly, setting her holographic hand on Elisa's shoulder.

"I know." Feeling doubtful, she looked away from her camera and drank more water. She had been afraid several times. One time being when she had to face Daryl Coflin's monsters and save everyone in the Press Room! Now, she couldn't afford that waste of time. Flooding her face in her cameras light, she vanquished that strong emotion, activated her wall panel connection to the Regency's matrix site, and homed in on Thornton Manning's profile. "From the day we left Earth, his *Addendum 1* appears daily at the periphery of each person's grid site." She showed the inscription to the camera. "All Regents make speeches, answer hails, and propose and ratify laws exclusively through a holographic interface, and everyone is required to post their votes to their designated Regent. If there is a problem; in a day, the Regent will respond, but virtually."

She set her camera back down on her table and then resumed her narration: "Since their Lock Out Day, they've intervened to resolve quarrels and disputes as well. They've mitigated cases with the Supreme Judges in our Courts of Law, and interpreted the *Guidelines for Living* whenever confusions or complications arise, especially with Enforcers. They consult with physicians; and twice lately, I've had to call them concerning a medical accident." She sighed in regret as she downloaded the *Guidelines* to a camera's memory. "But not too many people want to call a Regent and appear in one of his or her rendered realities, especially since complaints and concerns seemed to just disappear in the ether! At least that's the feeling I get…a *strong* feeling…and it's a dangerous reality," she whispered, "and why I've begun this old-fashioned recording mission. I thought I was doing it for everyone, but really, I'm beginning this journey for myself…to make sure I'm not going crazy with all the strange things people have been seeing.

Twin's eyes were round pools of unresponsive bright green

light.

Elisa didn't notice the lack of response because of the flashing low battery signal on her camera. She checked the power source under her table. She needed more electricity, and getting that amount for the rest of the day would set off an alarm. She picked up a few Velcro straps so she could hide the cameras inside her clothes. She said in a hurried voice: "For almost a hundred years, we've adapted to the Regents virtual presence and have made our opinions, wants, and needs known to them, but something feels wrong. Their lack of personal appearances, especially now, when we need their leadership the most, just isn't right."

## Chapter 4 - Avatar Companion

Elisa shoved away two boxes, pulled her chair next to the side of her bed, and said to Twin: "Begin recording *your* way now, Twin. I'll take this other device with me to work; then after work, I'll start shooting for some footage. Maybe we can catch some of the strange visuals, one of those protesters, or a Regent."

Twin didn't answer. She appeared stalled, her eyes bright green.

Elisa waved her hand in front of her avatar's face. "You're acting weird! What's wrong?"

Twin's head was cocked sideways, and she appeared to be staring into a great expanse.

"Hey, matrix! Whataya think? Where are you?" Elisa snapped her fingers in front of Twin's eyes. "Snap out of it!" she ordered her virtual companion, athletic and tall with brown eyes and brown hair in a ponytail.

Whenever she walks into work at Regeneration Corridor-15, she has Twin at her side. Wearing her same style of a white lab coat, Twin is her on-call doctor double. During the entire

# Astrocity Sagan

100 years, she's only needed to ask Twin a question twice—the last time being after an accident occurred a few days ago.

Twin suddenly surged back to life. "Elisa, I've run self-actuating diagnostics and three scans to detect anomalies in mirrors and your nano-walls. I have detected no malware, optical anomaly, or abnormality in color on the human or electromagnetic spectrum."

Elisa sighed in relief at Twin's sudden improvement. "Thank goodness you're all right!"

"I—I am, I believe," Twin said, but then hiccupped.

Elisa couldn't see any glitch. "Well *something* weird is happening around this place…and now it's happening to you too!" She felt a rush of fear. "Twin, stay with me, but in Invisible-mode so I can keep my eye on your connectivity."

"Yes, Elisa," Twin replied, modifying Elisa's matrix programming while Elisa waited.

Then Elisa had a profound realization. Twin had been with her for over a hundred years on their interactive astrocity. Although she had updated her several times, she maintained her original virtual form since Terra-III began streaming on *Sagan*, March 7, 2068. That was a week after people on *The List* for Nelta rushed off-Earth to take refuge on the burgeoning *Sagan*. After the War on Terror ended with the moon cracking, many people on Earth, whom Terra *hadn't* chosen to the voyage to Nelta, wanted to force their way onto the astrocity. They didn't want to join some colonization project on Mars or one of Jupiter's moons. But there was no room for more people than Terra had allotted, and that was a mere 75,000 with planned growth to 100,000 as couples under the lottery system were allowed to have children during the lengthy voyage to Nelta.

With green glowing eyes, Twin sat back down and began staring at Elisa. "I am resuming recording, and storing everything to Grid 1 of Level-2, Living Cube Area 1, Unit 202B."

# J.P. Osterman

Glancing around her little one-bedroom unit, Elisa suddenly felt nostalgic. "Well, I'm gonna miss this little place. Still, like so many other people packing up, I can't *wait* until I step on solid ground. Neltan ground! And hopefully, one day walk into a *new* home, a *real* home, with two rooms, a big closet, and cupboards. A warm anticipation filled her. "Twin, show me the beautiful Neltan suns."

In front of her, a rendering on the surface of Nelta illuminated: one large sun followed by a distant sun crisscrossing at Nelta's zenith and then setting in red-orange-green tones over mountain peaks, giant monoliths and rows of obelisks.

"It's SO beautiful—I can't wait!" She wanted to grab Twin's hand she was that filled with excitement. "Do you have my movers scheduled? No one knows an exact date and time since the details are still uncertain. But everyone who is planning to leave is fighting for disembarkation slots.

Twin activated her *Calendar Events and Schedules* over her wrist device. The day scrolled to the last day in February: *Monday, February 28, 3070, Real Time.*

"This is the day *Sagan* is supposed to arrive in orbit around Nelta, Elisa." Then Twin reached out and touched the virtual calendar that displayed *Wednesday, March 2*. "You have movers coming at two o'clock p.m. to move your things off-*Sagan*." Twin then opened up a side display to show her the giant craft scheduled to transport her and her possessions off *Sagan*. "You're on *The Chicago*'s last haul of passengers to Nelta. That evening, *Sagan* is scheduled to launch for the artificial celestial body that had stored The Matter Stream. This ship—"

"I know," Elisa interrupted, "this place needs an *entire* update! Don't we all know *that*," she chuckled. "Did you make provisions for the rest of my cameras, but without specifying that they're my hobbies?" she whispered. "Make sure of that please, Twin."

"Yes," Twin said, gesturing at one of the giant open boxes ready for packaging. Over Elisa's wrist device, Twin zoomed in on a small storage space inside *The Chicago* that had her name marked on the side. Because Elisa was a physician and Chief of a Regeneration Corridor, The Regents allotted her extra baggage weight. "I have a space in Cargo Bay 1A designated for all your equipment," Twin showed her. "I stipulated in the moving instructions that they are to position your boxes against the hull. That way, they will have additional protection and support."

"Great, Twin, 'cause I need every bit of that space," she breathed, feeling suddenly overwhelmed. "Gosh—I wonder where I'm going to live right after I arriving there. I don't think anyone's thought of that."

"I am receiving that same concern streaming to The Regency," Twin said, activating the astrocity's *Holosite News* at the center of her Living Cube. That ship-wide concern was at the 38% Red Bar Indicator, next to the Status Bar showing the environmental readings on all 9 levels, the astrocity's trajectory to Nelta, a *Calendar of Events*, and holographic bubbles Elisa could call *On*, peruse, or participate in as she dressed for work.

She began analyzing the 38% statistically significant *Call for Concern* Terra had compiled from the most recent Live Streams to the Regency. At some point throughout the day; either one Regent, many, or all of them—especially in an emergency—would respond to the *Daily Concern List*, either in a broadcast from their Conference Facility on Level-9 or their Reception Area inside their Living Quarters on Level-1.

Elisa remembered again that most of those concerns were left unanswered. "We're all packing up as if an invasion's coming, but we have no plan where we'll be settling. Send *that* concern to them in triplicate, please." As Twin's eyes flashed green, she felt she had been a bit too aggressive. "But retrieve two of those. I know Thornton has probably forgotten about me, but I still want to stay on his good side."

"I have added your landing and settling concerns to the *Daily Concern List*," Twin said.

Then she remembered a common friend they shared, Dr.

# J.P. Osterman

Lynn Altmin, who had died on Earth. She wondered if he still had her ashes. He said he wanted to scatter them on Nelta. "Even if I stream him a *Hello* message, he won't respond." Several of her colleagues had sent him holiday greetings but received only his standard *Happy Real-Time New Year*! "Well, maybe while I'm on vacation, I'll compose a nice little message and send it to him through Regeneration Corridor-15's Confidential grid.

"Good idea," Twin said, adding the plan to Elisa's calendar.

That idea made her worry about her sensitive camera equipment! "Oh-uh, I just had another thought." When Twin turned to her, she said, "Without advanced hardware and software, I can't keep my photography hobby on Nelta."

"Oh," Twin said, "hmm."

"Terra has the *only* Photo-shopping capabilities to allow my old cameras to transfer digital images for renderings. What do I do?"

After seconds, Twin's eyes lit up bright blue. "Your small development lab on Level-6 is connected to the Performing Arts Center. They have advanced blueprints. You can check to see what they can do for you after arriving on Nelta. Maybe you two can merge and help each other."

"That's a possibility," she said, tapping on the schematics of her private developing spot. She had secured it with untraceable crypto-currencies, and thus the tiny place remains a secret. It's situated behind a large kiosk where she plans to spend most of her final few days investigating and processing camera footage.

Twin looked at her with sympathy, placing her transparent hand on Elisa's hand. "I hope it's a solution.

Elisa sighed and smiled at the light touch of friendship as her reflection returned to her through Twin's yellow holographic light. "After I settle on Nelta, I know I'll be able to find an advanced projector so I can experience everything I've recorded since leaving Earth."

"And don't forget shows from other peoples' lives as well," Twin said.

# Astrocity Sagan

"Oh yes! I'll matrix-shop them as well in the next few weeks," Elisa said. She folded her nightgown, tucked it under her pillow and slipped into her Regeneration corridor's standard black leggings and a tight-blended, cotton, collarless white blouse. When her closet door slid shut, a full-body mirror slid out of the wall; and she smoothed down her blouse as the nano-fabric established its symbiotic connection with her so she couldn't even feel the cloth.

Standing next to her, Twin said, "As you instructed, I included your *Request for Special Hardware and Software* in your profile to the Neltan Welcoming Committee. They'll know what you want and need for your hobby."

Elisa swept away the display of *The Chicago* and enlarged the months of February and March over her wrist device. "Good, now we can only wait and see what happens." Quickly blowing a speck of dust off her precious camera on the shelf, she walked over to the liquid dispenser, added caffeine to her hot water, and then drank it down as the time flashed over her wrist device. It tasted every bit as good as the old "Starbucks French Roast" she used to love on Earth. "I better hurry or I'm gonna be late for work. I can't have *that* on my last day!"

"Fifteen minutes until Maglev-5 at Bow Station departs," Twin said.

"I'm hurrying!" She reached between two boxes, pulled a snack out of her small food replicator and began eating while peeking at the time. "I *hate* punching Regeneration Corridor-15's time clock. But after today, that's it…I'm done working…I'm free!" She felt relief as Twin's gentle holographic light wafted over her face. "I have vacation time and I've earned it." She felt proud and accomplished.

"Yes, you have, Elisa Holton…four weeks' vacation time to be exact," Twin said, showing her *Regeneration Corridor-15's Work History* that began displaying a summary of her working hours for the past two years. She hadn't taken a single sick day or a vacation day. "I have 30 days' vacation, and 3 days

Personal Time, beginning today, January 18, 2168, at 5:00 p.m., Space Fold Time."

"Sixteen minutes until Maglev 5 departs," Twin said perkily and closed Elisa's work history. Her image hissed and wavered. "It's 8:14 a.m."

Elisa winced at the hissing sound. "What's gotten into you today? This is the second weird interruption in you…" She hadn't programmed her to give a reminder until 8:15. "Now it's my turn to scan you, Twin." She tapped her wrist device that showed the Matrix uninfected and processing at 100%. "The time is not 8:15, Twin, not quite yet. You're off."

"Nothing is wrong, Elisa Holton," Twin replied in an innocent tone.

Elisa leaned into her a bit, not believing her. Then she remembered a news release from The Regency:

The matrix would be experiencing processing problems during the astrocity's final transition into the last wormhole leading to Nelta's M84 galaxy. Processing lags and glitches would briefly occur as Navigation—located over the bow of Level-1—began de-accelerating *Sagan* for its entry into M84, twice the size of Earth's solar system. "Dark matter and dark energy are mixing mysteriously there," Thornton Manning announced. "For the next two days, we need to diversify power and make alterations to the astrocity's interior to prepare for orbit. Several spaces are automatically beginning to restructure for the return trip to Earth. And please, continue to stream your intentions to either to stay on Nelta or return with us to Earth."

Twin said, "Fifteen minutes, Elisa, until Maglev 2's departure."

"You look fine, Twin…I just hope you *are* fine 'cause I need you," Elisa said. Standing to leave, she closed her Calendar, and raced over to the sliding door and its biometric Glow pad. She put on her white lab coat, brushed her hair, and pulled it back into a ponytail. All the while, Twin was reminding her not to forget any of her camera parts, and telling her the best corridors to take to reach her secret Area 64 Kiosk

# Astrocity Sagan

193 hobby lab after work. Elisa paused and looked at her reflection in the mirror. She felt suddenly confused. "Am I still scheduled for my last Regeneration tomorrow? Any changes in the Corridor's schedule? I hope not!"

"You have the prime spot of the day, Elisa." Twin opened up the Month of January and zoomed in on tomorrow's date and time: Tuesday, January 19, 2108 EDT, 2:30 p.m. "I am providing you Space Fold date and time, but I can include Earth Day date and time."

"Not *that* calculation, 'cause that'll make me look over a thousand years old. Now who wants that!" she laughed. She could read her age in clear numbers that Twin had set right in the mirror. "It's so hard to believe I'm over a hundred." She lifted the tube of light pink lipstick out of her lab coat and began dabbing her lips.

"One-hundred thirty-two years and one-hundred three days exactly, Elisa May Holton," Twin confirmed. "I can provide you with images after you were born as date/time stamps."

"Nope, that's fine, Twin," she said, inspecting her face for wrinkles. She spotted two long smile lines next to her mouth and a few gray hairs that seemed to appear overnight. "I hope my last Regeneration will eliminate the hair that's turning to gray and bring back my youth. I just want to be young again, and in my prime one last time. I always knew the day would come when the aging process would start again...but now it's here...tomorrow. The process saved us all from death, but now, those of us who step off Sagan will not only be starting a new life but coming face-to-face with mortality."

Twin turned toward Elisa's rainbow-cycling ceiling hub. "I will emphasize your concern to Dr. Pultoff who is performing your Regeneration procedure."

Elisa blinked into the Glow pad on her doorframe, and the door opened to the bustling wide corridor leading to several Maglev transport stations. People were coming and going on multidirectional moving walkways with their avatars and directional icons either hovering small over their shoulders or body-sized, and trailing alongside them like transparent cartoon characters on invisible leashes.

"Come on, let's go, Twin. Let's start our last day of work and begin our mission," she said, feeling confident that everything was under control and her day on schedule. She stepped outside into her corridor and directed Twin to notice every detail. Feeling sentimental again, she wanted to record *every* detail and point out every cranny. "Here's my little paved walkway that leads to the western walkway. It's a five minute, fast-paced walk from here to the Level-2 Central Station. Then I hop on a Maglev down to Level-5 where I work, and then I catch another one to the stern station, the location of the Regeneration Corridors."

As she merged into the crowd with other people west-bound, she tapped on her old iPhone 10 and activated Camera-mode to record from the button-cam under her collar. People ahead of her were busy organizing their days, messaging, watching renderings, or composing renderings. That she'd be talking to herself wouldn't be noticed, at least she hoped not, until she spotted an Enforcer on his craft gliding by overhead at sixty-miles-an-hour. Then he was gone. But there'd be more behind him.

She continued her recording: "Level-2's domed ceiling is a mile high, and set to early-morning. The atmosphere is bright and summery in keeping with Earth's circadian rhythm of the southern hemisphere in Australia. We voted on Australia as January's rendering on December thirtieth. A gentle breeze is constantly wafting in a controlled current, and trees and flowers are situated in parkways between all the moving walkways—complimented by patches of artificial greenery as well." She turned so her camera lens could focus on the East and West moving walkways. Twenty-five feet above them were the North and South walkways. "They're not too crammed, but still busy in the morning's traffic. At one-mile intervals throughout are all of the eateries, gathering areas, markets, kiosks, and cultural exchanges."

She had Twin capture images of people snapping pictures of rare birds, and a few people were recording their sounds on all sorts of portable devices, as well as taking photos of virtual deer and the rest of the AI animals created to keep us company. Situated at random places throughout *Sagan*, authentic creations of artificial wildlife moved freely among the citizens reacting normally as they would on Earth.

She said into her camera lens: "Scenes such as this one have been rendering our Earthly home since we departed." She told Twin to capture a 360° view. "This is going to be the last time I walk down this moving walkway at 8:30 in the morning," she smiled, noticing her reflection in Twin's light. "I can't wait! And tonight, *we* start four weeks of nothing but fun!" She felt suddenly dreamy and charged up, and gave Twin a high five until Twin reminded her of the mission that would be replacing her job.

A man turned around and leaned through Twin's body. "Lady, in four weeks we'll be stepping on alien soil!" He raced down the walkway toward Center Station, his avatar spinning in the air behind him and waved goodbye to her.

She noticed one of his eyes, two colors. *"That's* the fourth person with heterochromia I've seen in two days!"

Before she could lock onto his avatar's neck-ID indicator so she could look up his medical history later, he disappeared into the large throng of people dashing toward the giant Maglev platform now sounding an approaching warning tone and flashing green linear lights that looked like illuminated rods. Rushing to the back of the line to catch Maglev 2, she said to Twin: "At some point today, remind me to check and see if there's been an increase in heterochromia that's manifesting subsequent to the Regeneration process." When Twin's eyes flashed green, she continued: "I've seen four people with pronounced heterochromia, which statistically is quite suspicious as generally only 6 out of 1000 have the congenital mutation. The mutation in itself doesn't hurt anything, but it could indicate a problem or some unexpected medical complication during consciousness uploading or downloading into the matrix."

"Every step in the Regeneration process is monitored by Terra-IV," Twin said.

No genetic mutation has ever affected the population; but should any occur, the *Transparency Law* directs Terra and the Regents to inform the entire population through an Emergency Broadcast. Those affected would be immediately be whisked to Level-4's Medical Facility for an in depth evaluation, and if indicated, a rapid genetic repair.

"This heterochromia I've noticed is *definitely* a genetic issue that needs to be addressed, and I'm wondering why I haven't heard even a confidential message about it." Elisa stepped onto the Maglev as the threshold indicator read her ID and uploaded crypto-currencies for payment. Then she told Twin to operate on Invisible-mode, and Twin faded into her wrist device.

As the rectangular L-car prepared to descend, she strapped herself into a seat and remembered something about her special biology she had forgotten. Two weeks ago, Twin informed her she was sleeping less, and her dreams were becoming more vibrant—with images of Nelta. She was also drinking more water and craving high-protein snacks. I wonder what those symptoms mean. As the electromagnetic currents whipped around the Maglev and gravity decreased, she opened up a self-scan, and Twin's little body appeared over her device showing her the changes, but also displaying normal vitals. She whispered to her: "I feel fine, Twin. Just continue to override any abnormal biometric reading so nothing streams to The Regency, just like we talked about, ya hear?"

"Yes, Elisa." Then Twin faded.

Sitting back while trying to ignore chattering people and their annoying avatars, she blocked out the burgeoning changes in her body with gulps of water and bites of protein bars.

# Astrocity Sagan

## Chapter 5 - I Need a Break!

At work in Corridor-15, she felt the time, flying by. She was that busy! The *Real Time* holographic clocks were already imaging 3:10 p.m., and she hadn't eaten lunch, just popping high-protein snacks. Turning to the next patient on a hover gurney and asking her assistant Dr. Nick Burgess to don the woman's head with a Cranial Interface Net so they could upload her mind, Elisa saw an entire row of covered bodies that looked more like cadavers than sedated patients prepped for Regeneration. Stopping another gurney before it hit her in the hip, she felt inundated by the jobs ahead of her, but she had to finish by five. No way was she going to let overtime spill into her vacation time. She had plans, her private mission. Quickly, she tapped the app on her device and sent in the heterochromia issue into the Medical Facility at the center of Level-4. She touched her pocket. Under it was one of three concealed cameras. If she didn't receive a prompt reply by one of the doctors there, she'd go to Level-4 after work and fill out a personal report of the heterochromia manifesting in the population.

# J.P. Osterman

"It's almost quitting time, Nick," she said into the patient's forehead as she propped his head up toward the rainbow-cycling, beehive, ceiling hub—the processor responsible for extracting a person's consciousness into Terra. "In an hour and fifty minutes, my permanent vacation starts, and we'll have to figure out some different way to meet," she laughed.

"Ya sure are due a vacation, Doc," Nick said. He called on their station's information that rendered next to them. The Regents had already selected a new Regeneration Specialist to take her place, and the man's profile appeared next to their station's stats. "But I don't see any fun in taking a vacation now though. If I hadn't taken mine a few months back, I woulda used the time to pick up a second job and barter for goods for when I relocate to Nelta." He swept aside the profile and rendered the patient's biometrics. The man's heart rate and cerebral activity began hovering in front of them.

After Elisa acknowledged her patient's stable vitals, she accepted the ceiling hub's checklist for consciousness uploading, stepped back, and began waiting for the rainbow-cycling processor to glow green for *Consciousness Upload Commencing*. She thought of her hobby of restoring old cameras and the difficulties involved in transferring data to an alien system. Maybe she could invent an app to present to a Neltan scientist who could help her modify her old equipment to stream into the matrix. "I need a vacation, Nick. I have plans, and when that clock strikes five, I'm outta here, and I don't intend to see your face until I see you on Nelta, except for maybe having drinks somewhere." As he laughed with her, she saw a question surface in his warm brown eyes. He was going to bring up her ex-boyfriend, Carl Foldier. "No…we're *not* back together, Nick, and I don't intent to just sit in my living cube and ruminate over what went wrong. Been *there* done *that*. No more. I'm done dating. I've got better things to do." She didn't want to tell Nick about her plan to travel around *Sagan* to take pictures of ghosts, apparitions, and Regent hunting.

"You said that months before you met Carl, Elisa, but ya

still dated again," Nick said.

"Yeah, but I shoulda stuck to my decision and kept the hell away from that *Partner for Life* dating world. Look where I'm at now, Nick, partner-*less*!" She breathed and felt the drudgery of the time dripping like sap over all the patients they had yet to Regenerate. "I'm looking for permanence, Nick…like in the old times. I want marriage."

Nick waved in exasperation, his broad shoulders shrugging as he wiped sweat off his sideburns. He had strands of bleached white hair running through his black crew-cut. He had a baby innocent face, a dark tan, and bright blue eyes. After working hours, he was a swimmer on one of *Sagan*'s swim teams and a member of the diving team who performed stunts at the Level-1 arena pool.

The Arena is the largest public facility on *Sagan*, capable of seating fifty-thousand people and the location where the Olympics are held.

"Good luck finding love and marriage, Doc, 'cause if ya hadn't noticed by now—" He glanced around. "People aren't falling in love and gettin' married."

"Yeah, tell me about it," she moaned.

"Still, that's gotta change," he began, "because as a species needing to survive on Nelta, people will *need* to change their, well—"

"Sexually unrestrained habits? And settle down and have children?"

"Yeah."

"Yeah, right, Nick! I can't wait to see the day *that* happens."

Nick gave her an encouraging look. "You'll find someone someday, Doc. Heck, he might even be one 'o the guys in here!"

She winced and peered around the room partitioned off with barriers and buffered against loud noises. In the Regeneration Corridors, she could only see covered bodies,

# J.P. Osterman

heads meshed with cerebral caps, holographic body readings, and strong light beams uploading minds into Terra. One face appeared the same as all the rest, as did her long list of boyfriends she fantasized about marrying before they left her, or she broke up with them. She felt sick. "I don't see anyone I'd even be remotely interested in, Nick."

"That'll change, Doc, once ya meet someone who'll wanna settle down with ya on Nelta."

"But not now, Nick, never on *Sagan*," she said.

"You know the expression though," he winked. "Never say never."

As the patient's medical imager began scanning the man for illnesses and abnormalities that might need immediate medical and genetic intervention prior to the Regeneration procedure, she began recounting how the culture of the astrocity had changed throughout the decades...

# Astrocity Sagan

## Chapter 6 - Life Onboard *Sagan*

There are families on *Sagan*, and people do marry at the various Religious Centers at the center of Level-1. Then again, people also flagrantly divorce; so much so, The Regency and Judicial Committee at the stern of Level-1 instigated the Birth Control Mandate two decades into the voyage. All people wanting children must throw their names into a lottery. At adolescence, a birth control patch is mandatory and a passage into adulthood for those over fourteen.

Elisa remembered the time when several RIs had to be reprogrammed due to a massive malfunction that Terra couldn't override. Thirty women and over a hundred men began producing excessive hormones and nearly died when their RIs began producing miniature ovaries and prostates! Noticing the malfunction immediately, thanks to monitoring, medical technicians called Elisa to Level-2 to help devise a new nano-organic RI to correct the faulty internal expansion. No one died—but a death toll came close! Other comparable problems have occurred as well, but matrix techs and medical specialists readily corrected them by calling on human

# J.P. Osterman

ingenuity, Terra's quick-fix simulations, and nano-organic, genetic, and robotic designs. When the RI malfunctioned that time, Thornton Manning finally told Saganites—via a virtual-world appearance—about a clone technology they had discovered prior to leaving Earth. In case *any* person might die on the journey, they could clone the individual—worst case scenario. People were panicking at the time, fearing death and genetic mutation during the Regeneration process. Neither cognitive intervention nor medication helped. Concerning cloning, people voted on and approved Amendment I to Law IX, the Medical Experimental Law: *Only in a case of death is cloning necessary and permitted.*

That law and nine others, totaling ten, The Regents modeled after the ten Global Laws of Earth and the U.S.A.'s *Bill of Rights.* In a massive vote, Saganites decided to call the new rules and regulations, *Guidelines for Living.* After boarding *Sagan*, the Regents proposed them in their seminal forms, and the crew voted for them and approved them by the necessary 85%. Over the course of one-hundred years of spacefold traveling, comingling in a beehive-type community setting, experiencing life, and developing an Augmented Culture off-Earth; the laws evolved, and Saganites continued to modify the *Guidelines for Living.* No matter who authors a new law, proposes an amendment to an existing guideline, or alters an existing regulation, everyone over eighteen must vote on and approve the law, guideline, or regulation through Terra's Live Stream Media system: *Sagan*'s one-hundred-fifty channel virtual station. Public Channel 3 is the Voting Center. The approval point is set at 85%, more than a majority to deter discontent.

Throughout the first years of living on the astrocity, the crew decided on a belief and value system at the heart of the *Guidelines for Living.* The one mission statement is etched in glowing gold into the archway over the Center Transport Platform on Level-1: *Every person is vital; every job is paramount!*

Poverty on *Sagan* is nonexistent. Some people are rich, and most people have more than what they need of food, shelter and clothing. In a beehive-community, no one ever goes

# Astrocity Sagan

hungry, thirsty, lonely, or remain isolated. Every adult has a job. Some people barter, some trade their skills and talents, and some work from their living cubes while others commute on Maglevs through transport tunnels to their jobs. Nano-biological interventions, stem-cell cures, and preventions have almost eliminated the need for extensive sick time and disability. Tardiness and idleness are short lived. People realize they have a purpose and a value—especially to preserve the human species in the future on Nelta. Augmented realities and avatar interactive experiences insure individuals have close companions, helpers, and medical monitoring. Most times, life runs smoothly on *Sagan*'s 100-year spacefold journey to Nelta.

However, in the last six months, Elisa has been closely monitoring the *Population Count* on the astrocity's Home Holosite Page. She has to, as Chief Medical Specialist of a Regeneration Corridor. The count hasn't increased as Terra had predicted, but instead has remained hovering at a constant 99,727—most unusual, and lower than the maximum 100,000 number Terra had predicted and allotted. The current population count was off mark with the number of children the Medical Center reported as Live Births. And there have been *no* deaths!

Two hundred and seventy-three people are missing. How and where are they?

The crew began noticing the disparity four months ago and began streaming questions to The Regency: "Who are these people? Where are they? Have they left *Sagan* somehow? If so, why? Can they harm us or our ship? Have the cognitive scanners in the archways detected any criminal impulses?"

The CBRR hubs are *concealed* imagers only The Regents can locate. A technology from Earth but originating on Nelta, the Cognitive Behavioral Relief and Repair (CBRR) hardware is designed to glean brain impulses and interpret them into images. They're constantly scanning the crew for criminal intentions. The Regents special elite Clone Techs situated hubs in other locations discrete locations as well in case people might try to ditch one of the 27 archways leading in-and-out of the 27 transport platforms.

Because of the disparity in population numbers, some people have afraid of and suspecting a small uprising. In the past four weeks, invasive and incoherent messages have been seeping through firewalls, startling people. The culprit is using outdated code from early 2000. The messages morphed into ten-second scenes of cartoon characters pantomiming distress signals. Matrix Security Techs on Levels 7 and 9 could not back-track their location.

Three weeks ago, Thornton Manning made a special appearance from his private quarters at the bow of Level-1 where The Regents live but also have a theater-style conference area. He looked the same as he did a hundred years ago, like Beethoven the conductor, except taller and thinner than Beethoven. For that particular appearance, he had assembled his entire *real* Enforcer army, headquartered at the bow of Level-9.

From his red-curtain backdrop, he said: "We've combed every Maglev tunnel and sent robotics to inspect *every* niche. That should allay your fears that people are missing and conspiring to down our astrocity. And we have five-thousand armed Enforcers patrolling *all* the living quarters, hallways, and work areas. No one can harm *Sagan*, especially now, when we're about to fulfill *The Pact*."

He went on to tell the crew how cognitive monitoring and quick-tech response time were at their best in apprehending perpetrators, and relegating them to treatment on Level-7.

Still, people continue streaming their worries and concerns over someone possibly damaging *Sagan*. But no one can offer a sound explanation of why anyone would want to interfere with *The Pact*. All the evidence people have to present are copies of the startling messages and the backs of terrifying creatures and apparitions. The Regents have Terra working on compiling every outdated code and discovering the conundrum of missing people and the terrifying messages as well as those

# Astrocity Sagan

horrific apparitions. The population number is a big clue: 99,727. It's a number of beauty but complexity, and unity but disharmony in the cosmos. The number is acting like a palindrome, stymying Terra and sapping up her matrix energy.

The concern of a mutiny, *Pact* interference, and a matrix virus are daily snowballing, with Regents appearing in between their hourly updates on Nelta to try and allay peoples' fears. All fifty Regents are taking turns making public appearances. They all had the same message: "If someone *might* be conspiring to harm people or set off a bomb, Enforcers can capture him or her and send them without legal representation to neural intervention on Level-7."

Each Regent keeps maintaining:

"If we *do* discover a group of people in hiding and experiencing some type of collective problem or illness, we have an immediate solution to help them recover. You know the interventions and treatments, but we need *your* help us spot any strange occurrences, photograph them, and sent them to our holosite. We've experienced a few medical issues before; and every time, we've cured and healed people. Don't worry. If your fears are correct and Terra can locate some sort of off-matrix people, our Enforcers will find them and stop them. Again, *don't* fret! Go back to deciding what you want to do as you approach the end of our voyage. That's where your focus should be right now as we have just six weeks before arriving in orbit around Nelta. And if you decide to stay on *Sagan*, stream that decision to our holosite so we can make provisions for you when we leave Nelta to return to Earth. Again, as always, we have *every* medical, emotional, and behavioral treatment available for these *hypothetical* missing people. But let us not worry about them, *if* they exist, which Terra has not confirmed. That faulty population number and the matrix intrusions you're streaming to us could be part of the Neltans' Living Breath entity in Navigation to communicate with us and signal the end of our voyage. Only time will tell what is happening with these mysterious occurrences."

The speaking Regent would then continue to expound on all the great medical advancements we've had in place on our journey that have been keeping people alive and well:

"Advanced genetic manipulation, nano-organic technology, and stem-cell organ growth have been life-enhancing and life-extending medical miracles that are still making the 100-year spacefold voyage to Nelta possible—and full-body Regeneration. As medical specialists can utilize nano-organic biological interfaces to promote health, heal wounds, attack viral and bacterial agents, and cure illnesses; physicians can conduct more intense interventions using nano-biological agents as well, for example, dissolving kidney stones with cellular robotics and manipulating cellular treatments to grow teeth. Those latter interventions and organ growth—close to cloning—required more serious therapies than a simple nano-biological treatment, with Regent approval."

In spite of various psychological and behavioral interventions available through the Mental Health Center at the stern of Level-1, people can also call on avatar counselors, psychiatrists, or social workers to help them solve or intervene in relational problems, make decisions, and counter loneliness—the last of which is the most pronounced problem on the voyage. However, like shadows, some difficulties people can't notice themselves. Thus the invisible CBRR scanner in all 27 archways can detect "personality difficulties." The scanning hardware can "read" for crime thoughts through matrix-sensitive imagers. Upon receiving a *threatening impulse*, Terra streams the person's profile and location to Level-1's judicial system, where a large team assesses Terra's message between Code-1 through Code-10—*Danger to Self or Others*. Interventions range from light avatar counseling to a brief time of face-to-face counseling; from a minimal mental health committal period to an expanded treatment or even nano-organic cerebral intervention. Crime is almost nonexistent onboard *Sagan*, and people can also report potential "risks" to Enforcers who have kiosks on Maglev platforms and at the

# Astrocity Sagan

centers of all the markets at the perimeters the Maglev platforms.

Level-7's jail is small; however, the Rehabilitation center at the bow of Level-7 is five miles in diameter with over 1,000 workers helping 200 people recover, rehabilitate back into society, or simply receive more in-depth counseling treatments than Level-1's Counseling Center can accommodate. A few people who had entered there decades ago are still "residing" in that Level-7 rehab min-city, waiting for The Regents to reclassify them as *Fully Fit for Ship-Wide Assimilation.* Their numbers dwindled six weeks ago to 117, before *Sagan* approached the final intergalactic wormhole to Nelta. The Rehab center is transitioning to *regular* status as Terra continues tracking the biometrics of those 117 "questionable" individuals who are moving about the mini-city: their biometric avatars reading only as holograms, not real bodies.

Ship-wide scanning, tracking, and monitoring to prevent crime or predict danger are separate from medical monitoring. Of course, people believe that once they arrive on Nelta, all the rules, regulations, and monitoring will change!

Still, in the beginning, when people were vying for jobs on *Sagan*, everyone who replied 'yes' to Terra's Acceptance Message had to sign a ten-item *Terms and Acceptance* document. *Item 1* of the agreement mandates they take a two-week simulation class to prepare for the transition from living on solid ground to living on an astrocity. All those signed agreements are still in the matrix's storage grid—a permanent dash in the sand of time.

Lately, in a string of advertisements, The Regents have been encouraging Saganites to download renderings of Nelta and practice living in various settings and among the Neltans both in rural and urban locations. Terra collected every quantum-streamed image of the planet and its history prior to our Final Transmission with Ambassador Shaesar and *The Pact* signing ceremony on the night of February 28, 2068. Activating a rendering of Nelta and practicing living there is fun, but not accurate. No one has *any* idea of the status of Nelta or what might have happened there in the 1,000 years Real Time. These advertisements are just propaganda, frightening people to make a final decision stay on *Sagan* and return to Earth, or disembark on Nelta.

As of today, Elisa thought it odd that she had only seen advertisements, but no dates and times for those off-*Sagan* simulations. Remembering a rendering she had experienced after boarding *Sagan* that didn't prepare her for the heartache she would experience with men, she began blaming the way dating had evolved after leaving Earth:

People gradually grew accustomed to experiencing virtual dating scenarios and holographic "hooking up." *Anyone* can graphically create any type of virtual person, place or thing in their own quarters—and under strict guidelines, on the job—to act out fantasies, wants, and desires: a profile rendering. Singles, or anyone seeking companionship, can exchange renderings and experience one another artificially prior to meeting someone face-to-face. The astrocity's entire dating scene has evolved into quick scenes of sex, brief cohabitation, easy separation, and fast divorce experiment. Most heartaches people work through on social-media revenge grids or relegate their stinging emotions to Level-1's counseling center. In worst cases, desperate and angry people seek out neurological remapping at the Neurological Facility on Level-2 to eliminate painful memories, ruminations, or unwanted behavior patterns that began poisoning their social and working lives. Wanting to avoid the virtual dating scene, tiring of it, or just wanting permanent relationships but feeling frustrated because they can't find a "real match," some people create augmented homey settings for dating experiences, reflections of their desired way of life after working hours—usually photo-shopping an old-Earth TV show or movie. *The Brady Bunch*, *Modern Family*, and the current, reality holosite series *Moms and Dads* are the most popular grid sites people are down-streaming and activating as Surround Environments in their

# Astrocity Sagan

living cubes.   They believed they're creating their own safe families.   But even these false worlds with their fake interactive experiences tend to present problems when friends or relatives visit.

Elisa remembered rendering one of those several times; but afterwards, she felt worse.   Illusions aren't substitutes for face-to-face touch and love, and a rendering provides only piecemeal portions without satisfying the *real* need for human bonding, attachment, physical interactions and communication. That's what several researchers finally concluded after almost one hundred years of longitudinal living studies on *Sagan*.

She thought, in six weeks, our entire living experiences *will* change.

# Chapter 7 - Uncertainty

She groaned when she thought of how much time she had wasted in those *senseless* worlds. "No more dating! I mean it this time, Nick."

He laughed. "I just brought up the problem with taking your vacation now, because most popular tourist sites are becoming mighty crowded, Doc." Over his wrist device, he activated small images of the Grand Canyon grid on Level-3, the Great Wall of China grid on Level-6, and the Lanikai Beach grid at the back of the Recreation Site of Level 1. They were five-mile stretches of recreational, matrix-interfacing domes that people voted to keep as permanent holographic worlds in this last year of travel to experience after working hours. "See? They're at maximum capacity almost all of the time, and Enforcers aren't allowing anyone entrance there today. So if ya want a good participation experience, ya better get to one of these places before 6 a.m.!"

"Maybe I'll hit a Rec Center instead, Nick." She knew what she was doing, however, recording, and then processing them for renderings in Kiosk 193 on Level-6.

# Astrocity Sagan

He chuckled so hard, the patient bounced on his gurney, his forehead almost inclining into the unprepared *Upload Activation* beam. He gasped and quickly re-aligned the patient's cerebral helmet.

Elisa exhaled in relief when he showed her the man's stable vitals and the correction he made with the ceiling hub that was almost ready to receive the patient's consciousness.

Then he turned to talk to resume their topic of conversation. "I don't know if the main Rec Center on Level-2 is gonna be any different either, Doc. A pal of mine who was lounging there yesterday told me she couldn't find a place to set down *her towel* let alone her kid! And when she finally *did* find a spot, it took them *an hour* before they could rent space and start their virtual participation time. Her daughter couldn't almost finish her half-hour surf lesson. And those cost big bucks!"

Bucks are slang for crypto-currency, financial exchanges people make through the matrix's *Financial* grid, *Business* grid, or a host's personal grid.

"This'll all end in about six weeks, Nick," she yawned, staving off fatigue. "Just seventy-two more days, give or take a few, and we'll step on Nelta. But I can't wait that long for a break." She felt her vision blur a bit as she ran her sleeve over the side of her face that felt hot and perspiring. "I need one...now." She chugged down a tube of cold water, glanced up into Terra's processor hub and said: "I've worked *two* straights weeks in a row...two! With no days off. All these people are stampeding the Corridors!" She motioned at the long rows of sedated patients—and lines of patients *waiting* for sedation.

In distant facilities partitioned off with special glass, bustling physicians and techs were scrambling to up-stream minds into the matrix. After the up-streaming process is complete, nurses and techs glide patients into the northern, one-mile long, Full-Body Regeneration section, where more specialists monitor patients and wait for each patient's medical avatar to direct the patient to Full-Body Rejuvenation pods. Any patient a Medical Avatar diagnosed with a complication, specialists quickly glide the patient to Level-4's Medical Facility for more intensive stem-cell treatment, organ growth and surgery, or nano-organic intervention. Upon exiting a rejuvenation pod, the sedated patient glides over to another specialist who down-streams the patient's consciousness back into the patient's body—a ten minute process. When the patient regains consciousness, a nurse in the Recovery section activates the patient's avatar that then remains with the patient for another one-hour recuperation period, after which the Regeneration Administrator releases the patient back into the general population to rest for twenty-four hours and then resume his or her regular activities—looking and feeling like 25 to 30 again!

"I've *had* enough of all this, Nick," Elisa said. Not wanting to ask Terra to relieve her headache with an analgesic pulse just yet, she whispered to him: "The Regents seem to believe that we have super powers and can work straight through without breaks twenty-four-seven."

"That's a good way to verbalize their expectations, Doc," he said, sipping more water from a bottle he called over to meet his lips from a fifty-foot tall, Columnar Processing Dispensary. Modeled after the old cell towers of Earth but now infused with a special mix of electromagnetic energy and dark energy to stream Terra throughout the astrocity, MPDs receive their constant flow energy via Terra's Live Stream Field on Level-7, a secluded and partitioned zone.

"But I'll tell you one thing...we're not slaves to these last-minute procrastinators! It's their fault—" She pointed at the unusually long line of bodies waiting for Regeneration, not only in her Corridor-15, but also other Regeneration Corridors she could see through Plexiglas windows. "They should have scheduled their last-minute procedures months ago, and not pressure The Regents to force us to accommodate them." She looked into the rainbow cycling ceiling hub, hoping someone might overhead her and perhaps empathize with their fatigue.

"Yeah!" Nick said sternly, straightening the patient's holographic vitals that tilted, nearly melting the reading together until he re-aligned the gurney. "Wow, great catch!"

Laughing, she said: "Poor guy. That's *three* times you almost jostled his stats. If you blend the vitals, Nick, *you* sift through 'em and mend 'em yourself, you Juicer!"

They laughed, but that's the name people call specialists with the power and authority to perform consciousness *Up-Streaming* and *Down-Streaming*. After the Body Rejuvenation Pod portion of the two-hour-long Regeneration process, Juicers transfer patients' minds back into their youthful bodies. Because the crew counts on them to make *no* mistakes, Juicers must be physicians, have nano-technical training and Matrix Processing knowledge. Nick Burgess has been qualified for ten years; Elisa since after launching from Earth. Out of 20 Regeneration Corridors in the stern of Level-4, Dr. Elisa Holton is Chief of Corridor-15 and Nick's boss.

When a green light pulsed out of the beehive ceiling hub and landed on the patient's forehead, Elisa knew Terra was ready for his mind to up-stream. "Terra, I'm ready," she said, stepping back, waiting for a rainbow to appear on the patient's head. When the small circle of glowing colors engulfed his cerebral helmet, she commanded, "Begin Up-Streaming."

A yellow beam washed over the man's face and body. Terra was accepting his consciousness.

"I just hope what happened yesterday around this time won't happen today," Nick said, drearily while glancing at the time and washing his hands through a hygienic rinse.

Elisa peeked up at the 3:15 p.m. time that just scrolled down at several Smart Stat locations and quickly agreed. "But just in case, I called Cloning to be on standby with genetic material of everyone we process from this point on. Since I won't be here after day, I'm putting a warning into my replacement." Then she tapped on one of her cameras. The time of yesterday's accident was approaching. If anything should happen, she'd want another form of proof besides Terra or Twin's recount of the event. She tried activating Twin, but Twin wouldn't launch out of her wrist device. Something was already occurring, a miniscule scale, but still significant and she felt a foreboding feeling unlike anything she'd ever experienced.

"Smart move, Doc," Nick said.

She focused back on her patient, checking his Body Double imager. "If this guy—Dave's his name…if Dave here gets one of those rare aneurisms and dies like what almost happened to a woman in Corridor 11 yesterday at 3:25 p.m., I wanna make *sure* Dave has a back-up plan for his life…that he doesn't end up at the Cryogenics section with his mind lost in the matrix somewhere. No one's died yet, and we sure don't wanna be the first Juicers to have a black mark of death on our profiles!"

He gave her a dreadful expression. "Yeah, I wouldn't want that either."

"You think I did the right thing by notifying Cloning?" she asked after noticing a sudden spark of fear rise in in him when he glanced at a white processor beeping red in the corner— obviously a monitoring device. He looked frightened, of The Regents. "For *sure* no one's died that *I've* heard of…and believe me, Nick, we all would have heard something as profound as that!" She swallowed some cold water to quench her nervousness.

"No, I think you did the right thing to prepare that backup plan with Cloning," he said quickly.

She still felt worried about a possible reprimand and began trying to conjure up explanations should a Regent suddenly make a holographic appearance in front of her. Even though she felt angry at them for overstressing all the Juicers, she *really* didn't want to anger them, especially when she might need some type of provision to settle on Nelta. She remembered some advice her parents had given her before she went to college: *Just work with people. You don't have to be a buddy with*

# Astrocity Sagan

*everyone. Just get along with people.*

Nick touched her arm tenderly. "Look, Doc, even though we're supposed to get approval first through The Regency, you had no choice but to contact Cloning. And I'll back ya up. So don't worry."

After he exhaled in relief, she patted her chest in relief. "Approvals from them sometimes take an entire day lately. We don't have that kinda time when we're holding lives and minds in our hands…and relying on Terra to simulate worst case mind-and-body scenarios. The matrix is supposed to be perfect; but still, in spite of over a hundred years of living and breathing with her, I can't help but to believe that somewhere in our genius quantum processor, a flaw exists." She pointed to her wrist device and told him Twin wasn't activating. "And this morning, Twin experienced a processing flaw."

"A systems glitch?" he asked.

"Yep, and now, it appears to be worse." Having *two* cameras now on Record-mode to capture any strange activity or anomaly, she didn't want to worry Nick or ask other Juicers working around them if they had experienced the same type of processing issue. The Scan she activated after Twin's "glitch" returned to her three hours ago as a *Wormhole Transition Episode.*

Nick disagreed with the explanation. "It's a conspiracy of some type…a downright conspiracy I tell you!"

Telling him to be quiet, she decided to stream her concern that to *Sagan's* Home Page, hoping if others had experienced the same "avatar or icon glitch" they'd report it as well. Terra might determine the problem statistically significant, and alert The Regents to address the glitch publically, and immediately, and maybe even in an Emergency Broadcast!

"That aneurism that happened yesterday proves your Matrix Flaw theory," Nick whispered, but I'm not bringing it up to anyone…no way."

She took another careful inspection of Dave's 3D body: rotating it midair, assessing each biometric reading from brain to heart. "Perfect," she said, still feeling a warning call resounding in her gut concerning yesterday's "error" on Corridor 11. She streamed her concern about the accident and the glitch to the other Juicers working around her. "I'm ordering tight monitoring now, Nick." They had ten rows of patients on both sides of them, all sedated and waiting, their holographic vital signs appearing like miniature reflections of their hosts with heart rates beating, brain waves oscillating, and organ readings glowing various Health Ratings. "I don't know about the other Corridors, but everything looks good *so far* here. I sure hope the Regents' techs have solved the aneurysm problem." Nick asked his Avatar to run simulations for them and be ready with those simulations in case of an aneurism in their corridor. Dave's consciousness *Up-Stream* was at *75%* and uploading into the matrix with, *In Progress*, showing under his vital signs.

"Still, *any* kind of mistake doesn't look good, especially when people hear about them, and then confront us on the transport platforms—*rgh*!" Laughing with Nick, she added, "This morning, after I disembarked off our Level-5 Stern Platform, a lady stopped me, telling *me* right to my face that Terra might be malfunctioning. She's somewhere in here right now 'cause she said she had scheduled a Regeneration for today, around this time." Elisa knew it was useless to search for her in the field of white-clad bodies, but she couldn't help but try to locate her. The woman's distress was unforgettable, her face white with fear. She even appeared a bit disguised, as if she had on make-up and had inserted contacts in her eyes. The woman obviously knew something but was terrified to voice the knowledge.

"What did you tell her?" Nick asked.

"Well I couldn't say, *yeah, ya should be worried lady, and spread the word, 'cause someone almost died yesterday and we don't have a clue as to why...but a matrix problem could be why!*"

"Hell no—we can't say anything like *that*," he exclaimed, "so I hope whatever caused the error, or malfunction, or *whatever* ya wanna call it, is fixed, and Clone Techs are on standby, like you ordered."

When the yellow extraction beam disappeared off Dave's forehead, Elisa unlatched the cerebral helmet and handed it to Nick to place on the next patient. As they waited for a minute of down time, she noticed more patients entering and checking in at the Main Regeneration Center. The holographic stage at the entrance of her Corridor-15 was showing the date, time, each Corridor's capacity, personnel on duty, their profiles, their patient numbers, and their Regeneration progress. On the opposite end of Corridor-15—beyond the body pods infusing patients with biological solutions, cellular treatments and hormonal therapies— patients were sitting up, recovering, and happy—marveling at the years they gained, their new youthful faces, and energized physiology.

"I just don't get it, Nick," Elisa said, watching them.

"Get what?" he asked.

"Well, the matrix is failsafe, so these aneurysms don't make sense. Scientists proved Terra is accurate, infallible, and completely self-correcting. We've seen the matrix in action this way for nearly a hundred years!" Shaking her head and feeling stumped, she rubbed her eyes. "Whoever reported those perfect results *had* to have been a lying, Nick, or something way off kilter is at play inside this entire astrocity. Or…there's some kinda death-wish activating. I don't know! But an aneurysm has to come from somewhere when it happens. It's not the bodies that are at fault." She knew she was recording everything, every image and dialogue. Nick didn't know it. She couldn't risk him knowing her plan to record and expose any type of corruption.

Nick glided Dave and his Imaging stage over to a scurrying nurse so she could quickly send him into a Rejuvenating Body Pod. He grabbed a new patient and connected her to their station. All her vital signs droned on and illuminated. With a sickly expression on his face, he whispered: "Doc, you're implying that someone's *purposely* targeting people." After Elisa gestured positively, he added: "I know of horrible genocides on Earth that dictators instituted to control population and solve racial issues, but killing our residents? My God—I wouldn't even *say* that if I were you!" While Elisa situated the patient's Cerebral Interface helmet over her head, Nick acted as if he had overstepped a boundary when he glanced up at the ceiling and shot a coy smile at Terra's rainbow-cycling, beehive processing mount. Medical watchdogs and Internal Affairs were monitoring all procedures for performance evaluations and compliance. "Chief, don't even *hint* that someone high up—'cause *that's* where *this* kind of cold calculating maneuver could come from—could be targeting people with intrusive grid messages, devils and phantoms, and making aneurisms.

"Shh," Elisa whispered.

"Could that aneurism yesterday have been someone's murder gone wrong? If so, why? And why *that* person?" Nick's avatar activated over his wrist device as an automatic response; but then Nick flicked his wrist, and the tiny Doppelganger extinguished. With a fake smile still beaming on his blushing face, he waved at Terra. "We're almost ready for consciousness up-streaming here…just a few more seconds of prep time and monitoring! Nothing's wrong…we're just talking." The female patient's imager was still reading: *Diagnostic Scan, In-Progress.*

# Astrocity Sagan

## Chapter 8 - Tipping Point

Not wanting to cause an alert in case her own heated biometrics might trigger an alarm, Elisa thought up a distraction. She waved at Terra's ceiling hub. "Let's see this patient's profile, please!" Her profile began scrolling down all her information.

"About that lady who stopped you on the transport platform," Nick said, rotating the patient's vitals and then homing in on her oscillating EEG readings, keen determination on his brow.

Elisa inspected the patient's medical history after swiping away her insignificant employment history. "No problems that I can see here…but we have to wait for Terra to finish her diagnostic scan. Yeah? What about her?"

"I had the same thing happen to me after the first aneurysm occurred two months ago, only the guy started railing on me and scolding me," Nick said as he tapped *off* his in-ear device. He often had it *on* to listen to music or as white noise to block out all the surround sounds. "I started using this ear bud as an Image Interface with my collar to disguise myself in the transport tunnel."

"Wow that's drastic," she said.

"Even that underground group has classified all the weird stuff happening as death scenarios. That's how I got the idea of disguising myself. That's what those people are doing to move around undetected."

"I heard of the off-the-grid outsiders on my way to work this morning, but people don't consider them a problem," she said. "But on my time off, I'll keep my eyes open for them, and record them if I spot anyone *not* using technology."

"Yeah, send me a picture too, will ya? 'Cause they're all over this morning's Live Stream news and I'd like proof!" he said.

"Are they the two hundred and seventy-three missing people?"

Shrugging, he answered: "I think so. This morning, someone hacked into transport tunnel hardware. They projected images at the Level-6's center dome for ten seconds. Ten seconds!"

"People must have panicked like crazy," Elisa said.

"Oh yeah!" When he tried to open up the show that some people had copied for astrocity-wide streaming, his wrist device produced static.

Then a sudden Emergency rendering activated over his wrist device.

"Oh-oh!" he said, tapping his device wildly with his finger.

Executive Regent Manning's face appeared. He had his usual Beethoven serious features, stern expression, and black, slicked-back hair.

"Sorry, Sir...I—" .

"We have criminal activity occurring on *Sagan*." With his stern Beethoven eyes and square rigid jaw, Thornton Manning began displayed Level-6's Central dome over the transport platform.

"This isn't just me," Nick began. "People everywhere are seeing this broadcast."

At several locations throughout the Regeneration Corridors, Thornton was projecting his news rendering. He

# Astrocity Sagan

showed images of people waiting in line for Maglevs and Enforcers flying high-up in the domes in hovercraft, scanning for signals and targets. One particular scene unfolded on Level-6's Grand Central Station with the virtual sun at 3:20 p.m., the way the crew had voted on and approved the setting for January of 2168 *Space Fold Time.* To be there would be like standing in the station. The interior would appear so real, smell musky, and its outside rendering would have visions of a wintry chill.

Regent Manning continued: "If you see *any* illegal use of technology, overhear *anyone* discussing a plot against Terra, spot *any* abandoned kiosks, or see any packages out in the open, please, *please* hail your nearest Enforcer and stream The Regency immediately. Thank you, and follow us for updates on our Regency Home Page." The show stopped.

"Damn!" Nick kept repeating. The patient's diagnostic scan stopped, and he began attaching cerebral interface patches to her forehead. "*This* must be completely embarrassing for The Regency, huh, Doc?"

"Sure!" Elisa agreed.

With his head low, he began tucking in the patient and whispered, "Chief, you think The Regents are taking the focus *off* the matrix to blame this new group for all our latest problems? They *did* hack into secure sites."

"But not medical sites," she corrected. She puffed out two sighs. "I don't know. The type of manipulation we're looking at is so advanced. Could a Regent *be* so cold and filled with megalomania as to set up a conspiracy? And why?"

Nick looked frightened. "Maybe something *worse* than aneurysms, weird messages, and virtual monsters might pop up around here. Whataya think?"

"I don't know—shhh!"

"I'm tellin' ya, Elisa, someone or something is trying to get our attention or get rid of people. That's what I'm concluding…after putting two-and-two together. He mouthed the word, *murder*.

"Can't be!" she waved. "I think your imagination is running on overdrive, Nick," she laughed. "The aneurysms are just mistakes, most likely from working overtime." Suddenly, she believed that *she* or Nick might cause on error! Neither one of them had gotten much sleep in the past week. They'd been working overtime for days! It was her job to keep pressing the Regents for better working hours. She had streamed that complaint to them, along with her concern over the pronounced heterochromia issue, but she hadn't received a response from them or through Twin, who wasn't activating anyway. A bitter tang hit the roof of her mouth, pushing her toward a confrontation.

Looking around at the 22 Juicers rotating body scans or initiating mind transfers through Terra's yellow quantum beams, she noticed a few of them peek up at her, and she thought: No way am *I* gonna allow people to believe that *I'm* working 'em to death—that *I'm* jeopardizing patient safety. She felt a hallow loneliness as she waved at one Juicer who immediately turned away. Wow, she thought, Dr. Janet Melton looks so ticked off! I've been trying to make friends with her and a few others before I leave. That they're angry doesn't help.

She had a few friends from her previous job as Chief of Regeneration Corridor 3, but those alliances and friendships faded over a year ago after she became serious with Carl Foldier and made him the center of her life that changed her schedule. Then some of those old friends changed careers, which wasn't uncommon considering the increase in longevity. Elisa felt suddenly angry, at herself. Whether The Regents had manipulated her into working overtime or not, *she* had allowed all her waking time to morph into working time—mostly likely, to get over Carl.

"It's retaliation time...*right* after I get off work, Nick," she said.

After advising that she not retaliate *too* harshly, Nick called out, "I'm ready here, Terra," and a rainbow appeared on the patient's forehead. "Begin *Consciousness Up-Stream*." He backed away. After Terra's yellow upload light extinguished, he lowered the gurney, released the holographic vitals stage, and pushed the patient toward the Rejuvenation Body Pod suite. This patient had a requested a tropical cabana setting in the Recovery Center to awaken to after her full-body rejuvenation treatment. "Chief, I also think the problem is that we've had *twice* the usual load. This overload we've been experiencing is not your fault."

"You mean the Line Jumpers," she said, spraying her fingers with a quick-dry sanitizer.

Because some people were desperate to regenerate—especially those who couldn't decide whether they wanted to stay or disembark on Nelta—they were calling into the Corridors with emergency scenarios, trying to wheedle in between scheduled appointments.

"Like I said, Nick, I'm gonna do something about our overtime and being so overworked, *after* I get off duty, especially if I don't hear from Regent Manning."

The nearest clock was now reading *3:31 Space-Fold Time.*

"Tell our team *that* after I leave, will ya?"

"Sure, Doc, I'll definitely do that," he said softly. Then his face contorted in shock as he peered around their Corridor that appeared overwhelmed with sedated bodies. "Maybe, because of all these Jumpers, Terra's Cloud center might overload!"

"Naw, that can't happen, Nick." She tried to ease his panic by stopping the next in-coming patient gliding toward, giving him a brief break.

"I hope consciousness-crossing doesn't occur, Doc. If Terra mixes up minds or memories—my God!—identities!—we'll have a full-blown problem!" He was inhaling hard and rubbing his face. "That'll be a *real* mess that *we'll* have to clean up!"

"Nick, you're exaggerating," she began. "Drink some more

cold water, take a minute's rest against the processing tower, and I'll have Terra beam ya down a calming cerebral analgesic." She grabbed his arms gently. "Stop…breathe…we're all right, Nick." As he settled down and glanced at the new patient with dread in his eyes, she said: "You're thinking of a scenario that I'm sure is *far* from happening." Peering up into Terra's cycling beehive hub, she said into firmly into it: "See what happens when we're pushed too far? When you expect us to work so much overtime?" The Juicers around her gave her the thumbs up signal, smiled, but then immediately returned to their jobs. She felt energized and proud. "Terra, schedule me an appointment right after I get off work with Regent Jenkens, please. *He's* the one who mediates between us and The Regency…or let me see Executive Regent Manning himself, or any other Regent if they're available. We have problems here in all the Corridors, and I need to tell them about it personally, not just through a matrix connection." Now she began to feel the silt of sickness in her growling stomach that comes with anxiety, and anger. After gulping down some water from a bottle that another Juicer tossed over to her, she said: "Especially inform Regent Manning that it's me, Dr. Elisa Holton. He knows me, from our days Earth days." She didn't want to use that special advantage, but she believed she had no choice. She hailed Twin, again, and this time Twin appeared next to her. She put her on Copy-mode to stream her request to The Regency as well. She said into Twin's brown transparent eyes: "Regent Manning, you and I haven't spoken in years, but we *did* have an acquaintance in common, Lynn Altmin, and you recommended me for this job in the first place. I've had it since leaving Earth. Now, I need a few minutes to talk to you about some concerns."

She felt choked up when Lynn's face popped into her mind. Her best friend for years, Lynn died ten years prior to *Sagan's* launch from Earth. Since her death, Thornton Manning had become progressively withdrawn, ending in his ultimate act of seclusion: Lock Out Day. That's *not* how she remembered Lynn describing him though at all, completely opposite! Lynn loved him, and Elisa remembered noticing how he loved her on First Communication Day with the Neltans, even though Lynn told her prior to the *Greeter*'s launch that they had never consummated their love. Lynn was looking forward to taking a long vacation with him after *Greeter* landed. That never happened, only Lynn's untimely death. Elisa wondered: Did Lynn's death trigger a drastic alteration in his personality? Or did some bad experience after Lynn's death incite a change? Or did he *always* have a propensity to distrust people and isolate?

She longed to know the answers. "Please tell The Regency that I'll descend to their Level-9 Meeting Arena after I get off work, at five. I know they're busy rendering graphic appearances with the crew or creating holosite worlds, so I'll wait for them to reply. Emphasize to them Twin, We need to talk."

As a Lead Regeneration Specialist, she knew they'd have to make time for her. If not, she could create a social-media nuisance on their Home Page and force them to listen! She had that much authority as a Regeneration Specialist. She had never been outspoken before, and now, voicing her concerns and asking for results could jeopardize her future career. Her stomach felt raw, her skin numb for starting this unusual act of asserting herself. "I'll be off-Corridor duty for good after today, but at least I hope to make a difference for these employees I'm leaving behind, Nick." She noticed that all the Juicers had paused, attending to her every word. "I need ten minutes with *one* Regent. That's all I'm asking, please." After seeing a green beam of light flash in the corner ceiling hub and Twin disappear into their matrix grid to receive an answer, she turned back to Nick. "I'm going to the top of the food chain right after my shift is over.

Nick sighed and readjusted his in-ear device to waft in soft music. "I hope you can do something, Doc, 'cause *all* this overload and overtime is crazy making! Something *big* has to be going on around this astrocity. Someone's obviously hacking the matrix, inserting malware into messages, and rendering monsters to the crew. But what are worse are the aneurisms, and another can occur at any time. Something's not right, Elisa. I wonder *what*...don't you?" he asked in a whispered deep concern. Fear was also clamoring on his face, replacing his earlier heated panic that Terra relieved by emitting an analgesic pulse into his brain. Standing still with a new patient between them, she saw his uneasiness turn to a calm steady pace.

# Astrocity Sagan

# Chapter 9 – Aneurism

Suddenly, their new patient began convulsing.

Orange alert lights illuminated high above her gurney. Her vital signs were haywire! Simulations activated, showing various solutions as nurses, and more Juicers ran to their rescue.

"What's going on, Nick?! This alert's probably rippling everywhere!" Elisa cried, staring at the patient's face. "She looks familiar. Give me a name."

"I can't see through all these stats to *see* a name!" Nick shouted.

Quickly, she snapped a picture of the patient with her concealed camera as Nick hailed matrix techs and medical personnel.

"The Diagnostic grid is scanning her for an answer," Nick said.

Elisa inserted an IV into the patient's arm as per the Virtual Nurse's directive. Noticing Terra's rainbow processor circling at twice its normal speed on the ceiling, she ordered, "Terra, cut power!"

Nothing happened.

# J.P. Osterman

The sight of the convulsing body gave her a shot of adrenaline, and she raised the gurney and spotted a problem on the patient's Body Double imager. "There's a bulge in the superior sagittal sinus that needs a nano-biological treatment. We can't do that here! We need Stem Cells techs!" She pushed the patient's forehead under Terra's hub for immediate consciousness up-stream.

"Oh no!" Nick cried. Several Juicers around them repeated the dread.

"Oh yes!" Elisa countered, gesturing for her colleagues to get back to their duties. "We've got an aneurism…and there could be more, so get back to your stations and be on the lookout for any neurological deviations from your patients' medical renderings."

"But this one's worse, Doc," Nick began. "I see another aneurism…right next to the interior cerebral vein." He pressed more emergency patches on the woman's extremities that were streaming her biometrics to other medical labs and facilities. He then turned to the Virtual Nurse, this time, being directed from The Regency. "You better tell us how to proceed, 'cause if ya don't, this lady's *not* gonna be able to smell or count numbers *if* she regains consciousness!"

"What's this woman's name and what's her position?" Elisa asked, rotating the patient's virtual muscular-skeletal system. "Maybe some other type of implant is responsible…maybe a previous treatment we missed in her history—"

"Emma Jane Wright is her name, Dr. Holton," Terra replied, her Standard Form appearing in front of the patient's netted head.

A tiny, yellow rectangular icon containing a red body pod appeared under Emma Jane Wright's name, then a purple insignia with an eagle and four stars. The two images kept interchanging inside Emma Jane Wright's profile.

"I remember her name from somewhere," Elisa said, her thoughts sharpening.

"I don't!" Nick countered, touching Emma's cold hand.

# Astrocity Sagan

When Elisa noticed Emma Jane Wright's Regency Clone Tech insignia, signifying that Emma was part of their elite Clone Tech group, she said, "What's a Regent Clone Tech doing *here*? They have their own Regeneration facility on Level-9."

"My sentiments *exactly*," Nick barked, "but there's no time to wait for an answer. Let's get rolling! I'm sure other Clone Techs are probably on their way up here right now."

Elisa wondered: Did someone just dump her here to die? Or had Emma experienced an accident on Level-9 that someone was working hard to cover up as a mistake? But Terra wouldn't let *anyone* get away with something like that! Monitors are everywhere. A report should have rung out—no, blared out—if a Regent Clone Tech had gone missing. "Who sent her here and why?" Elisa kept whispering under her breath.

Nick kept parroting, "I don't know…and I'm not sure I *wanna* know!"

Then, a tiny picture appeared in the Emma Jane Wright's holographic projections. They were obviously slide shows of her first glimmer of life. "Look," Elisa cried, "her mind's already been up-streamed!" She said into the high ceiling processor, "What the hell's going on?!"

"She shouldn't be here," Nick said, turning every which way for old-fashioned medical equipment to help them. Little robotics were coming with them, but not fast enough.

Another Juicer interjected: "Terra should have all the information about all this *somewhere* in her grid…or The Archives."

Elisa whispered into her camera still concealed inside her white pocket, "See, I *told* you something very odd is going on."

A bright-red warning illuminated through all the Regeneration Corridors, and more Juicers and nurses dashed toward them, asking if Elisa and Nick needed help.

"Death is eminent for Emma here if we can't fix her brain

right now," Elisa said, catching more IV bags and blood enhancers, the latter which she applied to Emma's neck. A small brainwave activated on Emma's Body Double Imager. "Whew—almost! At least we've got artificial readings…but now we gotta find her mind!"

"A first death on *Sagan*, damn!" Nick said, gloomily.

"At least the first one we know of," Elisa whispered, realizing that if this had happened right in front of them, others deaths had to have occurred somewhere else. Emma was still on the verge of flat lining, but she filled with determination to make sure she wouldn't! She ordered the Regents' Virtual Nurse to make a Regent appear in person to get one of their special Clone Techs from Level-9 to her Corridor-15 station. As the nurse complied, Elisa hit her forehead in exasperation. "God—why me? Why here? Under *my* supervision!"

Another Juicer monitoring Terra's processing of minds said, "I'm receiving a surge in Terra's Up-Load grid!"

"Where?" Nick asked her.

"*Sagan*'s core," she answered. "Is that Level-9 'cause I've never heard 'o that place before."

Elisa felt spooked. The Level-9 area responsible is called the Live Stream Field—Terra's core processing center. "I don't' get this!" Then she was filled with an unprecedented intuition in the form of medical images, people operating. Her mind felt like a downloading conduit of surging vital information. I can save her, she thought. Turning to Nick, she said, "I have to operate manually and relieve pressure around that vein or Emma's gonna die of a hemorrhage." She pulled out an emergency kit from under the gurney and took out a drill. "Prep her, Nick." She had an idea. "Someone find and program a nano-organic feed that I can inject right into this area of her brain. If I inject it fast, it'll go straight to the damage and heal the tissue." She breathed. "I think we can save her."

Nick caught a tube of solution and began dousing a shaved area on Emma head. "You can do this, Elisa. You're the *best*!"

# Astrocity Sagan

"I'm trying," she inhaled through the pressure. Another Juicer handed her a vile filled with preprogrammed nanytes while another began calling in codes for their targets. Drilling sounds yielded Emma Jane Wright's brain. As she injected the tissue with a nano-robotic intervention and Nick guided the repair-bots to the aneurism, she kept repeating: "*God*, a Regent Clone Tech right here! But why?"

"It's not on her Living Resume, Doctor Holton," a male Juicer told her.

"Most of her history is missing too," Elisa said. "We can't even get an image of where she's been or what she's been doing that coulda caused this and made her wind up here!" Concentrating, she tried hard to block out Nick's, "It's not your fault, Doc, just keep up the good work, 'cause you're a whiz!" She felt everything around her fade as she continued the operation. *Am I* doing the emergency work, she wondered, peeking up at Terra's rainbow cycling hub, or are *you*? She remembered medical school and years of residency, but that was on Earth. Then she noticed her arm, and recalled the Neltan Encantado armband experience. She was operating, but with exquisite artistry and precision that Juicers around her felt stricken with awe.

*Something profound is happening inside me now. I felt it before, but now this fine-tuned skill is proof! The new influx of knowledge, skill and energy are surging through my body and soul, power and abilities making me focus and recall everything I've ever read, watched or experienced but forgotten*, she thought. My biology is now a channel and a conduit for the unexplainable. *In this emergency, I'm evolving in knowledge and being infused with new abilities! Where's it coming from? Who is all this coming from?* She felt amazed and suddenly strengthened by an outside force—so intimate and joining with her. *It's guiding me, coaching me on autopilot, and making me change and enhancing me.* "I'm at the bleed site..." The virtual instruments were like utensils in her fingers.

"Wow, Elisa...look at you work! You're gonna save her,"

Nick exclaimed.

Then, her entire Regeneration Corridor lost light, and a low drone filled the air.

"Now there's a matrix drain," Nick cried. "I don't get this."

Pops and snaps electrified the air, and then sparks flew from two, giant processor towers that looked like energized Tesla coils. Everyone began shouting and dropping to the floor.

"Damn! I hope this isn't a signal that something's wrong with this ship, or that we're about to go into wormhole spin," Nick gasped, steadying a few straggling gurneys.

"I hope not too," Elisa said, regaining her balance. Even in the dark, she was being guided by the light, the instruments easy fixes for Emma Jane Write's aneurism.

The Virtual Nurse showed her the nanytes' healing trajectory. They were almost finished cauterizing Emma's brain bleed, but noise was abounding everywhere.

"Quiet everyone!" Elisa wiped heart-palpitating sweat on her sleeve.

Noise in her Corridor stilled as the lights whirred back on and the processing towers settled into their normal Low-mode drone and whir. Terra's hubs hissed as they regained power, their little rainbow beams circling wildly.

"That power drain stopped—*whew*—and we're all still here—*whew*," she sighed, and everyone cheered as Matrix Techs ran into several Regeneration Corridors and began scanning for abnormalities and streaming their reports to The Regents. As Elisa applied an organic seal to Emma's scalp and irrigated the incision area, she felt something hot strike the base of her head. "Not me!" she screamed, reeling back from the *Consciousness Up-Stream* that had activated. She felt a sudden flush of strange words and images flood her mind. "Terra— cut processing! Your targeting me!"

She blacked out…then regained consciousness, focusing back on Nick's alarmed white face.

"I'm all right…I'm okay," she breathed. After standing up

and repeating that several times, she noticed the Up-Stream activity wouldn't leave Emma Jane Wright. She ordered Matrix Techs to divert the activity as strings of bloody spit began oozing out of Emma's mouth.

Elisa felt her chest pounding. "Terra, stop this Up-Stream mode! She doesn't have a mind *to* upload!" She grabbed the drill and swung it at the ceiling, trying to dislodge Terra's hub. "Kill power, damn it!"

Two Matrix Techs began fighting her, ordering her stop. "You can cause a chain reaction in this entire Level-5 section!"

But Nick punched them. "We have a life to save, so get a Regent down here and have *him* do something to help this poor lady!" No matter where Nick and Elisa moved Emma Jane Wright's body, Terra's yellow extraction beam kept targeting her, lighting on her.

"Terra, are you purposely *killing* this woman?!" Elisa shouted.

The malfunctioning hub crackled and sparked as it dislodged and flew off the ceiling, and Elisa pushed Emma's gurney over to another Regeneration station where techs grabbed her and lifted her onto a new gurney.

Nick slapped two pads on Emma's chest, sending surging current through her lifeless body. "It's not working, Elisa, should I prep her for deep freeze?" He pressed a button. A sealed portal opened in the floor behind them, and up hissed a fogging subzero body cylinder.

After two Matrix Techs replaced the faulty ceiling hub, the new hub was reading *normal* her station and Elisa ordered, "I need Diagnostics, Terra...not your Matrix Techs. What went wrong, and why...and why can't we retrieve any background data on Emma Jane Wright?!" Sirens were blaring at a lower level as Juicers rushed recovering patients out the exits. Escalator doors where grinding on their magnetic bars as steel sliders opened and thudded shut with wild new activity.

"Just a second, Nick, wait on the deep freeze option," Elisa said, waiting for a call from a Regent and thinking about the next best course of action for Emma Jane Wright.

Deep freeze? Or should I hold out for emergency cloning approval from the Regents' Clone-Techs? Cloning is only authorized in case of death, and only after Regency approval. But she still hadn't heard from them! Before enacting that option on her own, the Law directed Chiefs of Regeneration Corridors to adhere to protocol: cryogenic storage. But she couldn't authorize a cold stasis-existence for Emma whose neurological state was now on its way back to reading normal…*if* she could only locate her mind and down-stream it back into her body! Cryogenic storage would result in Emma existing in a frozen world while being completely aware of her chambered presence inside Terra's matrix. What would life be like inside a matrix? No one knew, and from the research she had read, no one would want to know.

"Cryogenic stasis would be *torture* for this poor woman, Nick," Elisa began. "At least getting a new body will give her a new life."

"Well…"

"I vote for sending her to Cloning," Elisa said. "And since the Clone Techs who are supposed to be doing their jobs aren't here, I say we start the process…and stream the lack of patient care and concern to the crew if The Regents don't respond soon and continue with my course of treatment."

"Huh?" Nick lamented. "It's gonna mean paperwork, and interviews with Internal Affairs, for *all* of us."

She felt her heart race with the urge to fight. Terra—or someone—had started this battle, for some reason, and she felt the call to strike back and defeat whoever was trying to take her, and Emma, down. She grimaced at Terra's rainbow-cycling hub—knowing that powerful people had to be watching. "I *will* resuscitate Emma Jane Wright, and get to the bottom of what happened here this afternoon, but the only way to proceed now is an Emergency Clone Procedure."

Nick gestured in resignation. "Emergency Clone Procedure it is then. I second the order. Let's get started."

# Astrocity Sagan

"Yes, Dr. Burgess, confirmation received," another Virtual Nurse said and then faded. Terra's ceiling hubs began cycling green. That directive had reached The Top—Executive Regent Thornton Manning. He was giving his approval. Every Juicer and Matrix Tech within one-hundred-feet of Emma Jane Wright began glancing at one another in trepidation. Soon, each one of them would receive in their person grids an *Order to Appear before The Regency*.

Even Elisa sent in a request to Level-1's Team of Medical Attorneys to advocate for her in the near future. "I hope I receive an immediate reply. I'm gonna need a good lawyer."

Nick Burgess eyes reflecting the whirling lights made him look alien. "I hope a Clone Tech get in here and takes over soon, Doc." He wrapped a band over Emma Wright's chest that began automatic CPR. Elisa infused Emma with two vials of nanyte serum that would capture her genetic code for cloning. "The cryogenic window of opportunity just closed," Nick said with resignation. The cold-steaming cylinder descended into the floor, and the clamp sealed it shut.

While murmuring expletives of anger and frustration, Elisa glided Emma Jane Wright's body under a special hub at the center of five Regeneration Corridors. A giant white light illuminated. Nick was standing alongside Elisa when she said, "Terra, transfer a grid from your Cloning protocol, *um…*" She had forgotten the precise code to override the Regency's restrictive order, but then remembered it was part of her birthday. "Level-5, 05010004, Clone Facility. Transfer ten stem-cell units to Center Stage, now."

Emma's body was now under a powerful white sheen as special tubing wound around her lifeless body, infusing her in select areas with potent cell replicators.

"Stem-cell robotics commencing genetic scan, Dr. Holton," Terra said, appearing feet away from Emma and monitoring the cloning process.

"You're hacking the Clone Lab," Nick cried. "The Regents

# J.P. Osterman

will have your license—"

"Authorization code 05010004," Elisa repeated, angrily eying a monitoring device high in the corner. "Transfer all remapping to the Clone Tech lab for immediate reproduction of Emma Jane Wright, Terra."

"Yes, Dr. Holton," Terra replied.

"Search for her consciousness, Terra, and when you find it, deliver it to the Regency's Clone Facility. Begin body remodeling of Emma Jane Wright there now."

The large rainbow-cycling hub descended and expanded over Emma's body as Terra replied, "Commencing cloning of Emma Jane Wright in Cylinder 1, Clone Tech Center, Level-5, Dr. Holton."

Techs on hovercraft, scanning several ceiling processors, backed their craft toward the escalators and elevators.

Elisa saw a terror of death spread across the faces of several of her colleagues. "You can leave if you want to," she said to everyone as she waited impatiently for Terra to finish mapping and streaming Emma's genetics to the Clone Facility, miles east of their Level-5 Regeneration area. "I know hacking into the Regents' Medical Grid is illegal, and I'll take responsibility for what I had to do here today to save a life." She saw relief spread like sunshine over their taut faces. "I guarantee I won't implicate any of you. You *know* me. And if you want to leave your stations and reschedule your patients for tomorrow, I'll vouch for your innocence with The Regency when they question me. I plan to appear before them tonight. I won't wait."

"They might interrogate you!" a tech called.

After an exchange of harsh whispers, groans, and frightening cries, most Regeneration Specialists and their assistants decided to stay while the rest stampeded to the escalators.

"Thanks for sticking with me, Nick," Elisa said softly.

"Sure thing, Elisa," he said, slipping off his magnifying visor. He looked tired, but then his face energized after he applied antibacterial cleanser on his hands. He suddenly

72

turned sullen as he nodded at the escalators. "Uh-oh, look who's coming."

Scientists dressed in yellow protective suits charged the special station. They were The Regents' elite Clone Technicians—very seldom ever seen on *Sagan*. Transferring orders into Elisa's wrist device, they pushed her and Nick out of the way of Emma's body as if they were anticipating a fusion accident. Elisa noticed a few Regeneration Specialists from nearby Corridors running her way while narrating their perspectives of the malfunction over their wrist devices. Elisa began to feel less afraid as she imbibed their moral support through encouraging statements they were sending to Twin. Turning her attention back to Emma's Body Double Imager, she said to one of the Clone Techs: "This tissue scan is almost complete. All you should have to do is to activate a full-body stem-cell formation in Clone Chamber, Cylinder 1." She hoped Terra had already initiated the full-body formation before anyone could override the initiative. An override would kill Emma Jane Wright and the clone. The Regency would *never* do that. *That* would be murder, the first murder ever on *Sagan*. She wondered: they'd never kill someone, would they?

As the three Clone Techs kept monitoring Emma's progress, the sirens completely stopped sounding, and normal environmental stats began projecting around the room: everything from temperature, population, and wormhole location, to date and time.

Wanting to keep Internal Affairs at bay for her workers, Elisa felt the need to justify her decision to everyone, including the Clone Techs. "I couldn't wait any longer for Regency approval, so *I* hacked into that medical grid and ordered cloning."

With his face concealed behind a special visor, a Clone Tech showed her a virtual shaping of Emma Jane Wright's body. On the bow of Level-5, in their Clone Tech facility, a body pod was replicating her.

# J.P. Osterman

"Stem-cell cloning at fifty percent," Terra called, until one of the Clone Techs asked her to stop the countdown. Terra disappeared from Corridor-15. The bright white, Center Stage, Emergency Clone Processor extinguished and ascended into the ceiling, and everyone began clapping and cheering.

Inhaling, exhaling, and feeling faint, Elisa almost collapsed in relief. "*Whew!*"

"We did it!" Nick cried.

The Clone techs grabbed the gurney, covered Emma in a white blanket, and left the Regeneration Corridors like pall bearers.

Elisa felt proud. She disobeyed the law, and might have to pay a price—but she had given Emma a new chance for a new life, now burgeoning in a clone capsule at the bow of Level-5. Then she remembered that Terra had begun processing Emma's body without ever replying to her request for the location of her mind. "Where is Emma Jane Wright's consciousness, Terra?" After Terra gave her the grid through which Emma's consciousness had streamed, but no storage site, she called the Clone-Techs who appeared over her wrist device. They were now on The Regent's private Maglev to the Clone Facility, showing an arrival time of ten minutes. "*Where* is Emma Jane Wright's consciousness?" she asked them, noticing Nick's somber expression as he pushed bloody gauze and sheets into floor panels for recycling.

The three Clone Techs standing at Emma's feet replied in a strange low voice, "A Level-7's matrix cloud." They repeated the location, and then extinguished the communication.

The clock above the escalator archways struck 5:00 p.m., and techs and specialists working overtime scampered back to their sedated patients. Watching them return to work, Elisa felt a dull ringing in her ears. She felt a bit dizzy and out of body as she recalled the interference that had occurred between her and Emma when Terra's consciousness Up-Stream went berserk. Had Emma's encephalographic void altered her own consciousness in some way? In thirty minutes, her shift would be over. She agreed to wind up all the details and work until 5:30. Then, she whispered her concerns about a mind-mix up to Twin and asked her where she could go for a safe and unmonitored scan of her own mind. Twin said she would search the astrocity for a private medical specialist. Tapping her camera and stopping the recording, Elisa reminded Twin, in a whisper, to include the abnormal biology coursing through her body.

As her discussion with Twin ended, Nick had already activated robotics and disinfectant sprays to clean up and sterilize the floor. Then he said, "Elisa, Internal Affairs has re-routed our last five patients to other stations. They say we're done for the day. They want my statement, now."

How much trouble would she'd be in? She couldn't guess. She told Nick: "Anything from a slap-on-the-hand, a note in my file, or losing my license so I can't perform Regenerations."

"Darn," he said.

She laughed. "Nick, we won't be Regenerating people anyway in the near future. A Regeneration revoke won't hurt me...and I have plenty of funds stashed up, so I have no worries." He appeared concerned about *his* future. "I'll tell them *I* made the decision to clone Emma Jane Wright, not you, Nick. Don't even worry about losing your license. I'm going to argue my case in person, to The Regency, right after work in exactly twenty-eight minutes." But before she left, she wanted to make sure that a malfunction wouldn't happen again. Standing on a platform intended to draw attention, she announced to her entire staff and Regeneration Specialists-Juicers—who were listening: "We only have a little time left on this shift. Make sure you check the buffer on *all* circuitry in the gurneys, and run diagnostics on *all* holographic projectors prior to accepting a new patient. Be on the lookout for wavering statistics on *any* patient's Body Double Imager. *Those* we just learned are early indications of surge-and-drain power issues." She didn't dare say 'malfunctions.' That might escalate into a ship-wide viral panic, if a ship-wide panic hadn't already been triggered. She had no idea of what the crew had learned. "After I'm gone…because after 5:30 p.m. tonight I'll be on permanent leave, make sure you have a backup gurney, and ensure the Center Stage Clone areas are ready to clone people." They began discussing her orders in mass. "I intent to take our case to *Clone Without Approval* to The Regency right when I log out of here." Their lips opened in shock. "I hope to procure emergency cloning for all Chief Corridor Specialists. I'm determined to fight for our rights and patients' rights." Her colleagues clad in white lab coats with Chief insignias on their collars appeared happy and uplifted. "I'll stream you my results of the meeting; but for now, I'm sending you all new protocols and that emergency clone code in case you might have to act fast in the face of an accident."

They streamed her positive emoticons over her wrist device with images of support as they returned to their stations. Regenerations slowly resumed as techs pushed in bodies from closed rooms and slid them into the queue. Nick Burgess sighed, "*Whew,*" and pointed to an incoming Regent Clone-Tech who was maneuvering around all the Corridors with a scanning device, obviously trying to retrace Terra's error.

Elisa felt a pounding headache coming on. "What went wrong, Terra?" Suddenly, she realized that being angry was getting her nowhere. She decided to talk nicely to the hub. "Answer me, *please.*"

"Sensors aligned, Dr. Holton," Terra replied, appearing right next to her. Nick jumped back when her processor light filtered on his face. "Power re-routed." All patients' stats were showing normal and ready for Regeneration.

Elisa didn't feel ready, and she clenched the rim of an empty gurney. "What the hell went wrong?" she asked the rendering of the tall athletic woman with brown hair— Standard Terra. "You still haven't answered me. It's like you *purposely* set out to kill Emma Jane Wright. Damn!" She felt madder than ever as she grimaced at the hub. A Regent Clone-Tech had just finished sealing the hub with nano-fabrics and was testing its performance. "Answer me, Terra, 'cause *I'm* scheduled for a Regeneration in here tomorrow, and I sure as hell don't want what just occurred happening to me!"

Nick said, "Have ya thought of rescheduling?"

Stretching out her fingers and then rounding them, she groaned, "No! I wanna be my best and youngest self, for Nelta, and to live as old as I can."

"You got it!" Nick said.

A rainbow light began cycling strong in the renovated hub.

"Well, Terra?" she asked.

"A Level-9 power surge occurred, Dr. Holton," Terra replied, "then a drain. That's what *went wrong*."

"Terra sounds pissed!" Nick said.

"Level-9, Nick." Elisa repeated. "What are Regents *doing* down there? And the drain in *our* power had to have amassed energy to power up something powerful somewhere else…but where, Terra?" She looked at Nick's puzzled face and added: "What the heck's going on? Six weeks until we arrive at Nelta, and there are *real* mysteries happening all over this astrocity!"

As she knotted up her hair in a bun and tapped her concealed cameras, Nick pulled the sleeve of her white coat and said: "Elisa, if I were you, I wouldn't look too deeply into all this. The accident's over. The surge and drain problem has been resolved. As for the accident, I'm sure The Regents' Clone-Techs will isolate the core of the mishap and fix it." Suddenly, an emergency message activated in front of several LED wall panels. Regent Manning appeared in his standard black suit, purple Regency tie, and shiny shoes. He began addressing the issue and the source of the disturbance. "See? He's showing everyone the error and telling us about the surge and drain malfunction…due to *Sagan* transitioning…resulting in a course correction inside the new wormhole leading to Nelta." Then he checked his wrist device. "Oh, and Terra just informed me she's closer to locating Emma's mind. Great news, right?" he sighed in relief.

Twin appeared, delivering the same message to Elisa. Elisa

wondered if they were the only two recipients since Regent Manning's short-lived broadcast just ended, and no one else besides the two of them received such a personal explanation. Their messages also closed with the same request: an order to present their accounts of what happened to Internal Affairs by the close of business tomorrow. "So just let everything that happened this afternoon just go away?" she asked Nick after their avatars extinguished.

"Yeah, Elisa," he whispered, "let it all go. Don't make trouble when there is none," he said, wiping his blood shot eyes.

She could hardly believe what she was hearing! He had suddenly changed from angry to compliant! A hissing static rippled through the Regeneration Corridors, making everyone stop and take notice. "I think Terra just agreed with you, Nick, or she's snapping back at ya," Elisa joked. The lights were now making her eyes feel fatigued, and she yawned.

"I can't wait to get off work," he said. "They've finished making repairs on the Level-2 Rec Center. I'm gonna hit the beach at about 3 a.m. when it's the least busy."

She breathed deeply, trying to stay alert and not sleepy. She still had so much to do, including setting up some of her surveillance equipment at her makeshift hobby unit at the back of a kiosk on Level-6, but only after keeping her appointment with The Regents. She had already instructed Twin to transfer all her funds to a new and secret financial account, and another grid to stay connected secretly to friends. She quickly checked her wrist device to make sure Twin had followed through on her orders. Twin returned, but via a message this time. She had assigned Elisa Level-6, Area 64 of 7,000 at the port, grid 85, Business Kiosk 193G. Twin had successfully activated for her a new business account! That meant she could fully proceed with her goal of exploring the astrocity, capturing footage, and processing her discoveries! Beginning tonight. She was finding it hard to contain her excitement, but realized she had no choice but to keep her mission a complete secret that not even Nick could discern. "I can't help it, Nick. It's just something about me. I have to know what happened here this afternoon…and a little emergency broadcast explanation just isn't doing it for me. And besides, I need to tell them personally that they're overworking people. Even though I won't be here any longer, someone needs to do something more than just send them complaints that they're obviously not taking seriously. " Again, she felt nerve-pinching mad!

Another patient on a gurney glided past them, and Nick doffed his lab coat, his way of winding down from the busy day. He sipped water, leaned against a processor tower, and opened up a snack bar. He appeared nonchalant and carefree. Elisa thought, *He seems so different all of a sudden, and so opposite of how he usually is.*

"Chief," he began, "really, I think it's a waste of energy to rehash the accident. Go home, get some sleep, and then meet me at 3 a.m. at the north end of the lake. Go surfing with me. Let off some steam that way." He moved like a surfer riding a wave.

"The smells though," she said, recalling the zoo beyond the artificial lake.

"All the animals will be asleep by then and the absorption panels will have eliminated their smelly messes. Whataya say?"

"I'll see," she replied, waving off his playful invitation. "I have a busy day tomorrow."

"Oh that's right, your Regeneration," he said.

She looked up into the large processing hub over their station. "Remember, Terra, *tomorrow* is my Regeneration at 4 p.m."

"Yes, Dr. Holton," Terra said, and then she faded off the station.

Nick picked up an empty bottle of disinfectant and tossed it to an android mop. "Doc, maybe that accident was a drill?" He threw another empty bottle at a chute, where an automatic vacuum sucked it down a chute.

"That was some sick drill then, Nick," she scoffed.

# J.P. Osterman

He had a look of excitement now in his bloodshot eyes. He was a thrill seeker, but the near-death accident on their shift would make them both look bad to everyone, in spite of Regent Manning's smooth explanation. He opened up several news renderings in front of them, but they could find no reports on the accident. But there was news about the new group was beginning to ripple quickly throughout *Sagan*! Were they the missing 273 of the population that was still hanging at a constant 99,727? That 273 was a perfect cosmological conundrum…unsolvable even for Terra. Thus far, The Regents' Matrix Security Techs haven't been able to detect their presence. From somewhere completely out of reach—throughout *all* of *Sagan*'s monitored premises—these people were operating, making noise, and stirring commotion. About what and why? She could only glean some facts from the gossip tricking down around her: Something on *Sagan* was *very* wrong. She already knew that but no one could provide proof or a culprit! Soon, however, she believed she would.

"Nick, someone almost died," she said, spraying off her hands. "Trying to cope with the accident by calling it a drill, or an exercise, is plain nuts. It was a near-death experience for Emma Jane Wright, and for us, who witnessed it. Most of us on *Sagan* have been alive for over a hundred years. A hundred years!" She felt the air in her chest move in and out as she closed her eyes, concentrating on each sensation and every voice in the room. Her biology seemed to enhance all her senses into finely tuned instruments!

"You all right?" he asked, grabbing her right arm. She pulled away her left arm, slightly aching. "Yeah, sure," she breathed, "but you have to understand something, Nick. Everyone who witnessed what happened came face-to-face with Death." She whispered, "Death." Watching him scratch his forehead and nod in agreement. "We've believed we'll live forever. That's not gonna happen. There's going to come a time when we're all going to have to step off this astrocity and onto real dirt…either on Nelta, or back on Earth. At some point, eternity-mindedness will all end." She turned around in a circle. "That's what we agreed on, no more life extension. No clone technology. When we step on Nelta, or step back on Earth, we leave eternity behind us." She felt her eyes sting. She couldn't remember the last time she had cried; and for sure, she didn't want to cry in front of *him*! The tears suddenly stopped when she inhaled in relief.

Nick stepped up beside her as if he might salute her. "Elisa Holton—you have a knack for homing in on what's going on, and a real ability of expressing ideas so people can understand the unexplainable."

Huffing off the complement, she said, "Come on, Nick."

"No—it's true, Doc! I think that's why most of the techs stayed and helped you. You have a real way of getting people behind you, backing you up, and supporting you," he said softy, tears in his pink eyes. "Including me. I'm gonna miss ya tomorrow…and days after that."

"*Ha*," she waved, still angry at the matrix and Regents. "Watch this. People will *really* like me now!" Glancing into Terra's Central hub, she said: "Terra, begin a formal recording now."

"Formal recording activated, Dr. Holton," Terra's voice resounded. Then Terra appeared in Standard Form at the Central Platform: a woman in her thirties, with short brown hair and an athletic build, wearing a white and purple form-fitted body suit. She looked powerful and unwavering, like a virtual sword wielder out of the old-Earth video game *Viking Queens*.

Elisa told her, "Terra, I'm ordering all dayshift workers to be relieved of duty after they finish Regenerating their current patients." She checked the time—now close to 5:15. As people cheered, she continued, "I'm ordering Corridor-15 to close in thirty minutes." After checking to make sure no Terra malfunctions had occurred on any of other Regeneration Corridor, she concluded: "The dayshift is over. Everyone start packing up." She then told Terra, "You can stop recording and send that order to The Regents."

"Yes, Dr. Holton," and Terra disappeared.

Several Regeneration Specialists began sending her farewell messages, also asking to see her again prior to stepping on Nelta. This was after all, her final farewell, and they were sending her virtual celebrations she continued saving so she could open them up and experience them later.

After touching her wrist device and sending her his farewell salutation, Nick said: "Emma Jane Wright didn't really die, Doc. She just got cloned. And there's *no* level of consciousness that Terra can't recover and download back into a brain, I'm sure. Tomorrow, I bet Emma will be bouncing around this ship and rejoining her Clone-Tech team—*wherever* they're working at these days."

Staring at Terra's rainbow-cycling hub, she said, "We'll see, Nick."

Since the malfunction, all the Regeneration Corridors had taken on a new atmosphere. Rotating holograms of patients' Body Double Imagers were flickering intermittently, accompanied by rumblings and droning. Terra had initialized extra filtration units to absorb bad smells and eliminate excess ozone from the very first emergency cloning procedure.

Making her way through lines of gurneys, Elisa took her final place overlooking her Corridor-15, except that tomorrow, she wouldn't be there. She watched the action, as if in slow motion through her sentimental tears: A technician was trying to calm down five patients who were upset at having to reschedule their regenerations. The nurse, last in line, after consciousness up-streaming and down-streaming procedures was scanning a patch of shaved scalp, re-growing the patient's hair. Glancing around, Elisa thought all the Corridors looked like a scene out of a snow-covered cemetery. Instead of tombstones, they had rotating body scans, and yellow Terra beams inhaling and exhaling ghosts; really peoples' minds—their entire lives, memories and souls!

As techs were busy cleaning up, Elisa believed she could finally get some answers as to what started that accident.

# Astrocity Sagan

Descending the five steps down into the control area under Center Stage, she said, "Terra, give me the real status of Emma Jane Wright."  Again, her name sounded familiar, but when she asked Nick and several others if they remembered Emma Jane Wright's name, they said they didn't.  But I remember her!  She tried recalling several variations of her name: E. Jane Write…no…E. J. W., no, EJ…that's it!  She learned the truth about her:  EJ was one of Captain Bartlet's crew!  "Hey, Nick!"

"Yeah?"  He was clean shaven now and ready for his off-duty fun.

You remember EJ Wright from The Archives?"  She quickly retold how she and Captain Bartlet had defeated the terrorists, but how they also launched a new weapon that split the moon.  No one else could recall Captain Bartlet or any of his crew members either.  She could.  They were fresh in her memory as if their entire battle had occurred just yesterday!  Why couldn't anyone else recall them?  She felt suddenly disoriented.  If she could remember them, but no one else could, that meant someone was interfering in mass with human memories.  That meant *real* trouble!

Yellow lights began flashing along a row of underground cryogenic tubes.  Pulleys began cranking, and magnetic rails locked into place as body cylinders re-aligned.  She felt encased in a laser-light show as Terra began arranging all fiber-optic fields to stabilize.

When all the noise stopped, and she could hear only techs checking out of the facility, Terra said, "Successful cloning of Emma Jane Wright, Doctor Holton."

Two green beams of light suddenly hit her retinas.  Up-Streaming beams!

"Drop, Elisa!"  Nick dove and pushed her to the floor.

"Stop Terra!  I'm Elisa May Holton!  You're supposed to be finding Emma's mind and fixing her!"  She held her throbbing head.  "*Ahhh!*"  The pain was radiating into her throat and her chest.

Suddenly, she saw bodies germinating inside of huge capsules. Then she recalled a sign at the end of a long white corridor: Level-10, Clone Core.

"What?!" Breathing deeply, she rubbed her forehead. "There is no Level-10!"

"Yeah, there's no Level-10," Nick parroted.

Then she realized the images were emanating from someone else's memory—experienced through someone else's mind. *What's happening to me?* Shaking her head and trying to slough off confusion, she climbed down the stairs and prepared to step out of Corridor-15. Techs handed her food, water, and her backpack. Gulping down some water, she said: "Tomorrow the mistake that occurred here today won't happen again." Nick told her he'd make sure of that! She was also counting on her Regeneration procedure repair what mind impulses crisscrossed between her and Emma Jane Write. "But where did all this start, Terra? And where is this Core Level-10 I keep imagining?" she whispered just before leaving Corridor-15. The most advanced AI in the known universe had to know!

"Level-9, Grid Station 1, Quadrant 1, Self-Aware activated, Dr. Holton," Terra replied.

"Show me, Terra," she ordered.

Over Corridor-15's Main Hologram platform, she rotated flashing images and spreading out specific areas Terra kept labeling "*Restricted.*"

She asked, "Can you be more specific? Give me a way to find the place?"

Terra appeared again, right next to her, in her Standard Athletic Form: "Self-Aware initiated, Doctor Holton. You said the word *three* times."

"What word?" Elisa asked. She touched Terra's hologram that immediately extinguished. "Damn!" Rushing through a row of recovering bodies, she called to Nick: "I'm leaving. I have to wait and meet The Regents on Level-9. I have to do whatever it takes to make sure another accident doesn't happen on *your* shift."

# Astrocity Sagan

"You okay though, Elisa?" Nick asked. "You look white as a sheet...and you're sweating." He raced over to her and handed her an energy pack. "Here, eat this."

After opening a protein bar, she ate it while resting on the ledge of an exit terminal. When she quickly regained energy and focus, she realized her changing biology was empowering her. "I'm fine, Nick, thanks. Terra's doing some pretty odd things...either by direct order, or through some type of program we know nothing about. But it has something to do with Level-9." She didn't want to tell him she had actually seen a Level-10, or he *would* report her for being nuts! "I gotta get down there, now!" She swallowed the final bit of energy bar. "Gosh, am I dreading going down there. Strange how people want the prestige of having a special clearance, but for me right now, it's like having a bad irritation!"

Nick chuckled sarcastically. "Level-9, Level-9. Aren't ya lucky to have access to Level-9." He was obviously thankful it was her descending there and not him. Level-9 was the Regents' private Tech Center, the home base for their Clone-Techs, scientists, experiments, and law enforcement agents they named Enforcers.

"Yeah, Nick, I don't know whether to feel privileged, or feel like a sucker," she began. "Besides, I have to give an account anyway of why I did what I did." After calling for one of the escalators so she could catch a Maglev shuttle on a transport platform, she said: "Wish me luck! I hope The Regents don't put me in a cell on Level-7 after I confront them on everything that happened this afternoon and rail at 'em about all our overtime!" She laughed, but part of her believed she might never see Nick again. It was a gut feeling. She wanted to run back against the grain of the escalator and cling on to him for dear life! She drowned out that idea as she gulped down a tube of cold water from her backpack.

"Tell me if Regent Manning has changed any," Nick shouted before the escalator door thudded shut. "Three months ago before his last regeneration, he looked about ready to die!" he laughed. "Call me when you get home if you wanna meet me for surfing," he shouted. Straightening a line of white lab coats on a rack, he added, "I'm done here now. I'll secure all the patients' records in the grid. Then I'm taking off for surfing."

"Thanks, Nick," she called, walking out into a busy corridor of people getting off work.

High up among policing Enforcers on hovercraft, were sky-lanes, guiding L-car traffic: various vehicles carrying people to-and-from the Level-5 Stern Regeneration Corridors to the Level-5 Eastbound station. "I might call you after I get home later on and let you know—"

The door shut, cutting off their conversation.

# Astrocity Sagan

## Chapter 10 – This Bad Window

She ran down a long corridor moving walkway and found the shortest line for the nearest eastbound L-car heading to Level-5's Stern Transport station. The oblong L-cars are aerial, the larger bullet Maglevs tunnel transportation. Strapping in and looking out the window as the L-car ascended into the air and launched toward Stern Transport, she could see rows of beehive Living Cubes lined with kiosks, cafes, and eateries. Below, people on moving walkways appeared to be ant-sized and crisscrossing—dashing east-and-west and north-and-south—on their way home after a hard day's work, leaving for evening meetings, or rushing to evening gatherings.

She'd have a five-minute ride on the L-car and then disembark at Stern Transport. From there, after getting a quick bite to eat, she'd head eight miles east on a Maglev to the Central Transport, the main station at the center of Level-6. Once there, she'd have to take one of the quick-lifts to the Descending platform, hop on the tunnel Maglev there, and begin the twenty-five minute descent to Level-9 to see, hopefully, in person although she doubted it, a Regent. She

# J.P. Osterman

felt fear sick, but also angry and determined. Every minute Twin called out to her felt like a shock in her gut.

Glancing around on the L-car, she saw people engrossed in conversations with their avatars (or messenger avatars), matrix-shopping renderings, and manipulating other forms of holographic images—from animals and icons, to objects and places. Watching them with Twin on Stall-mode 'cause needed to wind down from all the turmoil at work, she remembered how architects and builders had intricately designed *Sagan*: heavy, but also light enough to glide through dark-energy/dark-matter induced wormholes.

With a thick outer hull, the massive island-sized ship also has a recycling interior atmosphere, stable gravity, and is accessing outside power comparable to the luminosity of the entire Milky Way galaxy, distinguishing the astrocity and Saganites as a Kardashev Type III civilization, thanks to the Neltans. Over the one-hundred-year spacefolding voyage to Nelta, *Sagan* would be filled to capacity if those missing 273 residents could finally be located and numbered among the population! Shaped like the island of Oahu, it took six years and six space-stations to manufacture and construct *Sagan* out of new materials, fabrics, Neltan blueprints and Neltan-based technology. On the astrocity, the residents know of only nine levels, and each level contains a one-mile high dome with a quarter-of-a-mile of structural integrity in between them—electrical components, piping, and matrix connections. Each level is also twenty-four miles in diameter, making the astrocity elliptic in shape—with enough room to live and breathe comfortably, and commute via Maglevs. There are two exceptions to the design: 1 mile of spacefolding technology surrounding the ship like a chrysalis, and a mile-wide observation terminal at the top portion of Level-1's stern. Of all the nine levels, five are close to being filled to capacity. Some people camp out in the halls just to be near Level-2's Rec Center, Level-3's Arts Facilities, Level-6's Performance Center, Level-8's Sports Center, and Level-5's Regeneration Corridors. To ensure the conservation of food and water, years ago, The Regency began restricting water usage, limiting virtual participation time in certain sections of the astrocity, and implementing energy powering the food replicators, in spite of the plentiful gardens on Level-1, grazing zones on Level-8, and vegetation fields on Level-8. Each of those three, five-mile-in-diameter centers has processing sections and fabrication lines with robotic and android assemblers and movers.

Arriving at Level-5's Stern Station, she stepped around pairs of people and dashed toward the giant Maglev. Four virtual attendants were standing at kiosks and one Standard Terra conductor situated at the center of the large bullet-shaped shuttle. They all announced simultaneously and then separately the embarkation time and travel time to Central Station. The travel time to Central Station flashed: *fifteen minutes*. She checked her watch: 6:47. From there, she'd have another twenty-five minute ride! There's no way I'm gonna make it to The Regents' Level-9 Visitors' Center and Conference Area by 7:15, but that's the time Twin said it was closing, and she hadn't heard anything back from them to confirm the tentative appointment. Standing in line, high above her, she noticed people boarding the much larger shuttles—Maglevs and not L-cars. They were heading up and down to access other levels; and on distant platforms on her right and left, people were scurrying off and on more Maglevs. The departure bell was sounding. She had one minute....

Quickly the financial icon confirmed her crypto-currencies at the threshold. Then she sat down in an aisle seat and strapped in. Now, if traffic would just clear inside the tunnel, the ride to Central Station would take fifteen minutes. Time dragged on. Problems, again! As she noticed the station thinning out a bit, she said to Twin: "I wish I could rest on one tiny piece of grass at the Rec Center, Twin. But that isn't going to happen, is it?" Twin told her no.

But soon, the problem of overcrowding and living in an

artificial environment would go away when they'd disembark on Nelta. Soon, she believed, many would choose to leave *Sagan* and make Nelta their home. That's what happened in the mid-2000s when the first expedition to Mars left Earth to set foot on the red planet! There was no return ticket home. But this expedition has been different. From what people understand, they can return to Earth, but no one will have the details on the return trip home until after landing on Nelta, discussing options with the Neltan Scientific Committee, and making improvements on *Sagan*.

Her eastbound Maglev slowed and glided into a magnetic/electric-driven terminal inside Stern Station. Next to her Maglev was an approaching one that stopped and began syncing with the movement of her Maglev. After disembarking passengers, they'd trade directions. Outside, a long docking zone illuminated red. Stern Station came into full view as a downtown Chicago rendering with all the honking sounds, steaming rooftop projections, and bustling business noises. When her Maglev finally lowered and stopped, the walkway changed green—the signal for the craft's protective chrysalis to retract upward and disappear into the fabric of the shuttle.

After the sliding door opened, she stepped out into the open air and onto the loading zone. Seconds passed as several patrons entered after her, followed by the door hissing shut and the chrysalis sliding down, and the threshold sealing the insides against radiation. At the loading zone and standing at the edge several walkways, avatar officers and station guides were directing pedestrians to safety across the moving walkways while also streaming information with patrons and their avatars. She quickly dashed across the street, modeled after a busy Chicago L-car rendering, with Twin coaching her toward the escalator to the Regency's small way station. Once there, she'd need their permission to catch the descending Maglev to the Level-9 Regency Visitors' Center and Conference Center.

It was already 7:50 p.m., and a few schedule changes and an

unexpected bottleneck had stalled two shuttles! She'd have to wait for tunnel traffic to clear up. "That means I'm gonna be late to the meeting with Regent Thornton Manning," Twin. Through Twin, he had replied to her request and agreed to meet her at 9:30 p.m. *That's awfully late though*, she thought, *and so unusual that I didn't get at least his avatar to talk to me over my wrist device.* She had to eat. Seeing an old-town Chicago pizza sign, she dashed inside a kiosk eatery, pushed through a line using her physician's priority icon, downed a cup of coffee, and ate a slice of deep-dish pizza fresh out of a replicator. She had been experiencing a new type of energy since this morning and had to feed it or else she recognized she'd become a bit jittery. *Even though he didn't reply to me through his avatar, I can meet him...I can do this*! Her gut instinct, however, was giving her a growling warning.

She left the eatery, and Twin pointed the way to the loading platforms for the Descending Maglevs. There, she'd have to find the Regency's small station, stream them her profile ID, and get their permission to descent to their Visitors' Center on Level-9.

There are always eight functioning Maglevs stopping on every level—four descending and four ascending—but only one makes intermittent *direct* descents to Level-9.

"It's the last one for the day! Hurry, we can't miss it," Twin said, coaxing her up the lift.

Staying with a small crowd, she saw crisscrossing moving walkways and determined people driven to launch on time to various levels throughout *Sagan*.

The entire transport design of each level is 3D-hexagonal, with small Maglevs running north, south, east, and west; and the larger Maglevs ascending and descending, transporting heavier loads of people, mega-loads, and goods. These shuttles make scheduled non-stop runs, but not The Regents' two private Maglevs available only to them and for their private transport. She hadn't seen one of them yet.

# J.P. Osterman

Then she overheard a few conversations and learned stunning news about the missing residents. The missing 273 residents were off-grid renegades, believed to be hiding in the tunnels or spaces between levels. "They're most likely causing all our Maglev delays!" a woman said. The 273 group hadn't yet caused any type of damage, or made threats of sabotage, but one graffiti image had been found in front of the Regents' private quarters, behind Navigation at the bow of Level-1: a circle with a square in the center and a tiny nautilus.

"The symbol is a puzzle that Terra is working to solve, even though it represents the philosopher's stone from the olden days of alchemy," the woman's male companion said, checking his news rendering of the symbol.

"It's some strange mixture or concoction the group is brewing up, in Terra or our archives," the woman said.

Her companion added, "Well, The Archives are the storage site where every bit of information is also dispensed to us, so it makes sense that whoever is causing all the strange creatures to appear would be routing himself—"

"Or herself,"

"Or itself,"

"Through The Archives!" Then the three stepped off the moving walkway toward an exit from Level-5's Central Station.

Elisa wondered what the philosopher's stone had to do with *Sagan*. "Except the person responsible for blaring the image positioned it directly in view of the Regents!" she told Twin.

With her concealed cameras panning in her steps, she was determined to capture proof of the group, or the virtual monstrosities, or maybe even a Regent who might be secretly walking among them, watching them. She had their true images saved and ready for a comparative scan, and she also had a Facial app that could discern a real face from a rendering.

After finding the Regency's small private loading zone, she did what Twin instructed her to do, and stopped in front of a door with a purple star insignia, their symbol for *Sagan*'s representational style of government throughout the astrocity.

# Astrocity Sagan

Twin suddenly appeared out of sorts—fuzzy and filled with static. Elisa jiggled her wrist device and repositioned her small necklace device. No results. Twin's abnormal features wouldn't yield to a clear reception...so unusual given that everyone else's avatars were functioning fine and fully energized with 100% matrix processing power.

Twin said through her wavering image: "Elisa, Regent Thornton Manning ordered his private Maglev just for you. It should arrive in ten minutes to pick you up."

Elisa reeled a bit. "You sure, 'cause this is their *private* station?"

"You can board it once the automated hostess clears you," Twin replied.

The large Central Station was now almost empty—with Enforcers and their policing avatars directing stragglers on the platforms to leave for their final destinations. Because of 273 and what the disturbance their members caused at their private quarters at the bow the Level-2, Thornton Manning enacted a curfew for the evening: 9:00 p.m. The first curfew ever on *Sagan*! People and their avatars were objecting, making the Enforcers work harder, and the Level -5 transport platforms began slightly vibrating through the commotion.

When a light hit Elisa's face, The Regents' Terra receptionist appeared in front of their large regal door gilded in bright yellow. Elisa jumped back as the rendering looked her over with green scanning eyes, and then smiled. "Regent Manning and Regent Jenkens are expecting you, Dr. Holton. But given the problem with disguises we have been experiencing today, please give me a verbal description of yourself so I can match your voice patterns to my database."

Elisa folded her arms and sighed in a bit of frustration. "I'm Doctor Elisa Holton. My ID is my birth date, 05012043. I am Medical Director of Regeneration Corridor-15. I scheduled an appointment with Regent Manning to speak to him about a malfunction that occurred at my work station around 4:30 p.m. You should have my request…actually, about four requests! Well?"

The receptionist's eyes flashed green in acceptance of Elisa's identity. Dressed in a fitted purple skirt and white crisp blouse buttoned to the collar, she replied: "Please enter, Dr. Holton." The sliding door to the station clicked open, and the small station illuminated a vast grid in preparation for a rendering. "I can see no one's been in here in quite some time, Terra."

"Yes, Doctor Holton, would you like the names of predecessors?" The receptionist gestured for Elisa to enter.

"No, no thanks," she said facetiously.

"When the Regency's private Maglev docks, Dr. Holton, I will re-appear and guide you inside. Meanwhile, welcome to the Regency's Waiting Area, and please help yourself to refreshments, and make yourself comfortable in any kiosk resting spot."

Elisa felt suddenly uneasy, her biology triggering a bad intuition, and she sat stepped back toward the regal door. "Can I just wait outside until the station clears up a bit more?"

The receptionist's head turned in an expression of confusion but then she smiled and straightened up in clarity. "Yes, by all means, Dr. Holton. I have you checked in. You can enter at will." She showed Elisa a small glowing bio-scanner next to the doorframe. "When the Maglev arrives and if you're not inside, I will alert you on your wrist device."

"Thanks, but—"

The receptionist disappeared, and the sliding door to the little station slid shut in front of her. Feeling dismissed, Elisa stopped when she heard people walking and talking behind her as they headed toward a ticket kiosk.

Ticket kiosks are just for show, with artificial foliage and programmed avatars functioning around them as parts of the décor. This area in front of the Regency's small station is a replica of Chicago's Transit Authority and its rendering.

Remembering the accident that happened in her corridor and fearing they might recognize her from the news, she kept her distance from the small crowd. People enjoyed situating their avatars to eavesdrop, to record slices-of-life, to matrix-shop them and then watch or stream their renderings later on for residents to share and response. However, slander, coercion, and bullying are against the law.

A young couple pushing their infant in a stroller was about to pass her. They grimaced at her and began whispering. Obviously they had seen the Regeneration emblem on her white jacket.

"What did I do?" she asked, raising her hands in an innocent gesture.

The couple began walking faster. "Killing people!" the man called back.

She shook her head. "Hey, everything's *fine* in the Corridors. Really! I'm gonna look into the accident myself right now!"

They disappeared around the kiosk. Walking behind them, their avatars, programmed in Victorian era dress, shook their forefingers at her and then streaked back to join their hosts.

Fuming because she was working so hard to try to please them—to accommodate *them* before landing on Nelta—she had a mind to call-on Twin to chase after them and give them a piece of her mind! Again, Twin wouldn't render for her. "Darn wrist device!" She felt frustrated. "Ah, what's the use anyway," she huffed, watching a few shop owners at the outskirts of the station illuminate their red-flashing security lights. They were closing up shop as per Enforcer orders. How different from before leaving Earth, she thought, when people had to put bars on their doors and locks on their gates! A thief crossing over one of those red flashing barriers would get an instant burn; and hacking into any vending machine, eatery, kiosk, or Living Cube would activate a hologram of an armed Enforcer, or initiate a robotic deterrent, or unleash a burst of laser fire on the intruder. Only on rare occasions would someone be so bold as to attempt a robbery. Break-ins that had occurred were usually for fun or a prank: teenagers trying to have a robbery experience, like Bonnie and Clyde back on Earth, or someone trying to unleash a small robotic warrior on purpose to record the scene for social media. After a slew of those occurred years ago, a business entrepreneur opened up several franchises for people to experience virtual cops-and-robbers scenarios using Terra's Cognitive-Behavioral Safe Scan so fear-of-death kills couldn't damage their minds.

Suddenly, a group of teenagers with avatars dressed up in scary costumes as if for Halloween darted by her. They were out past curfew, and they knew it. She laughed when she saw their avatars poking them in ticklish spots. Obviously, their parents had secretly input a Security Guard app into their avatars who were nagging at them for being out late, prodding them to catch the emptiest shuttle, Maglev 5, up to Level-2.

Feeling tired, she checked the time: 9:17 p.m. She walked back to the small station, had the bio-ware scan her eyes, and then called the receptionist. "Terra, just in case you don't know, but you should know, tomorrow I have a *really* big day." She showed her the Regeneration procedure she had scheduled with Dr. Pultoff. "So please, help me out here will ya? Hurry the Maglev a little, will ya? It's past nine already, and after the meeting with Regent Manning, I have a Maglev ready to pick me up. I don't intend to stay at Level-9 for more than fifteen or twenty minutes."

The receptionist's eyes flashed green, and she smiled. "I streamed your message, Dr. Holton. Please enter."

Sitting down after she spied a long bench, she thought, God—I'm so tired! When am I gonna be able to rest? She felt a rush of mounting pressure as she hailed Twin twice; and just as she was about to give up, Twin materialized alongside her, startling her. "Oh, okay…well, I want to tell you what I need to talk about at the meeting with Regent Manning in case I leave one item out." She inhaled and closed her eyes. "Number one, investigate the surge and drain that caused the aneurism; two, explain why I ordered the Emergency Clone Procedure; three, tastefully and tactfully complain about all the overtime; four, tell them about Emma Jane Wright and how no one except me seems to remember how famous she is; five, take Maglev 5 home, 'cause that appeared to be the emptiest one; and six, sleep. Then, at 4 p.m.—"

"Your Regeneration procedure tomorrow," Twin said.

Then she felt suddenly dizzy. "My God—my body feels *so* out of whack." She took her pulse. "Wow, my heart's racing...but when I feel I need to sit down like I might collapse, I feel energized!" Then she believed she could see through a wall! She blinked in disbelief, until the thick concrete appeared as atoms. She walked to the containment field through which their Maglev was scheduled to appear. "I think I see lights in the tunnel!"

Her thoughts began streaming down the tunnel as if guided by a magnetic force. Her vision suddenly stopped, illuminating people deep inside *Sagan*. They were human, but clothed in special glowing body-ware, and wearing strange, shining grid-like facial masks. They saw her too, and began waved at her wildly. Then they appeared suddenly surprised by someone and disappeared. The magnet force stopped—uniting her thoughts with her body.

For a few moments, she felt as if the station was spinning. "They have to be wearing some type of camouflage clothing or cloaking technology!" she whispered. When Twin appeared, settling her down and showing where she could get a drink of cool water, Elisa wondered if the hallucination was part of what had happened to her earlier when the consciousness up-load beam locked onto her instead of Emma Jane Wright. "Oh—send a request to Dr. Pultoff to look for any neural impulses that don't match with mine. And send my request to the Regency as well. Got it, Twin?" She stood up, her dizziness gone.

Twin's eyes flashed green. "Done, Elisa."

"Great! You can fade, Twin. Just inform me when you hear the Maglev approaching."

"Yep." Twin disappeared.

Sitting down on a bench, she doffed her white lab jacket and began listening to the sounds of a desert wind blowing through a projection of Earth's starry-filled night sky. Watching them while feeling a warm wind waft over her arms and legs, she fell fast asleep.

# Astrocity Sagan

## Chapter 11 – Rampant Maglev

A bell rang, waking her up. Noticing she was still alone without The Regent's Maglev in the transport tunnel, she glanced at the time that repeatedly streaked through the virtual sky as a comet's tail. "9:36 p.m.! I've been asleep slept for almost half-an-hour! What the hell happened? Twin!"

No answer.

"Twin—where are you?" She jostled her wrist device. She checked her tiny glowing necklace processor, still working. Then she yawned, the sound echoing, and she noticed the small station and larger Transit Authority station completely empty, except for the occasional virtual Enforcer appearing intermittently as monitors in the latter. Sitting straight up and rubbing her eyes, she glimpsed at a 3D-movie on a wooden plank: A purple-and-white Maglev car stopping, the door hissing open, the time counting down. She had five more minutes to wait. "Darn!" she said.

Software designers had programmed this small waiting station to mimic a western train station. To the right, there is a participation kiosk with a virtual server standing out front and saying in an inviting voice: "For just one Euro, you can partake in your favorite game show! *Western Jeopardy* to *I Survived a Japanese Game Show*! For this and all your entertainment, choose the number one matrix-media expert, Phillips Corporation. Remember: Your Excitement is Our Satisfaction!" The voice turned soft as the server added, "One euro a minute, and a five-minute participation time is the minimum required."

She thought of other waiting areas, Virtual Realms, wherein she had participated in their themed shows. Accommodating thousands in some facilities, and hoping the Neltans will like to use their ever-evolving programs, businesses are yielding huge profits and always hiring actors and actresses to attract systems engineers, rendering programmers, vendors, and maintenance techs, especially in the stations and mazes of hallways and walkways where people access their Living Cubes. Companies are also in the business of conducting weekly competitions or lotteries and then holding award ceremonies on Level-1 or Level-6's Performance Center. Using these times as opportunities to dress up and display their avatars, friends and family members of winners attend the ceremonies, congratulating the winners who receive monetary prizes or special vacations on one of Level-8's Sports Centers or in one of Level-6's Virtual Spheres. But this Virtual Realm inside the Regents' Level-5 bow station was exceedingly small. Elisa surmised they wanted limited visitors here, and the purple ribbons and gold stars on all the slats and rails were strong reminders to special passengers that the Regents were regal, *Sagan*'s leaders, and the law.

Suddenly, a loud humming sound resounded. At the edge of the transport tunnel, space turned to rainbows. Electrified by dark-matter coils, particles began spinning, generating sparking and arching energy. The Maglev was approaching. She stood and began walking toward the boarding zone that flashed a long runway of red lights.

"Warning!" A conductor called out. He was dressed in cowboy attire as he materialized and extended his hands in

# Astrocity Sagan

front of her. "Keep back, Dr. Holton."

She ran behind the bench as the Maglev's boosters droned. The brakes screeched as clamps buckled down on the rail. The tunnel wind surged into a light static, raising the hair on her arms. The wind stilled as the Maglev stopped, rose, and began hovering. The containment chrysalis lifted. Wild currents began settling, but she felt quite unsettled.

Taking off her white jacket, she glanced at the time. "Something's not right, Conductor." She pointed at the time streaking by in the sky. "*This* Maglev is way off schedule. It was supposed to be here thirty minutes ago! Is something wrong?" Angry and tired, she showed them her wrist device. Twin didn't materialize when she called her on. "Is this a malfunction happening in this small station, or a total glitch in matrix processing?"

The doors to the Maglev slid open. The Terra conductor waved her inside. "You may board now, Dr. Holton," she said invitingly.

"I've got to keep trying to hail Twin!"

"Avatar capability is off-matrix during all Regency transports, Dr. Holton. A security precaution, you understand." Then the conductor disappeared.

Anger overcame her. "Hey! Come back and give me a better answer than that!" After no answer, walked slowly toward the Maglev and peering inside. "Hello?"

She smelled ozone, and touched the wet condensed doorframe. The vehicle capable of seating rows of Regents was empty.

When she stepped inside, it jolted, rocked slightly, but then leveled off. "Whew!" She grabbed a hand rail. The Maglev seemed to have a personality of its own. "Hey!" she called, steadying herself. "Conductor, where are you?!" No answer. Then she noticed the front seat with a giant purple stripe and one giant white star bas-relief on the headrest. She touched it, running her fingers gently overt it. "This is Regent Manning's *private* Maglev!" She felt all the oxygen leave her lungs. "I don't think *anyone's* ever been inside it, except during live broadcasts, when the crew can virtually step inside this craft and interact with Regent Manning whenever he makes an announcement." Walking to a headrest, she touched the gold star embroidered into the plush dark purple cushion.

"Wow, Regent Manning's personal seat," she marveled, remembering him from long ago and tapping the gold edge of the white star. "Just think, he was probably here, in this very chair at some point during the day." She had to ask Terra. "Conductor?" She glanced around when she received no reply. "You *gotta* be here *somewhere*! Answer me!"

Terra appeared, almost in front of her face: five-foot-eight-inches tall, medium skin tone, short brown hair, brown eyes, and a form-fitting blue-and-white body suit. "Dr. Holton, Chief Regeneration Specialist of Corridor-15. May I help you?" Terra momentarily hissed off, but then re-animated behind Elisa. "Hello, I'm here, Dr. Holton."

Turning around, Elisa gasped when she saw Terra's 3D-forefinger light on her shoulder. "Oh, there you are. Am I supposed to be in *this* shuttle? Regent Manning's *private* shuttle?" As Terra gestured for her to step farther inside, Elisa followed her. "Well, are you every going to answer me? You about took my breath away by disappearing back there ya know! You listening to me? Did someone program you to scare people half-to-death?"

A large rainbow illuminated around her from head-to-toe, and Terra blinked. "I apologize for the craft being late, Dr. Holton. Regent Manning has been detained. Please sit here, in this aisle seat, and the craft will launch per Regent Manning's request."

She realized she was deep inside the shuttle now. When those doors shut, she would be at the point of no return to the outside world until Thornton Manning would let her out.

Terra's outfit changed from that of her Standard appearance to a flight attendant in a light-purple A-line skirt and long white-sleeve blouse.

# Astrocity Sagan

Again, Elisa felt startled and covered her heart. "Look, Terra, access my avatar, Twin. I give you permission to bypass privacy. All I need is to keep a scheduled meeting with a Regent. I've put in quite a few requests. I have urgent business."

"Urgent business," Terra repeated, blinking. "Yes, I see your messages, Dr. Holton. Regent Manning received them as well."

"Is your processing off-kilter or something? You seem...well, strange...so unlike your usual self. Is something wrong?" Elisa remembered the accident. Concern felt mounting, like a bellowing scream about to erupt, especially when she recalled how Emma Jane Wright's mind had tripped through her own thoughts a bit. Perhaps Terra was picking up on the cognitive asymmetry, or detecting something amiss with her biology.

"I am processing on one-hundred percent power and at one-hundred percent efficiency, Dr. Holton," Terra began, "so please sit down and I can start the Maglev."

Looking at the exit and almost ready to bolt to it, she sat down in shock when she saw Terra's eyes, blinking wildly, just like the furious oscillation of her rainbow processor prior to that surge and drain. "Something is wrong! What's going on?" Standing, she grabbed the back of a chair. The car gave a quick jolt as if purposely throwing her back into her seat. Emergency visors and oxygen masks unleashed from the ceiling. She raced for the exit. "What the—"

The door swooshed closed just as she reached it, pinching the hem of her pants. "Hey!" Trying to free herself, she yanked the material. "What's going on? Terra!" Finally, the material ripped and landed on the floor where the carpet began absorbed it. When the Maglev jolted again—an abnormal lurch—she fell, hitting her head on a bar but then quickly pulled herself up. "Terra! Stop this thing!" She felt terror ripple through her arms and tried steadying herself through the rocking motion. The Maglev was launching! She wasn't strapped in! "Quit, Terra," she gasped, "emergency stop!" Running to the back of the car, she noticed a faint beam of light way in the distance. Imbibing the burgeoning energy within her, she felt her mind race toward the light. A power was guiding her—flowing through her—and she felt its special and mysterious infusion in her muscles and bones. She pounded on the window. The thick chrysalis encasing of the Maglev cracked. "Hey—help me! Hey! I'm in here!" Was someone inside the tunnel trying to stop the shuttle? Interfere with its run? Maybe someone had heard her cry and was racing to help her? In any case, she had to do something fast! The Maglev was definitely malfunctioning. "Terra! Stop this thing! Now!"

Terra materialized in front of Thornton Manning's seat. Her face appeared calm. "I cannot stop the order, Doctor Holton."

"Order? Whose order?!" Elisa shouted. Feeling a bump on her head, she knelt down. "What the hell's happening here?!"

A containment shield illuminated—the chrysalis covering of the Maglev repairing. "I cannot stop the order, Doctor Holton. Please sit down. Core Level initiated."

"Core Level?"

Terra faded.

"Terra—what the hell is a Core Level?!" Her chest pounding as the Maglev rose for launch, she raced to the exit. She had only five seconds before the transport bar would activate the dark-matter boosters and deadly currents surround the shuttle. She tried prying open the door. It wouldn't budge. Fusion thrusters ignited. The shuttle jolted.

She tumbled to the floor. "Terra! Let me out!"

Outside, she could hear voices and saw the beams of many flashlights circling around the back window. Clawing the carpet and trying to reach the back of the shuttle to hail the outsiders, she cried, "Help!"

The Maglev rocked and slowly launched. Outside lights extinguished. Crawling to her knees, she grabbed the back of a

# Astrocity Sagan

seat and slid into it as the Maglev began descending rapidly through the transport tunnel. As the disequilibrium of gravity ensued, she lifted off her seat. Gravity suddenly stabilized, jolting her back down, and a seatbelt wrapped around her.

"Whew!"

Blocking out an intense high-pitched screeching sound of a failing environment attempting to regain homeostasis, she covered her ears and tried to calculate the travel time: About a two-minute ascent or descent per mile. That's about ten minutes from Level-5 to Level-9, without stopping for residents on other platforms. But Terra had said, *Core Level.* She did what she could to calm herself down—taking in deep breaths of sweet-tasting oxygen and rubbing sense into her face and arms. "Where's Core Level, Terra? Where—damn it—where!?" She hit the armrests. How the Regents could be harboring a level she'd never heard of made her fume with anger.

Looking around, she spotted emergency mind-linking helmets dangling on the ceiling over each seat. It was the old technology, but still capable of transmitting a brain wave. If she could reach one and put one on, maybe she they would receive her emergency thoughts and let them know that a renegade Maglev might crash into their conference area. Brushing back her hair, she adjusted the mesh helmet on her head. Now, if the old-fashioned device was still working, Terra would be able to detect what she was thinking—all the images coursing through her mind—and help her. Waiting for the green mind-link signal to flare, she gripped the armrest. Nothing.

Then she saw a nameplate with the words, *Regent Ellen Markus.*

"Darn—so stupid of me! These visors are programmed to read specific brain waves! What now?" She tried tapping her wrist device and necklace processor to the visor's optics at the center of the mesh helmet. Again she thought of her emergency experience, hoping The Regents might receive the helmet's transmission. Only time would tell, and only she would realize if her attempt would be successful, if the Maglev didn't crash land. "Damn! Darn!" she moaned. "Now I'm not only trapped, but on a death ride." She thought hard: Help me...someone please help me!" She could only hope someone had heard her plea and come to her rescue. Now, she could only wait, descend into *Sagan*'s core—wherever that might be."

Outside, a shield illuminated to white as friction intensified. The interior was growing hotter. Huffing and puffing, she watched the white-hot beams. "Help!" She wiped sweat off her eyelids. A ceiling vent opened, releasing a cool breeze over her face, and she began picking at patches of her sweaty clothes that were sticking like liquid sugar on her skin.

Terra's voice suddenly echoed through the car. "Core Level-10, one minute."

Elisa tried unfastening her seatbelt, but it remained tight like a constricting snake. She strained hard to glance around the car, but all she could see were the useless visors dangling in a twirling dance. Confusion spun like the static around her skin. "Terra, there is *no* Level-10! Where the hell are you taking me?" A pinching sensation bolted through her chest, nearly suffocating her. Picking away at bits of the strangling seatbelt, she gasped for air. The more air she inhaled, the more fine-tuned her senses became! Then, images welled into her consciousness. She could picture their pieces finally uniting to form a cohesive memory:

Images of white-clad scientists and technicians re-arranging LED panels on dark walls. They were using a new type of magnetic/electric field capable of capturing, or generating, dangerous proportions of energy and power. But *Sagan* would have to terminate spacefold flight to actualize such a capability.

"For what?" she whispered. The memories suddenly stopped. "Is that the Core Level-10 that Terra told me about?" Suddenly, she recalled receiving those images in pieces when she began working on Emma, but she had dismissed them as being garbled symbols. They weren't! They were very real; and soon, she'd be seeing Level-10.

She felt a sting above her temple. "Ouch!" She tried whipping off the mind-linking mesh, but the tiny nano-organic clamps wouldn't peel off. Then she remembered the mechanisms of the old-fashioned technology. Unless a specialist would initiate a special Unlock command, the helmet would stick like glue to her—an artificial intelligence on her scalp. Realizing she was helpless, she sighed and gave up. She'd have to wait until someone at the end of her ride would realize the malfunctions occurring inside and outside the powerful Maglev and free her. "That's it!" she exclaimed. "Maybe this is just one giant mishap!" She kept repeating those words, hoping the brainwave program in the mesh helmet might alter and deliver her message to The Regents. "This is all one giant innocent mistake, that's all!" She laughed, and then repeated what she said.

Until her forehead began throbbing. Feeling her scalp, she touched a flap of skin. "Blood…oh God!" Growing dizzy, she searched the floor and noticed a red stain disappear into the carpet—the absorption fabric. She felt herself approach unconsciousness! As she was about to faint, she re-energized. Oxygen began working miracles in her lungs and brain, igniting her with a powerful charge. Touching her head and then looking at her fingers that a second ago were covered with blood, she saw nothing. "Healed? How? What's happening to me?" Pulling at the visor, she finally managed to yank it off her scalp. "Ouch!" The stinging and throbbing quickly subsided. *Perhaps my special biology has the ability to heal me*! When she looked for signs of blood again, they were gone. "What the heck is happening to me?!" she said, tears stinging her eyes. She began stretching her fingers and moving her arms— anything to remain fully aware of her changing physiology. "I'm fighting! I *will* stay alive! I *will* fight this."

Suddenly, the Maglev slowed to normal stasis. Swallowing

hard, she forced her thoughts to slide out of the abnormal gravitational fluctuation as well. The Maglev jerked to a stop, the door *whooshed* open, and her seatbelt unfastened. Fending off another dizzy spell while inhaling, she stepped onto the docking platform. The twelve-foot-high depot was dark in the distance where the air transitioned to blackness. She stopped. "I'm not goin' in there!" Looking up, she saw the ceiling, appearing electrified, like Tesla coils operating at full blast. They had to be pulsing electricity and some other type of wild force upward, into the entire astrocity—and downward, to Sagan's bottom-most hull. "Could these wild reactions be part of propulsion? Navigation?" she whispered. Feeling static rolling around her like ants on her skin, she felt suddenly lighter than air, as if she could walk on water. "I feel like I'm half-spirit…like forces are playing on my body!" She stepped back toward the Maglev, but remembered that awful wild ride. "I not goin' back in there though either," she whispered. She had only one choice: call a Regent for help. "Hello?" Her voice stopped in her throat—a knot, tongue-tying her. "Anyone-*cough*-here? Regent Manning? Regent Jenkens?" She tried hailing them on her wrist device. Nothing. Then she remembered the receptionist's words: "In the Regents' Maglev, all portable device connectivity had to be disabled as per security protocol."

She wondered: Shouldn't someone *know* I'm here? Then she had a worse thought when she glanced down at her left arm—the place where the Neltan Encantado technology had begun its abnormal interface with her and was now beginning to affect her in new marvelous ways: Could this place change me into something horrible? Not wanting anyone to know anything about her recent healing experiences, she thought: *shut up—don't even whisper that fact! At least I didn't crash-land and end up a clone!*

She breathed deeply in relief. The air smelled energized and ionized, and a strange pinching sensation was wafting over her body. *The laws of physics here are in no way normal down here.* Having no idea of who she might see, who might see her, or what she might see next; she knew one thing: no one, except for the ten Regents, had ever stepped on this Core Level-10.

## Chapter 12 - Core Level-10

"Hello? Help!" she called, walking slowly into a bowl of darkness. Approaching steel doors resembling those at the entrance of a movie theater, she opened them cautiously—the hinges creaking, the sounds echoing—and walked stealthily inside. Looking around another dimly lit arena, she noticed ten long rows of high-back seats and a small center stage. She remembered walking into such a place, although much larger, when she was ten, back in 2053, before the terrorist attacks when her mother took her to see the penguin sage, *Ice Capades*. "I'd give anything—*anything!*—to be back there instead of here!" she whispered, her voice echoing.

For a moment, she began seeing through the eyes of her little child once more. At center stage, her mom appeared…first as a transparent ghost, then as a tall blond-haired woman wearing a yellow and green flowered dress, the same dress she wore when she and Elisa saw those movies. It was one of the best days of her life! No way could Terra have captured that past moment to superimpose her mother into the current reality!

# J.P. Osterman

"Mom!" she called, rushing toward the stage. "Is that you, Mom?"

"Shhh...*you* are the answer, Elisa!" Her smiling mother pointed at her and disappeared.

Elisa rubbed her eyes, staggered backwards, and landed in a seat. "She was really there...I *know* she was! Where'd she go?" She recalled what she'd been hearing for the past several days on social media: some people had been claiming to see all sorts of things—mostly monsters out of old-Earth TV shows and movies. Medical Specialists and Matrix Security Techs were labeling the images viruses, and telling those people they were hallucinating. Now, she knew differently. "My cameras," she whispered, "that's what I brought them for!" Her white jacket was on the Maglev, and its electric/magnetic idling abnormally. "Damn!" But she had one inside her pant pocket. Pulling it out, she noticed the round glass had shattered. "Drats, it's busted."

The theater suddenly ignited with light, and she stood up, peering at the exit. Her loud voice had activated a prompt. A few overhead panels illuminated brightly, and a bluish-hue of glowing luminescence began spreading like tentacles on the ceiling. "This is some type of new skin combined with metallic technology...a living and breathing open system," she whispered, stepping away from center stage. "I don't remember seeing *anything* like this *ever* on *Sagan*...and definitely not on Earth, because as a Nano-Organic Genetic Researcher, I woulda been involved in its production and testing. Nope, this is *definitely* turning out to be one helluva horrible adventure!"

Walking up the aisle, she kept repeating: "Hello? Regent Manning? Regent Jenkens?"

Still, no one replied, but now she could smell hot butter and hear popcorn popping—both augmented reality experiences her voice had triggered for a participation rendering. "This must be the Regency's private entertainment center!" But when she saw giant processor hubs bulging on the ceiling and protruding from behind the red curtain, she stopped up in the middle of the arena and covered her mouth in shock. "This place is where they observe some type of testing. Those are Regeneration hubs!"

As she began walking down the aisle to investigate, she heard the sounds of scraping metal. She held her ears and glanced back at the entrance. From the ground up, about a kilometer high, glowing panels were unhinging, re-aligning, altering in shape, forming walls and a domed ceiling, and then sealing tightly.

"Someone is changing this entire place!" She could no longer see the steel doors she had entered. "So *this* is how someone's been able to conceal Level-10." The Maglev's idling sounds altered. She could hear a droning hissing sound—a launch upward.

"It's gone," she sighed, "and I'm stuck here…trapped, and waiting for a meeting that's obviously *not* going to happen." She called to The Regents again, but with no response. "Hey—you have to know I'm down here!"

Spying a large door now visible next to the stage, she walked over to its access panel. It couldn't read her fingerprint, eye code, or body aura.

"Terra, it's me, Elisa Holton," she whispered as to a friend. Looking up at the doorframe, she read a glowing sign: Core Level-10. "This is the exact same sign I saw when Emma Jane Wright's memory interfered with mine!" Then she realized she might need old-fashioned codes to access the area. She input her medical ID from Regeneration Corridor-15 into the keypad. The door wouldn't open. Then she input the code from her Living Cube on Level 2.

The door opened.

"Hey! Is anyone in here?" Again she called out for several Regents, this time, including Regent Sylvia Itonovich, the Regent responsible for representing the residents on Level-2.

Stepping inside, she walked down a long white hallway. Everything was quiet, except for a wavering, droning sound.

# J.P. Osterman

Following the noise, she walked down hall-after-hall. The place resembled a sterile hospital on Earth, except this Core Level-10 seemed completely empty. She knew *that* couldn't be true. "Someone who installed this place has to be her somewhere." She knocked, sometimes pounding on several doors. She felt trapped in an endless maze of white corridors! "Hello—anyone here? Who's running all the technology? Terra?" She listened for the sounds of Regents talking, or eating, or broadcasting their virtual speeches or programs.

No one answered.

After wandering several meters, she came to a dead end: a ten-foot white door. "Hello?" she called, knocking. "Definitely, the noise is coming from behind this door."

Suddenly, the door slid open. The suction pulled her onto a moving walkway. "Hey!"

She tried stepping off, but the material kept her glued to the black sticky floor.

"Let me outta here!" Her head began throbbing. She rubbed her aching forehead. "I *know* you know I'm here…so let me out! This is a huge mistake! What are ya gonna do to me?"

Electrical charges flashed around her, confining her in a pool of fright. She ducked for cover as static prickled in goose bumps on her skin. "I'm Doctor Elisa Holton! You—you have to—you have to let me go! I'm—"

A knot of energy exploded high above her.

"*Whoom!*" She ducked and covered her head.

When she was a child and had toured a museum, she had seen a giant Tesla exhibit. Now, she was gliding straight through the center of two huge rows filled with those types of high-powered rods! As the walkway moved her around another rolling curve, the facility altered into walls of multi-colored glowing glass. Seeing her reflection everywhere and appearing to stretch into infinity, she felt an ache in her left arm. The mysterious place had triggered a reaction with her morphing biology. She smoothed down her sleeve, making sure her arm was completely covered.

# Astrocity Sagan

"This place is a type of advanced Kaleidoscope…and it's replicating my DNA. But why?" Again she cried out for help, fiber-optic processors hissing and shining brightly everywhere around her—the fabric of Terra's matrix. "I'm in some type of preparation portal," she said as light began refracting into rainbows. "I've never *seen* such technology capable of *genetic* quantum processing!" Gasping for air, she felt a burning sensation in her lungs. "What is this place?" she heaved, trying to breathe. "What is this technology?" She screamed: "Hey! Answer me!"

No one responded. The conveyor was ushering her somewhere…to where, she had no idea. "I'm *not* the first one on this thing, am I?" She wondered who else had treaded in her steps. Pungent air wafted up her nose, stinging her sinuses. Her skin and lips felt numb. She licked her lips for moisture; but her tongue was so dry, it was sticking to the roof of her mouth. Panicking when she couldn't see her feet through a frothy, caramel-colored mist, she began fighting against the pressure that kept pushing her up whenever she tried bending down. If she could peel away from the conveyor, she could jump off the walkway before hitting a white cloud about fifty meters in front of her. But gravity was a thick cloud—confining her to the moving walkway.

Then, she had an idea. Prying out of her shoes, she leaped off the conveyor on to a wet floor. Breathing slowly, trying to catch her breath as she glanced into rainbows rippling through the air, she stamped out her fear of the unknown and stared at the direction from which she came. *I have a decision to make. Should I return? Hope I can make it back to the station without being discovered? Hope I can hide somewhere and then try to sneak aboard one another of their shuttles? Or should I go forward…and try to figure out what in the hell the Regents are doing in their Core Level-10?*

Her curiosity peaking, she dodged into the shadow along the fiber-optic baseboard. Breathing normally again, she tried to see through the sparking white cloud. Inching toward it on her belly, she felt irresistibly drawn to knowing the truth: What are the Regents doing? What's worth hiding? Doesn't the crew deserve to know about this place? "I just gotta know!" she whispered, "and then I can sneak outta here somehow and tell everyone."

Slowly, she stood and began walking through the parting white cloud. It looked like cotton, but was obviously an intelligent gas comprised of nanytes. Clusters of them began attacking her skin, creating tiny slices, but her morphing biology immediately healed them, also repelling them as if they had sensed her and knew her. "Oh my God! They targeted me as foreign! A green cloud descended on her—the biting stopping—and she inhaled deeply and exhaled: "Thank God, but what a close call!" She stepped back against a bright LED partition. "Did my wrist device might save me?" It was flashing the time brightly, 10:30 p.m., exactly an hour later than the scheduled meeting with Regent Manning.

As the green cloud dissipated, she spotted a figure in the distance. "Hello!" She ran toward it. Parting colorful strands and walking through what looked like seaweed, she stepped into a white room. In the center, enclosed within tall cylinders, were faceless featureless bodies. "These are stem-cell sprayers...and they're adding human cells, tissues, in layers!" She recalled the technology from the emergency clone procedure done earlier on Emma Jane Wright. "These are stem-cell pods!" The various gravitational-cloud areas she had just passed through had never been mentioned to the crew. "This is all definitely new technology...and must be Neltan in origin. But why, and what for?"

One cylinder illuminated and began hissing with cell-spray activity. A hologram of her appeared inside it.

"*Ahh*! This cylinder is processing *me* as a clone! No way!" She ran toward the cylinder, prying the door open just before it closed. When it opened, immediately her virtual mold disappeared. In the distance behind her, she could see her shoes she had ditched—now bubbling over with skin and flesh the cloning process had failed to replicate successfully.

# Astrocity Sagan

Technology was working to teleport her as a clone, but the process had failed horribly.

A siren resounded and red lights began cycling wildly. The facility lit up brightly. Cloning cylinders appeared in rows like caterpillar covers.

"These cylinders look like the Emergency Cloning Chambers in the bow of Level-5," she exclaimed, touching the door. "But these are so different." When she glanced up at the high-domed ceiling, she noticed more new technology. There were no Terra hubs for uploading and downloading minds, no matrix technicians, and no Juicers. "This area *is* a cloning facility…but no one's monitoring it. It's fully automated!" Automated for whom?

Stepping in front of another cylinder, she noticed Emma Jane Wright. She had just left her a few hours ago. This wasn't the woman she had worked on and saved. She tapped on the glass that had crystals of condensation forming on the inside. "Emma!" The body was in a state of gradual deterioration as Emma's hair changed from gray to white. Her face began dehydrating into deep wrinkles. "Someone! Open this! I can save her if I can get my hands on her—"

Too late. Emma had become a skeleton.

When Elisa looked at a tall, wet, formless blob of flesh in the tube next to Emma's, she noticed a new Emma forming. "What?" She rubbed the glass. "My God—she's cloning again?" The puzzle becoming more confusing than ever, and she asked through the blaring alarms, "Who are you, and why are you killing people and re-cloning them?" Now she could hear faint footsteps in the distance. When people would arrive, she would take a stand and confront the criminals. "This is completely illegal…this is murder!"

Turning around, she careened into another tube. She wiped off condensation, trying to discern a face. The features solidified, but she couldn't recognize the new person. Looking down, she realized he was a man.

# J.P. Osterman

His eyes popped wide open.

"*Ahhh!*" she screamed, stepping back into fiber-optic strands that encircled her, trapping her, tinkling like a band of tiny cymbals. "Terra! Stop! Now!"

There was no reply. Terra was obviously off-matrix to her in Level-10.

She had to secure proof of the Regent's illegal activities, but first she needed to know who they were cloning and for what purpose. Then she remembered the hallucination she had seen after disembarking off the Maglev. It wasn't her mother, but a ghostly imposter that (or who) had told her: *you are the answer.* Maybe this Terra down here, but not functioning on the above levels, is acting as a conscience and had brought her to expose all the illegal activities 'cause the matrix knew she was on her way down to Level-9 anyway? That possibility energized her with sticking power to discover the truth.

Her fingers now glowing in the attack on her body, she managed to thrash her way out of the special seaweed environment to inspect the man inside the cloning pod. He was currently only a muscular-skeletal form inside the chamber. But his eyes were open, and glaring at her. He seemed to have cognition and intelligence, and obviously terrified of his new surroundings.

"Oh my God—I woke him up prematurely!" She tried calling out commands to stop the awakening process, but no avail. "I'm so sorry...I wish I could help you," she said. "But I can't stop this process. You're gonna have to wait out the pain. Right now, I have to stop this place from creating *me!*"

One of his eyes suddenly formed a purple spot. A creation nanyte must have reacted to an influx of activity in the man's occipital lobe. She had triggered a bad reaction in the cloning process. "I'm so sorry!" she cried. Feeling sick, she held her stomach. She felt so powerless.

When the forming man raised his hand, she noticed more creation Nanytes swarming around her. "Anything caught inside this place tries to make a copy," she whispered, realizing that the people who were trying to track her presence might also be experiencing problems, 'cause that's why she hadn't yet been caught. When she put her arms in the air, the nanytes sped in clumps away from her left arm. She held her arm high into the air, realizing her special biology was keeping them at bay. But the man in the cloning chamber was reaching out to her with pleading eyes. She backed away, her wrist device glowing brightly as she tapped it several times, capturing his image along with other Level-10 objects and technology. "I gotta go! Sorry. But I'll bring back help for you...I promise," she cried, racing back to the moving walkway. She remembered the man's distinct eye color—his right eye green, the other eye green and purple. "He also has the heterochromia problem I've been seeing in people. Now, I know where it's coming from, some type of neural intervention, and I hope I can stop what's happening," she said, sprinting down the edge of the walkway.

Coming to the exit door and yanking hard on it, she couldn't open it. She pounded on it until she felt saliva choke in her throat. She could hear people approaching her. Looking back, she could see fire and smell smoke. "They found me! This *isn't* gonna be good."

She rammed the door, but it still wouldn't budge. "Open...open..."

Breaking the bio-tech security pad with her left arm, she then kicked the door. It dislodged, and she ran down the long white corridor, searching for the way back to the Maglev. Exhaustion and fear were working her thoughts into a haze. When she came to a T in the corridor, she couldn't remember which hall lead to the station. She felt trapped, doomed.

Still, she ran until she thought she might drop. Breathless, she stopped when she saw the same Regent insignia above a doorway she had raced past two minutes ago. "I'm going in circles!" she said, panting. "Someone must have closed the door leading into that Cloning facility I just left." Now, she felt more hopeless than ever. "I'm finished," she groaned.

# J.P. Osterman

Voices were getting louder. They were angry screams heading in her direction. Soon, she'd meet her hunters. If it hadn't been for what she had just seen, she would have run toward them, told them she'd accidentally taken the wrong shuttle. Maybe then they'd be inclined to help her, not capture her. Then she remembered her wrist device and all the scenes and images she had captured. If a Regent would find it on her—after what she'd just seen—surely he or she would kill her. Taking it off her left arm, she spotted a fire extinguisher. Feeling dejected though because she would no longer have crucial evidence, she shoved it behind the extinguisher's red container. Maybe later, if I can make it alive outta here, she thought, I can find my wrist device. Never give up hope, never. The only thing now giving her motivation to fight was the ghostly apparition's words: *You are the answer.* "I just have to hope that someone will help me."

Glancing around for another exit, she spied another door with a key pad. If she could break inside, she might find a hiding spot. Rolling up the sleeve covering her left arm, she noticed a change in her capillaries. They were like luminescent strands, glowing red under her peach-bright skin. "Wow—if not for what's been happening to me, I think I woulda been dead by now." She kissed her hand. "Thanks Neltan technology." Then she thought of the danger. "But we're gonna get caught soon…and I don't want us ending up as an experiment on a slab…so I better start thinking weak thoughts, and thoughts about being average and normal. But for now, just one more time, get me through this bad spot so we can figure out a place to hide and slip outta here."

With all her might, she struck the keypad with her left arm. It sparked, and the door unclamped. Smoke curled into her nostrils, tearing her eyes, and she coughed through the pinching congestion. "I'll hide in here," she huffed, entering the darkness. After motion lights illuminated, she jammed the door shut with a steel part she ripped off a miniature MRI scanner. The room was a storage facility for ancient technology. "They must be keeping this junk as some sort of backup plan," she said, the fumes abating. "Now…where can I hide?"

# Chapter 13 - Captured

Noticing a 2062 Model-I Regeneration pod at the back of the large lab, she raced toward its computer station. "An outdated Terra-I processor should be at its core! It operates on the old system my mom bought for me when I was a kid," she said, animating an icon on the tray that hummed, vibrated, and then illuminated a two-dimensional image of Standard Terra. "Yes! It works! Finally a break!" Now, she needed Terra-1 to update, and that would take some finagling.

Pulling the sensor patch off her necklace processor, knowing full-well that act was like stepping on the processing and making it inactive, she pressed the patch into the hologram platform. "Applying icon-sensor, fiber-optic technology is how they upgraded Terra-I to Terra-II. God, I hope this works 'cause I'm trying to upgrade to Terra-IV!"

Instantly, the terminal ignited into a bright yellow light. A holographic program was initializing—attempting an interface with *Sagan*'s Terra-IV. If she could remember her mother's old verbal password, maybe she could get Terra-I to upgrade to Terra-II, and then input her old Earth-based code to upgrade to Terra-III. Thereafter, upgrading to the fourth version would be a cinch.

Hearing a clanking noise as the door bar jostled, she realized she didn't have much time. People were almost inside. Their voices muffled, they were pounding on the door, banging on it with their bodies. "Open up!" a man was calling.

"We know you're in there…give up," another screamed.

Flicking on a green switch, she heard the terminal drone, and then she said into a tiny microphone, "On, Terra-II." She remembered her mother's information. "Mable Anne Holton, born December 18, 2008, *umm*, but I forget her Social Security Number. I do know it ended with 9000 though."

Immediately, the yellow hologram pad flared on, a miniature 3D Terra appeared and began spinning like a top. It solidified in front of her. It was the first Terra ever to appear in 3D to the world in 2066."

"You *did* upgrade to Terra-II," Elisa exclaimed, *whew*! Thank God you're here 'cause I need ya!"

Terra hopped off the hologram pad and grew to human size. "You don't look like Mable Anne Holton," Terra-II answered. "But wait—" She had her hands over her ears. "I hear loud noises." She appeared in pain. "Someone…no many people are trapped…and I can't release them and free them. Help me!"

"I need you to help *me* though," Elisa said. Hearing more shouts, she gasped and faced the door. "I'm in *big* trouble! I saw things…illegal things, and people are after me."

Now there appeared a sliver of an opening in the door. "We're almost in!" someone called. "Get the others!"

"Push harder," another screamed.

Desperate to link with the newest version or her avatar Twin, Elisa said, "Connect to Terra-IV now please!"

Terra said, "Identify yourself, please." She began glancing around frantically. "Who are you? Where am I?"

"I'm Mabel Anne Holton's daughter, Dr. Elisa Holton. But there's no time for long introductions and explanations. Just upgrade and interface with Terra-IV. Then we can help each other since you said you need help too."

"Terra Version Four?" The virtual woman began fidgeting with her fingers. She appeared distressed. "I don't know—I don't know—"

"Terra, calm down and listen. I'm Doctor Elisa Holton—"

A man's hand reached through the crack in the door. "Open up! We know you're in there, Doctor Holton!"

"Something is terribly wrong!" Terra cried. The lights in the lab began flickering.

Elisa gulped down air. "Just send a copy of everything you see happening right now to my private kiosk. It's *not* my Living Cube. By now, I'm sure some powerful people have taken it over."

As the upgrade continued to ignite reactions throughout the small outdated lab, Terra replied: "Okay, I will take you at your word, Dr. Elisa Holton, daughter of Mabel Anne Holton. You have Mabel Anne Holton's eye structure and some facial features in common. Therefore, I will carry out your orders. What is your address?"

She flicked her wrist, the wrist device activating, and she touched the Info app that began displaying her profile. "Send everything you see to Level-6, Area 64 of 7,000 at the port, grid 85, Business Kiosk 193G." She felt her breath cut off in her throat. "Got that, Terra?"

"Elisa Holton?" Terra asked. "Doctor Elisa Holton, of Regeneration Corridor-15?"

"Yes—that's me!" She sighed in relief as the lights stopped flashing and flickering—the lab stabilizing to normal. "Thank God for upgrades! But also, remember my own upgrade, the Neltan Encantado armband. It's beginning to change me lately, and I think I saw my mother. Did I?"

At the base of the hologram platform flashed a date. "I have your birth record: May 1, 2043, 2:13 a.m., Eastern Standard—"

"Yes, Terra, but there's no time for accuracy. Are you

# J.P. Osterman

recording everything? Will you send everything to my secret location? And make sure you keep the place secret!"

"I am recording, Dr. Holton." Terra's eyes flashed green. When the light hit a wall mount, the large ceiling hub flared green as the platform flickered: *Sending In-Progress.*

Watching Terra activate all five hubs that began shining brightly, Elisa said: "I need you, Terra, 'cause I don't know what's going to happen to me when those Regents and their techs come charging through that door. I need you to get a message to the crew. I've seen cloning technology, and mind altering technology, but I—"

Terra suddenly hissed out of existence and then returned. The old Terra who had been cut off for so long from the world was rippling through space/time, linking and transitioning to Terra-IV. The evolution seemed to be a painful experience for the artificial intelligence. Each time her hologram platform hissed and droned her image in-and-out of existence, she was cringing. "It is not me, Dr. Elisa Holton, but other people who are attempting to escape from the matrix...so impossible!" She appeared to be at the center of an attack.

"Escape the matrix? What do you mean?" Elisa asked.

More fingers appeared through the crack in the door, and people were attempting to break inside with objects.

Elisa whispered loudly, "Fade but still record, Terra! When this is all over, you should be in a better place, and stronger, at least I think so. And if I end up in one piece after all this is over, I'll help you...and whoever *you're* trying to help as well."

"Thank you, Elisa Holton." Terra faded, but the old computer station remained in Hibernation mode.

Elisa could see Terra's green afterglow-of-an-aura in a circle around the hologram platform. "Fade...fade..." Then her aura disappeared...just in time, except for a button of a white light illuminating in the ceiling hub over the outdated station. "Yes! There's still hope!"

The door broke open.

She turned around to face her captors. When she saw them

rush at her, she put up her hands. "Stop—I can explain!"

"Grab her," a man shouted.

Two men apprehended her by her wrists. They patted her down, trying to locate her devices.

"They're gone. I lost them when the Maglev malfunctioned," she said, her skin burning as she fought to escape their choke holds. "Look, I can explain. I must have taken the wrong shuttle, that's all. I'm Doctor Elisa Holton. I had an appointment with Executive Regent Manning. Call him. He'll confirm it I'm sure."

The men looked at her askance as if trying to match a face to figure. Two other women dressed in cream-colored lab coats joined them. "I have her resume here," one of them said as Elisa appeared in virtual form with her job history, education, and test results scrolling alongside it. "We're gonna need this soon," the tech then said.

"Need it for what?" Elisa asked. Now, she had to play dumb and stall for time. "You're the Regents' private medical techs, right?" After the two women replied yes, Elisa asked: "Don't you recognize me? I'm Chief of Regeneration Specialist of Corridor-15!" She gestured at her virtual resume showing her performing her duties. "I've been sending you and the Regency messages since 4:30. Check it out. I even had a 9:30 appointment scheduled with Regent Manning. How else could I have gained access to the private station and shuttle? Now come on—stop this! This is crazy—*uh*, what's your name?" Then she noticed gold stars on a man's suit. He was lurking behind the women. She'd try reasoning with him. "Sir, this has all been a huge mistake—"

"Move her outta of here," the man in the black suit with gold stars on his collar called out.

"No! No way!" she cried, fighting back with every ounce of kick and arm wrestle she could muster. "My name's Dr. Elisa Holton. What's yours, Sir? I'm reporting you! I'm reporting *all* this! Let me go, now!"

# J.P. Osterman

They pulled her into the hall where they stopped. "Wait here," the Regent ordered. He began talking to his avatar. She had seen the Regents in pictures and watched their broadcasts. She couldn't recognize this Regent at all…then again, she hadn't yet seen his face; but from the tossing and turning of his head, he appeared frustrated, startled, and unsure of what to do.

She believed she could help him decide. "I'm Chief of Corridor-15. I know Thornton Manning personally. Just ask him. We knew each other from Earth." The man gestured for her to wait a minute. "No…you can't hold me like this." Her shoulders hurt. The tight muscles in the back of her neck were pinching as she struggled to break free and talk to the man in the black suit directly. Through tears, she added, "Look, all this is just a simple mistake—really!"

The man in the black suit finally turned around and began walking toward her. From the dark circles under his eyes, tanned skin, and face features that made him resemble the comedian Jackie Gleason, she recognized him immediately from all his campaign performances on Earth. "Regent Jenkens!"

He leaned into her face. "Are you aware, Dr. Holton that this area is restricted?"

She writhed against the set of strong hands pinching her wrists, but she had to stay calm and collected in order to tell her story of what had happened. "I came here, Regent Jenkens, to *this* room by accident." She gave out a facetious giggle as she began reiterating her story: "You see, after I shut down my Corridor, I left to meet with Regent Manning. That Maglev, by the way, is dangerous, Sir." She gasped and coughed. "It malfunctioned and nearly killed me, and coulda killed all of you!"

"Uh huh," he said, folding his arms, nodding at the two buff men who then let go of her wrists.

She began rubbing them. "I needed to meet with a Regent to report why I ordered an Emergency Clone Procedure on one of your Core-Techs, Emma Jane Wright, who by the way, no one seems to even have heard of."

"Yes, E.J., we know," he repeated.

"Well, I remember her from Earth, but no one else who worked on EJ remembers her, Regent Jenkens. Doesn't that seem strange? I'd like to know, Sir, what's really happening on this astrocity."

"Strange? No, not at all, Dr. Holton," he said.

Not at all wanting him to know what she had *really* seen, she swallowed hard and closed her eyes. Hours ago she had treated Emma, but moments ago, she saw her decaying flesh! She'd change the subject. "There's a heterochromatic mutation that's happening in the Regeneration process with some people, Sir. You need to know that, and fix it before more genetic mutations manifest in the entire crew."

"Genetic issues? No, none at all," he said, tapping his wrist device. He seemed odd, unfazed, like robotic. Then, his avatar appeared next to him, showing him the most recent Regeneration stats that showed no abnormality in the human gene pool. Regent Jenkens waved off his avatar. "See? Nothing. So it tells *us* something is wrong with *you*, Doctor Holton."

She stepped back but the two buff Enforcer agents apprehended her. "Oh my God!" she cried, feeling cold tears on her cheeks. "You—you—pompous jerks!" She lunged at Jenkens. The men pulled her back. "You killed Emma Wright…one of your *own* scientists. She helped save Earth and helped win the War on Terror. She was a hero. You're like wiping her outta The Archives. Why?"

Jenkens stepped around her. "You also forget that Emma Jane Wright died. She crash landed on the moon with the rest of the crew."

Elisa suddenly stopped moving as she remembered what happened with Emma, Captain Robert Bartlet, and the rest of the crew onboard the astro-fighter-craft, *Spider*. They died, but obviously the Regency resurrected E.J. for some mysterious purpose. "You're cloning some people? Why?!"

Jenkens tapped his earpiece and called: "Prepare a Clone Cylinder."

"No!" she screamed.

Turning to her, he said, "Because they are special, and we need them." With his jaw clenched, he said right into her face, "Not even a Clone Tech can know our plans, Dr. Holton. Emma Jane Wright overstepped boundaries."

"Good for her," Elisa shouted, "and I'm stepping in where she left off!" She spit in his face, and he slid away from her. "But if I can't find and expose whatever plans you have in store for the crew or the Neltans, someone eventually will."

"The changes we have to make are complicated, Doctor Holton." Then he told the two men to handle her gently and not bruise her skin.

Those words suddenly stunned her. "Changes? What changes!?" As she suspected, Emma had uncovered something terrible and had tried to expose The Regents who then killed her. Still, however, they needed her, for they were attempting to clone her again and again, obviously trying to weed out some mutation or cognitive non-compliance. Elisa wondered what changes the Regency was trying to make: changes to *The Pact*, or perhaps a change in plans to return to Earth? Believing she still had time to talk herself out of sudden death, she realized she had better tread lightly on this dangerous water. "Please, tell me about the changes. But making your changes will kill people!"

She saw the curmudgeon Regent Jenkens mumble and grumble as he continued to talk secretly to someone. "We need her though..." His mumbling grew inaudible again.

She felt her cheeks turn cold and wiped her tears across her shoulders. Those were the wrong words to say! "God, why do I have the tendency to speak without thinking twice?"

"We're gonna change that, Dr. Holton," Jenkens said, "and soon."

As she continued to wiggle away from her captors, their grip still tight on her arms, she said to them: "Are you two men clones? Mindless blobs? Let me go! You know this is wrong, and holding me against my will is completely illegal." They were both the same height with crew cut hair and pot marked faces. Most Enforcers had that type of skin from repeated treatments after wearing cheek guards daily. "Is this what you do all day long? Parade around the ship? Kidnap people who act a bit off, or say the wrong things, or accidentally wander into the wrong places?" She shook her head in an expression of exasperation. "Duh—obviously."

They didn't reply—not even laugh, which she expected. They had to be clones. How many more of them were around the astrocity? She couldn't guess, and no one could. And arguing with them would be useless, especially since the Regents had to have subjected them to Cognitive-Behavioral Relief and Repair—no, some type of new mind-altering technology that was probably much worse.

Suddenly, heavy footsteps resounded down the hallways in a loud, steady and forceful walk. Regent Jenkens and the guards turned toward the sounds. When a tall shadow towered on the floor in front of them, Elisa felt numbing waves ripple down her arms and legs. The incoming Regent had to be a powerful person to instill so much terror that even Steven Jenkens appeared to tremble.

"Kidnap people? No, we don't do that. People go the Regeneration Corridors willingly," the man said, and then laughed facetiously. "Do we force anyone to change, Doctor Holton?" Again he laughed. "No, the changes we make *enhance* humanity with the most advanced technology." He stopped, his presence alone rippling through space/time in a powerful and energetic aura. "Change…it's the only constant, unless that is, if you're kept in a state of eternal stasis."

As he rounded the corner, Elisa recognized him. "Executive Regent Manning!" Her knees buckled. Her captors lifted her off the ground. "What you're doing inside this Level-10 is completely illegal. You're abusing your power and authority, Sir! The crew should clone *you* and change all of *you*!"

Laughing mockingly, he said, "Power?" He turned coldly solemn. "Or implementing a vision?"

She stepped forward so she could look at him directly in the face. "Accountability, Service, and the Common Cause are etched over *Sagan*'s entrance main entryway on Level-1, Sir. You need a knowledge boost. You need to relearn those *Guides for Living*...all of you."

"No, Elisa," Manning snapped back, "*you'll* be relearning a thing or two."

"*Rrr*," she groaned. "When did you choose to murder people, instead of foster life, Sir?" Again she struggled to free herself. Then she remembered their past relationship—a time when they had been friends, even though that was a hundred years ago. Perhaps she could remind him of those old days and use the past as a stepping stone to incite change in him. Quickly, she recounted their friendship with Lynn Altmin, a scientist he had loved but whom a tyrannical doctor murdered. He, Lynn, and Elisa worked together to establish the first communication with the Neltans. She then died, but she and Thornton continued her legacy of securing a force—the matter stream—from the Neltans that healed Earth's ozone. What she didn't remind him of, and dreaded to bring up, was the Neltan technology that accidentally fixed to her arm in the Press Room. Given his uncertain state of mind and how she was lately morphing into someone different physiologically, there was no telling what he'd do to her.

"That was a long time ago, Doctor Holton, when we were very different people facing dangerous circumstances," Thornton said, his head low, his face void of emotion. Yet he still had the same Beethoven facial features with dark serious eyes, his most attractive yet frightening feature. Advertisers sometimes referred to him as *The Conductor* whenever they used his image to promote Regency sponsored broadcasts or events; and people were always changing his style of dress, along with the clothing and hairstyles of the other nine Regents to create all types of characters and caricatures to insert in their own photo-shopped social-media shares.

When she was able to catch her breath, she came face-to-face with his jutting chin. The whites of his eyes looked like ocean foam, his anger an intense storm. Then she spotted the large gold stars on his collar. They were hypnotic, as if jettisoning some type of retinal barbiturate. "Darn you...and damn you all!" she said, unable to gain strength to fight them. As they talked among themselves, she watched helplessly as Manning and Jenkens called other Regents. They began grappling with what to do with her.

Now, all she could do was to try her hardest to knock some sense into them all. "How many people have you cognitively altered, or cloned? Huh? You scum!"

She looked into Manning's intimidating eyes and gasped at his hard-cold sneer. His powerful position could kill her. She'd better try another tactic if she were to ever going to get out of this mess. "This is all a mistake, Regent Manning," she said humbly. "Let me try to explain."

"Try what, Elisa?" he asked, folding his arms and checking the virtual time that spun on in front of them. "Regent Jenkens, please find out what's taking the others so long, will you?"

"Sure thing," Jenkens said and then quickly left.

She believed that maybe she could ignite a tender spark in Thornton's heart. "Look, I'm sorry. Like I told Regent Jenkens, I just finished working a double shift. I—" Her voice cracked, and she coughed. "There are line jumpers in all the Regeneration Corridors." She gulped down two deep breaths. "A—a malfunction—that's what really occurred that nearly killed—*killed* someone." She almost mistakenly said, 'Emma.' "I tell ya what...just give me a cognitive alteration. I'll forget everything I saw and we'll go on like nothing happened, okay?" Waiting for a reply, she added, "Well, whataya think?"

# J.P. Osterman

Thornton kept pacing the floor and glancing at the men holding her. He was obviously getting impatient, or figuring out a way to use what she had just told him to her disadvantage. She remembered what Nick had told her: "Let it go, Chief." She wished she had done just that, but, no, she just *had* to know the truth, just *had* to be the exploring type of person. She puffed out a grand, "Damn!"

"What?" he snarled.

"Oh, nothing, Sir," she said. "Damn that I did this...sorry." Watching his irritation wax, she thought: somehow, I *have* to defuse this situation...get him to believe that I have *no* malicious intention to interfere with his business. Think...think! She felt a sudden rush of anger pulse through her body. As soon as she could, if she'd *ever* get off this Clone Level-10 with her mind intact, she'd find a way to broadcast the recording into *every* matrix grid, stream it to every portable device, and even make peoples' avatars say it. But the illegal cloning and their new technology appeared to be only the tip of the iceberg. Much more was going on with the Regents, particularly their plans for Nelta. She thought: play coy, discover what's going on, escape with my life, and tell everyone. "I have a regeneration scheduled for tomorrow, Regent Manning," she said, sweetly. "All I need is some rest. That's all. I bet we can all agree that we're tired...right? It's been a long day...right? Just keep me here tonight, and tomorrow put me through my scheduled Regeneration procedure...of course, wiping this part of the day out of my memory. There, problem solved!"

Thornton grimaced. His cold eyes felt penetrating to the bone. "Take her away."

"Wait—you can't do this! What have I done? Nothing!" She felt her stomach sink in despair as she wrestled with her captors and kicked to get away, bus she couldn't. "Regent Manning—kidnapping is illegal. You can't just kill me...*or* clone me...or *make* me disappear. People *will know*! I'm a Chief of a Regeneration Corridor. People see me all the time and we talk on the Maglevs!"

# Astrocity Sagan

They led her down the hall and pushed her into a large white lab where a large rainbow hub processor was buzzing with activity. Tesla coils were towering in mazes everywhere—their shadows on the floor disappearing when bolts of a new type of energy struck the air. The light made people appear in double form—instant virtual avatars. Jenkens was already at the back of a station and performing vital functions. She could see his curmudgeon, Basset Hound face blaring commands. Then the lightning bolts stopped and a body cylinder opened. It was a hover cylinder. That meant they weren't planning on storing her body in stasis, most likely on Level-10, where no one could help her.

Marveling at the new Terra-V, she exclaimed: "This Terra is new—isn't it? The hub is obviously a brain-grid processor, but from the high resolution rainbow I'm seeing, this must be the origin of Terra-IV's matrix processor. You actually created a hard-copy conduit of Terra…to use outside of the crew's influence." She remembered the terrorists on Earth had done the same thing before they were annihilated—stolen the newest Terra, modified a part of the matrix, and began using their new system against their enemies to advance their war on terror. "Why don't you want people to know about all this?"

A tall blond woman dressed in a white lab coat glided in a gurney.

Elisa realized they were preparing to extract her mind. "No way am I getting on that thing!" She kicked the gurney. The shocking reality bolted through her entire body: This *was* really happening…happening *right now.* "Stop!"

Manning waved in more Regents. "Strap her down. Let's get this over. *Tsk-tsk-tsk*," he hissed. "This procedure should launch Phase I of our expedition to Nelta."

"What are you going to do to me?" she cried. "And what's Phase I?"

Sneering at her, he replied, "Tomorrow, you'll be gone until we need you, Elisa."

"Gone where?" she gasped.

"Stasis, of course," he replied, "and with the Mind-Meddling app we've installed in several places, everyone passing through those archways will forget you ever existed...*and* Emma Jane Wright."

"And whatever else she might have uncovered," Regent Steven Jenkens added. "But like you, she's brilliant, and we need her in the future." Disgust and anger were exuding around him. "If someone does remember and stream and question about you, we'll say we had to charge you with malpractice as the evidence show, and that you're in jail, in seclusion."

"No," Elisa cried, "that accident *wasn't* my fault. It was *your* fault! Your private Clone Techs insert her body into *my* Corridor-15 when you'd already up-streamed her mind. How was I supposed to know you'd done that?"

"But people *think* it's your fault," Thornton said, his strong widow's peak dipping into a crease high on his forehead. His dark eyes were churning with a calm fury.

She had to drive the truth of his error into him—had to fight for her life. "I was just doing my job...finding the cause of what I believed was a malfunction. What are you people *really* doing down here on this new Level-10 of yours? Has something changed on Nelta? With *The Pact*? Did something happen that we're not aware of?"

Manning didn't respond, but another Regent began arguing with him. "Regent Manning, remember. She has a technology...she *is* a technology."

Feeling exposed and vulnerable—but breaking free of one of her straps—she said, as the two men alongside her overpowered her: "You've known about my special biology all along. So that's why you kidnapped me and dragged me down here." As Manning and Jenkens began colluding some more while activating more programs on her stasis cylinder in the background, she changed the subject. "Convert the ship? What do mean?" She felt more confused than ever! But at least one person wanted her alive. Those words began pounding through her mind: Stay alive, find a way out, and hope Terra is recording everything. Because, *if* what she believed was about to happen was true, she'd wake up sometime in the future and completely oblivious to the past. They would extract her consciousness and edit her memories—Mind Meddling they just called it—which was also illegal. She suddenly remembered a word that welled out of her soul. It was a memory, from Emma Jane Wright. "Self-Aware." She screamed it: "Self-Aware! You hear, Terra? Self-Aware! Now! Self—"

Jenkens ran over and covered her mouth. He slapped a sedation patch on her arm. "It's not putting her to sleep," he said, stepping back in shock.

When Elisa saw a face move out of the shadow, she stopped fighting. "Regent Sylvia Itonovich!" Maybe she could gain *this* Regent's sympathy. "You're in charge of the Regeneration Corridors." She gasped for breath as she bit the thumb of a Regent trying to tape her mouth shut. "You know who I am! This is a terrible mistake!"

Jenkens moved in between Thornton Manning and Sylvia Itonovich. "Other people might have seen Dr. Holton enter our shuttle."

"Who?" Itonovich asked.

"Those people who have disconnected from Terra," Jenkens began. "They're using old-fashioned frequencies to hack the matrix and extract data. They might have been monitoring our station and saw Dr. Holton entering our Maglev." Elisa breathed through tangling fingers around her mouth, and he added: "Regent Itonovich might be right. A cognitive Mind Meddle might not reach everyone or redact her identity from every device. If Elisa Holton comes up missing, someone *will* investigate at some point soon, and expose us."

Thornton moaned and said: "I still believe we should get rid of her permanently. We can upload all her knowledge and preserve her body for its special cellular powers. We don't know them yet, but they could appear invaluable." He patted her neck, his fingers searching for a vein.

Elisa tried to twist free of the straps they were tying around her hands. "No! You can't *kill* me!"

Sylvia Itonovich began rolling a wand over Elisa's arms and legs as several technicians began applying patches to her body. The stasis pod was now next to her. It kept fading and re-appearing, her consciousness slowly changing. Soon, she'd be rendered totally brain dead...she knew the drill.

Itonovich tilted Elisa's chin up toward Terra's giant hub. "Begin up-stream, Terra."

Elisa saw a green beam strike the top of her head.

Itonovich looked at her wrist device showing a special small lab within their altered Terra-V system. It was fiber-optics, nano-robotic, and quantum-computing technology; but the lab was also filled with streams of bright static that appeared as water strands. There were warbling colors on the walls, and images of people, places, and objects fading in-and-out of existence—then streaming up to the processing hubs on the ceiling. The area was a dimensional portal. Elisa saw scenes of her life flashing intermittently throughout the entire room. Itonovich ordered, "Up-stream to Level-10 Clone Facility, experimental cylinder 4A."

The uploading of her consciousness had begun. Elisa could feel pulses of heat penetrating her skin. She realized an artificial intelligence was intruding into her thoughts. "You can't Mind-Meddle without my permission! I'm fighting you. See?" She wiggled and squirmed as the cloned Enforcers held her down. Her new physiology was working! For how long? She couldn't predict. Talking appeared to help. "This is *completely* illegal!" She arched her back, trying to peel free of the gurney. Then she realized that to struggle too wildly would increase a misalignment within the brain-grid extraction. She could become a living vegetable! She stopped skirmishing and lay still.

"Terra, begin with Elisa Holton's days at Duke University until boarding *Sagan*," Itonovich continued. "Let's get a

# Astrocity Sagan

Baseline of Significance."

Terra began projecting scenes out of Elisa's life, beginning with her first day of medical school. The images appeared in the small lab now showing over Itonovich's wrist device.

Seeing her past scrolling before her, she exclaimed, "You Regents are rationalizing all your illegal activities because *you're* determining importance!" She felt a burn strike her ear. "Ouch!"

"Remain still, Doctor Holton," Itonovich ordered.

Now their Terra-V was projecting her academic achievements and her volunteer work with shelters after the terrorist attack.

"Stop!" Suddenly, she couldn't hear her own words. She realized she no longer had the capability to speak, but she knew she was crying. She felt her heartbeat race in her chest. Her only hope was the old Terra system in the other room— that is, if she was still recording and could interface with the illegal Terra-V they were using.

As her consciousness continued to Up-Stream into the giant hub processor, Thornton Manning told his two Enforcers and two white-clad Clone Techs who were monitoring the procedure with Jenkens and Itonovich: "After the system finishes this portion of the procedures, put her body in the stasis cylinder, and sent her up to Level-5. Take *my* Maglev. It's secure."

"Yes, Sir," they said, and they continued fulfilling his orders.

# J.P. Osterman

## Chapter 14 – Body Interception

As Thornton Manning's workers made their way back to the small Level-10 transport station with Elisa's body enclosed in a stasis cylinder, a hole opened up at the edge of the transport tunnel sixty feet above ground. The station had morphed back into its former state as a small theater, hiding all the interior labs and advanced technology. Two people slipped through the cauterized hole and fastened themselves on the rim. Clothed in form-fitting technology, they synchronized time. With stealth agility, they unleashed ropes, harnesses, and stick fasteners to rappel into the tunnel to save Elisa. As of yet, she was too far away, and they needed a bit more time if they were going to blend in perfectly with the tunnel. Two Enforcers and two white-clad Clone Techs glided Elisa's body closer the docked Maglev, but one of the techs paused, calling Thornton Manning. They forgot one crucial piece of instruction on securing her body properly inside the Maglev. The two intruders had more time to secure readings and launch their attack.

Aiden Mathews and Jean Trent are members of 273—the

missing crew. They named the rogue group *273* because of the perfectly harmonious number incapable of being dissected mathematically. The number is also the solution to many unsolvable equations, especially when used to manipulate various algorithms, code, and hieroglyphics. Their specialties!

Four weeks ago, the group formed when its members woke up in a daze at the stern of Level-2 after completing their Regenerations. Several avatars appeared in front of them. Shocked and baffled, they believed the avatars were hallucinations. In reality, they were *Sagan* avatars—the astrocity's messengers. One of the hallucinations explained the onset of their appearance:

The Living Breath entity inside Navigation was experiencing a severe problem, and something powerful was preventing it from isolating it and fixing it. The Living Breath is a Neltan artificial intelligence that had combined with Terra-IV prior to leaving Earth. Its purpose is to fix *Sagan* automatically, guide it to Nelta, activate self-defense systems in case of any type of alien attack, and receive and send communications from Nelta. It had disconnected them and formed several high-tech areas, which they would have to keep improving on, from Terra-IV's matrix. They would only have strange avatars in the forms of animals and old-Earth movie stars to help them.

When Aiden Mathews asked the avatar, "Why did you choose us?"

A *Clark Gable* look-a-like avatar replied: "You are the answer to discovering the problem and correcting it. We will also bring you more help along the way."

After successfully re-routing communications networks so that no Enforcer, Matrix Security Tech, or medical specialist could discover the group's altered biometrics, several spots inside the transport tunnels opened, altering out of piping, tubing, connectivity, and new metals. One of the apparitions, Predator, from the old-Earth movie, *Predator*, told the group another piece of information. The Living Breath had altered all their Regeneration Down-Streaming procedures. There was a new technology inside all the transport archways, and the Living Breath saved the 273 individuals from experiencing changes. To assist them in their pursuit of locating and solving the ship-wide glitch, the Living Breath also altered the group's resumes, jobs, medical files, and provided them with false biometric readings, thus rendering them invisible but also visible among the population. In the meantime, they've all been trying to locate the epicenter and creator of the impenetrable disturbance while living in seclusion from the rest of the crew, and monitoring the apparitions who are appearing more frequently to people throughout the astrocity. But a *Hermes the Messenger* avatar appeared to them at 4:35 p.m., asking them to help Dr. Elisa Holton, now hopeless and in stasis.

"When do we move in and take 'em down so we can get to her?" Jean Trent asked Aiden Mathews. High up in the tunnel rim, they had just checked the time. They had only minutes to free her. Also dressed in wingsuit reflecting every nuance of light for camouflage, Jean sat perched upside down on the rim of the tunnel. She was a black woman, muscular and ready to pounce down on Elisa's captors.

With a bald eagle on his left shoulder, Aiden Mathews whistled, and the eagle flew out of the opening to Jean's shoulder.

"What's that?!" an Enforcer asked, her colleague and the two techs pausing to listen from their search of information. The Enforcer activated an animal icon on her wrist device.

"I think she's calling the zoo," Jean whispered and then laughed behind her voice-linking mask. "Wow, do they have a surprise comin' at 'em."

"When he screeches, we dive in while they're distracted and secure Holton," Aiden said, petting his young eagle with his gloved hand. He then directed it to circle high above her body.

"You sure we're doing the right thing comin' 'ere?" Jean asked. She was Jamaican, in touch with the raptors she had once managed at the zoo's raptor exhibit on Level-2.

"Definitely!" he whispered. "You heard what *Hermes the Messenger* said. She's the answer as well, so we gotta save her."

The eagle screeched, lifted off Jean's shoulder and began diving toward Elisa's captors.

The Enforcers pulled out their laser weapons as the white-clad techs lifted their wrist devices to call for help. A raven dove out of the smoldering hole in the tunnel, jointed the eagle, and they began attacking their wrist devices and flying through their avatars. The two Enforcers began firing on them, but the raptors were too fast and escaped the yellow death pulses. The wrist devices on the Clone Techs' arms began smoking—their flesh became arching electricity.

"What the hell are they?" Jean asked. "I don't see skin!"

Trent lifted arrows out of his sheath and locked them into his bow as the Enforcers again aimed their weapons at the raptors. "Focus…"

"Better hit 'em or we're dead," Jean whispered. "Then again," she laughed, "I've never known ya ta miss even the fastest movin' target, man."

Two arrows streaked through the air, and two gargantuan avatars appeared alongside the Enforcers. Aiden's arrows hit their weapons, throwing the Enforcers to the ground.

When one Enforcer spotted the giant avatar towering over him as if about to devour him, he shouted, "Godzilla!"

"I've got Predator next to me!" the other screamed. "I have no weapon!" He backed away from the encroaching ghostly Predatory. "No wrist device either!"

"Me either!" the other Enforcer barked.

Both Enforcers let go of Elisa's stasis cylinder and ran back through the theater; but a few partitions hadn't finished altering the station back to its previous theater state. Two sharp metal partitions swept down like pendulums, sweeping the two men off the floor and four automated beams quartered them as the two Clone Techs ran toward the Maglev in defensive positions. Just as the Maglev's door slid open, the raven and eagle swooped down on their heads and began clawing their special white visors. Suddenly, their heads dislodged off their bodies; and sparks, pops, and cracks echoed through the small station. Their heads toppled on the floor and began rolling into the darkness as their headless bodies wavered in cooling air with their flailing arms.

"They're definitely robots!" Jean exclaimed. "Wow—I never woulda guessed the Regents' Clone Techs are really robots! Let's go examine 'em, get parts of 'em so we can show people."

"Never mind them," Aiden said as the eagle returned to him and landed on his shoulder. Jean quickly directed the raven to return to their home base deep inside Level-2's Vertical Stern Transport station. "Let's grab Dr. Holton and get her outta here." He opened his wingsuit in preparation to glide sixty feet down to the station. "Go!"

"Right…but where we supposed to be takin' her?" Jean activated her wingsuit and began skydiving toward Elisa via a green-lit path the avatars had illuminated. Controlling her wingsuit's direction, she landed softly in front of Elisa's stasis cylinder. Aiden touched down next to her.

"I don't know where she's gotta go next though," Aiden began. "They never tell me until they want me to know the answers," he laughed. He looked at the giant *Godzilla* and held up his special glowing wrist device so the avatar could input coordinates. It was an outdated device, rounder and a bit more cumbersome than the popular cookie-sized ones. Meanwhile, *Predator* had disappeared but then reappeared at the bow of the Maglev and began re-programming the shuttle through its redeye connection with it.

*Godzilla* shrank to half its size and touched Aiden's wrist device. Both their devices illuminated a new Maglev map. Thornton Manning's shuttle would come to a dead stop a few miles inside the tunnel, where a few of their team members would be ready to meet them and spray it with a light-based camouflage coating. Already the Living Breath was re-routing other Maglevs in their path.

"We don't have much time, but Level-5 is where we're disembarking," Aiden said, calling in an order to his team to have different clothes ready for them, and disguises.

"Where do we take her? And how are we gonna downstream 'er mind back into 'er body?" Jean asked.

*Godzilla* disappeared and *Predator* waved them quickly into the Maglev.

"Like I said," Aiden shrugged, "We don't know a thing until they show us! Blame the astrocity…not me."

"All right," she huffed as they gently guided Elisa's stasis cylinder into the Maglev.

"Don't move her to fast though! We have no idea about this new technology," Aiden cautioned.

"Over here…there are seats missing and tubing, and an automatic connection," she said, sliding Elisa's body into the perfect space to accommodate her stasis pod. "In between the time she arrived here, someone must have set up this section 'cause, I never noticed any hookup like *this* before in their Maglevs." The system linked with Elisa's body pod. Her vitals illuminated over it, reading normal. Jean suddenly panicked. "We gotta go! By now, they know it's us…and they're gonna start a *real* hunt, for all of us. Our entire group's in danger!"

*Predator* set his transparent hand on her shoulder, and then shook his head no in a gesture of certainty.

"That's a relief," she sighed as Aiden secured a special hub above Elisa's head. Quickly it illuminated a yellow containment field into the stasis chamber. *Predator* motioned at it with his clawed hands, and the hub began a counting down the time until her mind would downstream into her body.

"Three days!" Aiden exclaimed. He looked into *Predator*'s beady black eyes. "Where and how are we gonna hide her for *three* days, huh? You better have something good up your techno armband for us to pull off three days of hiding!"

Jean said to *Predator*, "We can't do this…no way! They'll

find us all, round us up—"

White rays of light interrupted, illuminating several spots on Elisa's body. The light altered into cycling rainbows all around her.

"This girl's special! Even the light appears to know her…react with her," Jean said, perusing Elisa like a book. "She might look like a sleeping beauty…but there's a technology interacting inside this chamber, the likes that appear capable of lighting up this entire astrocity!" She stepped back, awe and fear exuding in her eyes.

As the Maglev activated its propulsion components, Jean and Aiden unleashed their boot clamps into the flooring, and fastened in securely at the base of the cylinder, staring at Elisa's hibernating body.

"I've heard of her," Jean began as she scrolled through images over her wrist device, information about Elisa and the aneurism that affected her work station. "But I wonder how she's going to help the Living Breath." She touched the cylinder, and her hand print imbedded on the special glass.

Aiden began wiping it off, but couldn't expunge her print. It appeared indelible! He gave up. "Ya jealous of her?" he asked, seeing skepticism in Jean's eyes.

"Naw, man, I never been jealous a day in my life!" She folded her arms in an impervious gesture. Then she pointed her wrist device at the last objects inside Level-10's theater station. "We must capture this and report it."

Aiden pushed down her arm. "No, not yet. Remember…we have to live in secrecy, especially with *her* in our charge."

She scowled. "Well I'm gettin' mighty tired of being in-cog-ni-to!"

*Predator* gave out a bombastic laugh from his alien gut as the Maglev lifted at full-speed on its trajectory up the tunnel toward Level-9.

"I hope we can revive her successfully," Jean said in a doubtful tone.

"It's all up to us and our friendly avatars," Aiden said. "But at least we got to her before *they* did. No telling *what* Manning had in store for her…and what the hell he has in store for all of us!" He stretched out his fingers under his tight gloves. The special wingsuit technology could be constricting.

"Until we get Elisa Holton down-streamed into her body and revived somewhere, the safety of this astrocity is up to Terra and the avatars," Jean said. *Predator* nodded and walked in thudding steps to the middle of the shuttle, his eyes shining a beacon upward into the tunnel—a call for preparedness for the rest of 273.

"And the Living Breath entity," Aiden added. "All we can do is hide, and work on her." He gestured at Elisa's body that appeared so alive in the light-based images swirling everywhere through her stasis chamber. "And when the time is right, help fix the problems that are plaguing *Sagan* and jeopardizing *The Pact*."

After seconds, Jean added, "But from what we just saw, the Regency *might* be one of the problems."

# J.P. Osterman

## Chapter 15 – Life and Soul

After Thornton Manning launched Elisa's consciousness into his illegal Terra-V system, Elisa could see herself—a white ghost—rending and splitting off from her body, observe herself lifting off the gurney until she disappeared into the giant processor hub. Streaking through the quantum-computer matrix was a windy world filled with lights, tunnel, and portals. Some tunnels were trying to suck her down into their worlds, until a bright hand grabbed her, saving her. She had seen that strong reassuring hand before—Twin! That meant Terra-IV, or someone else, had redirected her consciousness to safety, saving her from Thornton Manning's illegal system that would have resulted in death.

"Now, if you can only find my body and Down-Stream me back into it!" she called. But her words appeared as music trickling through the matrix where she doubted anyone could intercept them and translate them. "I better stay quiet, or worse things might happen to me," she whispered.

Then she began softly gliding through a warm environment. She remembered the kaleidoscopic structure she had wandered through in that Level-10. This same place had no ending or beginning—only infinity. Moving her fingers through one of the strands of light, she noticed a rainbow land on her fingers. Looking closer at it, she surmised the little strand of light to be a *living* data stream. When she picked out any strand of it from the kaleidoscope environment, she could see people performing their daily activities. Every color had an individual associated with it—like a special spectrographic signature. But try as hard as she could, she couldn't communicate with anyone. She was now only a sensing spirit—a soul. Some things she could remember: her parent's faces, her tenth birthday, the day the terrorists struck Earth's ozone layer; but some things she was beginning to forget the longer she remained inside Terra-IV's matrix. She began a desperate hunt-and-peck search—touching and picking up strands of light, hoping to reassemble her life!

Angry voices began approaching her from behind. She stopped. She could hear Thornton voice and several other Regents calling: "Get her back!" and "Where'd she go?!" and "Find her now!"

Screaming, she dove for cover, landing on a cloud of air that pulled her down through a thick white glistening fog. Looking up, she saw a monstrous witch-of-a-woman: a black-clad, nasty-fanged entity with scrolling data for a face and clothes, all code. The witch was clawing her way over rainbows, devouring light strands in her path. Little voices were screaming. Obviously they're bytes of peoples' minds that failed to Down-Stream during Regeneration! Elisa felt an ache in her left arm—a warning signal. She surmised the witch's purpose: to locate her, and devour her! How long could she hide from the ravenous hunter? Not long.

A bright small tunnel suddenly opened above the voracious witch who shrieked like a screech owl as it sucked her up into its vacuum. The kaleidoscopic room morphed back into calmness. She stood up, rubbing her left arm that stopped

# J.P. Osterman

aching. "Hello? Hey! Thanks for saving me, Terra...or Twin?"

A musical note in C major resounded, a calm soothing answer.

Elisa saw her voice stretch out like orange taffy into the shimmering sky of the matrix. Then she looked at her hands...now small—her body shrunk down so small. If she were on solid ground, she surmised she'd be the size of speck of dust!

In the distance, she spotted a large spinning wheel and ran to it—her feet carry her like winged Hermes. Suddenly, she appeared in front of a giant spinning wheel. A huge crowd was in the audience. "What is this place? Why am I here?" she asked.

When she saw the Level-2 prompt showing ten thousand people tuning in Live, she realized Terra had streamed her into a game show. The *Wheel of Fortune* show was still popular; and every night, people were participating in the game from their homes as well as those select ones who could attend with tickets. But instead of receiving crypto-currencies, they'd receive vacation time at various rec centers around *Sagan*.

Letters finally formed below the wheel: "You are the answer." It was Terra-IV communicating with her! The audience was stunned and began talking among themselves in bewilderment as many of them began rendering the show for the crew.

"You said that to me before," Elisa whispered, "so when can I go back?"

More letters spun out on the wheel: "Run run as fast as you can!" Lyrics to the nursery rhyme began playing on the game show. People rushed out of their theater seats like scattering ants, screaming and shouting for help.

Elisa began hearing chomping sounds. In the distance, she could see tiny mouths devouring white energy. They turned ninety-degrees and were moving straight at her. "Help! Save me!" She began racing toward the empty theater seats but wasn't moving.

# Astrocity Sagan

The wheel ground down its last, *flap-flap-flap*, and then stopped. After the square bars revealed the prize—3 days of gym membership on Level-2's beach—one woman who had remained seated at the center of the theater stood up. Her face was bright and glowing, like an angel. "Here! Elisa! Over here!"

The number 3 lifted into the code-scrolling air where the munching mouths guzzled it up, missing Elisa.

Then Terra appeared in her Standard form. She was tall and towering. She picked Elisa up by the collar and rolled her into a ball. "This is quantum-string Dimension-7," she whispered into Elisa's ear. She felt snug, protected, and secure—the first time she'd felt that way in days. "Keep your arms in tight! Here we go!" Terra threw her high into the sky and disappeared.

Elisa could see herself high on one of the domed ceilings. She was a giant yellow comet with a long white tail, much larger than the shooting stars and comets she'd ever seen in the artificial night sky. People must think I'm a deadly asteroid, she thought. Looking down on several residents, she noticed people recording her on their wrist devices and tablets. Their avatars were straight at their sides as if being directed by a powerful entity to stand at attention and divert everything harmful out of the sky—Enforcers and Matrix Techs trying to eliminate the mysterious projection, her. Minutes passed, and Terra continued to cycle her through a progression of skies until she finally spotted a white room, enlarging the closer she approached it. She was settling, coming back down to Earth. Obviously, Terra had just finished the safe haven.

# J.P. Osterman

## Chapter 16 – Lost Soul Bytes

"Finally!" Elisa said. "How long have you been spinning me around *Sagan*, Terra?" She noticed she had a transparent body and could move her fingers, arms, and legs. "Thanks! Does this mean I'm alive somewhere?" As she floated to the floor, she saw Emma Jane Wright. "Emma! It's good to finally see someone I recognize…even though when I saw you last time, you almost died." After touching down, she hugged her, but her hands moved through Emma's arms.

"Elisa Holton," Emma exclaimed. "Now we can talk!"

She had the same face Elisa had seen when Emma endured that horrible malfunction—actually not a malfunction, but a planned extraction from the crew. Her memories were dwindling, but she quickly recalled one terrible thing: Emma had witnessed something, perhaps The Regents' illegal Terra-V or a plan even more deadly. Elisa wondered if Emma knew what had really happened to her. Her original body was dead and gone, most likely shot out a chute and drifting in space.

Excitement shown in pools of Emma brown eyes as if she had known Elisa since childhood. "I tried catching you a few times, but I couldn't reach you. Not until Terra gave me a lasso so I could rope your feet." Emma laughed. She looked like a delicate Asian ballerina with fine black hair tied back a red ribbon. On Earth while working with Captain Robert Bartlet to defeat the terrorists, she was a computer genius who helped locate a Demon Terra system and defeat it.

"Where are we?" Elisa asked. She could hear a bellowing wind rage against their four white walls. Outside their safe haven, she believed there was a void filled with electromagnetic currents, laser-light processing, and throngs of flow-flares from quantum strings popping in and out of the various dimensions.

"Terra is protecting us against a new Demon system," Emma whispered. "This is bad, Elisa, *real* bad."

"For who?"

"Us *and* the Neltans," she exclaimed, tears welling in her eyes. When they fell in crescents on her lids, they glowed and evaporated—the white room evaporating them as expressive pain.

Elisa remembered Emma's clone inside a cylinder. It disintegrated into ash; and by now, disposed of by The Regents. She didn't have the heart to tell her they were most likely trying again to clone her. Why? Most likely for the same reason Thornton said they were preserving *her* "special body:" for a time in the future when they'd need her. They were working hard to find special human DNA, like Emma's, and perfect it. What Emma had just said about people being in danger had to be linked to Thornton's plan.

Sitting down and crossing her legs, Emma exhaled a long and lost, "*Ahhh.* I wish we knew more…like why we're here."

"Regardless, we need to fight to escape!" Elisa said, plopping down in a whit seat next to her. They had a bright-white table between them, but no food or drinks. Then she saw her hands—completely transparent—and Emma's body, a glowing ghost. "There's gotta be a way out, but I'm stumped…and I think fading." She felt helpless, her emotion turning her skin light blue for sadness, except for her left arm, still the same, never changing. She knew the powers in her arm were working with the matrix and synching with her outside body to keep her in one piece. She had to still be alive…somewhere! That thought energized her, imbuing confidence.

"Minds aren't meant to exist in a place like this," Emma began. "Terra is a Quantum Data Land, a processing dimension, where we have no bodies and a matrix is holding together our minds." She ducked down in fright. "And protecting us."

"No water, no food…and I'm not even hungry," Elisa said, rubbing her abdomen. Her hand passed through her body and she pinched the place where her stomach should be. The hollow spot squeaked like a toy. "Oh my gosh!"

"Don't mess with your heart though," Emma warned, "or you might end up in a purple room or in front of a red-eyed bull!"

"What?" Elisa asked, but she didn't really want the answer.

"After I arrived here, I lifted out my brain and I saw my first-grade teacher giving me my first crayons! Boy did I shove that thing back into my skull fast."

Elisa shuddered. "Aside from formless bodies and weird feeling organs, this place is like a lab facility…so sterile and impersonal." The fine static hairs on her arms stood on end. The ceiling began to bubble and smoke.

"Hell!" Emma pointed at crackling white paint on the ceiling. "The Outside is trying to get inside, so take cover under the table!" She dove under the bright-white table like a fish. "Terra should change the color of our clothes to camouflage us soon; then should scatter." They lay on the floor, their bodies turning to mounds of white light.

The center of the ceiling morphed into two angry blue eyes surrounded by black and gray shadows. Their pupils began darting in their bulging sockets, obviously searching for somebody.

"They look evil," Elisa whispered.

A gale-intensive wind blew through, followed by screams and moans. The eyes disappeared off the ceiling, and it turned white again.

"What was that?" Elisa asked, shivering, covering her face. The terrifying shrieks abating, she smelled rain and green grass.

"Terra lured her Evil Update away from us and sent her packing."

"That black teeth-gnashing witch I saw before I arrived here?" Elisa gasped.

"Yep," Emma replied, fear in her voice. "But the Dark Update won't be gone for long." Then she sat up, inhaling the freshness that had replaced the sharp, ionic devilish blackness. "Lilacs!" she added, sniffing the air. "They're my favorite." Like someone waving a magic wand over her, Emma's clothes altered from a plane white jump suit to a pink-hoop dress with velvet red roses on the hem. She looked happy now and calm. Then she turned serious. "I call the evil beings searching for our souls, Kinetic Monsters." She glanced hurriedly around the white room. "They've also taken over The Regents' minds and souls...at least that's what I think."

"How? Have I seen it?"

"They altered the CBRR technology we approved. Now, it's interfacing with their illegal Mind Meddling technology. Technology *they* programmed...hub devices only they can locate, and deactivate."

"So *that's* the name of their new cognitive interference devices, Mind Meddling technology! I think I heard that...but I'm having trouble remembering."

"Yes, and the devices are everywhere, but most likely they affected you differently because you're different," Emma said.

"Yeah...I'm finding that out the longer my abilities are no longer dormant," Elisa said. "But how does the Mind Meddling technology work? If we get back, *we* can destroy them."

"Running on their illegal Terra, the devices extract neural

impulses and alter them right on the spot. That's why the Kinetic Monsters keep trying to find us and eliminate us. The Regents have programmed them to devour all proof of their Mind Meddling."

"But the technology could be killing cerebral impulses of normal peoples' minds as well," Elisa said. "During Regeneration, minds are Up-streamed to a grid in Terra-IV. If the Demon Terra assesses any of those impulses as hostile, it'll eliminate them. When the person's mind down-streams, they won't be right, and they won't be themselves."

"I know, so in this place, we're always running away and hiding from the Kinetic Monsters, so get used to it, 'cause they're after you now too."

"Never! They've got a fight to pick if they mess with *my* soul," Elisa said.

Emma appeared suddenly energized with fight. "Good Terra is always battling them with us, but at the String level, so they can't see what's coming."

Elisa remembered seeing the Halite Being from Dimension-8. "Too bad we have to change into soul form to touch another dimension."

"Oh you don't wanna touch a Kinetic Monster!" Emma cried, blowing on her fingers. One or more of the sub-quantum critters must have taken a bite of her. "I once saw an experiment where a Regent succeeded in changing a man into subatomic particles. His name was Seamus Kelly."

"*You* participated in one of their nasty experiments?" Elisa scooted away from her.

"Of course," Emma said, turning somber. "*Many* of them. I had to! That was one of my job descriptions: To evolve Terra-III to Terra-IV right after we left Earth, and then, to advanced Neltan technology for..." She paused, thinking.

"For what purpose—for what reason, Emma?" Elisa wanted to shake her, but her hands encountered a strange white barrier. "We're *all* in danger, like you told me when I first arrived here. We have to do something. I gotta get back to my body! You have to help me...and I'll help you!" She didn't have all her memories, but the ones she was gleaning inside the matrix were sticking.

Shrugging, Emma replied: "I forget…darn!" She sniffled and then pouted. A weighty regret washed over her body as her cheeks flickered blue and then back to their Asian skin tone. "All I can remember is the private Maglev that whisks failed experiments away to Level-10 to fix them." Her face and arms turned light blue—the color of abject sadness. "Like me," she sighed. "A failed experiment. I'm dead."

So she knows what happened to her, Elisa thought, hating to see her so filled with hopelessness. "No—don't say you're a failure. You might be gone, right now, but *not* forever." She touched Emma's shoulder, and her fingers tingled. Everything is charged. "Something good is gonna come outta this, Emma. You'll see. And when I return to my body…'cause I will…I'll find a way to bring you back to life…restore you…or Regenerate you."

"Don't promise anything you can't fulfill," Emma said, her head low. "Like me, you're already forgetting that world."

"No!" Another idea occurred to Elisa. "I just know Terra will find a way to repair clone you right. New innovations are always happening! I bet—"

"Stop it, please." Emma held up her hands in an expression of discomfort.

"Sorry. I was only trying to, well, stay positive and encourage you."

"Thanks," she huffed, "but being positive isn't going to stop those sub-atomic Kinetic Monsters from returning. They always manage to find us…always. And one day, either you or I will be gone…nothing."

Elisa cringed. "You mean they could bite their way through this area and eat us up at any time! Whata we do?"

"Nothing, except wait for Terra to zip us away to another hiding spot," Emma shrugged. "The Kinetic Monsters—with that Demon Update of theirs—are like dogs sniffing for

DNA."

"Makes sense, because I heard voices when those things first appeared to devour me," Elisa said. She suddenly experienced a rush of fear in her chest.

"What's wrong?" Emma asked, her neck stretching like taffy so she could face her. Then she re-appeared on the other side of her.

"*Sagan* is in trouble…and the crew. Something wrong is happening right now…but I just can't—"

"I have the same irksome intuition. It's powerful," Emma said in resignation. "Sometimes, all I do is pray for a miracle that'll return me to *Sagan*."

"Hey—I'll be praying for miracles for both of us," Elisa said, firmly.

The white walls suddenly filled with rainbows. Faces emerged in the rainbows. They began whispering to one another.

"What the—" Elisa dropped to the floor.

"They're people," Emma said, walking up to some of them, observing them. "Too bad they can't hear us. They're the leftover minds that Terra didn't Down-Stream back into peoples' bodies during Regeneration. They're bits and bytes of cognition—"

"That need to be returned to the people they belong to!" Elisa said angrily.

"After a while, you'll get sick of just watching them, and *them* popping in on *you* and watching you," Emma said, her shoulders slumping. She had a lost expression on her face. She seemed to have given up, her hope zapped out of her. "There are so many of us here. So many failed experiments, thanks to The Regents Mind Meddling technology…*and* the Regeneration process that does *not*…in spite of what *everyone* says…return *every* brain impulse back into peoples' minds. And then there are the *real* failed experiments. That's what I consider myself to be."

"How many?" Elisa asked, frantically glancing around. "How many failed experiments? Do you really mean deaths?"

# Astrocity Sagan

The faces disappeared, and the walls whitened.

"*Failed* experiments, like I said," Emma emphasized. "People who accidentally stepped into wrong sections of the astrocity, or their minds improperly Up-Streamed or Down-Streamed and then some Matrix Tech or Clone Tech made them disappear from the astrocity and expunged all their profiles, IDs and archival records. I call them, and me, Cybernetic Misfits. If you're here like me and you, you're a Cybernetic Misfit waiting for a body, or you're bytes of consciousness waiting to be Down-Streamed into your body."

"So *I'm* a Cybernetic Misfit, right?" Elisa asked, yearning for freedom. Emma nodded yes. "So if I can return—if we can return—we can match cerebral impulses with DNA, clone their bodies, and give them back their lives. Easy!" In anger, she hit the floor that absorbed the blow. "This isn't right...this is *so* wrong...so unfair!"

Outside, rain began hitting the walls. There was a clash of lightning and rumbling of thunder. The light in the white room wavered. It began flickering on and off, and then stabilized as the outside downpour continued. It was Emma, crying on the inside.

"You're upset too," Elisa said. "I don't blame you."

"*You* didn't freeze me." Emma had a look of gratitude on her face and hugged her. "You didn't freeze me when you could have—wow!" She laughed. "You cared. Thanks."

"No, I didn't freeze you, and of course I care!" Elisa held Emma so as to not slip right through her. "We're friends now. And I *will* find a way to help you...and free everyone trapped inside this place." When she let go of her, the outside rain subsided to a drizzle and then a trickle. She walked over to the wall and ran her hands over it. It felt like cellophane with the thickness of Styrofoam. "I *hate* confined spaces!"

Emma laughed. "The longer you're in this part of the matrix, the more you forget how confined you really are though. It's a perfect correlation."

# J.P. Osterman

Seconds passed as Elisa tried to remember instances in her past when she felt trapped and caged. "Nothing!" she said. "My emotions are gone." She looked at her hands. They weren't shaking. "I don't get this."

"The Regents' rendition of stasis," Emma said.

The faces of those who had disappeared on *Sagan* suddenly materialized on the white walls. She felt as if her biology had somehow linked to them, and they to her. The pupils of their eyes began rotating and emitting rainbows.

"*Ahh!*" Elisa screamed, holding onto Emma.

"No—don't be afraid," Emma said. "We're just trying to put together what we know…all of us, and since you're here, we all seem to be getting along so much better…except of course for the Kinetic Monster."

"Oh," Elisa said, gliding over to one of the faces on the wall and touching it. She saw her reflection: a woman—half-human and half blank, as if her face was a blank slate in the process of being wiped clean. Obviously, they didn't have much time before Time itself would wipe them—or peoples' thoughts—out of existence. "I'm so sorry," Elisa said to the woman who was trying desperately to give her a message. All Elisa could make out were her words: *My child, please help her.* "I have to do something!"

Their faces became puzzle pieces, re-arranging and snapping together to form a partial picture.

"Lie down like me," Emma said, lying down face up on the glowing floor. "They'll add more pieces because they all have information from around *Sagan*. That's why they're appearing more frequently…to tell us something they believe will help us."

After lying next to her, Elisa watched more pieces of the puzzle assemble on the wall and then rotate up to the ceiling. "It's still pretty incomplete though."

"But there are *some* facts available," Emma said. "Regents are cloning people and their wicked Update is getting stronger."

"We know that," Elisa said reaching up to one of the

puzzle pieces—stretching her arms far so as to manipulate it. "This puzzle piece shows The Regents giving people new identities. They're also positioning androids as their Clone Techs around the astrocity. Why? Why do all this?"

The pieces reassembled.

"It's Nelta's solar system!" Emma exclaimed. "But the suns are different."

"This is some future scene," Elisa began, "because Nelta is burning up in a ball of fire!"

The puzzle unsnapped and reassembled into a collage of Neltans who had been broadcast around Earth a century ago, but who were now in Terra's archives. On Nelta now, they're in stasis under the planet.

"I hear screaming! They're *all* dying!" Elisa exclaimed. Before, she would have felt compelled to save them but now sighed in resignation. There were so many Neltans dying, an entire population. No way can one person save an entire race of beings...especially advanced beings who can't save themselves. "Terra is predicting the future if everything current remains unchanged." Watching as the Nelta's Matter Stream disappeared from around the solar system, Elisa exhaled in exasperation. "The Regents' ultimate plan must have something to do with the Matter Stream: the one-of-a-kind force that's in *every* universe and interacting inter-dimensionally to hold together the Multiverse." She searched the puzzle everywhere for the light-year-long stream of unique energy, the stabilizer for the four forces and matter and anti-matter. She found it nowhere in the Neltan solar system, except its lingering glow around the planet. "Looks like no matter how much we evolve, or how much technology we believe will improve humanity, some people still can't change their basic nature...greed, 'cause thing powerful had to have dispersed that Matter Stream into nothing, right?"

"Obviously you're right, but I don't know...because what we're seeing is only one possibility," Emma said.

# J.P. Osterman

Elisa tore a patch off her pants and threw it at the white wall. Maybe she could find a weak link and escape! The patch flicked out of existence, materializing back in place on her pants as if new. Instantaneous teleportation. No way out. "The future *really* looks bleak if we can't stop The Regents."

"And all these trapped impulses in here could help if they could return to their rightful minds. They know things. They've seen things," Emma whispered, extending her hands in the air and closing her eyes. As she inhaled, she rose into the air.

Thousands of faces appeared on the walls. They began whispering, talking to her, but then they disappeared.

Elisa clenched her teeth that felt like putty. "Do you know a way out of here and you're not telling me?" She felt anger burn through her. "Did you purposely bring me here, Emma?" She felt her left arm, heavy. Rolling up her sleeve, she noticed it was no longer transparent, but translucent. Her biology was working to teleport her outside the matrix! And someone or something was helping her.

"Me? Purposely trap you here?" Emma asked, shocked.

"Yeah—*you*! The whole cognitive-entanglement that occurred when I tried to up-stream your mind at my station."

Emma pirouetted, spun in the air, and landed in a smooth plié. "Oh yeah right, I remember that." She continued to dance. "No, Elisa, I didn't *purposely* bring you here."

"Hey, come back down and help me sort out this puzzle," Elisa ordered, pacing the white room. Her arm was beginning to ache—a new morphology occurring in the quantum-light energy.

Emma changed again. Now she was dressed as a child playing Hopscotch.

Elisa felt overwhelming frustration. "Come on—quit dancing and hopscotching. We need to figure a way outta here."

"Can't," Emma sighed. "No use."

"Then I'll make ya, Emma. I'm getting tired of your tip-toeing around all our problems." With her arms open, Elisa ran toward her. If she could pin Emma to the white wall, maybe the Cybernetic Misfits might help her infuse Emma with the will to break out of their entrapment. But half way to Emma, the air swept her off her feet. She flew through her, bounced off the wall and glided in for a landing, stopping at Emma's flowery patent-leather shoes.

Emma laughed. "You're gonna have to adapt real soon to function in this place."

Not feeling tired whereas before she would have felt exhausted, Elisa believed she could coerce Emma into being serious. "Let's bust outta here. Come on! Let's play like kids ditching school. Let's do it…just for the fun of it. You're the type of person who likes having fun—right?"

Emma folded her arms and parted her legs like a military titan. "I can't argue with ya there," she said. "But I can't. Like I tried telling you…we can't just think our way outta here."

"I'm gonna try." Clenching her fists, holding her breath, and closing her eyes tight, she focused on the Terra hub in her secret kiosk, the place where she had told Terra to send her secret message. Her left arm began pulsating with light.

"No use," Emma began, "even if you *do* have that special Neltan biology, ya can't escape the matrix."

Elisa believed her arm had the energy of lightning…but nothing happened, and she finally gave up. She couldn't will her way out of her caged dimensional world either. She wanted to cry, but couldn't. "My God," she exhaled, rubbing her hands through her hair. Now it was short! She hadn't cut it, but she remembered a hairstyle she had admired a few months ago on a virtual mannequin at the corner walkway down from her Living Cube. Believing she had time, she had been mustering up the courage to have Twin remind her to cut her hair.

"It looks nice, Elisa. You have an oval face, a slender nose, high cheekbones, and symmetrical green eyes. At least they're green now," Emma said.

"They're supposed to be brown," Elisa said. "Always brown in the real world. I even keep them that way on my avatar, Twin. There are some things I don't like changing, ever. Maybe that's what's kept me sane on this hundred-year voyage, a little stability, holding onto a tiny routine, and a few friends." As she recalled faces, a few precious memories popped out of her head as bubbles. "No!" she cried, trying to catch them before they floated into the white ceiling that absorbed them. She heard metallic chomping sounds as the dangerous Kinetic Monsters began chasing them, to devour them.

"No! Run! Escape!" Elisa cried, shaking her fists.

The white room became silent.

"I think your memories won," Emma said. "If they did, they'll stream into that secret grid of your. You'll get 'em back when—"

"You mean, *if*—"

"No—*when*," Emma said, emphatically. "Gosh—I'm giving *you* hope now!" She grew despondent. "I wish I had hope for me."

"I wish both of us could get out of here!" Elisa screamed, kicking the white floor. "Terra! Let us out! Pleeease!"

Emma sat down next to her softly. "When I first arrived here, I had this overwhelming urge to bust out...just like you want to do right now...to claw back to my body if necessary...and figure out a way back to my life. I thought that if I wished, *and* hoped, *and* begged, *and* pleaded long and hard, Terra might stream out of this place, or if not completely, to at least download part of me into someone else's body." She snickered like a child committing a naughty deed. "I know that's wrong...body snatching, but a person gets desperate here sometimes."

Nudging her jokingly, Elisa realized she was in the safety of the White Room because of Emma. "If I ever get outta here, and you don't, I'll do whatever it takes to bring you back, and our Cybernetic Misfits friends, and Down-Stream stolen thoughts into peoples' minds. I just want you to know that Emma."

"Thanks," Emma huffed, "if we ever become self-aware in body form again."

Those "self-aware" words made Elisa think more in depth about their situation. Was Terra *really* protecting her and Emma, or was The White Room just a Cognitive Safe-Scan program? There was a difference! If Terra could blend the two programs, the expansive matrix could acquire empathy. If instilled with empathy and compassion, Terra might become enraged at all the kidnapping of souls and thoughts, and seek justice those people.

"That's self-awareness might be the answer, Emma!" Elisa said.

"How?"

"Self-Aware!" She faced her. "That's the prompt you told me to speak when our thoughts exchanged in the Up-Stream attempt!"

"Oh," Emma said in a pensive look.

"I believe Terra might be evolving to consciousness…but without a body." Elisa felt suddenly excited, and hoped Emma might catch it.

"Terra becoming a person? Wow! When? As we're about to touchdown on Nelta I bet." Emma's face was glowing in a halo of beautiful yellow light.

"Imagine if we could make her appear on the astrocity in actual physical form," Elisa said.

"Now that'd be a *real* feat of technology!" Emma marveled. "But first, you have to get back to initiate the process…connect levels and processors I'm sure…not an easy task." Emma then shrieked out frightening expression.

"What's wrong?"

"Elisa, you have another problem even if you do make it back into your body," Emma said.

"What's that?" she asked.

"You might not remember anything that happened to you in here," Emma began, "or you'll have only bits of memories. Maybe you might forget me!"

Elisa recalled one of the pieces of the puzzle. "I *do* remember a Help code activation there...in a secret kiosk of mine...the Cybernetic Misfits also sent information there."

"Yeah!"

"If Terra can stream me back to my body...or into another body, I know I can change things. I can help you, and our Cybernetic Misfit friends. I just know I can find a program counter to the Mind Meddling technology and down-stream peoples' thoughts back into their minds." She began pacing around the white room, trying to plot her course of action. "I'd need to access Terra's processors. That's her Live Stream Field, and then link that place with her Cloud matrix on Level-7." She sat down the task appearing so difficult. Until another energy overtook her. "But it could be done...if I can get some help."

"Maybe," Emma sighed, "maybe. But like I said, I can't leave. I'm dead. And there's no body for me to go into...at least now."

As another idea flashed into her mind, Elisa believed she had achieved a bit of success as she stood up and pulled Emma up by her arms. "Until I can find a way to bring you and the others back in body and mind, you can do some spying for me, if I make it outta here.

"Spying? Cool!" Emma exclaimed.

"Find out more about Thornton Manning's Grand Plan, guide me to the places I need to go to help you and our friends, and defeat the bad forces in our astrocity, especially that Demon Terra-V and the person or thing responsible for attacking the crew."

"*Hmmm*," Emma said, her lips pursing in obvious deep thought.

"Yeah! You and our trapped friends can be my guides. You can use Terra's fractal, quantum-nonlocality matrix to help me in the human world. You're smart!"

# Astrocity Sagan

"I suppose that's possible," she began, "if we can locate you...find ways to communicate with you." Emma raised her arms and began rotating upward as if she were happily inhaling sweet smells. "Terra *is* calling me now. Someone's after me. I gotta go! Sorry, Elisa. Bye!"

Elisa jumped up, trying to grab Emma's ankles, until Emma's shoes slipped out of her fingers. Then she noticed her left arm, solid and glowing. Human flesh seemed to be creeping up her shoulder! Somewhere, someone was reanimating her body; and soon, she'd have no choice but to unite with it. "Stop—Emma! Get back! Think about what I just asked you to do! You and the others can help me warn the crew!"

This time, Emma's head hit the ceiling where the white fabric began absorbing her. "Remember me, Elisa. Remember me." She was gone.

A portion of the ceiling turned into facial outlines. The Cybernetic Misfits said in unison: "Terra will take you back. It's only been a day."

More white faces appeared in the ceiling. "A day," they said.

Covering her head because she believed they might lead the Kinetic Monsters right to her, she huddled down. "I *can* stop the Regents...if you help me."

Twin appeared!

Then Terra appeared next to her in Standard form. They had linked and were touching Elisa's arm. "She's the answer," Twin whispered again and again, almost a chant.

Elisa heard a child's voice—not Emma's voice—and a ball bouncing in the background. "Get me back into my body now, please." She felt a deep sorrow, and water on her cheeks. "Tears!" She touched them and looked at them. They were like diamonds in the light that was building flesh around her, reforming her. "Get me back to my body. You can do it!"

For what felt like hours, Standard Terra and Twin were in a

hypnotic trance. She could feel energy flow through her—driven by her special biology. For hours, she listened to children laughing outside the White Room. They had to be her Cybernetic Misfit friends—with Emma among them—playing, accepting their life inside the matrix. But she was still in the room, not with them. Terra had separated them intentionally, and was keeping them apart for a more important purpose!

Her throat burning, she surrendered to her situation. "I feel like I'm in a long-term waiting room, Terra. When's it all gonna end? Either keep me here, or let me join the others. I just hate this loneliness and isolation!" She yawned, fatigue like sap running through her body. She fell asleep. She dreamed she was on a surfboard, riding a giant wave on Level-2's simulated ocean. In another dream, she was sitting among people at an eatery and looking out a stern-side portal at the lights of wormhole motion-distortion. "Chicken soup...*mmmm.*" She walked quickly into a Maglev, and her dreams faded.

## Chapter 17 – Who Am I?

"Lady—hey, lady!" A tall buff man with a Mohawk, beard, and thin lips nudged her. "Aren't you one of them?"

Waking up, Elisa felt dazed, her left arm aching. "Where am I? Who are you? And am I one of whom?" She almost asked him if he was a wrestler, until she saw a musical instrument case on the seat next to him. They were in back row seats, and in seats in front of them were a few people. It had to be either very early in the day or well after working hours. The Maglevs were usually packed all other times.

"Just a second and I'll show ya." He began swiping faces over his wrist device like shuffling cards.

She noticed they were ascending, but to where? She touched her hands, felt her face, and smelled her fingers. "Wow, where have I been?" Rolling up her left sleeve, she noticed she didn't have on her wrist device—her only connection to her home, her avatar—whose name she couldn't remember—and her destination. "How'd I get *here*? What's the date, the time?" She rubbed her eyes and ran her fingers through her hair. Looking at her reflection in the holographic light resonating over the man's wrist device, she saw her hair, cut short, and her clothes and shoes completely different from what she'd been wearing that morning...at least she remembered wearing a black skirt and a white blouse. Then she recalled she had on a jacket—now gone. Somewhere along the line, she must have changed clothes. She had to have changed because she was now wearing a form-fitting body suit and ankle-high tennis shoes. She felt sick. They weren't her clothes, not any style she would have even bought! "Something's happened to me. But what? Damn it, what?!"

The man scooted closer to her and squinted in her face. Then he appeared elated. "Hey everybody!" He began getting the attention of the other passengers and he showed them her image blaring over his wrist device. He'd discovered her identity. "This is Doctor Elisa Holton! She's one of the candidates!" He pointed at a show running at the front of the Maglev. "Terra announced your name at the Navigation Terminal late last night as one of the candidates, Doctor Holton."

After telling him to call her Elisa, she said: "Late last night? Candidate for what?"

"Hey—come on, Doc, you're joking, right?" he laughed. "I know you candidates are shy and all...and tryin' to hide out before the special broadcast ceremony, but come on, Doc...how about givin' me your autograph?" He shoved his wrist device in front of her. Still dazed, she signed her name with her forefinger under her picture that didn't at all look like the reflection she'd just seen in the glass. "Boy you shoulda seen The Regents' faces when Terra called out your name, Doc. You'd 'a thought you had risen from the dead—ha!"

"What?" Elisa pushed him away, her heart skipping. "What's going on?" She had a metallic taste in her mouth. "I'm so thirsty!" A woman stood up, ran to her, and gave her a tube of cold water that she gulped down as if she'd been lost in a desert. "*Ahhh*, thanks," she said to her as a more people gathered in seats in front of her. Their avatars were also hovering and towering around, making her feel as if she was being invaded by quirky ghosts. "Please—get back!" she cried. When they deactivated their avatars, she asked: "Where am I? Someone, please start answering my questions."

"You got on in front of me at the bow of Level-9'sTransport Station…at least I think you did…and we're ascending to Level-2," the woman answered, taking the empty water tube from her and throwing it in a chute next to her seat. "Where's your avatar?  I think that's your problem, Doctor Holton.  You probably accidentally lost your wrist device somewhere."  After checking around the area, the woman added: "But after you disembark, I'm sure you can go to any kiosk and IT will immediately supply you with another. After all, you're famous, and we gotta take care of the first people who are going to represent us to the Neltans." She then asked her for her autograph, which Elisa quickly signed on her Signature app.

"No—you boarded with a satchel, Doc," the man said, picking it up from under her seat and handing it to her.

"Thanks."  Elisa rubbed her temples, trying to wake up some more.  She quickly unlatched the satchel and took out an outdated device that flared on, but no avatar materialized.  She fastened it to her wrist. "It's off-stream I guess."  She didn't want to sound crazy by telling them she had no idea how she'd even acquired the satchel let alone the outdated wrist device. "I'll have to re-initialize it with Terra when I get home." *Wherever home is*, she thought.

"Or trade it in for the modern one," the man said.  Then he turned pensive.  "I think I've seen some people walking around with those old devices lately.  They look like old Dick Tracy watches that can't do a damn thing!  I can't imagine being on-grid for very long while wearing one of *those* old things.  No offense."  He and the others laughed.

"Actually, I thought all of them had been confiscated years ago," the woman said, glancing at her suspiciously.

Rolling down her sleeve to try and hide the device, Elisa

said, "I don't remember that, but at least I have something." Later, she'd find a place where she could turn it on. Even if it was old, it had to have a burner app programmed into it. If what the woman had said was true—that those types of old devices had been confiscated—she'd need to discover the information on it, find its source, and then ditch it, fast. Someone had given her the device and satchel. She began searching the satchel's contents: an old camera, a pen, a laser pointer, a line of silicone processor beads, and a dime-sized shimmering crystal that appeared to be part of a necklace, perhaps a new type of technology? She didn't recognize anything. Still, someone had given it to her. "Remember, remember," she whispered into the satchel. She couldn't, although she realized she had something important to do, something vital and necessary. "That's it. I gotta help someone!"

"Who?" the man asked through an urgent expression.

"I don't know…a patient maybe?" she replied.

The woman appeared surprised. "You're not Chief of Corridor-15 anymore though, Doctor Holton."

Feeling shocked, she wanted to say, *I'm not?* But she kept quiet, listening to her instead.

"That's what Terra announced, Doctor Holton," the stranger continued, "and that's why she chose *you* to compete against twenty-one other people to be part of the team on the first expedition to Nelta. There's going to be a big ceremony, a Choosing Ceremony."

"Where? When?!" Elisa asked.

The woman looked at her as if she was weird and strange. "The Regents are going to announce the time of the Choosing Ceremony sometime this afternoon. Gosh, where ya been?"

Rubbing her head and inhaling deeply, she replied, "Maybe I ate something…or drank something that made me sick."

The woman handed her a small protein snack, and Elisa began eating it. The woman continued: "With all your high scores on everything, you're one of the smartest people on *Sagan*, Doctor Holton. I'm *sure* you'll win a spot on the expedition." She glanced at the Live Streaming news at the Maglev's bow. "Oh, Regent Manning just named it Expedition-1. It's so exciting! The most *exciting* ceremony ever launched for social participation, Doctor Holton, and I can't wait!" Then she turned downcast. "I wish she'd chosen me though. Of course, a lot of people feel that way," she laughed off her disappointment while others around her agreed with her.

As Elisa finished her snack, the Maglev rocked through a lightning contrail as the Institute of Standards and Technology projected its hourly countdown underneath the holographic conductor: "Ladies and Gentlemen, today is Thursday, January 21, 3070, eight o'clock a.m. Here is your hourly update. Nelta is five weeks and four days away. For a list of events, connect with our media site *at* Holodome One. Have a Holodome Day! Sponsored by the Regency."

"January twenty first?" She repeated as the little crowd dispersed, but the man remained seated next to her. The last time she remembered, she was leaving work on January eighteen. "What happened to me over the past three days?!"

The man with the Mohawk called on his wrist device, and the cover of *Space and Style* appeared on the seat screen in front of his seat. When the Maglev stopped at the Level-8's bow transport station, a few people waved goodbye to her as more people entered and belted into their seats. "Quite a bit's happened in three days, Doc!" He showed her the *Greeting* Update from Nelta. "The Living Breath finally received it! It absorbed the message into Navigation." The information coming from him sounded strange since only special people had access to that Level-1 bow section of the astrocity. *He must have some type of job*, she though. "And The Regents say we're heading through the last wormhole interchange to reach Nelta."

"Great—*whew!*" she said, feeling relieved but also deeply troubled, an internal disturbance like a quake that wouldn't leave her. Her gut intuition was screaming: Something's wrong!

The man appeared to understand her disturbed expression. "Yeah, I know what ya mean," he whispered. "People have still been seeing those virtual creatures and monsters everywhere, and every day their appearances are scaring the hell outta everyone." He showed her a Godzilla creature and the monster from the old movie *Alien* that appeared at the large Rec Center on Level-2, triggering a massive panic that had people stampeding to the Central Level-2 transport platform. "No one knows why, but there's no denyin' that we're being attacked."

"By who?" she whispered, glancing around as if another creature might materialize in front of them.

He shrugged. "Don't know. The Regents say they're checking into the matter...along with their Enforcers and Matrix Technicians who are working to solve the problem overtime. All the escalating appearances are a complete puzzle." He leaned into her. "You thought we were all anxious not hearing that Neltan Update? You ain't seen anything!"

"Puzzle...puzzle," she repeated, the word rippling through her consciousness. She couldn't remember but knew she had a giant puzzle she was supposed to solve, and every minute of her day was a waste of time until the solution.

"You said that word, Doc, right after you sat down there and fell asleep." He turned the page on his virtual magazine he had loaded into the seat screen in front of him. "You dropped that satchel, said you had to solve a giant puzzle, and then ya fell asleep. *Fast* asleep I might add," he laughed.

"Who are you?" she asked.

He extended his hand, and she shook it. "I'm Ernie Bentley. I'm in a band, The Forgivers. Ever heard of us?"

Yawning and pulling the satchel close to her, she said, "Nope."

He handed her his business card. When it tilted forward, the five band members in the little rendering began playing music. "We just finished playing at the BeJazz Festival at the Armstrong-Beiderbecke Center," he said proudly. "The band's my hobby and side job. During the day, I'm a Particle Physicist at the Navigation Terminal."

"A rare position," Elisa exclaimed, understanding how he knew so much about the Living Breath entity and wormhole trajectory to Nelta.

"Wow!" the lady who handed Elisa water gasped. "You're one of the scientists who are going to prepare *Sagan* to return to Earth after we acquire technology to fix the moon." She appeared so positive. It was obvious: she was one of those who'd decided to return to Earth.

He chuckled, blushing through an obvious wave of embarrassment. "Yes ma'am—*Sagan* should station over Verba where we'll all have a chance to disembark for a while before heading back…at least those who choose to return. We haveta update *Sagan*, and add some changes, as The Regents are planning."

Verba was the southern section of Nelta. That landing spot sounded wrong, perking up Elisa. "Not Tractum? That's the location of the Welcome Archway, where a team is supposed to meet Shaesar, the Ambassador." She grabbed the man's wrist and swept off his Verba landing site. "Check *The Pact* we signed. I'm confused…either that, or I've *completely* been in stasis because the document outlines our touchdown site as Tractum." He opened the virtual document, but Tractum— the fifty-mile-wide, Archway location at the center of Nelta— was written nowhere, or in any map form, on the sacred document. "This is wrong…I know it!" People began looking at her or edging away from her. "We're supposed to land there—" She pointed at the center of Tractum. "We're supposed to present Shaesar with human DNA, and he's supposed to initiate the process to heal the Neltans. That's the deal we made with them. Don't any of you remember?"

"I guess," Ernie Bentley replied, "but The Regents said

conditions changed on Tractum, according to the Update we received. For the past twenty four hours, they've had us working at Navigation to recalculate specific trajectories and dark matter containment fields. I, uh-oh!" He put his chubby fingers over his lips. He had caught himself revealing too much confidential information that made his words catch in his throat as he flicked off *The Pact* document.

"What's wrong?" a woman next to him asked.

"Aren't we supposed to vote on changes to *The Pact*?" a man two seats down asked.

Another woman stood and exclaimed: "Verba not Tractum? We didn't make that change!"

Elisa saw the eyes of all several avatars flash green. A mass-communication to The Regency would begin on their command.

"Stop!" the man cried. "Don't holomail anything!"

Everyone sat down statue-like, their avatars bobbing gently in the air like miniature ghosts, waiting for orders.

"I can't say more," Ernie whispered. "You all better not either!" He cowered as if someone had overheard what he already accidentally divulged. "Some decisions have to be made impromptu. When conditions changed on Nelta, The Regents had to act fast to correct for those changes. That's what they told us in Navigation after we received the Update."

"Oh yeah...right...I remember now," the confused woman interrupted, tapping her forehead in an expression of having a headache. "I guess I just forgot," she chuckled, and then rested back in her seat—stiffly and sedately.

Ernie had a red innocent expression on his face as he gazed into other passengers' confused eyes. "Besides, Elisa, no one's gonna get hurt by a little change in course, right? No one's been affected, right?" He stood up, waiting for more people to respond to his plea. "Just please," he began, whispering loudly, "*please* don't send any holomail! You'll get me in trouble!"

People turned away from him in dismissive droves. Some people vanquished their avatars and returned to reading magazines and watching shows in front of their seat screens.

# Astrocity Sagan

Elisa noticed someone at the end of their row. He had a cold, blank, white mean face. He had sent a message.

Feeling sad and sorry for Ernie who had made that slip-of-the-tongue, she felt compelled to help. She said aloud for everyone in their row to hear, "Oh yeah—he and I *both* have Security Clearances. Standing, she added: "We *both* sometimes have to make decisions on an emergency basis. It happens!" she shrugged. "That's life…life on a crammed astrocity, right everybody? Come on…agree with me…" Waiting for mass agreement, she suddenly felt dizzy, and her left arm pinching. She fell into her seat. Peeking up her sleeve at her arm, she saw intricate veins below her skin. Before anyone else could see them, she smoothed down her sleeve. At the front of the Maglev, she saw an avatar appear, disappear, and then re-appear next to the man who had streamed that message to The Regency. He appeared abnormal, but she couldn't see his face anymore. She broke out in a light sweat, felt her heartbeat race, but then it quickly slow. Some form of energy was trying to interfere with her biology while her intuition was continuing to give her a message of danger…directing her *not* to look at the man at the end of her row.

A woman in a seat in front of her put another tube of water in her hand and made her drink. Dabbing Elisa's forehead, she said: "What's happening to you, Doctor Holton? God—I hope nothing terrible! I should send word to the Medical Facility and get you some help when we disembark on Level-6."

"She looks white as a sheet," Ernie exclaimed.

Drinking water and grabbing the woman's hand before she could transmit her concern or an alert, Elisa said, "I'm fine, really."

"She's okay!" Ernie said, wiping his forehead with the back of his sleeve. "I used to be a medic, I know." After people turned around and settled into their seats, he inhaled and waved at a Terra hub. "I'll fix this, Doc," he began, "you'll have nothing to worry about." He called on his avatar that appeared as a little musician in front of him. "Diffuse what just happened," he whispered. "Route the incident through Navigation to Terra's main matrix. In the Subject Heading, send my Blue-Uniform Navigation profile, *not* my Cool-Cat musical profile. Bold the whole scene with quote-unquote, Damage Control. Now *Send.*"

His small avatar's eyes flashed green through its reflective glasses. "Yeah, man...cool dude—done." Then his beatnik avatar faded.

"*Whew!*" Ernie exhaled as if having released a great burden. After a long pause in which he drank water and recuperated from his verbal slip of the tongue, he looked down, sighed, shuffled his feet, and then glanced outside through the thick portals. The Maglev's contrails were wispy streaks of deadly beauty—forces in the tunnel generating hazardous currents and poisonous fumes, the latter being disposed of by *Sagan's* Living Breath, and Terra. Ernie seemed all caught up in the poison, his face yellow and languishing. "I wish I could find her," he said in a lamenting tone of voice. "I just wish I could find her." He was straining to contain his tears.

# Astrocity Sagan

## Chapter 18 – Beatrice McDuff Bentley

"Find who, Ernie?" Elisa asked. He had been focused on her; but now she saw an emotional ache wash over him. She had to help.

The Maglev stopped at Level-7's bow Transport Station. Just as people began disembarking, the automated Terra conductor appeared, announcing the Maglev's early arrival and hold for fifteen minutes. There was a malfunction in the tunnel, the conductor claimed, and techs needed equipment and time to fix it since the astrocity wasn't properly sealing key areas inside the tunnels. She saw the time flash over the conductor's head: 8:10 a.m., and she glanced outside at the crowds of people.

Level-7 harbors many workers: from Propulsion engineers monitoring *Sagan*'s fission-fusion engines at the stern, to people still residing inside the jail-rehab community at the northern bow, to recycling and technical manufacturing/assembly at the center of the level. Over a quarter of the working population—20,000 people—had jobs on Level-7! In fifty minutes, work would begin on this level and throughout the ship. People were racing, sprinting, and dashing out of beehive living cubes, partitioned in sections like modern apartment complexes, over a half-a-mile high, and lining the sides of two wide pedestrian corridors. They were racing to catch one of four Maglevs at the bow's three-story terminal: her ascending shuttle, the descending shuttle across the platform from her stalled shuttle, the east-bound shuttle on the second floor, or the west-bound Maglev at the third-story terminal. The rest of the frenzied people were rushing to two other places on Level-7: Center Station and Stern Station.

"I wish I could find Beatrice," Ernie said, interrupting her pensive stare while glancing at faces in the crowd. Their avatars bobbing alongside them, over them, and between them weren't helping his search! Ernie's one-foot tall, beatnik avatar was hovering over Ernie's shoulder. It was involved in the search as well, and began crying. Operating through a Reflective-Reactive app programmed to mimic the emotions of its host, the avatar made the expression, *wearing your heart on your sleeve*, true. Ernie's beatnik avatar repeated: "I wish I could find Beatrice—*ahhhh*. I can't locate her biometrics though," it cried.

Elisa shifted in her seat. "Who's Beatrice? Maybe I can help your search, especially if I'm going to be part of some special broadcast…which by the way, I better check into pretty soon so I can learn where and when I have to attend."

After telling her he'd give her all the details when he'd receive a response about his sent message, Ernie began telling Elisa his story: "Beatrice and I married forty years ago, and today would have been our anniversary. Today, January 21, 2168 or 3070, depending on how one views time. Beatrice disappeared—vanished—a year ago, after delivering a shipment of flowers to The Regents' private quarters at the bow of Level-1. Someone had sent the rare bouquet to Regent Sylvia Itonovich to congratulate her for something. The last public view of Beatrice was of her holding that bouquet of huge rare flowers." He showed Elisa the security caption of Beatrice at The Regents' triple doorway entry. He said Beatrice was born in India. She was tall and had black waist-length hair and a thin physique.

# Astrocity Sagan

"Regent Sylvia Itonovich, you say?" Elisa felt her stomach sicken.

"Is something wrong?" Ernie gasped, scooting closer to her. "Ya know something about Beatrice, Doc?" He quickly wiped tears off his lids and sat up straight—his eyes brightening. "Beatrice McDuff-Bentley is her name. Ya ever Regenerate her in your Corridor?"

"No—I've never heard of her, but go on." She felt suddenly dizzy, her mind spinning, her vision blurring into tiny sets of rainbow spots in front of her eyes until she drank some more water while watching Ernie's avatar tuning into her every word, obviously recording their conversation. Ernie had to have programmed it that way at the mentioned of Beatrice's name. "Sounds like you've been looking for Beatrice for a long time."

"Everywhere and always!" Ernie exclaimed through distressed eyes. "I've written songs for her, and held a concert for her." He pointed at a missing person ad on the other side of the aisle that he just up-streamed. "There's a picture of her." He wiped his eyes. "She was beautiful. She had jet-black shiny hair and memorable smile...plum-colored lips and sea-green eyes. And she was smart! She was a real taxonomist when it came to naming all the rare and exotic plants on the astrocity." The ad displayed the name of the company who had employed her.

After watching the *In-Search-Of* show depicting Beatrice filling a vase of rare flowers, Elisa said: "So she worked for Pineapple Lily, Hoya, and Calotropis?"

"Yes."

"They're well known! The Regents have the company preparing seeds for planting on Nelta."

"Yep," Ernie said with a lost and pining expression as he continued to stare at the *In-Search-Of* show. "Enforcers give me a weekly report on their search for her as well."

"Oh?" Elisa asked.

"Yeah, they're always looking for her too."

"Really!" She felt an internal alarm sound. Something wasn't right with why Beatrice disappeared, especially if Enforcers were involved. "Go on."

"The last time a monitor captured her was around this *very* shuttle we're on right now, but on Level-1, after she made that special delivery," he said, solemnly, touching the seat screen in front of him, and the magazine article he was reading extinguished. Leaning down covertly, he whispered: "One person told investigators they saw her running *into* the transport tunnel though! Can ya believe *that*? No one else saw that, so the investigators dismissed her report."

"No one can exist inside any of those tunnels. Maybe that's why investigators didn't' believe her," Elisa said.

"An Enforcer then turned on me, saying maybe she left because of me...*me*! Like they were blaming *me* for hitting her, or—or abusing her. Never! No way."

"You? No way!" Elisa patted his arm. "You don't look dangerous or murderous to me," she laughed. "From what *I've* heard, Enforcers are definitely jerks when they question people. But I guess they have to investigate every avenue and even interrogate people if necessary. After all, people don't just disappear." She suddenly stopped, those words repeating in her mind, giving her a contradictory headache.

Ernie brought up pictures of his wedding reception over his wrist device and began staring into the glowing recording. His band was there, and they had a large cake and two hundred guests. He seemed lost in the first dance with Beatrice. "Or if people disappear, it's because they get lost in a virtual world somewhere for a few days, realize their absentmindedness, and then return home."

"I might 'a done that once!" Elisa joked, but stopped at the seriousness of their topic.

"Yeah, me too once, but that Enforcer who accused *me* of causing her to disappear was nuts!" He stopped the *In-Search-Of* show, and his laugh morphed into a sad and lonely expression as he began whispering and staring out the portal.

# Astrocity Sagan

"Every now and then, outta the blue, I get a blank holomail. I try tracing it to the source, but no luck." He showed her a scroll of fifty holomail URLs that ended, *Sender Unknown*. I know Beatrice is trying to communicate…I just *know* she's somewhere, but I'm stymied as to where." He began crying. "I just wanna find her, *huh-huh*, find Beatrice." He tapped his business card that Elisa was still dangling in her fingertips. "On the other side is a place you can input information and send it to me if you ever see or hear anything about her." He had his face plastered against the giant portal.

The Maglev's conductor appeared at the front of the shuttle, announcing a final boarding call and one-minute launch time. Outside, people were lined up to board. The time was 8:20 a.m., and only ten more shuttles would depart before nine, before so many people had to ascent to other levels for work. Now the rectangular shaped, nose-coned shuttle was almost filled to its two-hundred person limit, and people were vying for seats and standing positions.

Ernie pointed outside as well, now a swirling force of magnetism and electricity with dark matter infusions for propulsions mixes. The portal was preparing for the shuttle to launch. "I wonder…if maybe the person who saw Beatrice enter that transport tunnel really saw her do just that? But why would someone lie? Especially to an Enforcer, who has the power to send her to the judges?"

After a protective chrysalis sealed around the Maglev, the shuttle rose in the air, unclamped from its magnetic tracks, interacted with propulsion forces, and launched into the tunnel. For a second, gravity destabilized, making people rise a little off their seats and feet until the Maglev accelerated to full speed, and the conductor announcing the Level-6 destination at 7 minutes, arrival time 8:32 a.m. Everyone settled into their seats.

"I don't think Beatrice could be in a transport tunnel, Ernie," Elisa said softly, "'cause that's one helluva poisonous world." But when the Maglev streaked through a transition separation, a bright corridor briefly illuminated. "What?!" she gasped, her face pressing against the long glass. Believing Ernie might pound on it, she said, "I'm sure that was nothing...only the astrocity fixing itself." After he settled down, she tapped Beatrice's face on the card, the gesture activating a miniature *Contact* link. "I'll be all eyes and ears for information for you though, Ernie. I'll inquire as to her whereabouts the first chance I get. If I find out *anything* about Beatrice, believe me—" She touched his hand. "I'll contact you immediately."

From the corner of her eye, she saw two figures slip through the standing crowd. She was at the window seat, Ernie at the aisle seat, and the two strangely clad people were standing next to him, towering over him. They looked like flying squirrels! Inspecting them out of the corner of her eye, she noticed their peculiar style of clothing: shimmering, form-fitting body suits with thin shimmering polyester flaps covering their backpacks. The cloth had to be infused with special technology to give them their strange appearance and heightened capabilities! She thought they were avatars; but taking a third look at their disguised faces, she saw they were indeed people—but so different from everyone else in their style of dress and sparkling makeup. They appeared to have a peculiar blue-red-and-yellow luminescence altering their true faces! Or were those masks? She couldn't tell, but she noticed one thing: the one who looked like a man had on a wrist device like the one she was wearing. His companion, a woman, was wearing the same large cumbersome wrist device! They looked at her, then at the man at the end of the row—the man who had sent out a warning message about Ernie to The Regents. Light was playing over the man like an aurora, although no one else appeared to see the aurora. She believed the two disguised people could also see his abnormal readings.

Her left arm began aching again, and the blank ad banner above the mysterious man's head droned on, but with no show or advertisement. Yet it was activating; and at any moment, a message, or ad, or broadcast would begin. Her gut instinct began telling her that something was so wrong with him, dangerous. When she looked at her arm and began rubbing it to relieve the ache, she saw her wrist device, glowing. It was activating! Lifting up her sleeve while keeping her arm out of Ernie's eyesight, she saw the display bar beneath the device's round optics pad. It was pulsing red and green. It would take at least five minutes to synchronize with whatever current was coursing through the air, obviously undetected by Terra-IV, or else an alarm would have sounded, avatar Enforcers would have appeared, and a lock-down would have initiated until real Enforcers could apprehend people and question everyone at the Level-6 bow transport station, their next stop. All she could do was to wait for some type of direction, and keep all three of them in her awareness!

"Thanks for offering to help me, Doc," Ernie said nervously, brushing his beard with his fingers. "I'm holding another vigil for her at the spot where Beatrice disappeared, tomorrow night, at the transport platform." After offering to send her the time, he said, "I think she just got lost, or disoriented, and is stuck somewhere." He wiped his eyes on his sleeve. "But I'll find her. I will."

Feeling suddenly lost again, and still trying to remember events from the past three days, Elisa asked, "So, you said I was here when you boarded? I'm trying to remember my last footsteps. What a nap! Can ya fill me in?"

"Yeah, you were here when I boarded."

She recalled Nick and the Regeneration procedure she had scheduled. She laughed. "Oh—I probably had my Regeneration, that's all, and I was on my way home from Level-5. I'm probably just experiencing a mild side-effect...a slip of the memory that I'm sure I'll regain in no time." Feeling tense and uneasy, she thought: But three days...*three* days of lost memories? I *shouldn't* be on a Maglev ascending from Level-9! She was in denial of something more serious than what had happened to her. She took stock of what was on her: no modern wrist device, just an old outdated one, and different clothes and a strange satchel that looked like a visiting doctor's handbag. Again, she looked up, and the two disguised strangers were glancing down at her. They suddenly turned away! She almost asked them why they kept looking at her, but that might make her appear paranoid, again triggering another alarm. Then she noticed something new about their behavior. They were exchanging images over their old-fashioned wrist devices, but their communications were in hieroglyphics, like a special cipher. At the end of the row sat the mysterious man covered in a strange glow who was intermittently sending his avatar around the shuttle. Was he looking for someone? He wasn't an Enforcer! Trying hard to peer around Ernie and others, she still couldn't see his face. But his fish-appearing avatar was bouncing off other avatars throughout the Maglev. Each time the man's avatar struck someone else's virtual character, the man's fish-eyed creature glowed yellow, green, or red. Were messages being exchanged and sent? Was he spying on people, or trying to locate someone? She could only see the man's black suit and silhouette, still glowing, although only she and the two disguised passengers could see the aura around his body. They were making gestures about the aura, as if analyzing the mysterious man's biometrics and reporting them to someone. With minutes remaining before the Maglev would stop, she had enough time to gather more information on the two disguised passengers and the mysterious man they seemed to be monitoring, and monitoring her as well.

She turned her attention back to Ernie, who was now a calm friendly force. "I just need some rest I'm sure. Then I'll search for my wrist device. I'm sure I'll catch up on everything in no time." She slid down into her cushioned seat, thinking: *I'll be back to myself in no time.* Then she perked up when she remembered Ernie's words when she first woke up. "What did you say about so many things happening in the past few days?" she asked him. Perhaps, knowing more current events might jog her lost memories.

# Astrocity Sagan

He leaned closer to her and opened up yesterday's news that showed a probe launch through a small wormhole to Nelta. "The Regents sent it to confirm the Update we received, but it failed to transmit back any data. Supposedly, the probe's meant to capture images and sounds on the planet. Nothing."

"My God," she gasped, "I never heard of such a mission! When did *that* happen?"

"Two nights ago," he replied, still scrolling through animated pictures of Beatrice. "Where *you* been, Doc? In cryo, or lost in a participation world?" he chuckled.

"No, just working…I think." She looked up into the shimmering faces of the two people who were continuing to watch her while exchanging hieroglyphic communications. Beyond them, over the head of the mysterious man in a black suit who had transmitted that warning message and whose avatar was still flying covertly around the Maglev, she saw the ad banner ignite with a code. The banner began displaying a map of Level-6, and her old-fashioned wrist device hissed on.

"What was that noise?" Ernie asked.

She peeked at her device, but quickly shoved her left arm close to her side. "My wrist device turned on. I'll check it in a second."

With a puzzled expression, he scratched his neck. "I haven't heard one o' *those* old things whine like that in years! Guess I forgot that noise."

She had to divert his attention away from the strange man and woman standing next to him. "Tell me more about that failed probe, Ernie."

He turned serious, his voice in decrescendo. "You're like me and have a special credential, so I'll tell ya what I know…but ya gotta keep what I say to yourself, alright, Doc?"

Noticing the disguised man adjust his wrist device toward Ernie, she realized he was intending to eavesdrop. But before she could stop Ernie from revealing his confidential information, she saw her wrist device glow green. Quickly lifting up her sleeve, she read a message on the pad: "Trust us. We're here to help you. You're the answer. You *are* the answer!"

Her head ached, and her left arm began throbbing—a deep energy pulsing inside it. She whispered aside: "You're the answer. I've heard that somewhere. You're the answer…" Those words were triggers, launching her thoughts into a world of confusion until the Maglev's conductor activated another announcement, and her thoughts stabilized. Glancing up at the two disguised people, she saw them nod at her. The message was from them! They had to know more about what had happened to her. They had to be able to fix her broken life! She nodded back at them in a gentle gesture of acceptance. She decided to wait until the Maglev docked, and then she could approach them on the platform: two minutes.

Slipping her sleeve over her device, she whispered, "Okay, sure, Ernie I won't say anything about the probe."

He slid his music case closer to him and swigged on his energy drink. "The Regents say they're certain the probe is lost, or was destroyed by someone, or some force," he began. "Early this morning, at one a.m., Regent Manning appeared at Navigation, saying the Regency was in the middle of preparing a crew for an exploratory mission to Nelta. Since the probe failed, they need first-hand confirmation that Nelta is still there, and to survey the planet to make sure the data Terra has matches the present. They want to launch a human expedition in two weeks! Expedition-1."

"*Sagan's* projected touch down is five weeks and four days. People will arrive *way* before *Sagan* arrives in orbit. That wasn't in *The Pact*. We're *all* supposed to arrive in orbit around Nelta." She pointed at the countdown—always first and foremost among all the life-streaming information.

"Yep, that's what we understood, but that's really not specified in *The Pact*," he said. "The Regents say they need two scientists from among the crew to accompany *their* scientists on the expedition. They're preparing and training those scientists right now, in seclusion, so the crew can't constantly question them or distract them from their arduous instruction. They gotta focus!"

"*Hmmm*," Elisa said, feeling a wave of uneasiness as she repeated, "preparing *their* scientists."

"People have been protesting a bit about the expedition...so that's why The Regents are allowing the crew to vote and pick two scientists in the Choosing Ceremony."

"He's right," the disguised man said, leaning down, finally talking to them and taking Ernie completely off guard. When Ernie began to dismiss what he'd said as speculation, the man with the shimmering, multi-hued disguised face enlarged the news over his old-fashioned wrist device and said: "Replay the failed probe segment." He gestured covertly at her left arm.

Quickly glancing at her wrist device, she read a message: *Disembark at Level-6. Go to Area 64 of 7,000 at the port side. Enter Business Kiosk 193G. Your new social media site is Terra-IV grid 85.*

A strange avatar with fish eyes darted next to him, and his disguised female friend activated her avatar. Their two avatars began a light dance in the air—obviously vying for control over location.

"What the hell is happening?" Ernie asked, swatting the fish avatar that suddenly morphed into a shark. The woman's avatar changed into a larger shark—biting for control of airspace.

The disguised man showed him the replay of the failed probe segment on social media. The newscaster was Dirk Hunter, a man in his early thirties who like to appear dressed as a Ringmaster of a circus, always wearing blue or black velvet suits, colorful orange ties, and outlandish tennis shoes. "Dirk Hunter is also going to be the host of the Choosing Ceremony. He's so good at being the intermediary between the crew and The Regents.'

"When's the ceremony?" Elisa asked the disguised man.

"Touch your wrist device," he said to her. His shimmering

face suddenly wavered in the light reflecting off the glass portal.

She saw his eyes—blue pools of dark lavender. "I know you! I think I've—"

"Shhh, we're tryin' to guard ya," he quickly said. He had an Australian accent.

Ernie had obviously seen her discomfort as the disguised man and his female companion began edging their way to the front of the Maglev. They were obviously preparing for a speedy escape. "Something's wrong with those two, Doc. I've noticed 'em for a little while but didn't say anything 'cause I like minding my own business."

The invading avatar, belonging to the mysterious man in the black suit at the end of their row, was still fighting the woman's avatar. His avatar was now winning the battle for air space. The two standing passengers were retreating little-by-little to the front of the Maglev as it slowed to stop. People were gathering their belongings. The commotion was intensifying—the invading avatar experiencing difficulty keeping track of the two disguised individuals.

Ernie slid his saxophone case in between his knees and picked up a briefcase. "I wonder what's happening with those two?" he asked wearily.

Elisa felt her aching arm. When she reached for the standing pole at the center of the aisle, she felt a burst of energy leave her arm and strike the mysterious man's invading avatar. It exploded in midair. Some people heard the pop, glanced around in shock, but then quickly returned to packing up their things to leave. The mysterious man at the end of her row was still surrounded by a silver aura. "Whatever just happened has to be a self-preservation thing that activated inside of me, protecting me," she whispered, flexing her fingers. Her entire body seemed to pulsate with energy. She felt as if she could take on any foe, and win. The shuttle's protective chrysalis unwrapped as propulsion mixes outside stabilized. They were docking.

"What's protecting you, Doc?" Ernie asked. He closed his

visuals of Beatrice, his eyes full of fear.

Not wanting an alarm to resound, she replied, "That noise is most likely just a warning for people to remain seated until the shuttle comes to a complete stop." She knew differently. Her body was now like a lightning rod attracting energy but like a magnetic field, repelling danger. The extent of her power, she had no idea…nor its ultimate purpose in her life.

He laughed. "Sure, I don't wanna blow to bits like that avatar that just sprayed light through the shuttle!" Then he picked up his instrument case as the front and side doors quickly opened.

An alarm sounded, and Enforcers who had been lately monitoring all the stations ran to the alert. Gun fire in laser bursts pulsed through the air. People began screaming, ducking, and running for cover. Peering out the giant portal to discern the location of the two disguised passengers, she couldn't see them. "It's like a hole opened up somewhere…and they disappeared into it."

"Impossible!" Ernie said, standing up to leave. Now, he was facing people in the row opposite them. Elisa began keeping an eye out for the mysterious man with the invading avatar who had sent an alarm about Ernie—and who knows who else the man had accused!

"I don't know…" Elisa said, as his beatnik avatar appeared alongside him to guide him to his next destination. The avatar reminded Ernie not to forget his saxophone. "I can't forget the event either," he said to his beatnik avatar. "I gotta a jam session with the band in two hours.

As she was about to exit their row, a young girl peeked over a seat and tugged on her mother's shirt. Just then, Elisa came face-to-face with the mysterious man who had been sitting at the last seat at the opposite end of her row. He still had the yellow-silver aura around him, now a bright hue that her arm seemed to share a connection. He reached out at her, and she covered her neck in defense. His hands stopped in midair—

his fish avatar igniting alongside him, obviously to assist him, but then it quickly popped and disappeared. The man appeared zombie-like and stunned. He had large brown eyes—shining large accusatory eyes—so unnatural. He seemed to need to grab her, but couldn't, as if a powerful force was restraining him.

*My arm*, she thought, as its power kept him at a safe distance from her.

A little girl suddenly came between them; and he backed off, mechanically making his way toward the front of the Maglev. He was like an empty person, void of personality yet flesh and bones. Elisa stood stone still as the little girl said: "Here's the lady, Mom. It's really Doctor Holton…in person! Wow!"

"Hi," Elisa said.

The man stepped on to the loading platform and disappeared in a crowd waiting to embark the shuttle.

Ernie was far behind her, maneuvering his large saxophone case into the aisle. "Hey, Doc, ya got my card. Holomail me, and I'll send you the exact time our band will be playing tomorrow night for Beatrice."

"Great, okay, Ernie," Elisa said. Then she noticed the little girl with her mother. Her mother seemed bland, unresponsive, and wouldn't acknowledge her when Elisa smiled at her. Then, she saw her face. One eye was half-blue and half-hazel. A memory scampered through her thoughts, making her shake with fear. "I've seen eyes like that before!" Another memory welled into her consciousness: a heterochromia problem surfacing in the crew. *That's what I'm supposed to do…help people…that's where I was going!*" She remembered a strange ride on a Maglev. "*I was on my way to The Regents to tell them more about the problem and ask them to fix it. But something happened…what?!*" She stepped out of the Maglev onto the docking platform. Hundreds of people and their bobbing floating avatars were scurrying to their destinations. She felt dizzy, surrounded, vulnerable, lost. Until her left arm began tingling, and her outmoded wrist device illuminated, showing her the next destination. She needed to find Area 64 Port Side, Business Kiosk 193G. There, she believed she'd find answers.

## Chapter 19 – Nanyte Invasion I

Looking for directional avatars to point her to Port Side, she peered high into the dome. Level-6's Bow Transport station resembled a giant sports center, at least the Matrix Techs designed this dome's rendering to reflect a sports-center setting this week. L-cars were transporting passengers around Level-6, and virtual ads and banners were sky-high and interfacing with people, advertising products and skills.

"Now, to find this place that keeps popping up on the wrist device," she whispered, taking the Main moving walkway westward. On both sides of her, corridors were teeing off in an organized web—all corridors leading up lifts so people could access two levels of living quarters with corner minimarts and business kiosks. Again she glanced at her watch, still giving her a directional arrow but now shining the number 64, Business Kiosk 193G. She was heading in the right direction; and not too far ahead was Gathering Area-1 where people could meet for business or pleasure—the first of four rest stops on the way to Port Side's Dead End—the

# J.P. Osterman

astrocity's thick hull—and beyond the hull, *Sagan*'s space-folding wormhole.

Twenty feet in the air, virtual Zeppelins continued to guide Saganites to various corridors, along with travel times in walking distance. She was at Area 20 of 75. She needed Area 64, another ten minute walk, and the moving walkway was progressively increasing in speed. At area 25, she could step off and take a break at Gathering Area-1. Monitoring the entire level from lofty elevations were Enforcers on hover cars. Some of them were assisting Matrix Technicians who were applying processor hubs in strategic locations along the curved ceiling. Each virtual rendition needed augmented hubs, and Matrix Techs were constantly implementing the designers' specifications who were instructing them from Level-7 and Level-9 Tech Centers.

Suddenly, a loud noise resounded, like clanging brass and nails scratching metal. Stopping, she covered her ears. People behind her were reacting in the same way, almost clashing into her! Stepping off the walkway into Gathering Area-1, she looked behind her down the long corridor. A Maglev had just screeched to a halt, and people were disembarking and embarking as currents in the transport tunnel began hissing and churning with electromagnetic propulsion energy. No one appeared to be in danger, but her head began pounding, her heart racing. She felt claustrophobic as more unusual sounds filled the air, followed by screams and shouts. Something horrible was happening there, and also affecting her!

Enforcers began taking notice of the strange loud hissing and droning noises that sounded like attacking bees and hornets. They began conversing over their wrist devices with Matrix Techs who were unleashing instruments to home in on the unusual disturbance. The entire area went suddenly dim, and people shrieked. The hissing and droning was intensifying.

Standing in a virtual park among real benches, vending kiosks, and entertainment booths; Elisa held the large black satchel against her chest. Her arm was tingling again; and when she looked at it, she noticed it was slightly glowing, along with her outdated wrist device. An interaction was beginning, and she felt powerless to stop it. People were taking pictures down the corridor, their avatars dispersing into the corridor in search of answers to the disturbance. Several reports returned. At any second, whatever was striking the tunnel would soon be in Gathering Area-1. Most of the Enforcers patrols began leaving to defend the transport station where people were shrieking and crying for help.

An avatar dog began chasing someone's 3D cat in front of her. The little girl who owned the dog called it back to her. Robotic squirrels were tossing acorns and scurrying up fake oak and pine trees. A blue bird landed on the top of a red bench across a tree-lined pathway. It had a most unusual body and face! If it had been black instead of blue, the mutant bird would have resembled Edgar Allen Poe's raven. She whistled at the bird. "Come here," she called gently. Others around her noticed the bird as well. One man claiming to be a Software Engineer said he had never seen *anything* created like that by *anyone* in his Level-7 facility. The bird flew into the air, circling feet above the crowd. Someone had left the remainder of a protein vitamin bar on the ground that the technology hadn't yet finished absorbing. The bluebird landed and began pecking at the food. "I know you're not real," Elisa said, "but you're sure beautiful…and weird."

The bird whistled thweeet-thwete as it flapped its wings wildly.

One little girl said, "That bluebird has red feet!"

"With stubs on 'em that look like toes," her little brother added.

"Weird! Don't touch it!" the children's parents snarled. They wanted to whisk them out of Gathering Area-1, but an Enforcer stopped them, telling everyone to stand back, to fall back into the crowd for safety as the children complained, "*Aaw—naw*! Don't hurt the bird!" They were trying hard to snatch it, but it disappeared into a white shimmering fog.

# J.P. Osterman

Then it reappeared on the ground far away from the Enforcers who had given up trying to catch it with their special nets. They went to help others fight off what appeared to be an attack emanating from the tunnel. Before leaving, several of them accused 273 members of causing the trouble, others were blaming a hacker, and still others were hailing The Regents.

Elisa snuck up on the bluebird. "Oh—so you think you wanna come to Nelta too?" She thought it was only a light-wave manifestation, a feat of virtual rendering that would innocently land on her arm or shoulder. It wasn't robotic since it disappeared when it entered the special cloud.

The bluebird's wings fluttered as it chirped, *thweet*.

"This bird's talking," the boy exclaimed, licking a sucker.

Another child knelt next to it. "Ya scared little critter?" She looked as if she might burst out crying. "This poor little bird's shivering, Mommy. Can I take her home?"

The bird flapped its wings excitedly and chirped, *thwete*.

The brown-haired boy kicked the chunk of protein bar out of the bird's reach. "Uh-oh, I accidentally almost hit it!"

The bird rose up frantically, flew in a circle, and began whistling bursts of terrified *tweet—tweet*...

"It does sound like it's trying to communicate," Elisa said as the boy's mother scolded him for almost hitting it.

"Sorry!" the contrite boy said, pouting.

As people watched, the bird landed gently on Elisa's left arm and calmed.

"What!" she said, trying to steady her arm.

"Mommy! Daddy! The bluebird landed. It's real!" the little boy shouted.

Two women hurried into the congregating crowd that was watching stunned-faced at what they obviously believed was impossible. Meanwhile, an influx of strange deformed wildlife entered the area. A speckled deer leaped off a moving walkway, and vaulted into a green graphic forest, followed by a line of rabbits. They began eating the protein bar. They had black gnashing teeth and sharp claws—not at all the friendly creatures of Earth. They also had little arms and feet extensions as if their DNA had mixed with human genetics.

"I'm a physicist," a man said, stepping out of the crowd and examining the feeding wildlife while taking off his glasses, only an accessory. "But I haven't seen *anything* like this anywhere." Pointing upward into the dim morning sky, he said, "Barely can I make out a Terra hub. But definitely it's synchronized with these subatomic critters."

"That means watch out!" a woman added. "They could kill ya depending upon their programming."

"And the person or people controlling them!" another said, panic-stricken. Then she pointed at a long line of hissing and droning particles. "What's that?"

Elisa felt a connection building with the bird still perched on her arm as she also tried making sense of the lines of particles trailing like contrails behind all the deformed wildlife. The bluebird felt light as a feather, but she realized it had powerful potential. "I think I know what they are...nanytes, in subatomic form, reacting with light, behaving like an artificial intelligence."

"I agree, and they have the potential then kill us," the Particle Physicist shouted, "so everyone, stay low! These are light-based...and dangerous!"

A red line of nanytes streamed down from the dimly-lit dome, materialized into a cardinal, and began circling through the air. A large hawk joined it, until an entire flock of birds assembled and began speaking in high-pitched distorted voices: "Remember us! Find us!" Gathering Area-1 was now teeming with deformed flying birds, disfigured flies, large buzzing bees, and gyring gnats—all swooping down on people, around their arms, and through their parted legs.

Crying in horror, people dropped to the ground and huddled in small circles. Back at the transport station, the Maglev had docked, its magnetic rails squeaking and the electromagnetic wind weakening. People were running to it, pounding on the chrysalis cover to get inside. Once open, they began clashing with disembarking passengers, even throwing people out on the platform. Huge fights were breaking out as wildlife kept swooping down and attacking anything with bare flesh. They hadn't hurt anyone, yet, but their frenzy reminded Elisa of Halloween back on Earth, except this manifestation of fright was real.

An emergency broadcast began playing on the twenty-five Zeppelin banners throughout Level-6; but dragon-like creatures attacked the large unmanned aerial vehicles, and the broadcasts fizzled out. The creatures sucked the light right out of them and then multiplied!

After the banners extinguished, several new deformed creatures turned their focus on the robotic squirrels, fake trees, and artificial flowers. They began chasing everything synthetic and artificial—destroying it all with their claws, hind legs, and teeth.

Enforcers appeared unprepared to respond, and they appeared apprehensive to open up with laser fire power. One Enforcer exclaimed, "They're not real, so if you shoot, your fire will go right through them and injure someone!" They and Matrix Techs were calling for help, and hailing The Regents. "We're definitely being attacked. It's a mass attack!"

"Impossible. Holograms and renderings can't change into physical matter!" the man who worked as a Software Engineer shouted. He and the Particle Physicist began capturing the scene on their wrist devices, until a giant wild hog disappeared from across the area, reformed ten feet in front of the Engineer, and appeared fang ready to attack him.

"Turn off your wrist device now," Elisa ordered them, maneuvering the bluebird toward the two men.

The Engineer said to his floating avatar, "Send this to the Regency!" But the wild hog leaped into the air, bit into his holographic avatar, and then disappeared with it in his mouth only to reappear across Gathering Area-1. It was shaking the avatar between his teeth! Just by touching it, the wild hog had altered the avatar's light source into matter, its prey.

"Maybe these creatures escaped from a participation

kiosk," a teenager cried.

"Now all we need is a donkey!" a woman said sarcastically.

A donkey galloped off the moving walking into the disheveled forest and began heehawing. All the strange animals began gathering around Elisa and the bluebird still perched on her left arm.

"Don't think about animals anymore," the Engineer ordered, "'cause I thought of a deer, and now there's one across the Gathering Area-1, licking a salt brick."

A crowd of over a hundred people were trying to communicate with the Regency; but then they stopped when they realized their attempts were being monitored, and consequently, making them targets of the new light-based technology. One woman heard one of the animals say in a high-pitched voice: "This is just the beginning!"

More attacks are eminent everywhere on *Sagan*.

A boy whipped off his wristband, threw it to the ground and stomped on it. "An animal jumped on my arm and ate my Robbie avatar!"

"Mine too!" screamed the teenager. "Mom, Dad! How can these freaky things come to life and kill avatars?"

"This has to be advanced nanyte technology…real entities that are capable of disintegrating and recombining at a sub-atomic and light-wave structure!" Elisa shouted.

The Particle Physicist agreed. "There's only one way to stop them. Discover who's activating their programs, and where. That's the epicenter."

"Like I said, no one from *my* Tech Center did any of this!" the Software Engineer proclaimed.

Elisa had to get everyone's attention. The bluebird on her left arm was glowing. The bird and her arm had synchronized. Perhaps she could figure out a way to repel the creatures. Still, she didn't have their source—the person and location responsible for the attack, or why. She needed everyone calm in order to think and concentrate. "Listen to me, people!" she screamed. The large crowd stopped and listened. "Whatever monsters and creatures people said they have been seeing are *truly* real."

"They're not illusions at all," a woman cried.

"So what are these things?" a man asked, trying to bat away an attacking large bumble bee.

Elisa extended her left arm in his direction, and the bee flew into the sky, slurped into the ceiling, and disappeared. "This is advanced nano-robotic technology! It's also synchronizing with our matrix and stored information."

"The Archives then," the Software Engineer said, holding out his hand to touch one of the animals that appeared frozen in space/time in front of Elisa. He paused before actually touching the glowing brown-and-white creature. "Somewhere is an evolving software app that is in quantum nonlocality with the visible spectrum. But I don't have a clue as to who input the app and the source code! I've *never* seen anything like this even partially operational…and I should know if a technology such as this exists because people I work with design, test, and input the apps for social-media participation." He was about to put his finger on the large porcupine that appeared to have venomous quills.

Elisa walked slowly over to him, stopped, and held out her arm. The Particle Physicist had his Level-9 app activated, monitoring the man's experiment.

A light-blue light wafted off the bluebird, striking the porcupine. The light appeared to have a taming effect on the venomous porcupine that lowered its quills and allowed the Software Engineer to touch it. "Now, I think you're safe. Take a sample of its code for study."

He touched his wrist device to the porcupine's back spine. "Got it!" Then he stood up and addressed the frightened crowd. "Just don't think into existence any more animals, or else Terra's CBRR grid will continue to read the symbols in your mind and creating them!" As he stepped cautiously back toward the transport station, he gestured for the Physicist to join him, and said, "Everyone…move slowly…don't react quickly, only slowly. I'm going to analyze this…that is, if I can make it back to my Level-7 lab without getting attacked. I think the source is Terra's Live Streaming Field on Level-9 and her Cloud Matrix Center on Level-7. Of course, The Archives…but I don't know their central programmable location. But those areas will be able to reveal who is responsible, why this is happening, and how to stop it."

Elisa thought hard about her new location at Kiosk 193G of Area 64: *Find me and give me a report.* When she saw her address appear on the Engineer's wrist device, she gave him the signal to leave, and they disappeared down the corridor.

A frantic woman jumped into the arms of a man who began hugging her, trying to get her to calm down. "Can this new App that the Engineer mentioned generate real monsters? Monsters capable of killing?" Gathering Area-1 was beginning to calm down, but many light-based creatures were still in attack mode and striking at several Enforcers and Matrix Techs who still had on their wrist devices. They were nano-photonic perfect!

"I can't answer that right now…I'm thinking…thinking about these creatures leaving us alone, and returning to where they came from," Elisa whispered to the woman as the bluebird on her arm lifted off with the last creature toward the domed ceiling. With the special connection they had formed, she knew she'd be seeing the strange deformed bluebird soon.

The light-based animals were high in the air when The Regents' faces materialized on the twenty-five Zeppelin banners, obviously so they could see the attack firsthand. The animals saw them instead, and began an assault on their images.

Again people screamed and children shrieked and cried. When all ten Regents' faces faded off the Zeppelin banners, the glowing animals slurped into the ceiling and disappeared.

People sighed and moaned in relief.

"I wonder if this happened here only?" several people

asked.

Rubbing her arm, Elisa replied, "If we can re-establish social-media connectivity, I'm sure we'll find out, but I can't hear any blaring siren." Gathering Area-1 turned silent as people began listening for an alarm on Level-5 or Level-7. Nothing, only gentle rumblings of the pipes and propulsion technology in between levels. Enforcers and Matrix Techs on hovercraft high up in the dome had activated special instruments to locate and analyze the attack and the strange new creatures.

As the commotion subsided and Maintenance crews began rushing in to fix all the robotics and artificial scenery, the dome hissed and its Sports Center rendering faded. Now the mile-high dome appeared smooth as silk, with black glistening connectivity processors and giant processing hubs. Everything was dark and void of settings and scenery. A Matrix Tech told everyone it would take two hours to fix all the broken technology and return the dome to its Sport Center rendering.

Several people tried activating their wrist devices and were finally able to get their avatars back on-matrix. A man said, "I just wanna know what that creature meant when it said, *remember us and find us.*"

"Yeah, me too," several others said. "I wonder who we're supposed to remember and who we're supposed to find."

On the empty Zeppelin banners, suddenly appeared a woman's face. She looked like the old-Earth movie star, Gina Lollobrigida.

"Who's that?!" People shouted.

"Anyone know her?"

"Where is she? Who is she?" a crowd called, as people climbed on to café tables and benches and began searching the crowd.

An angry man stepped on a bench and said, "All this 'remember me' stuff has to do with something terrible I'm sure!"

Another person cried: "Terra is *completely* malfunctioning. That's what's going on. We're *all* gonna *die!*"

# Astrocity Sagan

"No, wait," Elisa screamed.

The crowd still broke out into hysterics. Some people shrieked and began sprinting toward the transport platforms. Others fell to the ground and covered their heads. Children were crying and reaching for their parents, clinging to them in fits of fear and desperation. A few children were chasing the broken robotic squirrels and laughing, having fun.

Gina Lollobrigida's glowing image still showed brilliantly on the Zeppelin banners as she said, "Remember Emma Jane Wright. This is the beginning." Her image hissed and faded.

"Who is Emma Jane Wright?" people asked one another.

"*Who* is Emma Jane Wright?!" they questioned over and over again.

"I'm searching for that identity right now," a woman replied. "I'm trying several spellings."

"I did that," someone began, "but nothing."

"Yeah! If an Emma Jane Wright ever did exist—on Earth or here—she doesn't anymore," a man called out angrily. "Her identity's been scrubbed clean outta the matrix."

"Purged?" a woman gasped.

"No way! Maybe she's in cryo?" a young mother said, nervously cradling her baby.

After moments of watching people search the matrix for answers, Elisa finally asked: "So there's *no* Emma Jane Wright?" Yet she felt she knew the name…even remembered a face! But if others couldn't find an Emma Jane Wright in the matrix archives, what did that mean for her since she could remember her? Then she recalled what the Software Engineer and Particle Physicist had said: Levels 7 and 9—Terra's Live Stream Field and Cloud Matrix and The Archives—had to hold the answers to solving who had evolved technology to light-base creatures, why, and how to stop them. But first, she needed to find Area 64, Kiosk 193G. Was that home?

# J.P. Osterman

## Chapter 20 – Area 64, Kiosk 193G

After hiding among the crowd on the moving walkway while dodging people who were looking for her to tell her thanks for helping them, she stepped off at Area 64. This Area off the Main thoroughfare to Port-Side Dead End has a virtual rendering of Lido Key, Florida, with a sand-appearing floor, gentle reverberations of seagulls gliding in the air, an occasional sea turtle, pelicans, and the sound of lapping water. The ambiance is laid-back, casual, and not as crowded as some of the other five-hundred-feet-in-diameter areas on Level-6. On both sides of Area 64 are two, five-story, rectangular Living-Cube facilities with artificial façades resembling white Jerusalem stone. They're all up-scale, and most have penthouses for people who like to time share.

Kiosk 193 is large, white and crab shaped, and sits at the center of Area 64. It's a grocery store and storage facility in one, with a cafe and a small strip mall as extensions. On both sides are two moving walkways with residents traveling north and south. The people noises could be unbearable if not for more technological innovations! To reduce echoes are large circular hubs extending down from the domed ceiling that not only processor the Lido Key scene, but also contain sound-dampening technology only a Matrix Tech Project Leader can adjust.

Several sections around Kiosk 193 have small stations that resemble beach shacks with their wooden façades and scruffy shingles. But Kiosk 193 was constructed out of the same fabrics as other kiosks, corner minimarts, or cafes: self-repairing technology, and LED/hub holographic functions to accommodate social-media participation and ship-wide broadcasts. High in the dome, Zeppelin, small Unmanned Aerial Vehicles, and Enforcers are always monitoring the entire twenty-four-mile-in-diameter Level-6.

Noticing an Enforcer shining his spectrometer into the crowd, obviously trying to gather information on the wild disturbance back at the station, Elisa remembered seeing Regent Manning's face on one of the Zeppelin before a light-based creature attacked his image. That intimidating brooding Beethoven face ignited in her a deep disgust and repulsion. "I just have to let off some steam," she whispered while activating the vocal app on her wrist device. It attuned to her signature and began picking up her whispers to listen to later. "Since waking up, I've been feeling sick and angry at the thought of him, and my arm aches and begins developing bluish veins until I force him outta my head. "But then this sick feeling and metallic taste in my mouth returns! Then his face keeps blasting through my mind like a poltergeist is sticking to me!" She drank some water and paused while a few people passed her by. "This is one bad cycle going on inside of me where he's concerned, so Thornton Manning *must* hold the key to what happened to me. But how do I get to him or the other nine Regents in person?" Her app displayed to her the answer. "Yes! Tonight's Choosing Ceremony is my chance to get up close and personal to him." She extended her wrist device, and it showed a *small* rendering of Kiosk 193, also guiding her to her destination.

Walking around the back, she began searching for Unit G. "I just passed D…now F…here's G! Wow, it sure looks small, the size of a storage unit." Then her wrist device showed her a picture of a laser-light pen. "I guess you're telling me to take it out and use it," she said, taking the pen out of the black satchel and clicked it on. Its green light shone a pattern on the security keypad, and the small sliding door opened. After slipping inside where a small light brightened, she noticed bowls of freeze-dried soup on a small kitchen table, and she hurriedly doused one with water and nuked it in the food replicator. "Gosh I'm starving!" Then she saw a small cot on the left side of the room. A round hologram platform stood at the food of the bed. Over it, she could access Grid 86, her new social-media connection with the matrix. She could watch renderings over it, activate renderings on her walls, and link with all the channels. But this technology was old. "Most likely, there are some things I can't do with it," she said, taking her hot soup out of the replicator. She blew over a spoonful, and gently began eating. "Finally, I can also get some much needed information about what's been going on and what I was supposed to do three days ago!" While eating her soup, she sat down in front of the hologram platform. "Now, I want answers."

After calling on a calm beach setting that appeared all around her, she ordered, "Connect me, Dr. Elisa Holton, to Grid 86."

Nothing.

She repeated the command, louder.

Nothing.

She stood and waved her hands in between the round platform and the floor. "Maybe this thing is password protected." After pacing in front of the knee-high stage connected to the floor with a giant black tube, she gulped down more soup and remembered another object in the black satchel. She had seen a string of old processor buttons—

optics and sensor chips—the type people used on Earth to generate a social-media URL. After taking them out, she squished the buttons around the platform. When the last tiny processor blended in with the stage, the ceiling hub above it fired into action, and a bright yellow column of light shot down onto the platform—a functioning matrix connection. "Wow, someone *purposely* modified this technology for me! Who?" She hoped she hadn't set off an alarm to Matrix Security. They could be at her door and accuse her of illegal hacking!

After seconds of wait time wherein she couldn't stop wondering about who had altered the platform and why, the strange misfit bluebird with red feet and toe stubs suddenly appeared in the yellow holographic light. She stepped back. "You're the bird I saw in Gathering Area-1!" She looked at the small creature's structural integrity, and when the bird squawked and jumped, it altered a bit from matter to light. "You're light-based, but also solid…a unique quantum property!"

It responded with a light excited chirp. Elisa put her hand gently into the yellow holographic light to touch the hand-sized blue bird. Her forefinger sank through the image, but then she felt something prickly and energetic on her skin. "You're physical make up doesn't make sense!" Again, the bird chirped, and then grew in size two inches. Elisa stepped back. "You're *definitely* a hologram, although I believe you're also capable of amassing tangible properties." The bird flittered a little in the yellow light, hopped twice, and then chirped. "I'd call you a nano-photonic creation." The blue bird grew again, pecking at a few particles of yellow light. Elisa didn't know what to think, except to try and get at the bottom of the attack. "Okay, where did you come from, and who sent you?"

Flapping its wings wildly, the foot-tall bluebird chirped three times. And its bright orange beak began opening and shutting as if the bird were trying to vocalize.

# J.P. Osterman

Elisa folded her arms in frustration. "It's safe in here. No one can harm you *or* me," she whispered. After a pause, the bird calmed down, jumped on the rim of the platform, and materialized in solid form as it did in the park. Just then, Elisa felt a connection to the strange bluebird, and her fear subsided as the creature gently expanded its wings, took off, and glided around the room. "Hey! Come back down here! You'll wreck a wall or hub. Then what'll I do?" When she raised her left arm to coerce it to land, the bird landed on the back of her hand like a trained hawk. She softly set the bluebird on the edge of a chair where it flapped its blue-and-orange wings and then perched statue still.

"Do you need rest, or food?" Elisa asked, sitting down across the table from it. She took a tiny cup off the counter next to her small sink, poured a little soup into it, and set it on the table in front of the bird.

The bird's face rounded out a bit as it glanced at the food, hopped on the table, and began eying the noodles and carrots. It had dark brown eyes, human eyes if they were larger, and a blush on its cheeks, almost like applied makeup. If not for its beak and feathers, the bird would have human characteristics.

"Maybe if I eat some of mine, you'll try some too," Elisa said, tasting some more soup. "*Mmmm*, it's chicken noodle, fresh off Level-3."

After the bird swallowed a bite, its beak changed into a human nose.

Elisa reeled. "My God—what are you?" She stood up, glancing around the room. Someone had to be directing it. "Come on, give me some answers! Who are you, and where are you? And why are you scaring the heck outta people?" After no reply and checking her keypad for a security breach, she realized there was no off-site connection. The bird was alone, and obviously trying to communicate better. As the bird bobbed its head again, Elisa remembered a name that the other light-based entities had said during the attack. "Are you here because of the woman your friends mentioned?" She quickly recalled the name that no one could locate in the matrix.

# Astrocity Sagan

"Emma Jane Wright?"

Terra appeared over the hologram platform, shocking Elisa. "Do you want File 358 now, Dr. Elisa Holton?" The bird flew into the air and chirped twice.

Elisa remembered that those two responses meant yes. "So you know her. Emma Jane Wright?" Relieved but also more confused than ever, she scratched her head, and turned her attention to Terra. "Finally—thank goodness you're here! I thought I'd done something wrong. I've been trying to hail you with no results. Or I thought you might be experiencing a ship-wide glitch, especially after the attack in the station. And this bird's not telling me much." She felt dizzy again, sat down, and began sipping more nourishment. She felt suddenly drained. Is the strange bird, or Terra depleting my energy, or is something else sapping my strength? She didn't have time 'cause at any second, the matrix could falter again. She had to ask focused questions, ones that could help her. "Terra, what happened back at the station? Is *Sagan* experiencing some kind of serious trouble? Are people in danger? Do you know when the next attack will occur?" She had so many questions, but these were the most pressing.

"An internal alarm triggered, Elisa Holton," Terra replied. "An alien is among us."

Elisa squirmed in her seat as the bluebird began disappearing and reappearing around the room, actions signifying agitation. The bird was continuing to grow and its appearance change. But Terra's vision hadn't locked onto it, so the bird couldn't be the alien presence even though it was manifesting outside Kiosk 193. "An alien on *Sagan*? What are you talking about, Terra? There's been no report of anything alien or extraterrestrial permeating the hull." She showed Terra the outdated wrist device only displaying a *tiny* yellow column of signal connectivity. It then displayed *Sagan*'s Home Page, but Dirk Hunter the famous newscaster hadn't posted any alien invasion, ship-wide retaliation, or threat of an invasion on the page, except an intensified hunt for the new protest group now formally named *273*. "See? Nothing."

"I am not privy to Executive Regent Manning's directives, Dr. Elisa Holton," Terra replied.

"Well, the alien invasion proclamation you just announced sounds faulty," she grimaced as Terra shrugged. Then she remembered her avatar. "Where's Twin?" She began taking off her outdated wrist device; but the morphing bluebird fluttered in wild retaliation. "Okay, I'll keep it on." Then she sat down as the bluebird calmed. "At least let me link with Twin so she can schedule me a checkup at the Medical Center. That Regeneration I had left me without three days' worth of memories." She snapped her finger. "Zapped right outta me! I need 'em. The special Body Double Imager they have there should be able to retrieve my Up-Streamed memories that seem to have been misplaced."

"Twin cannot activate, Dr. Elisa Holton. Twin is no longer on-matrix." Terra's image froze. Furthermore, Terra hadn't stepped off the hologram platform. Most unusual. She was containing herself inside the yellow processing field.

"You're behaving like ya got a glitch again, Terra," she said, walking in front of Terra's yellow projection field. "And what do you mean that Twin is off-matrix? That would mean Twin is no longer available. And if that's true, she doesn't exist. And that means that I'm dead!" She waved her off. "No way...uh-uh...I'm here!"

"Twin is off-matrix, Doctor Elisa Holton," Terra repeated. She had a most mechanical appearance, not at all the modern Terra-IV. Perhaps the attack had altered the matrix and techs were working to fix it. She needed more data to draw a conclusion. Feeling disoriented as the bluebird perched on a shelf next to her, right up close to her ear so it could whisper secrets, Elisa breathed, and her rising blood pressure lowered. "Okay, let's try something a little easier. I need to know when the Choosing Ceremony is, Terra. A man showed me a broadcast wherein you chose *me* as one of twenty-one candidates for Expedition-1 to Nelta. When's the ceremony and where? I intend to talk to Regent Manning personally, even though the sight of the guy right now makes me wanna puke," she said under her breath.

"One-thirty this afternoon, at Level-1, Ceremonial Platform," Terra said, her image wavering.

Elisa called out a command to steady the interference, but Terra continued to infuse with intermittent static. Such electrical weave in the matrix's quantum fabric is unheard of! Then the time flared: 9:42 a.m. "Wow! I don't have much time to get some sleep and change…and the trip up there will take a half-an-hour."

The bluebird began chirping wildly. Its body appeared to have more human characteristics, and even a face and skin! "Who are you?" Elisa asked, stepping back and breathing. She lay down on her cot, and the bird landed gently on the cot's metal frame between her and Terra. "What about File 358, Terra? Maybe I can activate Twin from there. The wrist device keeps showing me that file." Her fatigue felt like an ice berg. "God—I can hardly see straight I'm so tired. I need sleep, but I also need to catch up on what happened to me in the past three days." She forced herself to sit up. "Do you know…what happened to me?"

After a pause, Terra replied, "I have several messages I diverted from Level-2 to your new Grid 86."

"Level-2?" she asked, the place like a fog. The bluebird chirped several times and performed a brief dance. "I think you just told me I used to live there…at a Living Cube on Level-2." The bird nodded yes. When she looked more closely at the bird, she noticed it had short black hair and brown eyes. "So you're telling me I'm here for safety reasons?" Elisa asked, touching her throat.

As the morphing bluebird chirped happily in reply, Terra said: "Ernie Bentley holosited you just now." Terra illuminated Ernie next to her.

Ernie began: "Hey, Doc, nice to have met you this

morning." He still had his Mohawk and wrestler-like appearance and his saxophone carrying case. "The concert I told you about to raise money to expand my search for Beatrice is next week, Wednesday at 7:30 p.m. I just received a permit to hold it. Funny, Matrix Security assigned me a space on the level *you* disembarked on. What a coincidence, huh? Anyway, my band will be at the Louis Armstrong Center. I hope to see ya there, Doc! And let me know if ya need any help, bye."

After yawning, she said, "Schedule me in, Terra, and set my standard reminder."

"What is your standard reminder, Doctor Elisa Holton?" Terra asked.

Her jaw dropped. "An hour. That's my standard reminder. Gosh—you're acting like I'm dead to the matrix! I'm not. I'm here. See?" Noticing Terra's eyes flash green in reply, she fluffed her pillow while watching the bluebird continue to evolve in appearance via light waves emitting from Terra's holographic platform. Under the bird's blue and orange wings were now tiny thin arms. "Did anyone else call me?"

"Carl Foldier," Terra replied.

Elisa grabbed her pillow and threw it before Terra could produce his image. "Remember what I told you to tell that guy the next time he calls?"

"No, Doctor Elisa Holton," Terra replied.

"That's strange, 'cause we had a long talk about that," she huffed. "I told you to tell 'im to take a hike." Her image flickered. Something wasn't right at all but obviously couldn't be corrected. Another Terra popped into her mind...a foreign matrix no one knows of. But that can't be! She was going to delve gently into Terra's strange nature. "*Who* are you, 'cause you're *not* the Terra I knew three days ago! At least I remember that!" She sat on the edge of the bed; and as she watched Terra's eyes change color at every question, a revelation occurred to her. "You're *not* Terra...Terra-IV." She could be in serious danger, and she had to tread lightly and humbly.

# Astrocity Sagan

When Terra didn't step out of the containment field or answer her, she said: "Something strange is happening." Rubbing her forehead, she felt as if she was in a dream. "From those weird birds saying, *Remember me*, to Emma Jane Wright, to those unnatural creatures that attacked the transport station. Something is really wrong onboard this astrocity…something worse than any type of alien invasion."

"The attack at Gathering Area-1 is Live-Streaming everywhere, Doctor Elisa Holton," Terra said. "An alien *is* on *Sagan*."

Elisa felt angry. "But there's been no announcement of an alien infiltration." When Terra couldn't produce proof, she added: "Please, quit calling me *Doctor Elisa Holton*. You always call me Elisa, not all this doctor this and doctor that! Quit it." She walked over to the sink and drank some water. Drops spilled down her sleeve, her arm soaking them up. Now that had never happened before! Feeling suddenly exhausted as the evolving bluebird began lightly chirping out a tiny melody, she yawned. "*Please*, don't go haywire on me anymore, Terra. Not you…not now. I can't stand it! I need you."

"Yes, Elisa."

When she looked at where the bluebird had landed, she saw it standing on the little table. It had completely changed into a half-human, half-bird creature. She clutched her blanket. "You—you have a face! A body…and arms…and fingers on your wings! What the—"

"It's me, Elisa," the blue bird blurted out in a high-pitched light chirping voice.

Elisa rubbed her eyes. "Emma Jane Wright?" Historic images welled into her mind. "It's you…yes…I remember!" Emma was now twelve inches height, with tiny webbed human feet, expansive arms as wings, and blue boney knees. She had dark brown eyes and short black hair with pink bows around several blue feathers on her neck. "Did you go through some type of light-wave technology that made you change?" More memories of Emma flooded her thoughts: Emma Jane Wright had been a famous IT tech on Earth, but died while saving it along with several other crewmembers on the *Spider* who crash landed on the moon. Regent Manning announced that none of those ten heroes had survived. After arriving on *Sagan*, they had to have cloned Emma back to life, but someone had killed her in her Regeneration Corridor three days ago. After that memory, her memories hit a wall. Were more crewmembers from the *Spider* alive on *Sagan*?

"EJ. That's me!" Emma Jane Wright said happily, not at all sounding dejected at living in her altered state.

"Why would someone want to kill you, EJ?" Elisa turned sick, ran to the sink, and vomited. Regent Thornton Manning and his mysterious theater room were attacking her thoughts and she felt disoriented and out-of-body. She then remembered seeing large processing hubs—all illegal technology. He had implemented a secretive, powerful Mind Meddling technology everywhere, light-based waves capable of expunging impulses from peoples' minds, inhibiting them from remembering select events. But the first step is to walk under any one of many special Mind Meddling hubs. They're all over the ship. She thought long and hard. "But I'm unaffected by them because I remember everything about you, EJ." She glanced from her the fingertips on her left hand to her shoulder. Recalling her special Neltan abilities, she touched her left arm. The nanyte enhancements to her cellular structure weren't only in her arm, but all through her—and obviously beginning to synchronize with the astrocity. It was a communications technology—a teleportation technology. Stunned, she sat down. "That's why, with your help, EJ, I was able to defeat those creatures at Gathering Area-1."

"We beat 'em!" EJ exclaimed, her wings flapping excitedly.

"Wow, I never realized I had this kind of ability…power to direct even light," she marveled as she rubbed her arm and shoulders. "It's scary though."

EJ began circling Terra's yellow containment field. Terra stretched out her hand, and the bird landed on it, changing into a holographic image. "Shhh," EJ began. "You're the answer."

Elisa gulped down water, staggered back to her cot, and lay down. Little by little, she realized her memories were returning, and she had Emma's to help her more, her special powers that continue to strengthen, this different Terra in front of her, and time. "God—I need medicine, 'cause I think I'm going nuts! All these memories aren't making sense, and I'm the only one unaffected by the Mind Meddling technology. So how am I going to get other people to help me stop a future attack?" She felt small and helpless. "*Sagan* is in danger. That's all we know right now."

Inside the containment field, EJ began slowly rising toward the ceiling processor. Whenever she spoke, her voice was high-pitched, her words were soft, but their resonance was cut off. "No you're not crazy, Elisa. We talked just yesterday, and I helped save you."

Exhaling in frustration, Elisa touched her forehead with her left hand. Suddenly, another memory welled. She fainted.

After seconds, she felt a gentle spray of water on her face. Regaining consciousness, she inhaled back to life. "I died!" She felt a suffocating slow death, followed by her mind lifting into a rainbow. "But someone resurrected me!"

"Resurrected," EJ repeated. "Yes, that's the word that could describe what happened."

Elisa stood up, glanced at the time—10:01 a.m.—and then she plopped down on her cot. "So that's what happened to me. And that's how I know you...from inside the matrix, where we *actually* met, where we talked about things I still can't—can't remember. Damn!" she said angrily, gesturing at EJ. She felt as if someone had smacked her in the face, and she rubbed her cheek. "Regent Manning. Thornton Manning keeps coming into my mind like a life sucking demon." She trembled, and EJ appeared to shiver as well as she hovered high over Terra's holographic body. That's why Terra kept showing everything about her as being dead. To hide her.

"I'm still in danger," she whispered. "*Someone* wanted to get rid of me, kill me." She believed she tasted blood. It was a strong memory of Thornton Manning and the strangulation hold he had around her neck. "My God!" she began repeating, and crying. "He, they, wanted to kill me…but they, they didn't, 'cause they said, they said they need me for something." She wiped her tears. "But what?" That small fragment of a memory returned to her, along with the Terra in front of her, but nothing more. "What else…what else happened?!" She tapped her forehead, frustrated at the unknown. "I just can't remember, drats!"

Terra stood still as EJ said through proud expressions in her blue wings: "But you're not dead. You're alive. I made sure of that, and the reboot of your memory,"

"But without *all* my memories," Elisa cried, "I'm completely vulnerable, like an ant."

A small commotion welled up from outside the door, and Elisa stopped moving. Every sound began magnifying as she remembered what Ernie Bentley had told her after she woke up on the Maglev. He said Thornton Manning appeared white with shock when Terra announced her name as one of the twenty-one candidates. Suddenly, she laughed. And EJ laughed, but then a chirp stuck in her throat as Terra whispered, "I just received an instruction for you, Elisa. Call open, File 358 in your new Grid 86. I set it for *your* voice and biometrics only."

After sipping more water, Elisa said, "File 358, open." A camera appeared over her wrist device. "I know this!" She reached into the black satchel and pulled out the rectangular camera. Back in the mid twenty-first century, it was the newest device, verbal-based and image driven with instant connectivity to the iCloud and immediate availability on any system. She activated the camera. An entire wall unit opened up behind her, revealing fifty cameras. She touched a few, and remembered specific details about when she acquired them. "That's right! I had them moved here. I paid a company to pick up my things and move some of them here as well as to the disembarkation area. I'm planning to remain on Nelta…I think." Later on, after the ceremony, she could return, activate the devices, and hopefully watch her life story, or at least part of it that might help her and her mission to discover the source of the attacks—the alien invasion—stop the attacks, and free the crew. But the Mind Meddling technology continues stealing events from peoples' minds! The consequence is an altered crew! Then, another memory welled into her consciousness…an evil, chomping entity, slowly eating up minds. "People needed to be found. They're desperate for help," she whispered, trying to slip out of her daze.

"Special movers helped you then, and after I stream back into a special grid," EJ whispered, looking suspiciously around the room, "I can get more help."

"Who helped me back to life in the first place?" Elisa asked.

"273 movers," EJ replied. "That's how you got back to your body, 273."

Again, Elisa felt faint, but fought off a descent into unconsciousness by pacing the floor. "No way…this *ain't* happening to me…no way!"

"But it is," EJ said in a light and buoyant voice.

Elisa ran right up into Terra's yellow projection field. EJ was fluttering by the ceiling hub; and at any moment, would disappear high into the processor. "So what do I do now?"

"Keep following me," EJ replied.

"Follow you where?"

Terra finally had File 358 as a ball of images in her hand. One by one the images began forming a picture. "You left yourself this message…and 273added to it."

Elisa felt like smacking Terra. "Everyone keeps mentioning that group…and EJ said they saved me! Who exactly inside 273 save me?!"

Another image formed in front of Elisa as Terra's hologram filled with static. The interference was intensifying, and EJ appeared to become progressively more anxious with her bird-waving gestures. Someone *might* have discovered her location, and Elisa had only seconds to communicate with them.

"To stop the attacks and help the crew, you'll have to unite Terra-IV's Live Stream Field on Level-9 with a special code inside the Cloud Matrix on Level-7. I am Terra-III. I helped you, but I cannot help you any longer."

Then Elisa remembered that *this* Terra-III was only temporary. This Terra had re-activated only to help out of a murderous situation. She would never see *this* Terra again. She felt powerless, until she rubbed her left arm, a reminder of the opposite: she could make a big difference and possibly help the Neltans if they were in trouble, especially if she could secure a place among Thornton Manning's Expedition-1. But other saving deeds had to come first! "How can I ever infiltrate Level-9 or Level-7? Level-9 is Terra-IV heart and 7 is her brain! Besides, making the kind of connection you're talking about could take days, or weeks. And I have to consider mining The Archives for information. The Archives are like Terra's nervous system, where every image is processed and routed. I don't have enough time to intervene before another attack...time someone might kill me," Elisa gasped, and then plopped down on her cot. "The security at both places is astronomical...and I don't have clearance. Furthermore, I'm sure people are stalking me." She remembered the strange man on the Maglev, the one who had reported Ernie to The Regents. What he was, she had no idea—human, robot, or clone—but he and others like him would be dangerous obstacles, for they had to be the eyes and ears of someone powerful. Ultimately, The Regents are at the top of the food chain, the ones responsible for her death and Emma's death, and perhaps the deaths of others.

"But you also have friends who will help you...friends you don't even know yet, like me," EJ said, cheerfully. "You are the answer!" She pointed one of her human-bird wings at Elisa.

Then Elisa remembered an update she had programmed three days ago. It had assigned her Kiosk 193-G as a secret base from which she could investigate strange visions people were claiming to see everywhere throughout the astrocity. And if not for *this* Terra-III diverting all her personal information, arranging 273 to empty out her old Living Cube, and EJ keeping her safe from all those attacking creatures, she might not be here. She sighed in relief and wiped tears off eyelids. "Thanks, EJ…Terra. I owe you two my life. So I'll trust you…trust that you'll help me when I need help to stop whatever is happening, and save me along the way."

"I'll be there to guide you when you need me," EJ began. "I'll be watching…and searching for the special code you'll need when you arrive at the Live Stream Field." Her little blue body sagged in obvious disappointment. "That's going to take some work though—whew! 'Cause I have enemies too," she chirped. "But I gotta go now, or I might die, again," EJ said. Then her bluebird form disappeared into the ceiling hub processor.

Elisa still had Terra-III. Not for long. She felt suddenly dejected, her energy fading as she glanced at the time. "I have to appear in three-and-a-half hours for a ceremony. I can't make it to Level-9 and then Level-7. And I have limited technology."

Before Terra disappeared, she whispered, "Sleep, Elisa. You do have a special technology." Elisa understood her. She had innate Neltan technology inside her, strengthening. Terra's repeating song was lulling. "Your alarm is set for 12:30 p.m."

Elisa felt herself falling asleep. "That's just enough time to get dressed and leave. Then, I'm goin' right up to Level-1 and after the Choosing Ceremony, confronting Thornton Manning! Thanks, Terra…bye."

# J.P. Osterman

## Chapter 21 – Choosing Ceremony

Disembarking on Level-1 at 1:20, Elisa spotted a Terra avatar holding a sign with her name of it. As she walked to meet it, she felt sentimental about the past and a hint of regret about leaving *Sagan*. This is my favorite place, she thought.

Architects built this small Ceremonial Platform at the heart of the four religious centers to replicate a Roman stadium with cushioned bleacher seats. A half-a-mile above it, a section of the dome ceiling was transparent to the rainbow contrails outside *Sagan*. It stands at the bow of Level-1 and has the only view into space and *Sagan*'s spacefolding trajectory. Residents must to purchase tickets three years in advance to gain access.

Then she overheard an Enforcer say that The Regents ordered them to increase their numbers at the Ceremonial Platform. They were on the lookout for 273 members, whom people accused of attacking Level-6 although no one had any proof.

Following the Terra avatar, she met up with the twenty other candidates, and they began walking down a long red carpet toward a semi-circular stage. On both sides of the carpet, people were cheering them on, their avatars hovering around them and over them to record them for a rendering. High above UAVs and patrolling Enforces on disc-shaped hovercraft continued monitoring the entire Ceremonial Platform area that looked like a small stadium.

Sizing up the huge cheering crowd while also noticing processor hubs at two major thoroughfares that had to contain the illegal Mind Meddling technology, she shivered in fear of their cognitive snatching capabilities. People were walking under them. Their minds altering! She lifted her wrist device and quickly captured one picture. She'd see Thornton Manning soon, and would confront him. Most likely, he or another Regent would realize that she was unaffected by it, and she'd have to divulge more about her strengthening abilities, her Neltan and human biology. She'd have to maneuver away fast so he couldn't capture her and try killing her again—if her biology is what he was after in the first place. She still couldn't remember all the details.

She then stopped to watch pedestrians walk unaware right under a droning processor hub. *I can't stand seeing this and not doing something!* She whispered into her outdated wrist device: "From now on, conduct an intermittent, 360° photo shoot of everywhere I step until you finish photographing *all* the hub processors. Work off peoples' avatars too since they have visual access to this entire level. When you finish, compare and match the pictures with the old hubs." A slice of her wrist device glowed green and began increasing in diameter. When the pie completed, she set in an icon to send in Confidential into her grid.

She then remembered her mission to save the crew: She'd have to link Terra IV's Live Stream Field on Level-9 with an unknown program at Terra's Cloud Matrix on Level-7. This Choosing Ceremony would be the first step in gaining access to Level-9. But she'd need help, and more verification of illegal tampering with technology. *If I can gather enough concrete evidence, even though people are being blinded from noticing it, I'll be able to broadcast proof to the crew.*

"This place is so full of people that I can feel the floor vibrate!" she said to one of the candidates behind her who had noticed her outdated wrist device and was snooping. Elisa was trying to distract her before Enforcers would notice her concern and descend to investigate. "I hope it doesn't collapse!" She covered her ears and pushed her wrist device under her cuff.

"My informational tells we're safe," the woman said, her avatar's eyes flashing white. She introduced herself as Dr. Debra Pickering, a Cartographer qualified for Expedition-1 since she had helped generate a map for humanity after First Communication Day. "Currently, there are ten thousand, five hundred, and twenty-two people on Level-1, but only half of them are here at the Ceremonial Platform. We're safe."

The stadium-sized area has a rendering of a manicured landscape; and beyond a park and garden is The Regents' regal, triple-door entryway to their private quarters. Seeing the doors that have the appearance of castle gates, she remembered what Ernie had said: his wife Beatrice was last seen delivering special flowers there. Before that, she believed the gates were creative illusions. Now they appeared like an entrance to a frightening medieval dungeon.

As she continued to follow the line of candidates toward the center of the Ceremonial Platform, she waved at some people who had called out her name.

How do they know me? she wondered. Perhaps the Mind Meddling technology not only alters thoughts but also imprints images into minds! Or they could be people I helped during the attacks and I can't remember all of them.

At the end of the long red carpet, she saw the candidates ahead of her begin climbing up a stairway as the famous newscaster, Dirk Hunter, waved them onto a large center stage. The farther she moved from the crowd, the more she could see into the distance, at the far edge of the Ceremonial Platform. There were history kiosks under action-packed banners, with signs and waving avatars trying to attract customers to participate in renderings. She remembered entering one kiosk on her left a few years ago. It was a rendering of the Hindenburg, with the virtual experience ending prior to the Zeppelin's explosion.

Climbing the stairs behind Dr. Pickering, she heard a Maglev hiss loudly—its rails screeching to a halt on Bow Station's electro-magnetic clamps. The station was two hundred feet away, but the settling sounds of the rails and currents were like cracking lightning. She gasped, jumped a bit, and then stopped, dropping her backpack. Two candidates behind her nearly fell down the bottom steps.

"Sorry!" she apologized. The two scowling candidates scurried ahead of her, and she lost her place in line. "Oh well," she exhaled. "That noise was sure different from the *other* Maglevs."

The candidate behind her said: "That's because it's The Regents' *private* shuttle. You act as if you've never heard it."

Grabbing the handrail and feeling dizzy, she steadied herself as a gray-clad Enforcer glided down and maneuvered in front of her. He had on a black visor. She couldn't see his eyes but wanted to stop his inquisitive stance. "I'm all right!" He quickly glided away.

The candidate behind her picked up her backpack and handed it to her. It also contained the black satchel she had found, and water and a few snacks. "After the crew chooses two scientists for *Expedition-1* to Nelta," he began, "the winners will get to ride in that car down to Level-9 to begin preparing and training for it."

She thought of all her cameras in the secret anteroom at Kiosk 193and how she needed them to help her with her memories. And she remembered EJ! Could EJ, in bluebird form, infiltrate all the way down to Level-9 to help her? She needed to go there anyway as a first step on her mission, but she never realized she'd be leaving so fast and possibly not be able to contact EJ and warn her. "Don't we get time to pack if we're selected?" she asked him.

"Nothing to be terrified about," the man replied through a puzzled expression. "This is an opportunity to become famous...uh, what's your name?"

"Doctor Elisa Holton." She shook his hand. "Elisa."

Tall and lean, the man had bushy white hair, bright blue eyes, and pale skin that appeared untouched by sunlight. Every now-and-then, he blinked in rapidly, most likely from being cooped up inside his living cube and avoiding *Sagan*'s full-spectrum lights. Elisa called people like him, Photon Phobic. "What's your name?"

"Doctor Walker, but just call me Walker," he replied, reeling a bit, obviously reacting to Elisa having sized him up. He had on a black suit, a shirt with small antique cars, gold cuff links, and white tennis shoes with bright green socks. He appeared washed out—unrecognizable if not for his bright style. "If you're a winner today, Elisa, you might be able to procure a political position if you decide to stay on Nelta, or a lucrative production deal. You could make millions!"

The woman in line in front of them turned around. "That's what *I'm* hopin' for!" At the edge of center stage, Enforcers had stopped all the candidates. They were searching the small orchestra pit, really a media area where reporters and rendering specialist had set up their equipment. "I'm so excited! Aren't you?" She was giddy, chattering to everyone who would listen to her.

Elisa didn't want to encourage her to talk a mile-a-minute. She was feeling nervous, even though her special Neltan-driven powers were giving her more confidence; but only after quiet moments, drinking water, and nibbling on protein energy bars. Still, the idea of competing against people was anxiety wrenching. "Money and fame won't be the same on Nelta as they are here I'm sure," she told the chatty woman.

"This is only the *third* appearance The Regents have made since Lock Out Day," the woman said. "I can't wait to meet them! I hope they let us shake their hands. Ya think they'll let

# Astrocity Sagan

us shake their hands?"

When Elisa finally saw the woman's eyes in the bright stage light, she stumbled back. One of her eyes was deep blue, the other half-blue and half-hazel. "I've seen this condition before," she whispered back to Walker who steadied her. Suddenly, a memory welled up: She had just finished work and was on her way to inform The Regents of her discovery of a mutation in the Regeneration process. She remembered catching *that* Maglev, the one that had *just* docked. Almost fainting, she gasped as another memory flowed through her mind: Someone was suffocating her...and then sedated her. Her arm began aching through the returning memory as she recalled Thornton Manning's face, again! He wanted her dead, and she needed to know why. This was the *second* time she recalled him murdering her! She began seething with vengeance, and she felt an ion current whip all around her into the air! High up, she saw a spark ignite under the view of their spacefolding wormhole.

"What the hell was that?" Walker asked.

"I don't know," Elisa lied, tripping a bit up the steps.

Walker propped her up and then quickly let her go. "Wow!" Obviously, he had felt that strong electricity and got a slight shock. "Why did you trip? Ya skip breakfast? Maybe *I* did, 'cause it sure feels suddenly cold in here," he giggled in a shivering gesture.

"No, I'm fine, just thirsty," she said, smoothing back her bangs. She took out a bottle of water from her backpack and began hurriedly drinking it. *What the heck just happened? I can't be interacting with light now, can I? I hope this water stop it from happening again!*

The woman with the heterochromatic eyes turned around with a serious look on her face. "Yes...what *is* wrong, Dr. Holton? And whataya keep lookin' at me for?" Her tone of voice sounded dangerous. Her jaw appeared clenched in anger, and her face had a yellow tinge. She was a light-skinned black woman with red hair, and her face was shimmering from her glitter makeup. She looked strikingly beautiful, and had to be brilliant for Terra-IV to have chosen her as one of the candidates. "Well, what's wrong?"

"Your eyes," Elisa replied, hoping the woman might know about her heterochromia.

"What about my eyes?" she grimaced, walking up another stair. She began waving her hands in front of her face as if shooing flies, but there were no insects, only the flow of a slight breeze.

Walker stepped between her and Elisa. "Hey, Doctor Chermont, no need to be so competitive. Or are you *trying* to get Dr. Holton to flub up? 'Cause if she does, *she'll* lose and everyone will vote for *you*." He said into Elisa's ear, "Strategy…*that's* what's in play here."

I'm not a cynical person, Elisa thought, but I wonder what's motivating Walker, and what strategy *he* has in play to win? Hearing Dr. Chermont's condescending huff as she turned toward the front of the line, Elisa brushed off her skirt and walked up another step. "Thanks, Walker but didn't you get a good look at her eyes? I'm seeing a lot more cases of heterochromia."

"Heterochromia," he repeated. "I never noticed, but then again, I haven't been out much," he laughed.

"Well, *I've* noticed," Elisa exhaled. "It's becoming like an outbreak, Walker."

"That bad?"

"Yes!" Then she toned down her voice. "This morning, on Level-6, during the attack, I—"

"You were there and saw that?" he interrupted, inspecting her from head to toe.

"Sure did."

"My God!" he exclaimed. "Matrix Techs and Systems Analysts are conducting all types of scans to discover the culprits! Did a prankster cause the attack? Or that new protest group…I think they call themselves 273?"

She recalled EJ's words. Someone from *273* had saved her

and brought her back to life; and someday, she hoped to thank the person. She wanted the word to start spreading that they had to be good and not destructive. "I don't know, and no one knows, but if *273* want to enact some *real* damage, they woulda done it by now. So I can't believe they're out to hurt or kill people. Someone else caused that light-based attack," she replied. She had another thought: Perhaps on her way to Level-9 and Terra's Live Stream Field, she might encounter the ones who'd saved her.

Walker's blue eyes suddenly rounded. "Hey—if *you* survived *that* wild light-based attack, people will most likely choose *you* as one of the two who'll scout Nelta! You're a survivor, Elisa." They were last in line now, and Walker called out to a few individuals in the crowd: "Hey—this is Doctor Elisa Holton! She survived the nanyte invasion!"

"Shhh, stop it," she said, feeling her cheeks redden. *This is not what I need right now, Thornton Manning seeing me when I want to surprise him.*

Yeee-*a*-ah!" Walker cheered. People were recording her on their device, and their avatars' eyes were flashing green, capturing the scene. Later on, she'd be all over the astrocity as a picture invitation for people to experience virtually the Choosing Ceremony.

She whispered into her wrist device, "Make sure my Grid 86 is buffered and all mail diverted to a matrix-dumping site." It flashed green in compliance.

"Did a light-based nanyte attack you, Doctor Holton? If so, how did you survive?" a woman shouted. She had left her family, broke through the crowd, and managed to get close enough to touch Elisa. "I was a half-mile away from there, at the Hungarian center when the invasion happened. When representatives from the other 195 countries heard, we dropped everything and headed home to our families."

"Communications were down for minutes," another woman added. "A strong interference interrupted the *entire* matrix. We were like dead in the water!"

"The anomaly scared half the residents," a teenager boy said. "I thought *Sagan* dropped out of spacefold flight and left us stranded!" He showed Elisa a special Navigation scene playing over his wrist device. *Sagan* had just entered another wormhole conduit. She recalled Ernie's words. He works for Navigation. He said there would be *no* other wormhole trajectory. The last wormhole conduit was supposed to deposit *Sagan* at the edge of Nelta's solar system. Then it would be only a week until touchdown on Nelta. Another conduit trajectory sounded wrong. Is it a temporary detour so *Expedition-1* can launch and scout the planet while *Sagan* goes in circles? The boy began showing her images of the nanytes trying to topple Enforcers off their hovercraft. "I think they're trying to kill people!"

"Now, Frankie, some *273* prankster was probably just manipulating the lights to make their point," his mother chastised.

"What point is that?" Walker asked.

She wrinkled her nose and shrugged. "I don't think anyone knows yet."

After calming down the crowd with his loud speaker, an Enforcer moved people away from the stage, and Elisa said, "The nanytes didn't hurt anybody though."

"But they *did* do some serious damage," the teenager called out, showing her sliced up and disheveled props and artificial scenery that Maintenance was still repairing at Gathering Area-1.

A man asked, "Has anyone found Emma Jane Wright yet? When they do find her, maybe the attacks will stop."

Elisa didn't want to disappoint him by telling him the truth about EJ. He would never believe her anyway; and divulging a morsel of truth now would only lead to panic. She needed more time, and evidence.

Another man screamed over an encroaching Enforcer: "I own the Detect and Untangle Agency on Level-3 just outside the beverage factory." She tried to see him through the bright light. She recognized his Australian voice but couldn't match it to a face. "Come visit me, Doctor Holton! I can use your help since you defeated the light-based nanytes. Come visit my shop!"

Looking through an ocean of cheering people, she suddenly spotted several Regents step off the docking platform. "Here they come," she said to Walker as she filled with determination to seek justice for his attempt to kill her. Floodlights illuminated the tops of their heads. Music played. People were applauding—their avatars morphing into colorful banners of support for them and enthusiastic sayings, such as, *Nelta or bust*, and, *We're Almost There*! It wouldn't be long before The Regents would climb up the stage and she'd be face-to-face with them. *Good, 'cause I've got some serious words I'm gonna whisper into Thornton Manning's ear. To ever think he was my friend—huh*! She felt like spitting in his face. *Now that would really make history*!

Walker suddenly grabbed her elbow and pulled her next to him. "I just did a search of that guy's Detect and Untangle business through my secure 107 Grid, Elisa. Watch out."

"Why?" she asked through the droning of Enforcer hovercraft cutting through the air in crowd-control formation.

"My avatar sent me information no one else has access to. I'm in the Technological Procurement business, and I know *everything* about *every* business profile. See?" A tiny hologram appeared over his wristband screen. He flicked his hand, and the numbers 273 materialized inside a white light under the man's Detect and Untangle license. "I think the business is a front, and the employees are *273* members." He showed her the logo of a graphic unraveling a binary code, also the company's active description. "It's *273*'s way of staying connected to the *Sagan* and the population without living among us so they can keep track of everything that happens." After she read all the information on the company that appeared inconclusive, he added, "My avatar automatically monitors even the most secret of matrix grids because of my job."

"What exactly do you procure, Walker?" she asked, again trying to allay his fear. They had saved her. Still Walker might be able to help her in the future as well as Ernie Bentley whose address she had neatly tucked inside her backpack.

"I'm always on the lookout for new stuff," he began, "and mediating between The Regents and businesses to license their technology for public use." He looked from side-to-side, obviously fearing the Enforcers, until the crowd cheered. "I'm a sort of spy...a good spy, trying to make an honest living."

Another loud cheer and echoing applause resounded through the Ceremonial Platform. The Choosing Ceremony was about to begin with Dirk Hunter as Master of Ceremonies. He was now at center stage and entertaining the crowd with a few jokes as The Regents slowly approached the red carpet in preparation to walk toward him. Ten small Zeppelin suddenly opened their airlocks, releasing confetti, balloons and streamers.

Walker coughed, sniffled, and blinked until his watery eyes. His light phobia was obviously beginning to affect him, and he appeared to be struggling hard to stay. Turning slightly away from all the lights, he said, "I heard through several of my colleagues, that if Enforcers even suspect someone of being part of *273*, that person gets an automatic Regeneration, even though they mighta just had one." He swallowed hard as his eyes filled with fright. "Talk about a real brain-scramble job, huh, Elisa?"

"For sure." She felt speechless, but Walker was adding to the mystery of why EJ might now be a light-based bluebird. She knew secrets, Top Secret information she must have been leaking to people, perhaps *273* members who were obviously waiting for the right moment, like she was, to come out of hiding and present a solid case of illegal activity to the crew.

"*I'd* never put myself in a position to get brain scrambled, Elisa." Taking out a wad of Kleenex, he blew his nose and stuffed it into his back pocket.

# Astrocity Sagan

Folding her arms, she said, "I'm a Chief of a Regeneration Corridor, and I can't remember *once* performing a duplicate Regeneration."

He pulled her away from Dr. Chermont who was standing within earshot of them. Then he whispered: "Not even a clone procedure?" He coughed—an accusatory gesture.

She suddenly remembered ordering a clone procedure for Emma. Her arm began aching, and she recalled another memory, this one fearfully riveting. She had seen Emma Jane Wright in a special clone chamber, her body rapidly decomposing. Someone was trying over-and-over to clone her to a specific set of criteria. She gasped, her breath cold in her lungs. Illegal cloning *is* being performed!

"So you *do* have proof of people being cloned?" he asked again, obviously seeing the rapid change in her.

"Shhh," she ordered, lowering her head.

"That's what those light-based invaders are saying is being done in secret somewhere on *Sagan*, Elisa, and cloning is *so* illegal!" He looked white with terror.

She moved him behind others standing in line on center stage. "How do you know all this?"

He shrugged. "I've been surfing the matrix in between jobs."

Glancing over the shoulder of one of the candidates, she spotted a large glowing processor hub in the archway between the station and a rectangular kiosk. Most people pass through the kiosk for information, guidance, or snacks on their way to and from the station. Obviously, it contained Mind Meddling technology; but because Walker worked from his living cube and hadn't stepped outside for quite some time, he had avoided the Mind Meddling machinery interfering with everyone's reality. Mostly likely, he was a rare person.

"Some people are clones and don't know it, Elisa," he whispered. "It's awful! But telling someone'll get me killed...and cloned." He shook his head vehemently. "Not me!"

"Shh," she ordered, "and keep away from Central Kiosk-1." She gestured toward the station.

"Why?"

"Because you'll forget this conversation on your way back to your living cube, that's why," she began, "and I can't have that, 'cause I may need you in the next few days."

"Need me, for what?"

"To help me," she replied as a look of disbelief wafted over his face. "Quickly, give me your exact, 107 grid address." She touched her outdated wrist device to his, but the two different devices failed to interface. Hurriedly, he jotted down his Living Cube number and matrix URL on a piece of paper and thrust it into her hand. Now she had his and Ernie Bentley's contact information. After folding it carefully and sliding it into her backpack, she saw a team of Enforcers approach The Regents in preparation to escort them toward center stage. Again, the crowd cheered and applauded. She didn't have much time to finish her talk with Walker so she could call on him to help her after she'd amass more evidence. This clone evidence was now becoming as important as the Mind Meddling technology! What else were the Regents doing? And where? She felt determination like an energizing potion calling her to accumulate as much evidence she could find to put Thornton Manning away for good. *I'll make sure he pays*!

"I wish I could come up with some type of test to detect a clone," he said. "Believe it or not, last night, I came up with a plan to develop one."

"But then what, Walker?" she asked. "What would we do if we discovered that some people *are* clones?"

He took a little kit out of his pocked and pulled out needle. After sticking himself, a speck of blood oozed out of his finger. He held it out to her, obviously to make a point. "I'd like to know the location of the *real* me. If you were a clone, wouldn't you?"

"Well, yeah, if my original body is not dead," she said. He was still missing the point.

# Astrocity Sagan

"I'd wanna know *why* someone cloned me." He turned serious. "I mean, isn't that why we're here? For a purpose? To champion a cause and make a difference for humanity?" He looked intensely at his red blood. "Can a clone do all that?" He was about ready to suck the little speck of blood off his finger. "The entire DNA of my ancestors is ingrained in this little drop. Everything about me is here…inside the red." He appeared in tune with the things ordinary people take for granted. She had never seen such a touching expression of awe about the universe. Then, his blood dropped to the stage floor, and the self-repair materials soaked it up.

His avatar appeared inch-sized next to Elisa's shoulder. "Doctor Holton, are *you* a clone?" it asked, whispering in her ear.

When she turned to answer Walker's avatar, it popped out of existence as an Enforcer's laser-light weapon shone brightly on it in preparation to fire.

"No avatars on stage, Doctor Walker!" the gray-clad officer hollered, and then glided away on his hovercraft. People heard the warning, and they began talking among themselves as if trying to decide whether to vote for Walker.

He peered down at the stage floor and tapped it with the tips of his tennis shoes. His gesture showed failure and lack of self-confidence. "No one'll choose me for the expedition anyway," he said. Then he perked up. "But would *you* like to have coffee, or dinner, or—*uh-uh*—lunch with me sometime, Elisa?"

She smiled and felt a sharp blush on her cheeks as they stepped back in line with the other candidates. "Well, I guess." Then she remembered Carl Foldier, and recalled a promise she had made to never date again, at least until she disembarked on Nelta. But who did she say that to? After struggling to remember, she recalled what someone had said to her about her previous dating failures. She had an assistant…Nick Burgess! Where was Nick now? She had no idea. Most likely, if she could locate him, he wouldn't remember her. Mind Meddling technology is everywhere, and extracting nano-bits of peoples' minds. She had to divert Walker's attention away from dating her. "Oh, and thanks for de-escalating that situation with Doctor Chermont. It's good to know someone's got my back. For sure, we'll keep in touch. For sure, I'll call you." She tapped her backpack where she had stuck his information. She knew she'd need him when the time was right, if he could escape all the Mind Meddling technology and remember her. He has valuable skills—and has to be able hack The Archives! That's the place she'll need his skills for sure.

The crowd erupted into waves of cheering people as floodlights illuminated The Regents.

"Here they come," Walker said.

Screaming people began rushing the line of Regents—their pounding shoes echoing like a stampede. Another band of Enforcers glided down, lined up high on both sides of the long walkway to protect them.

The line of ten incoming Regents looked like a purple snake in the crowd as they side stepped Enforcers along the red carpet. At the front of the line, she spotted Thornton Manning who had two gold trophies in his hand, one for each candidate the residents would choose for the Expedition-1. High above them, Enforcers were inspecting the dome, waving their detection devices that flashed green for "Clear." A "Red" signal would mean a breech in security, which would mean, as earlier in the day, another invasion. Some Enforcers were positioned with guns and special nets at the tunnel entryways and kiosks, obviously preparing to trap and apprehend *273* members, or anyone not displaying their ticket somewhere on their person.

Children, their parents, and miniature avatars were waving hysterically at The Regents. Ceremonial Platform appeared like a filled stadium with people cheering from cushioned bleachers. At center stage, a spotlight illuminated on Dirk Hunter, the Master of Ceremonies; and his avatar materialized out of a black curtain wearing a zoot suit and a fedora hat.

# Astrocity Sagan

"Ladies and Gentleman," his avatar called, "before I announce the names of the twenty-one candidates, I would like to introduce you *personally* to the Regency." After a flood of applause, Dirk Hunter stepped through his avatar and opened up his arms invitingly. "Lock Out Day is over!"

As cheering and applauding flourished, The Regents stopped at a bright red line, a barrier between them and center stage. They began waving to people from their safe distance.

Elisa couldn't wait to come face-to-face with Thornton. She would not only shake his hand, but shove her very face right up into his. She already had the words planned: *You didn't kill me!*

Suddenly, strings of brightly-colored, hissing-and-droning nanytes began streaming out of the station tunnel and dome lights. They began weaving through the air of the Ceremonial Platform.

The crowd gasped as people in the bleachers ducked for cover. Enforcers began firing at the descending nanytes, but their firepower passed through the light-based entities. "Don't fire up! You'll hit the Observation dome!"

One nanyte cloud began writing orange letters in the sky. As what had happened at Gathering Area-1, virtual creatures and monsters began materializing in midair and touching down among the audience. This time, however, more were appearing; and soon, they'd be tangible attackers! Because there were many more people present here than at Gathering Area-1, many more varieties of creatures were manifesting.

Elisa showed Walker the statistics that her wrist device was compiling from all the creatures and the people they were terrorizing. "Their programs must to be streaming through the Cognitive-Behavioral Relief and Repair hubs and The Archives."

Walker opened up a tracker on his special working grid. "That makes sense. Those hubs are meant to detect criminal activity, but they can also pick up peoples' fears. And you mentioned the illegal technology someone's stuck up there. It's making the nanytes manifestations worse!"

She rendered the blueprints of the legal CBRR technology over her wrist device. "Whoever is launching these light-based creatures into the population is rendering them from spiders, ghosts, monsters, and demons, all peoples' worst nightmares! But they're mutated and deformed." She closed the blueprints.

"It's because The Archives are processing them, and mixing up images with extracted thoughts and fears," Walker added.

She wondered if Terra-IV might be in on the commotion as well. Maybe the matrix is rebelling against illegal technology? It was programmed to do just that after Matrix Techs evolved Terra-III to Terra-IV, after *Sagan* launched from Earth. If Terra was experiencing a counter reaction, the attacks would only become progressively deadlier, like the little boy had suggested earlier. "Well, I can't get at the source of the attacks and until I can infiltrate the Live Stream Field on Level-9." Walker agreed, and lifted up her backpack that almost feel to the floor when a light-based cloud flew over their heads. Furthermore, EJ had to provide her with vital information she'd need very soon. She wondered how she'd ever make it to that Live Stream Field facility and unite EJ's special code to the Cloud Matrix on Level-7!

When Thornton Manning's nine colleagues fell to the floor, Thornton remained tall with his fist in the air. Looking his usual Beethoven conductor self, he called out to Enforcers: "Stop them from transforming! Locate their points of entry!"

"It's a chamber leak that's fueling them, Sir!" an Enforcer shouted back.

Two, giant, gold-gilded eagles solidified in midair and began circling high in the dome, obviously hunting for a specific target. They were glowing gold—laser-light renderings—and their vast wingspans were brilliantly radiating light. All weapons' fire was streaking through them. The eagles began spitting out letters…and words began forming.

"A chamber leak?" Elisa asked, reading them. "What's that?"

# Astrocity Sagan

"I don't know," Walker replied, kneeling so as to hide for them.

More nanytes swept into the Ceremonial Platform, their entryway the transport tunnel. Covering her ears, she screamed, "This place sounds like musicians tuning their instruments! The creatures are using light…and sound…manipulating the four forces and using them in new profound ways!" Metals in the dome made loud slurping noises as clouds of colorful nanytes began absorbing into Smart materials.

"They're becoming part of the ship!" people screamed, dropping to the floor and lying down on the bleachers. Children were crying, their parents consoling them and huddling around them, shielding them.

The nanytes began evolving into all sorts of flying monsters as they turned their hunt on The Regents. Enforcers swooped in to protect them, but the creatures counter maneuvered. Enforcers began falling off their craft. Some were grabbing the edges of their out-of-control craft, trying to hold on for dear life as special nets unleashed, catching them before a dark fall. Still, others pummeled downward, unprotected, where they landed on the floor and began screaming and writhing in pain.

Alarms resounded. Sirens blared. A ship-wide, *Alert-4* activated. *Sagan* could be in potential danger.

Brave people were snapping images and recording the scene on their wrist devices while also calling for help. Matrix connectivity appeared lost—dead—as their avatars stalled and hissed in-and-out of existence.

The eagles' shrieks pierced the surging air, and their talons etched out the final words of their message: *The Answer is at the core.*

Feeling her arm ache while gaining an unexplainable internal strength, Elisa walked to center stage where Dirk Hunter had just shielded himself behind his eccentric cowardly avatar. She stretched out her hand and watched holographic monsters descend into the bleachers. They were emitting ear-piercing cries, terrifying everyone, and blinding people with bright lights. Light, electricity, magnetism and molecules in the air were combining in new ways with Sagan's technology to form a multitude of AI creatures. Even Thornton Manning was backing away from their power, shielding his face from their talons.

Elisa thought she might try talking to the creatures. Her special abilities that had been intensifying the closer they approached Nelta might stop the attack. She couldn't see EJ, but she seemed to have communicated with at least her at Gathering Area-1.

"Are you trying to get people to listen to you?" she asked, talking to a glowing gold eagle that had just stationed itself fifty feet in front of her, obviously to target her or attempt to communicate with her. It shrieked at the other eagle, and they both glided straight at her, stopping ten feet in front of her face, their talons pointing at her. When they lowered their sharp glistening weapons, she noticed they appeared mesmerized. *I should be afraid, but I'm not*, she thought. *So let me try again.* "Instead of terrifying everyone, tell us what you want and how we can make this astrocity return to normal," she said, extending her arm into the air. Again she looked for EJ. Surely, EJ had to be somewhere among all the strange virtual creatures. She wasn't.

A beam of light escaped the eagle's eye and struck her arm. The round dial on her outdated wrist device glowed bright gold, and a glob of white bright nanytes infused into its rim, making her wrist shake, her body vibrate in the powerful exchange. "Ahhh!" she cried, but she felt energized, and experienced a split-second vision: a column of quantum-computing power, light-based but nanyte driven, completely new nano-photonic technology. However, a light-based strand was disconnected from the whole and missing from the Cloud Matrix on Level-7. "That's one of the missing elements EJ had talked about!" she said, collapsing on the floor. Then she felt suddenly exhausted, zapped of energy.

## Chapter 22 – Globbed

More Enforcers fired again on the eagles that had plucked a few officers off their hovercraft. Cornering the fluttering creatures whose wingspans morphed into fifty feet, they fired on the shrieking raptors that exploded into diffusing puffs of black smoke. Their golden sparkling message, *The answer is at the Core*, scattered as glow dust in a powerful wind.

People in the crowd began calling out questions: "What core do they mean?" "The interior of something?" "Some kind of fundamental warning?" "Where could a *core* be located?"

Standing stun-face at center stage, Dirk Hunter smoothed back his shiny hair while his tall lean avatar bobbed up and down, catching white nanyte particles in his teeth, eating them. All the kiosk lights, pole lights, and hub processors began vibrating. The strange nanyte swarms were continuing to disappear and absorb into those components.

"Someone called them off," Elisa whispered to Walker.

"Thanks to you…or this place might be ash," he returned.

# J.P. Osterman

"They're gone, Ladies and Gentleman!" Dirk Hunter called to the settlings crowds, and he began patting down his shiny black overcoat.

People turned their attention to him, sighing in relief, and enjoying the fresh oxygen flowing through high vents.

"*Whew*—is everybody okay?" Dirk shouted. He looked at his shoulder, rubbed it, and exclaimed, "I just got globbed!" He laughed and pecked a few dust particles off his Master of Ceremony's black coat: "Repeat after me, I just got globbed!"

Laughing, a few people repeated, "Globbed."

"That's right. Now say it again!" he called, bouncing a little, and then dancing with a red cane in his hand. He began twirling the stick like the leader of a parade. He was obviously trying to make a joke out of the disturbance as maintenance crews began fixing everything broken and medics began healing injured Enforcers with stem-cell sprays. A few medical personnel were quickly gliding covered bodies into an L-car for quick removal. "No one's dead folks!" Dirk exclaimed. "Injured, but not dead.'

People exhaled in one giant expression of relief.

Hovering next to Dirk, his avatar pointed at a frothy white mound rapidly dissipating into the floor. The mound was really an emission from the advanced nanyte technology that a few white-clothed techs began taking samples of.

"Globbed," the avatar cheered.

A bouncing ball appeared in a large hologram at the top of the stage. As Dirk sang, "Globbed," the audience joined in unison in an uplifting musical round. People rapidly changed from shocked and terrified to laughing in hysterics.

Elisa noticed tiny black and white particles still lingering in the ceiling where Enforcers were trying to capture them with shield nets and laser-light devices. The particles were eluding all confinement; instead, racing around Enforcers' faces, cutting and scraping them. As a large comet with a long gold tail streaked through the lighted dome, she noticed words written in gold: *Emma Jane Wright lives.* The gold beam struck the Regents' private shuttle, reflected off it, and disappeared into the churning ion current of the transport tunnel.

Walker whispered, "I think half of the population is looking for Emma Jane Wright even though The Regents just broadcast she never existed. This doesn't make sense!"

Elisa knew the truth. She had to trust Walker. He had avoided the Mind Meddling technology, so he could help her should she encounter any problems on her journey to Level-9. "Emma Jane Wright is alive," she whispered in his ear as Dirk Hunter continued to entertain the crowd. Looking through the mass of people, she counted eight Regents standing at the center of the Ceremonial Platform, but they were being secured behind a circle of Enforcers. Two were missing? Who, and why? After Walker gasped several times, she gestured for him to stay quiet. "I'm working for her. I call her EJ, and she's alive."

He had an expression of awe on his face. "You've got to be mighty special then, Elisa Holton," he said, blinking wildly, the bright lights again beginning to affect his vision. "Is EJ guiding you to the Core those nanytes wrote out in the sky?"

Watching The Regents who were about to announce the finalists, she replied: "I'm not sure if where I'm going on Level-9 has any type of special core attached to the area." Biting her thumbnail, she added, "The word, *core*, means, *the central or innermost part*. I can't imagine the bottom of the astrocity having any such special compartment." Images began flooding through her mind—again, her arm aching—but she couldn't make sense of them. Perhaps arriving at Level-9 would make them coalesce into a solid memory and understanding.

Walker stepped toward her. "Well, to answer that question, you're gonna have to find the uttermost bottom of *Sagan* then." He huffed out a laugh. "Good luck with that, 'cause from everything that's been happening with the nanyte technology, Terra must be evolving, and fast, in order to figure out how to counter the attack. It's her program."

"I just wonder where the Live-Stream Field is on Level-9. That's where EJ said I have to go."

He suddenly appeared happy. "Oh—the LSF facility is about eight miles into the interior after you disembark from their shuttle." He gestured fearfully at the Regents. "Like I said, Level-9 is the place where the winners will train. If the residents select you, you're half-way to Level-9."

"So if I'm chosen, my job becomes easier," she said, feeling more at ease and grateful for losing her place at the front of the line and meeting Walker. If not, she wouldn't have never have learned so much and also formed an alliance.

"But is Level-9 also connected to some other type of core or facility?" He paused, suspicion washing over his white face. "Only the Regents know."

"How do *you* know about the location of the LSF facility?" she whispered.

"Oh, as you're a Chief Regeneration Specialist, I'm always interfacing with the Regents' and software engineers. I hear a wealth of information concerning genetic programming and DNA archiving when brokering deals."

"The Regents probably need you all the time, and you're probably on-call for most times. Gosh— I thought *I* had it bad!"

Suddenly, Dirk Hunter's avatar waved the twenty-one candidates to the rear of center stage. As colorful floodlights illuminated the men and women dressed in regal purple, a drum roll resounded as Dirk prepared to announce The Regents' names. Dirk Hunter shouted: "*Here* is Executive Regent Manning in person, to present the trophies after I announce the results of the vote!" He paused in a gesture of suspense. "Ladies and Gentlemen...*who* will launch to Nelta?"

People applauded loudly, their gasps of awe and whistles echoing through Level-1. Some people in the bleachers appeared about to faint while a few people stormed the steps of the stage with outstretched hands to touch a Regent. Enforcers ignited shields that stopped them from penetrating the ten-foot safety zone they were maintaining around them.

# Astrocity Sagan

The crowd continued to applaud wildly until Manning put up his hand. "Thank you…thank you, everyone." He had a strong quaking voice, wide-beaming smile, and perfect white teeth. He kept repeating the greeting as he waited for his audience to settle down. For over a hundred years, he still retained the mesmerizing appearance of the wild-haired Beethoven, thanks to the Regeneration process. He had a jutting dimpled jaw, deep brown eyes, and a sophisticated presence in the way he slowly gestured with expressions of style and class. On Earth, he had begun his career at the Russian Academy of Science and Astronomy. After terrorists poisoned the ozone, he soared in world-wide fame as the physicist responsible for contacting the Neltans, humanity's saviors. Thereafter, the world elected him Executive Regent; and in his White House Oval Office, he worked alone, communicating with people only through pre-approved Skyping.

"He looks like Beethoven but moves and talks like Marlon Brando…that twentieth century movie star," Walker whispered to her as Thornton posed in several positions for holographic recordings that appeared behind him but in front of the candidates.

"He definitely likes being center stage…and praised," Elisa said as virtual advertisements appeared high in the dome, stringing out between drones like spider webs. Whoever was not attending had to be watching the ceremony. A Smart bar above the Information Kiosk at the entrance of the Ceremonial Platform was indicating 90% of the population.

Then she noticed a few abnormal advertisements to the far right, their glowing singed corners eaten up by an invisible entity. "The nanytes are still here in full force," she gasped, "and preparing to reassemble all around us!" She showed Walker two 3D posters of Thornton in the distance, now half gone, their fringes bright gold and fiery. Realizing her wrist device wouldn't function with Terra-IV, she asked Walker to record the rapid disintegration and transmit it to Enforcers.

"Nothing!" he said as people continued applauding for more Regents as Dirk Hunter presented them to the crowd. "Everyone's totally clueless to what's happening! Even the Regency. Whata we do? This entire Ceremonial Platform will become bedlam again soon."

"The nanytes are definitely up to something," she said. A cold draft of stinging air hit the backs of her legs. It felt like static electricity. "They're crawling all around here, Walker. You feel them?" Looking down, she saw a stream of light-based fireflies swirling around her legs, keeping their safe distance; and she felt imbibed with strength and energy— empowered.

Walker stepped away from her. "You communicated with them before, but maybe this is their way of communicating with you."

Stepping behind several other candidates and gesturing for Walker to follow her, she repositioned her arms downward, and the bright lines of swarming nanytes glided to the floor where they began hover and glowing, waiting. She thought: *Just stop. Alter to my biometrics and eliminate processor hub frequencies. Then wait...wait until after Thornton Manning announces the winners. Then do what you need to do. Just make sure I get enough of a distraction to travel to Level-9.* She repeated the command, knowing she was connected to them; and they were listening and obeying her.

Glancing at his feet after Elisa assured him he'd be okay, Walker asked: "Doesn't anyone but us notice these things?"

"Nope," she replied, peering at the candidates in front of them and everyone in the bleachers. "I have them synching with my biometrics, and filtering out the processor hubs. Only people not exposed to the Mind Meddling technology can see this. But we're standing behind people, and I'm trying to hide us from full view of the audience."

"Wow, you're actually communicating with the light-based beings!" he whispered. "God, let me continue to be your friend," he joked, as the audience and Regents focused on

# Astrocity Sagan

Thornton Manning and Dirk Hunter. Standard Terra suddenly appeared, stepped between them, and the crowd applauded. With her forefinger outstretched, Terra began writing in virtual letters the results of the vote for posterity: *Dr...*

She gestured for him to look up into the far right bleachers where a few people were pointing at her and snapping photos. "Walker, some people in the audience are also seeing them!" She moved back farther into the shadows, but the light-based nanytes climbing up and around her began glowing as they began attracting photons. She stepped quickly into the stage light.

"If a few people here are noticing them, people who are *not* present at the ceremony must be noticing them as well," he said. "Perhaps they're *273* members...people who have been off-matrix, and like us, avoided the Mind Meddling technology."

As two small transparent avatars began recording the deterioration of Thornton's 3D posters high in the dome, Dirk Hunter stepped alongside him. A yellow floodlight burst on, illuminating the twenty-one candidates.

Feeling blinded, Elisa covered her eyes and gasped, "*Ahhh!*" The nanytes rose around her, encircling her up to her neck. She could feel their curling whips of special electricity and tried to steady her breathing. She was managing to keep them stationary, but couldn't predict for how long. They were intensifying in current and power. "I think they're protecting me," she told Walker. "The closer Thornton Manning comes to me, the more their movements increase."

"Maybe he's *their* enemy too," he said.

Her powerful thoughts could no longer stop their swirling cycles. "What do I do?"

Walker stepped in front of her to keep her from being noticed by the crowd, and his avatar began speaking for him. "The nanytes are processing at the lower spectrum of visible light, Elisa. Stay still. I think they're absorbing your fear...and will feed off all intense emotions." He reached behind him, and Elisa touched his hand, the light-based entities uniting the two of them as friends. His avatar said to her: "If the light-based entities were going to attack people, they would have done so by now. Just stay calm and stand still. If an alarm sounds, this crowd will break out into hysterics. People will be trampled...and given the damage these entities have done thus far, who knows what'll happen to this place then."

"Worse than what happened this morning I bet 'cause the attacks keep getting more intense and destructive. I've got to find out why, and from where they're originating." She inhaled and wiggling her toes for feeling, and then a sense of calm spread through her thoughts.

"What's wrong?" the candidate standing next to Walker asked. "You two have been talking for over five minutes! Terra's about to write the names for the expedition, and then Manning is going to announce them."

A few more candidates exhaled a stern, "*Shhh*!"

Not wanting the nanytes under her control to swarm at them, Elisa stood perfectly still. "Fine."

Dirk Hunter continued to speak: "Last week, Executive Regent Manning announced an expedition to Nelta." Pacing at center stage, he began talking to the crowd as if they were his best friends. "This expedition will land at a protected site, assess the conditions on Nelta, and plant sensors. The Regents have a special crew currently training for this expedition, but they need two more representatives from among our residents." He began walking in front of the twenty-one candidates. "*You* are the top candidates Terra selected for the job." Terra had finished writing only the letters, *Dr*, in two rows, in front of her. Only their names needed filling in.

The crowd stilled. Like someone greeting a relative, Dirk opened his arms and exclaimed: "And here are the special candidates!"

People clapped wildly, their applause clamoring through the Ceremonial Platform like clapping lightning as Terra wrote out the name of the first winner.

# Astrocity Sagan

Dirk Hunter's avatar tapped danced in its zoot suit, and the crowd applauded again.

As the nanytes descended around her feet, Elisa whispered to Walker: "I hope Terra finishes the names soon, 'cause those drones responsible for illuminating the advertisements will send out an alarm very shortly." She gestured at two half-disintegrated ads that were about to disappear from view. At that point, surely everyone would see the attacking nanytes. But what they'd do thereafter, she couldn't discern from the ones protecting her.

Dirk said to the crowd, "Two specialists will accompany a crew already in training right now on Level-9." A drum roll resounded. "And who are your candidates, Terra?" he asked the holographic athletic woman, Standard Terra-IV.

The spotlight veered down the long line of nine other Regents, finally illuminating one of the chosen people as Terra wrote down her name at center stage. People applauded— their cheering reverberating in waves of gasps and amazement. "Doctor Janice Kiplin, Virtual Programmer and Statistician!"

The crowd stood up and applauded in one giant wave, and then people sat down and stilled on the edges of their seats. When Dirk Hunter took her hand, Janice moved slowly forward in strong steps. She was a short athletic woman with long black hair in a ponytail. She had an American Indian insignia on her collar—an outward expression of pride for her ancestry.

"And the other finalist, Terra?" Dirk asked.

Elisa crossed her fingers, closed her eyes, and prayed, "Me—me!"

Walker said: "Me—please!"

"Doctor Elisa Holton, Regeneration Specialist, Biotech Engineer!" Thornton Manning proclaimed. There was a flat sound in his voice and a cold expression on his face as he turned and looked at Elisa. Dirk Hunter appeared shocked and cut off. He was supposed to have announced her name, not Thornton; and the crowd also appeared surprised as a vibrating gasp trickled through the arena.

Elisa felt a shock wave sweep through her body. Staring at Thornton and feeling hot revenge stinging her eyes, she took Dirk Hunter's hand and began walking gracefully toward Thornton Manning. His face was enlarging in front of her now, and she wanted to charge him and slap his cold strong cheek. Even the nanytes trailing low and close to the floor behind her were swarming upward, her anger igniting their direction and intensity. She could feel their stings, and healing powers, at her ankles. Those few people in the crowd—outliers—were loudly chattering, obviously seeing the nanytes and trying to get others to notice them as well. At her thought command, the nanytes would attack Thornton—her enemy, her killer. The closer she stepped toward her hated adversary, the more intense the shadows under his eyes appeared like saucers, reminders of his murderous words and animosity toward her—aversion she still couldn't understand, except that perhaps he needed her body in the future to experiment on her special Neltan properties. When she was within feet of him, and his dismal expression and angry face were the focal point at the end of her short tunnel of revenge, Dirk Hunter quickly positioned her next to Janice. Her anger surging and her heart racing, the noises in the crowd shrank in comparison to the vengeful feelings twisting in her gut for Thornton. *Soon I'll get to him...soon no one will stop me. It's only a matter of time.*

Walker stepped up next to her and hugged her as the other candidates began congratulating Janice and her. The crowd wouldn't stop cheering and applauding, and the entire astrocity was on fire with excitement, the Live-Stream Viewing bar depicting 95% viewership. As Dirk Hunter handed her a special insignia, an *Expedition-1* patch, she realized she hadn't yet greeted Janice Kiplin, the woman she'd soon be attached to like glue on a fast trajectory to Nelta. She was trying to step closer to Janice, but Dirk and a few other Regents had Janice surrounded, congratulating her, and answering her questions. "I'm sorry you didn't make it, Walker," Elisa called back to him as Dirk Hunter pulled her out of line to set her in the lime light. "I'll call you soon! Remember to dodge obstacles—" She glanced upward at the extra-large hubs that obviously contained Mind Meddling technology. "And stay as secluded as possible!"

People were sweeping her away—the nanytes retreating—as Walker called back to her: "Will do! I'll be waiting for your call!" He moved back quickly, making his way off the stage and then disappearing into the crowd.

Nanytes began floating away from her and pecking at the eight Regents. She could no longer contain the light-based entities, and they were swirling into the air, high into the dome. She felt their trajectory and purpose: to call for more and attack. *They're on a particular clock…behaving as if they're on a schedule.* A few clumps of bright-white nanytes were also settling around Dr. Chermont, the woman who disliked Elisa and had intimidated her. The nanytes morphed into a mirror, reflecting her heterochromatic eye.

"Stop it! Go away!" Dr. Chermont ordered. "Help! They're attacking me!"

Suddenly, armies of nanytes escaped the lights high in the dome as the half-eaten banners popped and exploded. People began screaming and racing toward four Maglevs on the transport platforms.

As troops of Enforcers swooped down and tried scattering the nanytes with new laser-light technology that didn't at all repel or disperse them, Elisa watched Dirk Hunter point at more incoming streams of light-based invaders. They were entering through the four transport tunnels where all the currents were processing. The nanytes had evolved, their creator imbibing them with new capabilities to meld with metals. Men, women and children were dropping to the floor in shrieks, cries, and screams of terror. The nanytes hadn't yet killed anyone—except for injuring a few Enforcers and disabling their craft—but a new and more intensified strategy seemed to be imbibing them with objectives and targets. Enforcers on large hovercraft swooped down and began embarking The Regents on their craft toward. Another Enforcer swept down, stopped at center stage, and called: "Dr. Holton! Dr. Kiplin! Hop aboard! I gotta get ya to safety!"

Jumping on his craft, Elisa grabbed Janice's hand; and they glided around a major Mind Meddling hub, where a disfigured nanyte eagle had positioned itself purposely to detour them away from it. If she could find a way to reverse the Mind Meddling, she thought about revamping it to input some sense into Regent Manning, and the others if they too were involved in implementing it on unsuspecting victims. She believed they were. After the Enforcer passed the glowing gold eagle, Elisa secretly gave it the thumbs up signal, and the shrieking mutated bird soared high into the dome where it disappeared into the tail of a virtual comet. There, she spotted EJ, and she quickly raised her hand toward the soaring blue jay. The nanytes that had absorbed into her while she was standing at center stage left her fingertips and flew into EJ, who in turn replied by streaming to her shiny silver nanytes. They entered Elisa's arm and made her wrist device glow silver. It was a message, perhaps the element she'd need when she'd infiltrate the Life Stream Field. After arriving on Level-9, she could activate the message. Hopefully, it would contain the missing piece from the matrix with instructions how to connect those missing elements to Terra's Level-7 Cloud site. Then she could find creator of the nanyte entities, discover why they were attacking Saganites, and stop them.

"Don't worry, Janice, they won't hurt you," Elisa began. "I've had experience with these light-based entities just a few hours ago," she chuckled. She had to see if she could trust Janice. Hopefully, she could since Janice would be accompanying her to Level-9. She only had a little precious time to convince her to trust her! With the intensity at which the attacks were occurring, she guessed they only had a day or so before the light-based creatures would evolve more and kill everyone—men, women, and children. She felt suddenly panicked. Who would do such a thing? *Who* would want to kill everyone and stop *Sagan* for eternity in dead space? Surely not *273*. They'd be killing themselves too. The same for The Regents! The more she mulled over the problems, the more intense the nanytes swarmed. With her thoughts she commanded them to leave her and join the other attackers, permanently.

"I'm glad you can laugh because I sure can't!" Janice's hands were shaking as she swept back her black bangs streaked with sweat. The Enforcer then launched them on a race with another nanyte creature to the other Regency shuttle. The air was whipping chilly as she and Janice clung to the edges of their seats, holding on tightly not to fall.

On their approach to the Maglev, a black-and-gray clad Enforcer with Colonel Insignia had the shuttle barricaded but quickly opened the sliding door. The nanytes were swarming around the transport tunnels. They were amassing energy from which they were growing in numbers in the light, magnetism, and matter-and-antimatter tunnel currents. All types of monsters, creatures, ghosts and demons began appearing and frightening people who were face down on the floor. Other residents were racing to the Maglevs, stampeding the moving walkway, and dashing into every open kiosk. Lightning began striking from the dome, and vibrations resounding. A rumble of thunder made the floor quake as if it crack open and swallow everyone. Everything artificial began exploding with smoke curling through the pungent air.

Elisa and Janice ran inside the empty shuttle and dove into the front seats.

The nanytes are about to break through the safety zone we've manage to hold," the Enforcer helping them said, his eyes obstructed by the thick translucent glass of his protective visor. Behind him, tiny white nanyte globs were circling around the back of his head, obviously eavesdroppers for their

# J.P. Osterman

Creator.

"Elisa! I've been seeing these things for the past hour, and some around you," Janice said through a concerned expression. "Are you all right?" She breathed deeply, as a look of relief moved over her tan sweat-streaked face.

"Yes, I'm fine," Elisa replied, also thinking: Since Janice had noticed the nanytes, she hasn't been exposed to the Mind Meddling technology. Perhaps I can trust her with my mission.

The Enforcer began angrily swatting away several attacking nanyte clusters, and his black-gloved hands appeared scratched to his skin as he continued to hold open the door. "We believe this attack is an assassination attempt on the Regents! Strap in, Dr. Holton and Dr. Kiplin. Hopefully, we can get Terra's matrix back up and functioning. Another pretty bad intrusion seems to have infected it," he huffed. As Janice reeled from the news, he added: "Right now, Terra's off *everywhere* around Level-1, and maybe off-matrix throughout the entire astrocity!" He set the inside control panel that began flashing front-and-center: *Level-9*. Then he left to open up a side panel to input codes manually, change the Maglev's schedule, and clear the way for a rapid descent into the transport tunnel.

# Astrocity Sagan

## Chapter 23 – Janice Kiplin

Shaking, Janice opened her eyes as the oblong Maglev hummed in preparation to launch. The journey would take twenty minutes—a minute of travel per each level, including the spaces between levels. The shuttle suddenly dipped and rocked. A few people were jumping on the enclosing chrysalis that appeared suddenly stuck, unable to sync with the transport tunnel. Their bodies just slid off the chrysalis and back onto the loading platform. Light-based creatures in the forms of vampire bats were flittering around the tunnel rims above and below their Maglev. They were solidifying on the fuel rods in droves, sucking energetic juice from the magnetic/electric current pulsing everywhere throughout *Sagan*. Their Maglev needed that vital juice to launch!

Seeing their escort in trouble, Janice reached outside and grabbed the Enforcer's hand. Together with Elisa, they pulled him into their tilt-awhirl shuttle. He was injured; and if not for her rescue, the wild currents and outer chrysalis would have torn him apart. He began regaining his breath on the landing and their Maglev slowed and steadied. His outside interference had worked! As Elisa helped Janice elevate him, Janice gasped in fright, gesturing for Elisa to look out the murky glass window at the platform filled with panicking men, women and children. "A nanyte cloud just swarmed down and is morphing into a giant masked cowboy!"

Feeling her stinging left arm, Elisa noticed the veins moving like streams of blue flowing-glowing technology. She kept it out of Janice's line of sight and touched the glass window, concentrating on the monster. A transfer of bright-white energy struck the cowboy creature that popped apart in midair, and the nanytes dispersing into the dome.

"Wow—that force looked like it came from this shuttle!" Janice said, glancing around.

"I don't see its source though," Elisa coughed, sitting down, trying hard to direct the nanytes away so they could begin their descent to Level-9.

"The attacks are getting worse, Dr. Holton," Janice said as she offered the semi-conscious Enforcer that he drank voraciously.

"Call me, Elisa, please," she told her while the Enforcer splashed water on his face.

He blurted out his name. "I'm Ben Johnson." He looked ready to collapse, again!

"I feel helpless that we can't do something to get out of this mess!" Wiping away tears, Janice peered out at a thick window into the chaotic world.

Elisa knew she could fend off this attack, but helping everyone else appeared impossible until she could find the Creator of the attacks. "When we make it to Level-9, Janice, I believe we'll be able to help people. We'll be the only ones down there since most Enforcers are defending all the living quarters." As the recuperating Enforcer confirmed her information, she drank some bottled water Janice had tossed to her and then tossed her backpack on the seat next to her.

Outside, the light-based bats suddenly fled their roosting spots as large strange creatures began hoisting screaming people over their shoulders into the tunnels. "They're kidnapping people!" Janice shouted. "What are they gonna do with 'em? My God!" She fell back into her seat and grabbed the safety rail as their car rose again in another attempt to engage with the tunnel's propulsion currents. The countdown began to descent: 01:45.

With renewed strength, Ben Johnson pried open the sliding door, cracked open the chrysalis, and began firing on the creatures above them. "If they stay solid, this weapon will make a difference." He fired, and a hole blew open in one of the creature's legs. "The weapon's new software detects the target's electromagnetic signature and then adapts its fire power to eliminate the target." With thick angry eyebrows, powerful chin, and flushed cheekbones brimming with sweat and determination, Ben checked his wrist device, displaying a special space/time algorithm. He gasped. "The tunnel entrance above us is initiating a dimensional portal!" The portal started as a small shimmering pool of crystal-like water but continued expanding into a circular translucent view into an unseen but very real new world.

"Thank God we're going to descend though, right? I mean, we are, aren't we? Or we'll get caught up in the altering reality!" Janice said.

Then Ben's device projected the total number of operational Maglevs in all twenty-seven tunnels. "All regular shuttles are on automatic shutdown. There are some stuck inside tunnels, but not this one. Only two Regency Maglevs are operational…this one and the shuttle they're using. But if the dimensional portal enlarges—" He gestured with dramatic intensity at the round, bright-white portal above them. "It could suck both Maglevs right into it." Almost breathless, he pointed up and to the left. "The other Regency shuttle is revving over its tracks, so they must be safely inside it, but threatened as we are." After Elisa showed him several alarms blaring outside and ship-wide messages illuminating on ads, banners and AUVs, he added: "*This* disturbance is definitely worse that the others 'cause Terra just sounded an *Alert-3!*"

An *Alert-1* would mean spacefold collapse—and *Sagan* in jeopardy of dying in space. Outside, people were racing to all shadowed areas and cramming crowded places, abandoning their attempt to escape into a Maglev.

After Ben's military avatar appeared in a static image alongside him, he called into his green-flashing neck device: "This is Enforcer Ben Johnson, on Regency Maglev-1. I'm preparing the two candidates for descent to Level-9. We are under attack at Bow Transport-1." He exhaled, and then tapped his neck device that had fizzled off but then reignited after a boost in processing power. Meanwhile, Elisa was concentrated hard, focusing on protecting their Maglev and dispersing the creatures as far away from them as possible. Enforcer Johnson continued: "I need reinforcements ASAP! I we have an active dimensional portal above us on the ascending rim. If we want the candidates and Regents alive, you need to take countermeasures, now!" His avatar began manipulating the round recording piece, but the transmission arrow would not steady.

Janice interrupted. "Now the virtual invaders are taking *two* people into the dimensional portal!"

He grabbed the silver-dollar sized neckpiece connecting him to the matrix and set it over his wrist device to gain power, but the connection remained frozen. Several armed Enforcer crews were lining up in columns at the tunnel entrances and preparing to open up laser fire on the creatures and their dimensional portal. Ben said they also had special weapons— new Smart adaptive guns. "There's no way the creatures can survive with what they're hittin' 'em with," he added with confidence. Enforcer teams launched all their firepower into the creature that turned and began shooting nanyte arrows back at them. Two Enforcers dropped, and the creature picked up another screaming person, set her like a teeter totter on its shoulders, and began slurping into the shimmering dimensional portal. "The creature appears to have targeted that person out of the crowd," Ben said. When he stepped back into the Maglev, he had a shocked expression. "Now the creature has taken *three* people into the portal. I don't get it! It seems these creatures know our technology and can immediately counter. Where the hell did they come from? Who the hell created them?" He wiped sweat off his strong face, paling in surrender.

"I intend to find out, Ben, but first we have to launch outta here," Elisa said, grabbing a rail while still *thinking* down the light-based attackers.

"Now *five* people!" Janice shouted, watching a parade of creatures force screaming people into the dimensional portal. When the last creature fled into the swirling pool of cycling energy, the portal closed. Janice gestured at The Regents' large shuttle facing north two-hundred yards above them. They were about to take a detour.

Elisa wondered where they were heading to, and what that meant for her and Janice in the future on Level-9. "I hope they'll meet us when we dock, or else we'll most likely be quite alone, and on our own." She felt a tremor of fear move through her as a memory welled into her awareness: Would she and Janice *really* be docking on Level-9? A red blaring sign flashed into her mind: *Level-10*. The words quickly faded to black. Falling back in fright, she saw Ben order his military avatar to request further instructions from The Regents personally. The connection was in Wait-mode, but embedded with an *Urgent Reply Needed* as his avatar complied with Ben's request. Then he stuck a special booster button on the side of Janice's wrist device that glowed as the signal booster connected Janice to her personal holosite grid. After he instructed her to monitor her grid for a reply from The Regents, he called, "Go," and tapped the launch button. Janice had her eyes closed as Elisa watched the attack subside outside their thick windows. Then Ben jumped out onto the loading platform just before the chrysalis of protection lowered around their Maglev. The tunnel currents brightened, sparked, and began swirling in propulsion power. The oblong car settled and aligned over its tracks for launch. Over the intense droning and hissing sounds, he called: "The Regents should meet you at Level-9 soon! Take care!" He hit the side of the Maglev in a gesture of a blessing. "See ya both again someday!" He ran across the platform, joining several Enforcers who were calming down shocked people and taking their statements. The Maglev vibrated and then began a rapid descent to Level-9. Gravity quickly stabilized—the sensation of simply sitting—as a time stamp appeared over the car's Informational bar: Twenty minutes. After a relieving breath and strapping in, Elisa handed Janice a bottle of cold water that a robotic dispenser had offered her; and then it quickly receded into the aisle.

"I don't get *why* the creatures kidnapped *those* particular people?" Janice looked up at a small ceiling portal, inhaled oxygen from a flow of fresh air, and then slumped down into her seat. "Why?" She was checking her messages for a reply from The Regents, but still only receiving a *Wait-mode* answer. "At least the signal booster Ben applied is functioning. Where ever we go, we should have enough processing power to get ourselves out of any complicated situation," she laughed, brushing back her sweaty bangs.

"I believe this same attack scenario is happening all around *Sagan*, Janice," Elisa said. She took a protein bar from her backpack, tore off the wrapper, and began eating. Every time she had communicated with the light-based entities, she felt zapped of energy. Water and protein helped her regain strength. Then she noticed her arm, now normal without the bright blue glow of Neltan technology. But the abnormal spread of it was intensifying. She thought, if I can communicate and direct those light-based beings on a small scale, I wonder what I could really be capable of doing. She felt suddenly frightened and sick. Am I human? Who and what am I? She peered over at a contemplative Janice, still drinking water and recovering from shock. Luckily, Janice hadn't seen her abnormal abilities, or she might have accused

# Astrocity Sagan

her of being a new type of robot! As they would be spending more time together, at some point, Elisa realized she'd have to tell Janice everything about her. But first, she had to prepare her for the truth, slowly.

"Wow—I'm surprised you can eat at a time like this, Elisa Holton," Janice exclaimed. "But I better too." She took a fruit bar Elisa handed to her. "Ya never know when we'll be able to eat, or sleep again." She began slowly eating.

Then, Janice's tiny avatar clad in a white lab coat with black rim glasses vibrated on, appearing in front of her. "There is an intense stream of energy being emitted from the center of Level-9, but dropping…into a deep well—" The avatar then disappeared, its signal disrupted by a flash of bright-orange light.

"That's the location of Terra's main processor. But dropping into a well? The core that creature talked about a while ago?" Janice raised her arm in an expression of wonder. She began whispering the word as if conjuring a spell and then exclaimed, "That's what those creatures were talking about…a core! I bet we'll get close to finding it. Then we can stop them."

Elisa scooted closer to her, their tunnel descent now rapid. "*Someone* has to be programming in those areas and causing the light-based nanytes to assemble into Self-Aware creatures…sentient beings. Such an evolution in transformational optics and quantum processing didn't happen by chance from anything inside Terra."

"Neltan technology then," Janice said.

"But I believe some form of biology, organics, is at the heart of the creatures." She touched her arm—feeling a strength move into her chest and neck.

"You're right, Elisa!" Janice said, experiencing a breakthrough. "Perhaps organic technology." Her eyes appeared to be reading a newly discovered equation. "Transformational optics capable of manipulating light and quantum-processing capability is colliding on the nano-level to produce *real* entities!" Her avatar suddenly rematerialized in fuzzy reception. "Can't you pick up anything from Level-9?" Janice asked it. "If so, Elisa and I can locate a hot spot, and after we dock, we can get to the place, investigate, and try to stop all the attacks."

"One program is a subversion directive from Earth," Janice's avatar said in a squeaky voice. It illuminated a circular algorithm—alien to the avatar's translation and thus alien to Terra-IV.

Elisa saw her wrist device glow. It definitely recognized the program and quickly began deciphering the code. "Someone is working this outdated device from somewhere to help us."

"I hope whoever it is, is onboard *Sagan*, and not outside," Janice trembled.

As more compressed code solidified into comprehensible words over her wrist processor, Elisa turned the circular frame, and words clarified. "It's in the Neltan language…but not a modern translation. It's half-hieroglyphic, ancient Neltan, twenty-five percent modern Neltan, and twenty-five percent something else."

Janice's avatar added lines of compacted codes containing every language on Earth. A sudden translation appeared. "This signal from Level-9…or some other deep location…is piggybacking in a Fractal Pattern of Interference so that no one can detect and eliminate the message."

Reading the translation again, Janice and Elisa said simultaneously: "It's a thousand-year-old Neltan Failsafe!"

For seconds, Elisa tried to recall a Failsafe code but couldn't even though she was involved with the earliest communications with the Scientific Committee on Nelta. She felt stymied. "A Failsafe to stop what? We would have *known* about a failsafe if someone had implanted one! Everything we programmed, or the Neltans programmed into Navigation, everyone knows about, and we're automatically informed if any changes are made along the journey."

"Are we really?" Janice asked askance.

# Astrocity Sagan

A Terra conductor hissed on at the front of their shuttle. She was Standard Terra dressed in a shiny blue and white uniform. "Doctor Holton," she nodded at Elisa, "and Doctor Kiplin, please remain seated. Help yourself to refreshments..." She continued her speech on safety as the automated server wheeled over to them, cranked left and right, and offered vials of drinks and packages of food. Elisa dismissed the robotic dispenser; but Janice grabbed several drinks and food bars, and then quickly gestured for the server to leave. Terra ended her speech: "We will arrive at Level-9 in fifteen minutes. Please remain seated, and I will be at the exit upon disembarkation to direct you to your processing point." She disappeared.

"Wait!" Janice called. "We have questions and need answers!"

As she slumped back down into her plush seat, Elisa felt anger coursing through her, "Obviously, that message was preprogrammed for us, and not a question and answer session."

After a slight chuckle, Janice's brown eyebrows forked a bit in agitation while her green eyes continued to show gentleness and sustained calmness. She obviously had an unshakable personality in the midst of encountering unpredictable situations. Her steady collected nature had to have been fostered as a natural way of life—most likely learned from her parents and Native American cultural practices. She asked: "But why a Failsafe now when every protective measure to secure our mission to Nelta is on-schedule and being directed by the Living Breath Entity?"

Elisa listened to her postulate answers; and when she saw Janice embroiled in turmoil, she took compassion on her. It was time to tell Janice the truth, take her chances that she'd sympathize with her and keep everything about her Neltan biology and her lost three days confidential. Rolling up her sleeve, she showed Janice her powerful left arm flowing with nanyte technology. "I have some things I have to share with you," she began. She let Janice touch her skin in an examining gesture, and Janice told her that her entire body most likely had changed. Her biology was human but also Neltan. "They're billions of years more advanced than us, so who knows how they've managed to alter themselves. Now *you're* part Neltan. Cool!"

The more she divulge, the more relief she felt. "And my abilities appear to be protecting me with a shielding technology. I can communicate with the light-based creatures."

"Maybe you can even communicate with the astrocity itself! Or the Living Breath Entity!" Janice said, eating a bite of food while appearing enamored of Elisa's future possibilities.

"Only time and experience will tell," Elisa said laughed. Then she explained to Janice the gaps she was experiencing in her memory and the start of her problems three days ago. She told her what she could remember: from her close relationship with Thornton Manning during First Communication Day, to her encounter with the Neltan Encantado technology that had wrapped around her arm and infused her with her unexplainable powers. "I'm only beginning to discover and use what's developing inside me, Janice." Exhaling, she felt suddenly drained, and Janice gave her more water. Water was definitely having resuscitating and healing properties. But she had finally told someone her secrets, and the truth. But what would Janice do now? Possibly report her behind her back? One thing she knew for certain: she hadn't had a close friend in years. Experiencing unlimited virtual worlds had almost replaced the need for human contact and friendship. Janice appeared quite opposite—at easy in initiating conversations and being authentic. *I can definitely learn quite a bit from her, and maybe trust someone again.*

"Wow, Elisa," Janice said, impressed. "This is powerful stuff you've been dealing with, and coping with...and all alone." A glow of sympathy appeared in her tearing eyes. As their Maglev rocked and the aerodynamics of its fission-fusion engines decreased in preparation to stop at Level-9, she said, "The failsafe we intercepted, like your dormant powers, Elisa, might be similar to a dormant virus that's suddenly come to life." She tapped her full lower lip in deep thought. "But why did it activate now? That's what we have to figure out…and where it's coming from—"

"And who's responsible for it, so we can stop it." Elisa thought of the new *273* group, and told Janice they had saved her life. She told her about EJ, the missing woman who was still very much alive, but changed, and now one of the virtual entities. With a perplexed expression of being suddenly overwhelmed with shocking information, Janice huffed in deep breaths and checked her wrist device for an update on the protest group's activities. Nothing.

"They couldn't be responsible for the light-based attacks and disturbances anyway," Elisa countered, "because they haven't announced any answers as to what the *core* is or its location. Their purpose seems focused on keeping people alive, not dead, and exposing illegal activities, not developing illegal technology." She quickly told her what she could remember of Thornton Manning trying to kill her; but the group had saved her, even though she couldn't recall their names or faces except for the strangely dressed people she'd seen on a Maglev with Ernie Bentley. "Oh, he works in Navigation! Send him what we've discovered. Maybe he can keep us on standby and help us out when we arrive." She took Ernie's information out of her backpack and handed it to Janice who called on her avatar, told it about the failsafe, and asked Ernie to investigate any type of anomaly or abnormal code. Janice added, "But Elisa says to make sure you stay away from the large processor hubs at all the stations' entrances and exits! They extract memories…and you might never retrieve them as they slowly steal away your identity…your very soul!" She sent the message.

A return icon displayed Ernie's grid homepage and a

confirmation icon. He had received it, but not read it.

"He's probably at work on an emergency, and most likely involved in discovering solutions for the attacks." There was a Post It rendering at the bottom of his Return icon: *01:57*. It was now 3:59 p.m. He might not read all his hails until well after 6 o'clock tonight. Elisa wondered where she and Janice would be at that time. They might really need Ernie!

"I feel so jittery when I'm forced to wait," Janice said, jokingly.

Elisa felt suddenly under pressure. "If the dormant Failsafe is now a spreading virus that's manifesting as those virtual invaders, *everyone* could die in hours if we don't locate the source and stop the attacks."

Janice stretched her legs and wiggled in her seat. She was obviously trying to get comfortable but feeling squeamish. "Well, because I worked on calculating statistical data for the past few weeks, I surmise the data I input into my wrist device will show that this Fractal Pattern of Interference—this Failsafe—evolved because of some type of ship-wide glitch or serious problem. What kind of glitch or problem? I don't know…but I'm angry as hell and wanna find out!"

"Me too, and we're gonna do just that!" Elisa calmed down and began eating some more of her energy bar. After disembarking, they might not have time to take a break for hours! Janice reassured her they wouldn't starve by showing Elisa the food she'd stuffed in her backpack and pockets. Elisa said: "I'm fine, but I did lose three days' worth of memory after my Regeneration on Monday. I'm hoping anything—something!—can help me recall the pieces I seem to have forgotten." She leaned back in her seat as the Maglev's clamps descended in preparation to dock, and currents outside sparked in a decrease of fuel exchange. "I know Regent Manning tried to kill me, but people saved me." She breathed, striking the frosty glass in frustration as Janice touched her arm in a sympathetic gesture. "I want to remember. I've been trying so hard to remember! Even EJ's been helping me…and she's a bird!" She wiped tears out of her eyes, and then heaved in a breath of resolve.

Leaning across the aisle, Janice touched her again in a compassionate gesture. Then Elisa noticed three strands of small beads under her round neck processor. By the colors, the ensemble was obviously an outward expression and constant reminder of her Native American Indian culture.

Janice touched them in response and the beginning of a sad story shone in her eyes. "After my regeneration two years ago," she began softly, "I forgot my husband and three children for *three* weeks before an Enforcer found me lost and wandering in the Engine Room on Level-4." She called on her avatar, and it began projecting the information surrounding Janice's attack of amnesia: September 30, 3025, Real-Time; followed by a moving image of a dazed Janice standing next to a giant, contained, glowing column of propulsion power. Beneath the information were Janice's list of ancestors, one being Joyce Dugan, the first female elected chief of the Eastern Band of Cherokee Indians. Janice said to her tiny avatar dressed in authentic Cherokee costume, "Please send my husband my standard greeting," she sighed with longing in her green eyes.

"Yes, Janice," her avatar replied as its eyes flashed green.

"And tell him I love him…moon dream to sun beam," she added, pressing tears out of her eyes.

"What?"

Janice blushed. "That's what we call each other now when we message, especially after having experienced something as terrible as getting lost, and having no recollection of who I was and where I lived."

"Wow!" Elisa said, feeling hopeless, and unable to help the woman who had obviously experienced a terrible trauma. She had troubles, but Janice did too. "Go on, what happened? We still have a few minutes."

Janice quickly regained her composure. "Let me tell you, Elisa, after my husband and children cornered me, trying to convince me who they were and who I was, I endured one helluva long hard recuperation time."

Elisa remembered a scenario that had occurred back at that time, but not in her Regeneration Corridor. "I think I remember you...not you specifically, but your case."

Flicking her wrist device, Janice showed Elisa more holograms of that distressing time. "I went through two days of intensive CBRR in the Counseling Center to regain my memories. I had to get to know my husband all over again, and my children. They had to locate my memories inside the matrix...inside it!" she gasped, as if reliving the entire event. "But before I knew it...just as I was about to leave home permanently...I remembered everything. I just needed a little time and, well, cerebral assistance." As she sat reclined in her seat, she began toying with her special necklace beads—comfort items for her. "Would you consider trying a CBRR treatment to regain your memories?" she asked. "It worked for me. And the relationship between my husband and me, and my children and me, well, we're happy!"

Elisa touched her throbbing forehead as an onslaught of memories—screaming, chaotic, stranded voices—began thundering through her mind. She tried to match faces to the voices; however, there were thousands of words, in a giant crucible of thousands of voices forming nonsensical gibberish as if they were all trying to coalesce into a real person in search of someone who could help him, her, or it. "No thanks, but thanks for reminding me about that option." She turned to watch the slowing contrails outside their Maglev. She felt lost in them, as if they were whipping around her, making her cold and lonely. She shivered and gripped her armrests.

Janice patted her on the shoulder. A contrail outside sparked as their shuttle edged around a small corner to dock. "Thank goodness I have the love and support of a family who helped me get through that disorienting period of my life," she whispered. "That's when I began wearing these beads around my neck. They help me stay grounded, so I'll never forget who I am or my family." The tinkling beads glowed when she touched them. "My husband calls these jewels, *pearls of knowledge and love*...and my kids sometimes blow on them before we all go our separate ways in the morning. My husband, Doug, says they're unique gems...jewels he manufactured himself out of corundum...with a special technological infusion."

"Where did he accomplish that feat? He must have some magnificent job!" Elisa said. She had another thought and perked up. "Could the beads contain an advanced tracking mechanism?"

Janice shrugged as she softly pinched the yellow strand. "I don't know. Doug never told me where he synthesized them or if they contained any unique qualities. I guess we'll just have to wait and see if he comes looking for me...like he did that time two years ago when he couldn't find me." Again she paused in abject silence but then recovered. "But he swears I'll never get lost again so long as I keep these on my person!"

Watching her quickly bounce back from her terrifying experience, Elisa wanted to know how she always seemed so calm and steady. "Do colors of the beads mean something holistic?"

After a Terra conductor appeared, announced a two-minute docking time, and then faded, Janice held up the strands of beads and picked one up into her line of sight. "This green one is a symbol for hope. If I feel lost, I touch it, and the future look bright again, and I'm reminded to live in the moment and not the past."

"*Hmm*," Elisa said, touching one of the tiny warm green beads. She also felt soothed as if she were being flooded with a stream of trickling calm water in an oasis. "I think they feel like...like Time Stamps...good memories during sad times." She laughed and Janice laughed. "What about the yellow strand?"

Janice's teeth shone as bright as the whites of her eyes. "This yellow strand is like that hologram show playing above

# J.P. Osterman

our heads."

Elisa began watching a show of the sun rising through the Grand Canyon. "Beautiful!"

"Yellow is the sun, moon, stars, electrons...you know—everything light," Janice said.

"Beautiful." Elisa felt tears stinging her eyes.

"And the indigo strand is for twilight and deep water," Janice began. "I learned how to scuba dive as part of my recovery at the main Rec Center. Ever since then, I've been spending a little of my spare time in virtual scuba worlds. While swimming through reefs, among turtles, and all sorts of fish, I reflect rejuvenate. Most times, I think about Nelta."

"What about Nelta?" Elisa asked, picking up her backpack as the Maglev lowered to dock.

"What I'm gonna do after I disembark on the planet...and where me and my family might live." She inhaled deeply and then sighed. "*Ahhh*, the future...who really *knows* how it's gonna turn out."

"Nobody," Elisa said. "I guess that's why you have to keep touching your green strand of beads. The future's so unpredictable, so out of our control, I—" Laughing uncomfortably as the shuttle's claws interacted with a strong aerodynamic beltway, she said, "I'm completely opposite you."

"How?"

Elisa crossed her legs and folded her arms. "I'm the go-here-run-there Type A person. I'm active, always trying to learn something new, always keeping up with the latest in technology and medicine, which I have to do anyway because that's my job. People depend on me to make them young again...and keep their minds unharmed in the process."

"So you *always* stay busy," Janice said, dropping the beads and pressing them under her collar. "Do you have anyone you're close to? A husband? Children?"

As the Maglev's underbelly claws clamped onto its tracks and the outside chrysalis unwrapped, Elisa remembered an ex-boyfriend, Carl Foldier, who had left her for a virtual world and his new virtual mate, *Hot Victoria*. Inhaling the sadness, she sat up and brushed Janice's words out of her thoughts. "Nope, no one." She had to change the subject. Her palms were sweaty, her fingers trembling, her mouth drying. Suddenly, she saw something move outside in the distance, and she began wiping off the window.

"What's wrong?" Janice inched toward her and peered over her shoulder.

"I think I saw something…but I'm not sure." While Janice began whispering possibilities, Elisa perused the dimly-lit empty station. The Regents were somewhere else and on the run from the light-based sentient entities. "No sign of Enforcers, medical personnel, or Matrix techs…but still…I think I see something," Elisa said, caution creeping through her bones. In all the shadows around the kiosks, she detected movements. To get a closer look, she unfastened her seatbelt and walked down the steps toward the exit.

"What's out there, Elisa? The creatures? If so, I say we skedaddle! And let someone else try and stop this mess and save everyone." Janice left her seat and began searching her wrist device for codes that might sync with the large keypad at the front of the car. Standard Terra appeared—static and fussy—obviously useless except for a verbal warning, and then Janice quit her attempt at a matrix intervention. Terra remained transparent, but stall—a glowing, 3D static-filled animation.

"Forget her. She's useless now." Elisa lifted up her backpack and heaved it over her shoulder. "I don't see any attackers outside, but we can't stop just when we're so close to discovering some answers." She saw Janice's apprehension. She was touching her special beads, obviously more concerned about her family living without a mother should something bad happen. "Look, Janice, you can stay here, and wait for me while I go on and search for answers." Elisa checked twice to make sure she had water and packs of snacks on the sides of her backpack.

"Oh all right," Janice said, after a moment of stern contemplation. "I can't let you do *everything* yourself and be the only one taking all the credit," she laughed. "Powers and all...ya need me...admit it."

Elisa felt embarrassed.

"Come on..."

"Okay, I need you," Elisa said, waving Janice toward the sliding door. "Come on, let's get outta this car and go find Creator and his—"

"Or her!"

Elisa huffed, "Sorry, or *her* hide out. I have special abilities that'll help us, but I don't know how much more I'm capable of doing."

"A *lot* more I hope," Janice whispered as her green eyes enlarged in encouragement.

As the door slid open, over a mile above them in another tunnel running east and west, Elisa heard an escalating drone and motioned for Janice to stand still. "That's a Maglev...it has to be The Regents...but they're heading somewhere else." The noise was electro-static, swift and swooning, and then faded into a soft whirr and murmur of the typical sounds flowing through *Sagan*. Her arm began aching—her intuition preventing her from taking a step onto the unpopulated platform. "I've got a bad feeling."

"What's wrong?!" Janice asked, standing rigidly on the step behind her.

## Chapter 24 – Level-9's Maze

Elisa stepped slowly down onto the platform and could finally see more of the domed station. "I can't believe it!" she cried, pulling Janice down to the ground. A giant breeze swept through the station—uprooting artificial trees, searing processor hubs off the walls, and whipping tiles off the roof of an Information Kiosk yards in front of them.

"What the heck!" Janice shouted.

"Look up! A giant pterodactyl is heading *straight* at us!" Elisa said.

With a white wingspan of over fifty feet, the light-based creature had the head of an alligator and the body of a dragon. Elisa raised her left arm toward it, her thoughts focusing on the words: *keep back…stay away from us…I have a mission…leave us alone.* If her powers had helped her before and could fend off this attack, she'd definitely have proof of a special Neltan technology powering up inside of her. The giant shrieking creature flew away from them, straight into the Maglev. Janice shrieked, and Elisa moved her arm over Janice's body in a shielding gesture—directing a flow of current toward into the sentient dinosaur. It flew into the stalled Terra stewardess, and the figure began pulsating with near blinding energy.

"That conductor looks ready to pop! It could kill us!" Janice cried.

"I'm working on it..." Elisa said. She had her left arm outstretched at the shuttle, directing her bodily flow of special current into the creature and the captured stewardess. The conductor altered into a giant bright-blue bird with a human head. She recognized her. "EJ!" She began focusing hard to make EJ leave the Maglev and the creature's intense grip on her.

"I thought you said EJ was a *little* blue bird!" Janice said.

Suddenly, EJ exploded into a cloud of bright, blue-and-white, buzzing-and-droning nanytes. Swirling through the shuttle, the chattering nanytes wrote a message: Demon Terra! Go east! Don't stop!" The writing was cut off by a cluster of attacking, black nanytes as the two groups engaged in a vicious fight. The wind began gathering as a swirling bright portal at the northern-most entryway into the transport tunnel. A dimensional was activating, and the Maglev began rocking in place—its claws vibrating off the tracks.

"Get up and run!" Elisa called, and she and Janice dashed for the Information booth, now a skeleton of shimmering steel in repair-mode. Little robots, builder-bots, and UAVs were working wildly around the booth like frenzied rodents building perfect nests, *Sagan*'s standard renovation and restoration robotics. Elisa knocked a few of them out of their way so they could decide whether their hiding spot was safe. Before Janice bounded for another disheveled kiosk on the right, the Maglev lit up like trees on fire, snapped at the seams, and broke apart. Chairs began whipping around in circles as grinding metal collided, forming a vortex. In seconds, the dimension portal sucked up the Maglev, leaving only artificial tree limbs and plants floating in the sparkling air—their parts gently drifting onto the tracks.

Standing, but her balance a bit shaky, Elisa breathed in relief and grabbed a pole that had just self-repaired. Janice couldn't stop talking as if doomsday was approaching. "But it's over, Janice. Let's make a plan. We're safe now."

"You're right," she agreed, peering cautiously around the one-hundred foot station now appeared calm but in the ramshackle condition of a great magnetic storm. "I believe we have to go east. That's what I heard, and I trust the source. And we know we're also facing another problem."

"Can there be more?" Janice said facetiously.

"Yep, a Demon Terra." Elisa suddenly remembered a vicious chomping entity. "I can't remember, but I actually encountered a dark shadowy creature…but I can't believe it was real…because the thing was like a witch with fangs…devouring souls!"

"That's a soul sucker!" Janet said, followed by a quick description of an evil creature in her Native American culture. "A soul sucker can't die 'cause it's already dead." She exhaled in confusion. "This trip we're taking is getting more interesting for sure! And frightening."

Elisa felt sick as a memory struck her to the floor. Something was hunting her down, trying to gobble her up. Janice shuffled through the backpack, gave her some water, and helped her back on her feet. "Whatever happened to me occurred recently," Elisa said.

"When?"

Elisa splashed water on her face and little robotics slurped out from the floor, sucking up all the spilled drops. "Where the hell was I over the course of three days?!"

After a pause, Janice answered softy: "You had to have been in some type of stasis, 'cause coming face-to-face with a soul snatcher doesn't happen to people. Your mind had to have been inside the matrix. I just wanna know how you survived, and are alive."

Appreciating her concern, Elisa said: "You're right. I had to have been *inside* the matrix, and experienced something horrific." She couldn't breathe, but Janice gave her more water, and an inner desire to fight back revived her. "Okay, I'm ready to move on. I'm so pissed off, and need answers. Let's go."

"Well, let's find east then." Janice launched a Compass program over her wrist device. It pointed east into a dark area with sparks igniting high in the dome. They began quickly walking.

"I wanna find out who's causing all this mess around *Sagan* and how to pull the plug on Demon Terra," Elisa said. With Janice's Compass program illuminating a small yellow light in front of them, they walked stealthily for five minutes and then stopped when they approached a reception area filled with 3D waterfalls, lounge chairs, and empty food carts. Janice tried hailing someone again, but no one replied as Elisa walked through the zone's cooling technology that sprayed her face with a light mist.

In the rising temperature, Janice ripped the collar on her blouse, tearing the lining out of her suit coat, and wrapping the outer layer of the light jacket around her waist. "I have a two-degree rise in temperature since we left the station," she said. "It's gradually warming, or something is interfering with this level's homeostasis."

"Lose the jacket then," Elisa suggested.

She took it off but shoved it hard into Elisa's stuff backpack. "We can't. We might need the special fabric as bandages or tools."

"Makes sense, so let's move on," Elisa said, and they continued on their trek. Trying to discern a broad dark area in the distance, Elisa noticed movement on the floor, and light and shadows playing on structural beams of kiosks, eateries, abandoned robotics, and L-cars. She had Janice illuminate them with both her wrist and neck device. An analysis returned.

"It's a species of creeping-crawling algae!" Janice said, showing Elisa the bright-green signature of the organic composition. It had a question mark at the center, indicating the species was new and foreign to the matrix. Then she ran a

# Astrocity Sagan

Fourier analysis and received a crystalline structure. "We don't know its solid state, so we need to make sure we sidestep it. They're non-photosynthetic algae, combined with nanoparticles."

"It appears to be spreading through a field of unusual density," Elisa said, sidling carefully between a broad growth of the bright green algae. "We better go fast, 'cause this stuff is like a wild vine...obviously searching for anything to wrap around and suck the life out of!"

"I'm picking up a magnetic effect...and dark matter interference as well," Janice said. "Combined, the two are like air, dirt, and water—"

"Add heat too into the equation," Elisa added.

"Yep, they're the perfect medium for the genetically-engineered algae to spread, maybe throughout the entire astrocity!"

Suddenly, an image of a giant white maze appeared over Janice's wrist device, its processing speed increasing.

"This infected space must be a conduit that's boosting our signal, together with that silicon booster Ben Tucker input into my wrist device. Great—we need a break!"

Elisa recalled seeing blueprints of the area. "I remember this model from when I worked at *Research Station II*, when the Neltans transmitted the plans to construct *Sagan*." She waved Janice past the darkness that gave way to automatic lights. Then she returned to studying the illuminated map in front of them, guiding them east. The center of Level-9 had a circumference of five square miles. From the station where they disembarked, she could see several paths highlighted in bright yellow. "These are five corridors, one ending at a conference area, one at a laboratory, one at a research facilities, another one at a medical facility, and the last one ending at an experimental facility. The map isn't specific though 'cause all the information is classified." Only Corridor-1 connected with a conference-style meeting area—the place she remembered having to meet Regent Manning three days ago. "I'm glad we're not heading there!" she said, her memory foggy, her sense of direction skewed. "Actually, I don't have any recollection of disembarking at that place at all, where I should have disembarked, hm." She told Janice about her confusing experience; and Janice reassured her they'd get to the bottom of it as soon as they could complete the mission and meet Thornton Manning. Then they returned to studying the map, and Elisa noticed miles of barren space around the entire circumference of Level-9. "Shouldn't the empty area be filled with technology to power *Sagan*...and a robotics manufacturing facility?"

"That's what I see," Janice said, enlarging the massive horseshoe-shaped area.

"I don't. The place is empty." Then she saw a constant undulating light emanating from the center of Level-9. "I know this technology!" She showed her several key empty locations, but Janice maintained she could only see bustling manufacturing-and-assembly areas producing all sorts of robotics. "You can't see what I'm *not* seeing, Janice, because whoever is hiding this area is using transformational optics and bending light waves to manipulate objects."

"You mean I'm being tricked into seeing everything?" As Elisa nodded, Janice's face reddened in anger. "Damn! Why aren't *you* affected?"

Experiencing a flash of understanding, she gestured at her left arm. "Just as my abilities are shielding me from the Mind Meddling technology, they must also be making me impervious to whatever stealth technology is at working on this level to hide this place from the residents."

"Darn!" Janice said angrily, tapping her temples, obviously enraged at waves interfering with her brain. "This is *not* right!" She pounded the air in fury. "People need to see this after we investigate the Live Stream Field...which is somewhere around here," she exhaled in resignation. "Let's move on, so I can give those Regents a piece of my mind!" After unclenching her fists, she asked into the map guiding them: "Give us the location of Terra's LSF Facility. It's supposed to be down here somewhere…and streaming with Terra's cloud center on Level-7." A small, bright orange column illuminated. "This distance is two miles straight ahead."

"This is the origin of the stealth-optics waves as well," Elisa said.

On the map, the pathway to the LSF facility appeared unapproachable by a maze of hallways—obviously a deterrent. "The orange flowing column *must* be the point of heightened processing activity, and Terra's Live Stream Field."

The map returned with a low-automated voice filled with warning: "All sites on Level-9 are Safe-Rite protected and classified. No further access permitted, Dr. Kiplin. Tracking procedures activating."

Almost throwing off her device until Elisa tapped it with her outdated device that deleted its internal tracker, Janice said into her device, "I conduct classified work, you idiot!" Several directional arrows appeared on the guiding map. "Wow— where did *these* come from?"

"I guess combining technology…and outside help," Elisa said, almost wanting to kiss it and remembering EJ's words, *people in hiding saved you.* Then she told Janice to re-focus her guiding map. It immediately burst to life with colorful food icons that would remain steps ahead of them as untraceable directional beacons inside the map. "These preliminary arrows are a start, and will definitely keep us from being discovered, but not good enough to find our way to the area of heightened activity." Then she had another idea, and she increased power on her outdated wrist device, waiting to see if what EJ had input into it earlier in the day could help them. A 2D visual of a little bluebird appeared, and Elisa quickly swept it into the map. A message materialized over the map: *Pattern of Interference present.* Pacing the squeaky floor, she did as Janice suggested and touched the forefinger of her left hand to the map. A yellow light began cycling through the center, and then solidified into three white beams. "One of these is the way to the Live Stream Field. We need to break through the interference and locate which one."

"Yes!" Janice exclaimed. "I'll compile the statistical information as we go forward. The delta should be significant, but an outlier will appear, and that outlier will be our way to the LSF. Meanwhile, let's take the center path."

With the illuminated map moving in front of them, they rounded a hexagonal station and began walking through a thoroughfare filled with towering transparent partitions that looked like a sea of glass walls and shelves stretching high into the sparking domed sky. Each little square contained an image from inside the astrocity. Their noises were on mute; their intensity on diminished, or else they'd be so bright and loud, they'd outshine and trumpet throughout the entire level.

"They appeared self-replicating," Janice began. "The more images they receive, the more their programs either decrease their numbers or increase their monitoring capacity. Hovering at the sides of them were images of people performing various duties throughout *Sagan*. "This is obviously a special monitoring facility for Matrix Security techs."

Janice grimaced, her anger appearing to rise like the images high into the dome. "These people are clueless that they're being watched! This is creepy! I bet we were being monitored too!"

Elisa stopped and watched one of the live-streaming holograms. A woman with dyed-white hair and a blue heterochromia eye was standing in the shadows of a participation kiosk at the Level-6 Stern Transport Station. She was recording people with her wrist device and had two small avatars standing in front of her so she could avoid detection. "I've been noticing people with this condition!" She quickly explained to Janice how she'd seen many cases lately. "Could one of *them* have triggered the attacks?" Elisa stepped back and looked high into several images playing out over their heads. "Or someone else whose life is on display in one of these things?"

# Astrocity Sagan

"I feel like we're invading peoples' private lives," Janice said, distaste pursing on her lips. "Let's get outta here, please. This is disgusting. I don't wanna see *anything* private."

Slowly walking onward, Elisa asked, "Still, I don't think anyone we've seen here could meld optics with nanotechnology to create such invading light-based anomalies."

"You mean hologram monsters!" Janice corrected, following so close behind Elisa that she could feel her breath on her neck. Janice now had her fingers wrapped tightly around a strap on Elisa's backpack.

Elisa noticed the outlier they had been waiting for. It appeared over Janice's device and then flashed bright green on the map in front of them. A dotted white pathway illuminated. "It's the direction to the LSF! Yes!" They walked quickly around several small partitions. "After we get there, we need to find the direct interface with Terra's Cloud Center on Level-7." She didn't want to overload Janice with more information, but she was feeling under pressure, and waiting to hear from EJ or another mysterious helper, so she could input a special code into the LSF. As of yet, she hadn't received *any* code or element to link the two areas and discover the true source or creator of the light-based entities. If we arrive at the LSF without that necessary information, the trip will have been a waste, she thought. But she couldn't have made it this far unless EJ, or some other powerful people, were helping them along, as they just eliminated the pattern of interference.

"Finding this place is a *real* piece of cake!" Janice scoffed.

As they walked inward another mile among various robotics, UAVs, abandoned stations, empty little recreation areas, artificial workers, and inquisitive virtual avatars; Elisa could hear Janice's special beads collide on their strands. She had to be worried sick about her husband Doug and her children. She assured Janice they were okay, and she'd be reunited with them soon, but she appeared dejected at times; at

# J.P. Osterman

other times, anger fueled. Suddenly, they entered another highly-advanced monitoring area, this one more condensed and more concentrating on targeting specific residents. A glowing food icon on their guide map displayed their current position: approaching the fringe of Level-9's center. They stopped to take a quick break and drink water in the humid warming air. The area was morphing into a jungle of mangled abandoned technology with automated lights illuminating as motion sensors.

"I almost feel like we're under a strobe," Elisa said. Then she remembered three sets of special eye glasses she found at the bottom of her backpack. Digging down deep, she pulled two out, handed one to Janice who immediately put them on, and then donned her pair of glasses. Just in time, before fainting from a dizzy spell.

Breathing in relief as well, Janice asked: "You think we can make contact with some Regents through one of these monitors? I wonder where they're at?" She stretched to see images of people praying at a religious center on Level-1. "Hello...hey—hello!"

"They can't hear you," Elisa said. "This is just another spy center, Janice. At some point, I'm sure *we've* been their object of study."

"My kids! Doug!" Janice said, concern moving across her face.

Elisa grabbed her hand softly. "Don't even say their names, Janice. This technology is most likely voice activated and also processing with all the Mind Meddling technology."

"Then let's get the hell outta here!" she said, running ahead with the guide map illuminating her steps.

They ran away from the spy area and approached a giant virtual banner flashing, *Corridor 5*. They doffed their special glasses, and Elisa stuffed them back into her backpack.

"Keep close, Janice. It looks like we enter this place next." She saw yellow beakers and atomic numbers on the base of the guide map, an indicator of the contents of Corridor 5. "It's a giant laboratory," Elisa said, directing Janice inside. After stepping under an archway into Corridor 5, they stopped, walked over to information kiosk, and began watching a show. Throughout Corridor 5, tiny robots, smart machines, and worker-bots were repairing kiosks and resupplying them with equipment from 3D printers situated in camouflaged places. Even this secluded place leading into the interior had suffered an attack.

"This show is a replay of what happened after the Choosing Ceremony," Elisa said.

Standing next to her shoulder, Janice launched a Visual Comparison program alongside their guiding map. "This VC program will tell us if the creatures have been inside this area. It picks up residual signatures."

Elisa read the time, *3:15 p.m.* "That's when we entered the transport tunnel…and when they left. Any indication yet if they're anywhere here?" With her abilities, she could disperse them, but wanted a detour if they were near!

Janice appeared shocked when a giant eagle jumped out of VC scan, materialized over the guide map, and began pecking at it. She paused the analysis. "Their language is metaphor!"

"What?" Elisa asked.

Lines of literary works and light-based images began scrolling over Janice's wrist device. She stopped at the first line and picture. "Everything is code, Elisa, and quantum mechanics, and those hieroglyphs we've been trying to translate," she answered. "I'll show you."

Elisa glanced around quickly and checked the time, 4:48 p.m. She motioned for Janice to hurry. "You're the expert in programming and statistics, so start, so we can get movin'. Or maybe you should stop running the analysis." *Then again, maybe this is one way we can discover the necessary code, algorithm, or image to input into the LSF and stabilize the matrix on Level-7.* She told her to keep the comparison running. They had to stay vigilant and open to every new bit of information.

Obviously feeling pressured, Janice's fingers were shaking

and her look hard and intense. "Here's what the results are so far."

"Okay, whataya got, Janice?"

A proud gleam spread across her face. "In Alfred Lord Tennyson's poem, *The Eagle*, the majestic bird stands for truth and leadership."

"Okay…" Elisa said.

Janice picked out the eagle image, and set it next to their guiding map. "The dragon is a Chinese metaphor. Ancient Dalai Lamas believed the Earth was sculpted by the dragon's wings and that the dragon's tail carved out all the steppes, mountains, rivers, and valleys." She picked out the dragon and set it next to the eagle.

A holographic show activated in front of them. They jumped back. Even the robotics stopped all their renovation and kiosk repair. "Something is synching with them," Elisa whispered, and then she told Janice to proceed, but with caution. Janice ordered the show to play, and an historic account of the creation of Nelta and its solar system began. "Wow, I didn't expect *this*!"

"Me either!" Elisa agreed, examining elements in the show. "This giant, bright-white energy line looks like Nelta's Matter Stream. But what does *it* have to do with the nanyte attackers?"

Glanced rubbed her eyes in a gesture of fatigue. "Well, one of the virtual entities had the head of an alligator and body of a dragon—"

"And the giant I saw earlier on Level-2 was half Jolly Green Giant and half Japanese gardener," Elisa added.

"Yes…let me think." She paused, then continued: "I remember something that might help us," then she gasped, putting her hand over her heart.

"What? What's wrong?!"

Janice exhaled. "When I was at the Navigation terminal last week and inserted a new algorithm for approval, Terra sent back a reply coded in two, *two*, virtual strings of grid ending in pictures of tails." She excitedly walked under one of the Terra hubs high up in the dome. "Let me see if I can get a visual on one of those morphed creatures so my app can analyze its components, run a comparison with the two grids I received, and order a spectrographic pattern."

"What'll that do?" Elisa asked.

"If my guess is right, those morphed creatures aren't attacking residents," she answered.

"The Regents?" Elisa asked.

"Or maybe the specialists they took into the tunnels," Janice speculated, peering into various scenes of Nelta.

"I wonder why…and what they have to do with the planet Nelta, the Neltans, or the Matter Stream?" Elisa asked. "Let's keep going," she coached, asking Janice to re-align the guide map so they could follow the white directional light to the Live Stream Field. "Keep your Visual comparison up-and-running next to the map though. We might be able to use an image from it when we arrive there."

Approaching a transition area filled with high-tech transparent screens, Elisa called out for someone again; but other than the holograms and avatars that automatically began projecting around them, no person answered.

Janice was still deep in thought, analyzing the information about the light-based entities. "These creatures have to be warnings," she whispered. "I'm trying to find more images that someone might have taken of them, but—"

Elisa stopped walking. "I know where some might be!" She slipped off her backpack, grabbed the satchel she found when she awoke from her stupor, and took out the worn over-the-ear GoPro camera. It might have synched with other devices and recorded something from earlier. As Janice marveled at it she was greeting an old friend, Elisa thrust it into her hand. "I think the chip inside this GoPro is sensor driven, so any data should transfer to your wrist device. Hopefully, there are some captures in the old thing that will add to what you already have in your grid. If we can get some advanced help around here somewhere, I'm sure we'll be able to locate the place where the creatures are holding those people, and help them. And I can't wait to get my hands on the person who created the things illegally using Neltan technology!"

"Maybe the people are bad and will kill us!" Janice said. "We can't tell who's bad and good anymore."

"Or even trust our own eyes," Elisa added. "Anything can be hidden anywhere, and we're like walking ants."

Entering another large area, Janice told her she had successfully synchronized their two devices. Then they spotted images of Nelta and its solar system, reflections in a thousand mirrors in front of them. "We must be standing inside a study arena …or an analytical area…or simulation zone," Janice speculated.

"Wow!" Elisa marveled. "The artificial sun around Nelta appears to be in a state of death."

"That's a good thing," Janice began excitedly. "It means the Matter Stream left its artificial containment field and has rejuvenated Nelta. Yes!"

The distance between the artificial sun and Nelta was displaying a numerical two light-years from Nelta, and Nelta's binary star system was feeding the planet life-generating energy. At twice the size of Earth, Nelta has two giant oceans divided by one equatorial land mass circumnavigating the entire planet.

"This must be what Nelta's solar system looks like now," Elisa said, motioning at fifteen planets in perfect elliptical orbit around Nelta's massive suns. "The Matter Stream has definitely healed Nelta. "Now, we just have to land there and reanimate the Neltans!" She felt like jumping and clapping in celebration as a jubilant Janice jumped and gave her a high-five.

Over Janice's wrist device, a flash of red light appeared, and she turned to read the message after she shrank the guiding map. Suddenly, she dropped to her knees.

"What's wrong?!" Elisa asked kneeling beside her.

Pointing at several light-based creatures inside her Visual

# Astrocity Sagan

Analysis program she had running next to the map, she replied, "My guess is that a scientist on Nelta—on Nelta!—pre-programmed these creatures into Terra *before* we left Earth. They're advanced nano-photonics, processing beyond quantum mechanics, perhaps neutrino based *and* light based. We can't even detect neutrinos."

"Are they the Failsafe?!" Elisa helped her stand up.

"Everything from the color of their skin to the way they move and their fingers—" She paused, enlarging one of the creature's hands.

"They're slightly webbed...*definitely* Neltan!" Surprised, Elisa stepped back as she continued to make sense of the creatures. "These images we're seeing of Nelta have been taken recently! How?"

"I don't know," Janice replied. She had her arms tight over her abdomen, obviously sick; and Elisa handed her a bottle of water. In between sips, she said: "The attacks *must* be an activated Failsafe. And the clues to solving the problem that triggered it are embedded in codes, a grid in Terra's matrix, and Hologram site addresses." She appeared in contemplation again. "Hologram sites..."

"What about them?"

"*That's* how the creatures are determining which people to kidnap!" Janice wiped her hands on her smudgy pants and then quickly repositioned her light-jacket around her waist.

"But maybe the creatures saved the people they kidnapped," Elisa said.

Janice kept open an image of one of the creatures, and then enlarged the map. "I'm seeing if we can get a real connection to this creature...and see if we can communicate with it."

"Are you kidding!?" Elisa said, moving her into the shadow of the giant archway entrance.

"What harm can it do?" Janice asked. "We're surrounded by monitors, and I'm piggybacking on their signals ...so I know I can get a location on just one of them."

"Stop!"

"Shhh!" Janice returned, pointing her wrist device at a giant black shadow wandering down one of the northwest areas on Level-9. "Got it!"

The shadow began coalescing…suddenly molding into a solid gold glowing eagle that appeared to be stalking empty corridors. It had round human eyes, large webbed feet, and fingers at the tips of its wings. The map showed it twelve miles away from them, at the opposite side of the Live Stream Field, their destination.

"I think it's hunting," Elisa whispered.

The giant nanyte creature stopped, glanced high into a ceiling hub, made a 180° turn west, and shrieked. They couldn't hear it at their location; but through the augmented reality, the creature's eagle-piercing cry reverberated right through them.

Elisa felt her gut ache. "Now ya did it."

"Did what?"

"The creature detected us," Elisa replied. "We better run, 'cause that LSF facility is the only place we stand a chance of surviving." As they began dashing down another corridor, Elisa spotted another *Alert-3* message on a hologram stage. They stopped, she tapped on its Activate icon, and an image appeared of terrified people running away from a Level-2 Rec Center. "Look!"

Boosting the power on her wrist device, Janice said: "There's more bad news."

"What now?!"

"There's interference coming from below us…a giant gap between here and the hull. Right under us…now!" On their guiding map, the column of energy at the LSF was displaying more of its intensity and revealing more of its composition. "The closer we get to this expanding power source, the more we're learning about hidden things. We're definitely in unchartered water, and illegal territories."

"And it's becoming dangerous, I know." Elisa rolled up her sleeve. "But remember, I've been able to protect us."

# Astrocity Sagan

"Thank goodness, 'cause we're gonna need your special protection soon." Then Janice called on a visual of the bottom of the astrocity. "Dark matter coils on Level-7 are constantly powering the ten engine turrets at the bottom of *Sagan*."

"Right…"

She showed Elisa the problem: a tiny rainbow string of energy streaming out of one of the tubes, dispersing like a funnel into Level-7's Center Transport tunnel. "This dark matter is combining with the gravity already present in the tunnels. It's interfacing with *every* hologram, the historical archives on *this* level, and The Regents' Clone-Tech Center."

Elisa rubbed her eyes and finished drinking her water. She was trying to piece together the puzzle pieces. "We have rampant energy forces at play, weird matrix processing, illegal Mind Meddling technology, Regeneration technology interfacing with all three of them, and live images from Nelta." She laughed. "I feel like I'm in a nightmare with some mysterious crazy wizard at the helm of all my bad dreams!"

Janice tried again to transmit a *Request for Information* to the residents on *Sagan*, but she noticed the message still stalled. And they still hadn't heard back from any Regent as to their location. "We have absolutely no connection to the upper levels." She shook her wrist, hoping the jostle might help her device. "Nothing. We can't send…and we can't receive."

"Hey! There's another invasion occurring, Janice," Elisa said, as a new show began playing. "I don't understand why there's spying and current events streaming down here, and why we aren't having stable matrix connectivity."

In the show, Enforcers were launching saucer probes inside all transport tunnels.

"This is no invasion," Elisa began. "The probes are searching for those 273 protesters."

Janice heard the description. "Not protesters. Enforcers are calling them outlaws…and criminals…and there's a shot-to-kill order straight from the Regency…those murderers."

# J.P. Osterman

"Ya won't get an argument from me on that!" Elisa said as Janice pointed to a giant shield inside one of the tunnels. The saucer probe failed to detect anyone. "Yes! Good for *273!*" she said with a rally tone in her voice. "The protesters obviously have hidden sanctuaries, and technology that can deflect the probes' frequencies. No way will those Enforcers ever find them."

Elisa was becoming more curious as to their identity and remembered what EJ had said: two of them had saved her life. "They seem to be gaining in number and strength."

"I still wonder if *they're* responsible for the virtual invaders," Janice said.

"Well, the creatures did take five people," Elisa said. "The protesters must have encountered them at some point."

Suddenly, one of the Enforcer's probes exploded in front of a Maglev that had just slurped out of a tunnel on Level-8. Dirk Hunter ran onto the docking platform with his avatar in tow, and his many portable devices illuminated and ready to document passengers' stories.

Janice and Elisa watched Dirk's announcement:

"From their emergency calls, we've learned that a giant monster with the body of a polar bear and the head of lion appeared at the bow of a shuttle, and stopped it! It entered the shuttle—passed right through all the metal!—and began whizzing through avatars as if in search of someone. Who these creatures are looking for, no one knows…except we have *not* been unable to locate a Regent anywhere. I repeat…all Regents seemed to be off-the-grid and unavailable."

Dirk Hunter's personal Terra enlarged behind him. It was his way of receiving more information. The avatar began displaying words on a giant teleprompter for Dirk to read:

"Ladies and Gentlemen," he began, whispering, an optics hub getting a close up of Dirk's body. "I just received word from a Lead Enforcer that The Regents are traveling incognito. Indeed, Ladies and Gentlemen, the nanyte invaders…these infiltrating virtual holograms that are sentient and living…appear to be hunting down the Regents. Please Stream with me Live through my Safe-Site at Dirk Hunter, Premier Story-Byte Chaser. The Regents have begun scrambled communications. Contact me through my site only, because for the duration of this crisis, and until the nanyte creatures can be stopped, I will be your eyes and ears to the Regency. Be attentive to the *Alert-3*, remain where you are, and do not—do not!—venture outside. ..."

Dirk Hunter then flicked his wrist, and his avatar shrank down to an inch. As Elisa and Janice were about to leave and proceed on their journey to the LSF, Dirk Hunter said, "Doctors Holton and Kiplin. Are you there?" He repeated the call.

Two panels illuminated next to them.

"He's talking to us," Elisa said, turning back with Janice who activated a Recording program so her wrist device would capture his every word.

"We're here, Dirk," Janice said.

"Not so loud," Elisa said, "just whisper. Remember, we might have one of those creatures you communicated with tracking our scent or frequencies."

After Janice agreed, Dirk Hunter whispered: "Doctor Holton, Doctor Kiplin." His image scrambled, but then quickly recovered. "Look for Regents Asa and Ruth Stein." A boomerang signal returned his words, "Asa and Ruth Stein." An image of a sleek red car with a retractable hood appeared. "This vehicle should be there to pick you up right about now. Regent Manning ordered it for you, and told me to tell you to board it. It will take you to the Steins, and then they'll tell you where to go from there." Dirk Hunter's face hissed off the screens. Replacing his face, the planet Nelta began appearing on every screen. The magnitude was bright, almost blinding, and Elisa felt a protective type of warmth and comfort circulate through her body. Suddenly, a small, red shiny electric L-car appeared out of the darkness. The front lights and interior lights weren't on. Elisa's inner glow turned to fear.

"It's here!" Janice called, racing to the red car.

When it stopped in silence, a stewardess appeared—not at all Standard Terra—and announced the car's fifteen-second departure.

"Should we do as Dirk said and take it?" Janice appeared hesitant as she peered inside the door, inspecting the car's dark interior. "I don't know…"

"I know what *I'm* doing," Elisa began. "I'm staying." She backed away while shaking her head no. "I have to stay, Janice. I can't trust Thornton Manning. He tried to kill me, remember." She waited for Janice's decision. "I have a mission to complete. If I don't, I have a feeling everyone's going to die." She didn't want to leave Janice alone with the empty car, but time was running out. "If you want to take a chance and trust him, by all means, go. I understand…and I know you're worried about Doug and your kids." Janice was pacing a bit, with her hands on her hips, trying to make up her mind. "I believe Regents Asa and Ruth Stein are here, and trapped somewhere." She felt her arm, paining her. She knew to trust those warning signals. Every atom in her body was telling her to run away from the L-car and proceed to the center of Level-9.

With a conciliatory expression on her face, Janice walked away from the car. "I guess I'll go with ya. After all, *ah-um*, you need me."

Elisa laughed as the guide map appeared in front of them, and they began running east, their previous trajectory before stopping to watch what was happening to people on the levels above them. After five minutes of power walking, they heard a detonation, and the power of the explosion shoved them to the vibrating floor. Plumes of smoke curled into the dome. Materials began thudding to the ground. Elisa could hear shattering glass and robotics contort, whine, and squeak like fingernails scratching metal. A pungent smell filled the air.

"That L-car just blew up!" Janice said, fidgeting with her special necklace beads. "If we woulda been in it, we'd be dead right now!"

Panting, Elisa knelt on the floor as streams and swarms of robotics with parts clutched in their joints and claws scurried, hobbled, and lobbed around them in drones, whirs, and clatter. Avatars were appearing among them—directing them to the explosion site. In ten minutes or so, they would have the evidence cleaned up, all the spyware in the area re-assembled and working, and the stations and kiosks rebuilt without a scratch.

"Dirk Hunter, Thornton Manning, or someone in a powerful position had to have been responsible," Janice said as a small robot stopped and handed her a white cloth. Then it took off and joined the other automated builders. "Or it coulda been just an accident," she said, wiping her face with the cloth, tears filling her eyes. "Are we gonna make it outta here? Are we?"

"Yeah, right some accident!" Elisa said, collecting herself and then patting Janice's shoulder. "And of course we're going to make it out of here alive. But to do that, we need to move forward and solve what's happening." She touched her arm and gave her a protein bar. "Eat, and let's go."

"No," Janice said, throwing down the bar, her eye sight fixing on a monstrous distance. "Let's run like hell to the LSF!"

# J.P. Osterman

## Chapter 25 – Dark Destroyer

As they slowed down their pace, connectivity with the matrix strengthened so Janice could hack into several processing grids. She and Elisa queried the Level-9 Human Resource grid to discover up-to-date information about Regent Asa Stein and his wife Ruth. Elisa had met Dr. Ruth Stein on First Communication Day, but hadn't seen her since because of Lock Out Day. "Come to think of it, Elisa said, "neither she nor Asa were at the Choosing Ceremony with the other Regents."

"Yeah—I only saw eight of them!"

"I wonder why," Elisa said, "and why Thornton Manning wants them out of here."

"I wonder *where* they are," Janice inhaled. "I think, since we didn't do as he asked, he blew up the car." She patted her neck in a saving gesture. "Maybe we were meant to extract the Steins from their present location, and then *boom*—explosion! All four of us were meant to die."

"I don't know, but we're gonna find out, and ask the Steins what's going on when we find them," Elisa said.

Their guiding map began displaying their location that appeared as a gigantic dimly-lit cave. Green shimmering slime was creeping slowly up the curved towering partitions. Situated throughout Level-9, adjustable partitions separate corridors, labs, moving walkways, and facilities. Janice coughed and leaned into Elisa's ear. "Elisa, whoever tried to kill us might realize we're still alive and try to killing us again." She showed Elisa the walls, slime, and a few light-lasers that appeared to be special matrix processors. "Technology down here is so far advanced. All the robotics and assembly machines are at various stages of intelligence. And the strange genetically engineered algae could morph into anything, given time and the right conditions. And a Demon Terra is on the rampage. So many obstacles!" She appeared drained.

"Well, I also have special abilities and I can fight against anything that anyone throws at us," Elisa began, coughing, half-believing her words. But she wanted to show overconfidence and not be so under confident. Hope, she thought, we gotta hold onto it. She showed Janice her arm with a bit of blue glow under the skin. Then she had another realization that felt revitalizing. "I've noticed the algae are keeping their distant from us, and the robotics have backed away from us when they could have targeted us and attacked us, *hmm*."

"You have a deep connection to this technology on the ship, Elisa," Janice said through awestricken eyes. "I don't believe you've even begun to know the scope of your connection and capabilities."

Elisa waved her off. "Okay, enough of calling me Super Woman. Let's take one step-at-a-time and deal with what one obstacle at a time. Then, we'll be outta here."

The guiding map was a colorful network of lines over a yellow holographic tapestry with one, strong white stripe pointing the way to the interior of Level-9, now only a mile in front of them. At the finish line the map was displaying the Live Stream Field's column of orange power, its height intensifying the closer their approach. Then, one heat signature materialized next to the LSF; and next to the map appeared Asa and Ruth Stein's images.

"This is Asa Stein as he usually looks," Janice began.

Then his current Regency position appeared.

"He's a Lead Archivist, and managing other archivists who are responsible for directing peoples' information, recordings, and virtual worlds into historical archives for future use on Nelta," she added.

Elisa noticed several of his strong facial features. "He looks like that famous actor Robert Redford. I remember when photo-shoppers on Earth rendered the movie *Butch Cassidy and the Sundance Kid* for virtual participation, except Asa Stein has a mustache and brown hair." Rotating in *standard* form next to Asa is Dr. Ruth Stein. "She's also an Archivist, but has a classified title with a medical symbol under her name. But I can't identify the yellow pod symbol surrounding the caduceus symbol for medicine.

"But she sure does looks like Marilyn Monroe!" Janice marveled.

"She always has, since the day I met her," Elisa said. "But Ruth Stein doesn't sound at all like the ditzy characters Marilyn portrayed in her movies. I think she just admired the way the actress looked and dressed, and decided to copy her style."

"Weird though, and a bit creepy…copying someone *else's* style *all* the time," Janice said.

"To each her own," Elisa shrugged, gesturing at her full-bodied profile.

Ruth Stein has full ruby lips, bleached blond hair, and deep blue eyes traced with a thin stroke of dark eyeliner. Her long black eyelashes and perfect thin brown eyebrows make the blue pool in her eyes mesmerizing, and her short, curled hair against her pale skin gives her a delicate look. In her profile, she has on a rose-patterned, A-line dress and ruby-red shining shoes.

"Just think," Elisa said admiringly, "it's like Marilyn Monroe, right here—"

"And night now," Janice interrupted.

# Astrocity Sagan

"That's what I believe the Archivists do," Elisa said as they continued to walk on, while gleaning more information about the Steins. "These scientists see time as non-linear, and preserve and monitor all of history—both here and from Earth."

Another image suddenly appeared alongside Asa Stein: a tall Black Jamaican woman in her mid-twenties with straight bangs. She had red barrettes clasping bits of frizzy hair over her temples, and slightly large ears. A further identifier appeared: a genetic marker.

Enlarging the woman's slender body, Janice said, "Terra shows only a few Archivists working on *Sagan*: Asa, Ruth, and *this* woman….Doctor Jean Trent."

"And she's special because of a DNA manipulation she had on Earth," Elisa said.

When Janice said the name, *Doctor Jean Trent*, her Visual Analysis program activated again over her wrist device, but she didn't check the information. They were startled to find themselves entering a large experimental lab. All the robots and androids were on Pause-mode because the lab was void of technicians and researchers. There were artificial human bodies and body parts in containers, chambers, and compartments; and finished and half-finished organs suspended in liquid solutions. Various silicon patches were lined up on tall, long LED-lit panels being infused with a red-orange glowing liquid—blood-like. Some of the patches were sizzling, and some had little wiggling knobby protrusions, as lifelike as artificial baby toes and fingers. Many were beating, in tiny ticks and taps of rhythmic perfection. "Oo," Janice winced. "I can't tell whether someone botched up some of these experiments, or if some of these parts are supposed to fit into a wacky android prototype, worker-bot, or AI drone!"

"Just stay away. They're definitely creepy, and I'm taking pictures," Elisa said, waving her back, fearful that one of the wiggling, pulsing or throbbing parts might morph and reach out and snap her or bite her. She held up her wrist device, and it captured a 360° panorama.

Signs were everywhere—from genomics to nano-organics, from nano-technology to microbiology—all study and work stations. Surrounding several experiments in the distance were illuminated processing hubs, and active automated instruments craning, cranking, and flailing in a whirlwind of undirected movements. Elisa saw a shutdown station, and began extinguishing all the booths and stations as Janice gathered up a few tiny straggling robots, powered them down, and stuck them inside Elisa's backpack. "I can reprogram these, and maybe use them as a defense."

Meanwhile, Janice's Visual Analysis program synched with a monitor, and it began playing the scene of the earlier attack. Watching one of the virtual invaders pick up Doctor Jean Trent, Elisa said: "She's one of the people the light-based creatures kidnapped!" She looked closer. "I recognize her from a Maglev I took earlier...after I woke up and realized I'd lost three days!" She asked Janice to message both Ernie Bentley and Dr. Walker whom she had befriended, along with an image of Jean Trent's unique genetic marker. "Hopefully, we can find out more about her." The messages were streaming *In-Progress*, although she remembered Ernie wasn't off emergency duty yet; but Walker might be able to answer their questions concerning Jean Trent because he had connections to all sorts of advanced technology. She recalled what she could about the mysterious woman: "Jean Trent had on a weird mask—obviously a disguise, but I recognize her from her almond-shaped face...and her ears...so peculiar and unusual!" A message icon illuminated on Janice's wrist device, and they paused to watch the rendering when it appeared in front of them.

"It's Walker," Elisa said as Janice worked to resolve his static-filled face. He had bad news concerning Dr. Jean Trent, the Archivist. An hour ago, Enforcers linked her to the 273 group. She was on a growing Most Wanted list as a saboteur, hacker, and traitor. Enforcers, Matrix techs, and The Regents' special medical personnel were using Jean's genetic marker—and DNA signatures of the rest of her gang—to hunt them all down. Worse yet, The Regents proclaimed them responsible for the light-based attacks and gave Enforcers shoot-to-kill orders for anyone matching their DNA. "Jean Trent is as good as on death row," Elisa said, angrily. Then she told Walker to remain in his Living Cube, to continue working, and to scramble all their conversations through another communications grid so no one could accuse *him* of being in *273*.

"But why would the entities take Jean Trent?" Janice asked Walker before his image extinguished.

"The Human Resource program where you're at triggered Dr. Kiplin's Visual Analysis program, so Jean Trent has to be connected to Asa and Ruth Stein *and* The Archives," he replied. Then he signed off-grid.

Elisa expanded Ruth Stein's profile, and Jean Trent's image disappeared. Then a flood of multi-perspective views appeared around Ruth Stein's profile.

Marveling in awe at the vast collection, Elisa said: "We just hit a goldmine! Terra's is compiling *everything* about her—"

"And Asa Stein's profile is expanding behind hers!" said Janice. "I'm even receiving peoples' thoughts! It must be the Mind Meddling technology downloading right into this program, wow!"

Elisa felt suddenly weak, began shaking, and collapsed in disorientation as thousands of whispering voices flowed into her mind. She covered her ears as Janice searched the backpack for an analgesic. "Nothing'll help!" Elisa breathed. "I'm hearing thousands of people…and they're stranded! Their voices are driving me crazy!"

"You're being attacked," Janice said, kneeling next to her and offering her water. "Concentrate on one just one of them, and maybe your abilities will ward off the rest! You can do win…come on!"

# J.P. Osterman

Elisa's began experiencing a vision—a shadowy human figure trying to merge all the voices to form one consciousness. "He or she is crying for help—for release from the matrix," she screamed, her head throbbing. She felt her consciousness being used as an energy conduit for the new forming entity. "Stop! Get outta my head! Help!"

High in the dome, a swirl of blue light appeared and formed a cloud of bright nanytes that dove down and began swirling over Elisa's head. There was chirping noise and a shrill call.

Janice scooted away as a rumble of thunder and claps of lightning formed high above them. The hot lightning illuminated a giant partition in the direction where the car had exploded. On the partition were the algae, now whipping, sharp tentacles heading straight toward them. "We're definitely being attacked...and this time, we're good as dead," Janice screamed.

EJ materialized inches above Elisa's head. "Don't move until it's gone!" She flew into the heavy cumulous storm and disappeared inside a thick wall of green.

Bolts of blue lightning began striking the attacking green tentacles, and Elisa felt herself slowly recover. In the direction they were heading appeared a white light, and holograms began soaring at them. Elisa felt a surge of energy well within her, and she pointed her left arm at several images that began popping and exploding.

A great breeze blew in around them as Janice activated her wrist device, boosted a matrix connection, and began receiving information on their location. The map was illuminated, but small on the floor. "We're so close to the Live Stream Field, Elisa, so we must continue stopping what's preventing us from reaching it. We're so close!"

Elisa believed if she could plug into the matrix, she could amass even more energy and defeat anything. "I'm like an electrical socket to this flow of energy in here, Janice. No telling what'll happen when I connect with all the optics in that room ahead!"

# Astrocity Sagan

Through static, explosive pops, and cracking bursts, Janice gestured upward while monitoring new incoming information. "I see what's happening in here. All the light is interfacing with the processing hubs. Someone is processing information beyond the Singularity...true cognitive nonlocality processing."

Stymied, Elisa asked, "Do you mean a *sentient* consciousness is existing in multiple places and trying to escape the matrix using images and the algae?"

"Yes," Janice yelled.

"Oh my!" she reeled. "I just had a vision of what you just described...but I never thought such a creature could exist!" Light, the images, and the algae had formed a little ball of physical matter that quickly fixed to Elisa's left arm, thickened there, and began absorbing holographic images from the distant room. "I'm holding something...touching what feels like skin...but it's not."

"Whatever is working hard to birth into our space/time is throwing one helluva fight to take you over, Elisa," Janice said, almost ready to splash water on Elisa's arm.

EJ swept down yards in front of Elisa's face and gestured for Janice not to make that countermove. "More friends are coming to help! Water will only fuel them 'cause they're also fusion based!" Then she flew into one of the white-bright ropes of energy that turned a splash of blue, weakening the data stream.

Elisa's arm suddenly returned to normal, but the bluish Neltan tinge remained. "I think I'm okay, but we still have rampant energy to dissipate, Janice...and that wall of algae. It's heading right at us."

"I say we have about a minute of life left!" After sending another round of explosive robotics to the algae-blooming wall, Janice turned around and began pointing at a large figure solidifying under one of Terra's large dome processors. "What the...look!"

Elisa pulled Janice down to safety under a small dead robot, and they watched nanytes rotating like a hurricane around a white-hot epicenter. "One of those light-based entities is forming!" In seconds, a giant winged man appeared. "It looks like an angel." Janice's Visual Analysis program was compiling an energy frequency and location. A partial result appeared. "The Live Stream Field appears to be the fabrication center of all the virtual invaders."

"Dark Destroyer!" the gargantuan creature roared through a static-filled wind. It hovered in the air, bellowed again; and on wings, soared over them toward the wall of glowing crystalline algae that had been impervious to Janice's attacks. When Dark Destroyed struck the wall, a bright flash of crackling light detonated, rendering the green infestation defeated. No sooner had the explosion dissipated, and then a cleansing indigo beam undulated throughout the entire area.

With the data attack won, Elisa collapsed to the floor. Through tears of relief, she looked at her fingers. "I thought we might die there for a few seconds!" She marveled at her life as Janice lifted her off the floor now shimmering with repairing properties.

"That Dark Destroyer saved us, Elisa…a light-based entity—wow!—who woulda believed it! I thought they were attacking humans, not helping us," she exclaimed, and then a terrified expression wafted over her face as she glanced around in suspicion. "Some powerful data stream almost won over us, but thank goodness for your friend, EJ."

"And Dark Destroyer," Elisa added feeling a flush of calmness. "Now, we know two things: one, for some reason, someone is creating the light-based creatures; and two, the Regeneration grid is evolving to take on actual physical properties and attack people. If we can't contrive a program to separate the impulses of peoples' minds that have been uploaded into that grid, they'll eventually, and pretty soon, form one intelligence—one entity. And no telling what kind of artificial intelligence we'll have on our hands—"

"Especially if the new being gets ahold of a real body!" Janice added. "We've got to do something, and fast, to stop everything that seems to be snowballing out of control. I bet it's also involved in fabricating these light-based entities."

More creatures began materializing in the distance beyond their line of sight. They could see them over the map guiding them forward. Their birthing data streams were like brilliant whipping yellow contrails—beams of electrified information—processing in Quantum Nonlocality. She and Janice could only hear their roars, shrieks, cries, and shrill screams as their hot creation zones birthed them into existence. They were like new stars inside giant multi-hued clouds of nebula high up in the dome. After they appeared, they began a slow move toward the transport tunnels.

"I know we've got to do something," Elisa called to Janice over the commotion. "We also have to move on—" She gestured at the map. "Find the LSF that isn't too far east of us, and stop all this data creation before these creatures do some *real* damage to the population and *Sagan*."

Janice then received a Kill-code visual over her wrist device, a type of destructive malware hackers in the mid-2020s input into Photoshop games. The code was the signature of a deadly entity about to form right in front of them. "We've got to think of something and fast! Unlike the other light-based entities, this one is emerging from a ubiquitous bandwidth—magnetism and electromagnetic energy combined into a new emerging waveform. So many new waveforms are emerging and merging all around us!" She showed Elisa the most confusing but innovative Kill-code frequency that was an image of a long staff. Her wrist device was also receiving a musical major chord in G-major. Elisa decreased the volume, but couldn't turn off the sound. "If this creature escapes to the upper levels, my family's in danger!" Janice said, trying to stop the G-major noise that appeared to be responsible in part for nurturing the creature's form.

Seeing its frame materialize some more, Elisa remembered the Grim Reaper—a deadly character in the on-line game

*Skeleton King*, and Janice retrieve more bad history on the character: several countries outlawed the game for its harmful neuro-linguistic programming and subliminal messages. "I think the object materializing is a staff...with a scythe blade at the end. It's most likely programmed to—" She had a terrible thought: slice people to bits!

Janice was holding a small squirming robot close to her chest as if terrified to unleash it on the Grim Reaper for fear it would devour them. "We have to find Regents Asa and Ruth Stein. Maybe they know how to stop this—this creation Data Stream!"

"I don't know. I'm thinking...concentrating...focusing hard to blow the thing to bits," Elisa began, feeling energy leave her mind and penetrate the heaving chest of the deadly Grim Reaper. "I'm trying to stop it from growing and leaving here—"

"Well, here's a shot of nitro, you beast!" Janice screamed at the creature, and then fired spays of extinguishing coolant at it, but her attempt to stop it failed. The scythe wrote a message in the air: *A Sentence of Death.* Janice gasped, as the letters began glowing in yellow flames.

Running to a section of broken LED panels that were warped and twisted on the floor, Elisa grabbed some of the circuitry, broke it apart in her hands, and unleashed a stream of glass at the creature that shrieked, turned to attack her, and began turning purple with escalating anger. "Well, that experiment failed...now I have to think of something else."

"And fast!" Janice said, tearing off a boost that Enforcer Ben Tucker had given her for her wrist device. She extracted several small robotics out of the backpack, and linked them together with the malleable booster putty. The robots lit up into miniature flood lights of powerful potential energy. "Activate a one minute explosive!" The timer on her wrist device began the countdown at fifty-nine seconds.

"Good thinking!" Elisa said, ducking, avoiding a current of retaliation from the Reaper that whipped over Janice's body. "It's not touching me...it knows I have the ability to fight it off, but it's using *Sagan* energy to exist."

Seeing dread, fear, and fatigue wearing on Janice as she continued to spray the creature, Elisa said, "Now we have to stay alive. Ya ready?"

Janice replied, "Ready as can be!" She grabbed a scrap piece of aluminum from the trash and wrapped the line of explosives around it. Pointing her invention at the Grim Reaper, she gestured at several processor hubs up high, glowing with energy, "If we detonate the creature, I think we also need to destroy those hubs. They appear to be connected to the Live Stream Field that's feeding the creatures...with the matrix as a medium...and Mind Meddling scanners that have been receiving peoples' fears and using them to enact a death sentence on the crew. At least I think that's what's happening."

"So we explode the creature and program a ricochet effect into the hubs," Elisa said, searching through her backpack. She found the laser in the satchel, and she quickly extracted its chip, and set the explosion to spread to the hubs after penetrating the Grim Reaper.

"Now let's pray all this synchronizes and works!" Janice cried.

As the countdown struck fifteen seconds, Elisa motioned to a bright light in the distance—another entryway. The white streak on the map was pointing in that direction. "Run!" She picked up two extinguishers and threw one to Janice. "We'll get a backlash...so spray them when I give the signal!" They dashed toward the bright light.

The Grim Reaper had completely formed and was slowly heading their way. It had yellow current energy for eyes, an orange angry gaping mouth, and was shrieking and screaming in retaliation. It had noticed the countdown. The distance to safety was thirty yards. The feat looked impossible as Elisa fought off a disabling numbness in her left arm. "Ready?" After Janice unclasped the nozzle of her extinguishers, Elisa cried, "Now!" They began spraying coolant behind them, and an explosion pummeled them to the floor, propelling them toward their new entryway.

Looking back, Elisa saw a white swirling cloud that looked like a ghost where the Grim Reaper had exploded. Streaming through the air like kite tails caught up in a tornado, the white nanytes began hissing and making scratching sounds. The ceiling hubs were smoldering, but self-repair systems were working hard to restore their processing capacity.

"The explosion worked!" Janice called. "The processors should now stop creating light-based creatures!"

"At least in this area of Level-9," Elisa said, gasping in relief. "But there's on old saying: when one door closes—"

"I know, another opens," Janice said, scooting up next to a partition leading into another corridor. "But don't say that applies to light-based entities."

"It's true," Elisa said, handing her some water while watching the hubs return to their normal processing structures. Just then, a white angelic figure appeared over the cloud of nanytes, inhaled them, and then retreated into the hubs like a vacuum suction.

Janice threw down her extinguisher as a *hazard* siren blared. Streams and columns of robotics began flowing across the floor to the explosion area. "You definitely have friends in strange places, Elisa."

Puffing out a laugh, Elisa continued to watch the robotics head to their fix-it destinations. "I really wanna cry...I really do!" Wiping flame retardant off her the back of her hand, she stomped on a patch of white foam the floor began to slurp into oblivion. "We have no idea why this is all happening, their point of origin, and their creator!"

Janice put her hand on Elisa's shoulder, leaning on it for support. "Well, let's move on and find out. We're close!"

Another Self-Repair program activated. The floor rumbled. It was absorbing everything broken and foreign. Quickly, they stepped into an entryway. Looking back before a door shut, they beheld the decimated area that was like a valley of repairing junk.

"Now, back to the business of finding Asa and Ruth Stein, and the Live Stream Field facility," Elisa said. The G-major sound had subsided, and she smoothed down her pants and blouse—eliminating the static. After moments of listening to diminishing noises, realigning Janice's guiding map, and getting a solid position on their location via Elisa's outdated wrist device, a light fog began settling around their feet as glowing virtual butterflies, dragonflies, and ladybugs gathered around them from on high, forming a human figure. "It's Terra— Standard Terra!" Her heightened senses fine-tuned to every little nuance occurring around them, Elisa felt relief, but also skeptical about *this* Terra version. Anything could attack again—from anywhere and the elusive mysterious Creator. Nothing is as it appears in this strange central Level-9 area!

# J.P. Osterman

## Chapter 26 – Bubble Worlds

After she motioned for Janice to step behind her, protecting her with her left arm, she said to Terra, "I'm Doctor Elisa Holton. Are you Terra-IV?"

"And I'm Doctor Janice Kiplin," Janice introduced herself, straightening the delicate strands of beads that had gotten tangled in all the commotion. She released a fluttering, Purple Spotted Swallowtail off her finger as Terra stabilized. The receptionist nodded yes, and waved them through the large white entryway and down another small corridor into a lab filled with various transparent monitors. The guide map had them only feet away from the Live Stream Field. "So this must be the place where we have to prep before we enter the LSF," Janice said to Terra who was walking ahead of them and activating a secure grid for transmission.

"The Regents are in hiding, but they instructed me to give you a message so that when you find Asa and Ruth Stein—" She gestured forward to an area north of them, "you can give them an essential code that will help you restore habitability on this level." A flush of red static wavered through her image, along with a red emergency code—an obvious attack on her matrix—the red signifying death and approaching total disconnection from the residents. "If you cannot locate Asa and Ruth Stein in the next five hours and discover the origin of all the light-based entities, *Sagan* will venture out of spacefold propulsion and be in a stranded state of disability."

Janice whispered, "That must mean the onset of the Failsafe we discovered." A round panic appeared in her green eyes. "We can't be disabled in space! We'll all die!"

"I know," Elisa said, "that's been my mission all along, to find the source of the light-based creatures and stop the Creator who's been intercepting peoples' fears and then terrorizing them."

Janice and she were now inside a multi-colored lab, fifty-by-fifty feet in diameter. It appeared concave at the center—although quite straight—making Elisa feel a bit dizzy. Janice whispered that she felt as if she might slide downward, and clutched Elisa's right sleeve for stability.

"Doctor Holton and Dr. Kiplin," the receptionist began, "welcome, and—" Her image turned to hissing static when she motioned at a special center stage flooded with white light from the dome.

"It's a monitor and cloud architectural center!" Janice exclaimed as her wrist device illuminated data on their location.

Suddenly, a full-static transmission broke up Terra's image, and she disappeared. Just as they were about to take refuge behind a tall sleek monitor, a brilliant hologram activated on the bright stage, containing stats and images of Nelta and its other fourteen-interplanetary neighbors: Two newly regenerated binary suns and the newly regenerated Nelta. Another visual bubble appeared next to the show of Nelta: several light-based invaders stalking several abandoned Living Cube halls throughout *Sagan*.

"Thank goodness people are staying inside though, and the creatures aren't pursuing them there," Janice said. "We must have been right. The entities are solely attacking Enforcers."

"And Regents!" Elisa added. "That's why they're in hiding and need us to locate the Steins. But this appears to be data we also need—information concerning Nelta's current status."

"Which, by the way, seems impossible since we won't even approach the solar system for another four weeks," Janice said, checking her Saved Homepage information on *Sagan*'s current trajectory. "I do notice a spacefold slowdown though…I guess the beginning of that Failsafe we've gotta stop."

"It's another puzzle piece," Elisa said, feeling confused as another scene from the past popped out in a visual bubble on the brightly-illuminate stage feet front of them.

"Elisa—it's Asa and Ruth Stein!"

Asa and Ruth Stein were in a rowboat in a calm river, and Asa was rowing. The date, time, and location appeared: The Mississippi River in Wisconsin, before the attack of June 10, 2057."

"They looked happy," Janice said, "but I wonder why this image is here right now and if they're this together right now?" She began peering around their small facility as hums and Self-Repair systems continued to clean up and refurbish all the destruction outside their location.

Elisa saw more pertinent information. "This was taken when they graduated from MIT."

Janice began shivering and rubbed her arms. "These two Regents are connected to everything that's been happening. I just know it." Untying her jacket off her waist, she donned it; and Elisa did the same. "Oh gosh—we gotta find 'em. Time's running out!" Janice exclaimed, shaking her head in a gesture of hopelessness. "I don't like this…I don't like this at all, Elisa." Rubbing her hands together, she added, "God, it's cold in here." She looked down at her feet. "Fog!" She began lifting up her feet as if the fog contained a contaminant.

"Looks like it's coming inside here now," Elisa said, trying to connect her outdated wrist device to the special hologram platform. "If we can link with this thing, maybe we can enact some changes and make this zone a bit more user friendly," she joked.

Janice didn't appear humored. "Maybe it's just a gut feeling I have," Janice began, her green eyes appearing spellbound by the show of Asa and Ruth Stein. "I have a bad feeling…a bad gut feeling…"

Elisa also felt her intuitive compass of dread-and-fear move up a notch. Those instinctive dark premonitions were like expanding seeds whenever she tried to remember the past three days that someone stole from her life. "Well, let's just keep close. Bad things seldom happen to people who move in pairs, right?" She was trying to be positive and encouraging even though she felt terrified. Then she remembered her special powers and abilities. They had protected and shield them for the past several hours. They had fended off a few creatures that could have inflicted serious electrical/magnetic damage and killed them! The proven alien technologies morphing inside of her were like warm chocolate flowing through her insides—soothing and reassuring.

"Hey, if someone wants to put an end to someone else…kill us, I mean…no amount of data, whether a perfect positive or a perfect negative correlation, will stop a person from hunting us down and murdering us…you know that from past experience," Janice whispered angrily.

After she spoke those words, several of Asa Stein's images appeared around Ruth Stein. In all his pictures, he was a head taller than Ruth, had short sandy-colored hair, and seemed to make it a habit of wearing stripped shirts with blue jeans. Because she knew how the Regeneration matrix grid stores private patient information, she asked Janice to connect the Visual Analysis program with her Regeneration Corridor-15 user name and password. Private and detailed data began flowing at the base of their bubbled images. Elisa slowed down the scroll of data. "Asa Stein is still married to Ruth." Ruth Stein's image and more data streamed in at them. "She's a Genomics Specialist turned Archivist Engineer," Elisa said. "She's now helping him process recordings for *Sagan*'s return to Earth and for those who want to remain on Nelta."

"So they're responsible for what the entire crew can access

and be denied access to," Janice said. "They're like mediators between The Regents, Terra-IV, and the residents."

"They're obviously powerful people," Elisa said, remembering Jean Trent, one of their employees who was now missing and considered a criminal.

"They must have done something, or *failed* at something that relegated them to this place when all the others managed to escape before the light-based attacks began on this level," Janice said.

Elisa directed her to watch more information on the two missing Regents. "Ruth's maiden name was Ruth Eleanor Herbert. Her specialty is stem cell Research and Development."

Janice lifted Asa Stein's image out of a bubble from the past and set it next to Ruth Stein's youthful face. "Research and Development combined with stem-cell genomics means experimentation." She glanced back at the foggy entrance. "I don't like this. I don't like what I'm reading one bit." She breathed in fear. "I feel trapped. All these robotics we've seen…and I'm sure confidential archival information… can get us into huge trouble!" She was touching the yellow strand of neck beads that appeared to calm her down.

Rolling up her left sleeve and showing Janice a bit of her glowing wrist, Elisa reassured her, "No one's gonna mess with us, trap us, or hold us here. I've proven that. I'll just call back that Grim Reaper!" she laughed. Not really.

Janice blushed. "Okay…I believe ya. I guess if you can explode that thing, you can direct just about *any* source of electromagnetic energy. It's like the spectrum knows your name." She fist-bumped her right arm—an expression of humor.

Elisa then saw a historic program of Asa and Ruth exchanging their wedding vows. "Look, it's December 21, 2063, two months after Terra-II activated around Earth. But so much has changed since then." She couldn't help recalling the terrorist attack, her parents' deaths, and the way the Earth—and humanity—changed forever, especially after First

# Astrocity Sagan

Communication Day.

"So Asa and Ruth *can't* be bad people, right?" Janice asked. "*She* can't be evil, and he some kinda freak Doctor Moreau just because she was a former Genomics Engineer and *he* a former Medical Engineer."

"Of course, not—" *I hope*, she mumbled. "But if they are, they'll have a helluva fight if they try something experimental on us!" she exclaimed, holding up her left powerful special arm. With the bright center stage still showing data, still revolving in visual-virtual bubbles, she whispered, "Let's leave and move on." She saw the time on her wrist device: 6:16 p.m. They had spent the last ten minutes of the five hour countdown gathering information. But they to *encounter* the information—the creator—and stop the light-based creatures.

Janice again unleashed the guide map from its hidden program and projected it in front of them. "The Live Stream Field is near—"

"Just down that hallway," Elisa said, inspecting the map and pointing east. Walking toward a giant steel door, she called firmly: "Come on, let's find Asa and Ruth Stein."

# J.P. Osterman

## Chapter 27 – Morphology

As they meandered down a sound-proof hallway, they paused when a wall-mount processor droned on another ship-wide, *Emergency Alert-3* message. Dirk Hunter materialized in front of them. With yellow cat's eyes, fake red lips, a Victorian suit, and a false moustache, he was using another eccentric disguise and false identity to communicate through another rendering to the residents. This time, Dirk was speaking to people from inside one of the oldest post offices in the United States, The Old Log Post Office, built in 1802. On the other side of him was a welcome arrow, inviting social-media participants to enter other historic mail offices from the Old Wan Chai office in Hong Kong to the mailroom of the 1688 office in Bombay.

"Wait!" Janice said to Elisa who was about to dismiss his alert. Janice stretched the blue strand of her necklace beads. "Let's see what he has to say. It might help us."

"I guess losing a minute won't hurt," Elisa said, stopping and watching his announcement. "I hope the guys not long-winded like usual. We don't have time to waste on a clown act."

In obvious panic, Dirk Hunter stooped down and began whispering: "On temporary hold is *Expedition-1* to Nelta. Matrix Analysts have intercepted these holograms from

# Astrocity Sagan

Doctors Elisa Holton and Janice Kiplin who are trapped on Level-9, with Regents Asa and Ruth Stein—"

"That's us!" Janice cried.

Dirk Hunter continued: "Thus far, the other eight Regents have managed to evade the light-based invaders that are appearing at random throughout our astrocity. Right now, they're only frightening people and attacking Enforcers, but The Regents' Special Agents believe they're actually hunting down The Regents...and they're beginning at Level-9 and working their way up to the rest of us. We have a countdown before total takeover: Four hours and forty-six minutes. We can only speculate what will happen to all of us at that point; but for now, Matrix Techs and Enforcers are working their hardest to locate the creator of the entities and stop him or her from attacking us through the matrix."

Dirk began showing a current event occurring on Level-3. A swarm of pint-sized, virtual mutant bees were sweeping across the dome of the Center Arts Facility. They had owls' eyes, bats' wings, but the bodies of bees. Their stingers were glowing in a deadly blue poison.

"The analysts are now convinced the invaders are hunting down our Regents," Dirk Hunter said in a serious tone as he walked into a Pony Express rendering located in the Wild West. Glancing around, he whispered as if terrified of being stung: "As soon as someone can disengage the program that is creating these invaders, Executive Regent Manning insists that he and his colleagues will remain on the run."

A loud gasp and moan resounded in the background, followed by stomping feet and sounds of a stampede. It was a dubbing program Dirk Hunter often utilized to advertise his social-media grid and spin sound effects. After the dubbed applause and caricatures of residents faded, he continued: "Ladies and Gentlemen, there is no need to panic." *Ah-ah*, he breathed, *ah-ah*.

"He sure looks panicked to me," Janice whispered. "I bet

the crew's gonna pick up on that emotion and start a ship-wide manhunt to find the Regents and hand them over to the invaders!"

"I hope not!" Elisa said, glancing around and down the hallway leading them closer to the Live Stream Field. The Level-3 alert began subsiding; Dirk Hunter's voice fading.

Janice continued to watch the dregs of his broadcast: stills of a few Regents moving incognito around the ship. At several points, virtual invaders—in the forms of a bee, a vulture, and a miniature lion—honed in on a Regent and attacked him until a Terra hub fired an interference shot, disintegrating the invaders into a cloud of multi-colored nanytes. "No one knows what we know and has seen what we've seen," she exclaimed solemnly.

Elisa stretched out a hologram of Thornton Manning who was obviously in hiding and working in one of the Regeneration Corridors on Level-5. "There he—"

"Shhh," Janice interrupted when the image of him whirred, but then quickly altered into an image of an old-Earth, Delta airplane terminal in tropical Florida. "The matrix sees and hears everything...and so do the light-based creatures!"

"That's right, I forgot," Elisa said, and she jumped up high, grabbing on to the wall processor hub responsible for projecting Dirk Hunter's broadcast. "The light around this thing is sputtering." She saw a frequency: electromagnetic and sound. "There is definitely a ship-wide alteration in progress— a new system *someone* initiated. And the change is occurring in *all* the hubs."

"Starting from down here...and coinciding with the attacks," Janice added.

"Yep," Elisa said, capturing more images from the old iPhone device she had grabbed out her backpack. She had vaulted an abnormal twenty feet into the air to retrieve the hub information. After Janice asked her to take a sample from the base, Elisa did just that and then said after she noticed a strange absorption occur in multiple bandwidths and waveforms: "The new system is receiving and changing electrical impulses, from some type of cloud architecture, even human impulses gleaned during Regeneration…and then the matrix is processing the altered impulses with images from The Archives."

Janice added more new developments. "Then the Data Stream combines with the new hub technology, Mind Meddling technology and Regeneration technology to alter space/time which in turn interfaces with the matrix and manufacturing—"

"That's the glue—the cement for the creator of the light-based entities!" Elisa exclaimed, dropping down to the floor. She noticed a dark center at the end of the hallways. "Shh, look!" Janice cowered. "The creator of the light-based entities is hearing our every word!"

The three-foot-round whirlwind of dark froth down the hall was beginning to reflect their faces like a mirror.

"Don't think anymore," Elisa said.

"How the hell can't I do that?" Janice cried.

Elisa grabbed her hand and pulled her along the side of the wall around the frothing nanyte entities. She felt a shield of hot protection surround them as she heard millions of chattering, whirring, whipping, and mixing sounds—the nanytes forming a sentient entity. Her checks felt bitten, her feet filled with lead as she pulled Janice around the cloud of foaming nanytes. As they dashed down the hallway, she told Janice, "Any more thinking regarding The Regents, our location, and the Live Stream Field will most likely create some type of virtual invader."

"We don't want that," Jan ice shouted, her face red as if she'd survived a hail storm. "I forgot that this place hears," she whispered.

Then Elisa's wrist device began glowing. "A message!" A visual appeared over it: a necklace with crystal beads. "These were inside the satchel someone left for me on a Maglev," she said, rummaging through her backpack. She pulled out the satchel. Another image appeared, prompted her to snap them off and stick them behind her ears. Giving two to Janice, she followed the directions. When she experienced no ill effects, she motioned for Janice to do the same. Her wrist device activated an orange icon that linked with a grid somewhere between Level-3 and Level-2. "These are Mind Meddling inhibitors," she told Janice, after she noticed a portion of a processor hub explode over her wrist device.

"Just what we need to keep the creator of the entities from digging into our thoughts again," Janice said, breathing in relief while walking down the hallway leading to the LSF.

As the nanytes dispersed behind them, Dirk Hunter's hologram appeared clear in front of them. They stopped to listen to his newest emergency message: "Matrix Techs, Quantum Physicists, and Nano-Biologists are working around the clock to eliminate the light-based invaders. Please avoid all transport stations, remain inside your Living Cubes, and if you're at work, stay there. We've discovered a biological component to the invaders. Disinfect your hands, your clothes, and even your bodies. And don't touch strangers. No hand shaking or shoulder bumping...that's what the experts are cautioning." Dirk Hunter put on gloves and a scarf. "These invaders, these misfit creatures, are evolving up the chain of evolutionary sophistication."

A hologram appeared, depicting a nanyte cloud circling a woman's virtual pet cat she was walking down a pathway outside a café. As the woman screamed, her cat morphed into a half-cat half-fly, bit her on the back, and then began barking and buzzing as it lifting off and flew into the domed sunset. Enforcers began firing on the pint-sized creature as a physician sprayed the woman with stem-cell healers. They carried her off on a gurney and into one of many emergency centers they had erected to deal with these new attacks, now focusing on the entire population. The countdown was at four hours and thirty-five minutes, with more attacks pummeling people by the minute. "Level 4's Medical Center is filling with people presenting with some pretty serious injuries as we speak," Dirk

# Astrocity Sagan

Hunter explained. "Genomic Specialists are creating antidotes to counter these strange nanyte bites right now. The maintenance crew is installing misters and stem-cell healing chambers as quickly as the Manufacturing Facility on Level-7 can assemble them."

A group of people charged passed him as an Enforcer on a hovercraft chased a creature with the head of a tiger and body of a zebra. The attacking creature was morphing back-and-forth from nanyte cloud to creature, its offensive maneuver to avoid being dispersed by the officer.

Dirk Hunter's avatar appeared and began whispering in Dirk's ear. "Go away! Get back inside the matrix!" Dirk shouted at it as the avatar began crying in disobedience but finally disappeared. "All avatars could lead to a physical attack," Dirk said, gasping for air. "I'm sorry, Ladies and Gentlemen." He slicked back his black shiny air. He looked hot and sweaty as if suddenly stricken with the flu. "All quantum computing seems to attract these creepy creatures. So keep your avatars Off-mode for right now." Then he appeared serious. "I just received more information about their specific targets."

A hologram-within-a-hologram flashed on. At the center of Level-1's Religious Center appeared a line of body chambers with people entering the glass fixtures followed by a gaseous disinfectant surrounding their bodies.

"The invaders are specifically targeting Regent DNA," Dirt continued as he sipped water and walked into waterfalls inside the virtual Trevi Fountain. The delicate motions of undulating water appeared to be protective shielding as he took refuge far inside the majestic running streams. Still, the projectors were able to outline his image so residents could see him. "If you are genetically related to a Regent or have genetic markers matching one of the Regents on Earth prior to our launch, a Biotech Engineers should be contacting you right now and whisk you off to a protective area. There is a live round-up occurring *right now*, to help you. Everyone except the children seems to be targeted. The entities aren't at all attacking children under sixteen…and we're not clear yet as to why…but we're grateful they're all safe."

He then directed everyone's attention to a high-ranking Enforcer who was busy chasing a virtual invader that had morphed into a 1967 Corvette Stingray. Dirk said: "See everyone, we *are* under attack! Someone instigated it, and scientists are doing everything to find the source of the invasion and stop it!" With sirens whirring all around the base of his hovercraft, the Enforcer was in full pursuit of the rampant yellow Stingray that began laughing at him through its back lights. "This reminds me of that Disney *Cars* series from a few hundred years ago, Ladies and Gentlemen," Dirk began. "You can summon the shows and order an encounter right now for twenty euros and some odd cents." The Corvette Stingray disappeared into the wing of a giant pterodactyl that shrieked and spiraled high into the dome. The Enforcer suddenly stopped. He was groaning in frustration and failed retaliation. Dirk Hunter had a warning expression on his disguised face. "The Stingray is sure to appear somewhere around *Sagan*. Watch for the bright yellow, almost blinding paint job," he said, blinking, and then wiping his red bloodshot eyes. Then he perked up. "A Regent just contacted me from an Antarctica rendering!"

A snowy hologram appeared in the background.

"Here is Regent Jenkens!" Dirk announced. Even though he was standing outside Jenkens' world of snow, Dirk shivered as his hair and black suit became wind whipped. "Sir," he shouted through a blizzard in Jenkens' Antarctic world, "please tell us what you just told me as to how one can evade an attack should they find themselves cornered by one of these critters."

Clad in a blue-down snowsuit with a thick row of black fur around his face, Steve Jenkens pulled down his frost-covered gloves and shouted to the audience: "If you find yourself trapped or cornered by one of them, quickly enter any rendering, and immediately engage with your holographic surroundings. The interaction tricks the matrix and the attacks stop—" He appeared suddenly cornered. "But not for long—*ahhh*!" he screamed as something or someone had obviously spotted him and was about to assault him.

"How does an inanimate place stop an attack, Regent Jenkens?" Dirk shouted.

"Interference, Dirk! Can't talk now. Gotta run! But changing scenes scrambles their hyperspectral processing abilities and offers a short-term reprieve," Jenkens yelled through a blustering wind. "Snow dogs have been pulling me on a sled for over two hours. I've been able to avoid detection for two hours, but not much longer than that."

His holographic dogs began barking. In the not so distant background, large penguins with green glowing eyes were waddling toward him as if in Attack-mode.

"Here they come! gotta go!" Jenkens cried, and then he disappeared in a thick cloud of snow.

His cold, frostbiting rendering hissed as it faded into a black-and-white network, leaving Dirk scrambling for an explanation. "Well, Ladies and Gentlemen, *ah um*, one moment please," he said, tapping his earbud. "I cannot divulge Regent Jenkens' current location, but at least you have a solution should you yourselves become trapped by a light-based invader."

The Terra camera zoomed in on Dirk Hunter's smiling face.

"Run into a rendering and quickly participate!" he shouted, and then he entered a Tahitian virtual world. He was now wearing shorts, a flowered shirt, a lei, and flip-flops.

Still watching Dirk Hunter's show, Elisa said to Janice: "Well, *we* don't have the luxury of entering a rendering."

"And too bad we can't get more of these crystal protectants to people," Janice said, activating a scene on Level-2. It was showing people coughing and gagging as they exited body chambers after having received Dirk's recommended disinfectant treatments. "So many people are in trouble, and we're running out of time." She looked at her wrist device, her eye signature opening up and displaying the four-hour and thirty-minute countdown. She held her chest as if she was having a heart attack. "Elisa, if we don't stop this invasion, this gosh-awful infestation, people will become infected *permanently* on the cellular level...the damage irreparable!" She appeared faint. "My husband—*ah-ha*—my children—I—"

"Stop!" Elisa grabbed her arm and pulled her out of the virtual world in which she had become suddenly absorbed. "I see the time, but look...even though the Regents are in hiding, they're still in control. And technicians and Enforcers are everywhere. People are okay...your family will be all right. We're working hard to locate the creator of these virtual monsters."

After she fended off her spell of fear, Janice said, "Come on then, Elisa, let's keep walking and find those missing Regents."

They were nearing a giant archway with a green neon monitor on the right side. In the center was a giant red eye spinning out-of-order. Something had disabled the monitor during a powerful attack. "Something's definitely ravaged this hallway," Elisa said. Seeing a laser trip light that could inflict severe burns, she put her left arm into the spinning eye, and the harmful rays backfired, striking and exploding the malfunctioning eye monitor. Then she and Janice dodged into another hallway and were surprised by two, tall transparent robots that began ushering them onward: "Corridor 5A directly ahead," they kept repeating—their programs stuck.

"Just a little bit more and I know we'll find those trapped Regents," Janice said. Then she suddenly stopped. "Hear that?" The robots kept progressing down the hall, leaving them.

Elisa heard a faint voice. "Someone's screaming!" They both activated their spectrograph programs to receive heat and sound signatures, and pinpoint the location. "There's so much interference though, coming from everywhere..."

# Astrocity Sagan

"Darn light-based critters!" Janice said, her wrist device projecting conflicting data on the voice's Doppler readings.

"Help! Please! Here!" cried a woman. The words kept repeating.

"Is it real? Or another trick of some kind. Maybe an attack on us?" Janice whispered, linking her wrist device to an eye scanner on the side of a doorframe. When the Break-In alert sounded, Elisa smashed the scanner with her left fist. The scanner began smoldering, the door unjammed and lifted into the frame, and Janice ducked into the illuminated room for safety.

Then Janice received an *Urgent* reply from Ernie Bentley. He was finally off work from his Navigation job and responding to Elisa's request for information regarding the Navigation Failsafe that was endangering the residents and *Sagan*. He told Janice and Elisa the dire situation of everyone onboard. The light-based creatures were biting and clawing everyone related to a Regent; but a prominent physician, Dr. Nguyen, was working on a cure for the debilitating bites that were leaving victims comatose after an incubation period of thirty minutes. Urgent Centers had opened on every level, but not all the human targets could take refuge in those shielded places without being snipped, or bitten, or clawed, or stung by one of the many weird entities stalking the astrocity. "But I can send you a Homing app that has the ability to break through any kind of interference," Ernie said, showing them a dime-sized glowing processor button. "The Homing program gathers waveforms and bandwidths, and then weeds out interference...the kinds of noises and obstructions the light-based entities feed on to survive. My invention," he blushed, pointing to himself in pride. "That Dr. Nguyen is experimenting with, along with a biological, could heal everyone who's been attacked. But we need a specific signature from the Live Stream Field. Since you're there, you can locate the breakthrough signature and send it to the location I'm streaming to you along with the Homing app."

"That's where they're emanating from, Ernie, right here," Elisa said.

"And we're awfully close to the epicenter and locating their creator," Janice said angrily, followed by a hostile rant of what she intended to inflict on the creator personally.

After Ernie streamed them the app and a virtual world they could launch inside their hallway that would allow them to walk to the Live Stream Field undetected, Elisa told him about their hunt for Asa and Ruth Stein. Again they heard a woman scream. Ernie's Homing program began eliminating all the other noises, heat signatures, and electromagnetic frequencies so as to locate the origin of the screams that had to be coming from someone experiencing severe pain and distress. Elisa then told Ernie about Asa and Ruth Stein's jobs as Lead Archivists. "Their work is definitely tied to the light-based entities. It's imperative that we find those two missing Regents and fast." She gestured at the Failsafe countdown: 04:20, 04:19, 04:18...

"Go!" Ernie said, shooing them on, "but first activate the rendering I just streamed to you and enter it quickly. And be safe...and send me that special signature so Dr. Nguyen can mix an antidote!" Then Ernie disappeared.

Watching the Homing program focus on the direction of the scream, Elisa said jokingly, "I'm glad I woke up next to *him* after having lost three days' worth of memories." Janice activated the rendering Ernie had sent. Their surrounding altered, and they found themselves standing in a green grassy roundabout with four pebble pathways diverging into four white hallways. The Earthen sun was low on the horizon, a light balmy breeze wafting, and a strange bluebird circling in the distance over a giant oak tree. Elisa recognized the bird as EJ, now their guide and lookout for trouble.

"I definitely feel we're on a road less traveled," Janice whispered as she cautiously stepped over crunching pebbles, echoes of their augmented surroundings. Their curved path suddenly dumped them into a white hallway, and Elisa stopped when the voice grew more pronounced.

"Help! Please! I'm here! I can hear you...but I can't see you!"

Elisa felt puzzled. The voice sounded mechanical. "Could those be the sounds of a *real* person?"

Janice forced shut the door behind them. "Wow—a bad storm just developed in that world we were in!"

"It's the Failsafe countdown, or the creator of the light-based entities who has discovered our close proximity to his or her creation zone," Elisa said. They quickly arrived in front of a door with a tiny gold sign: *Lab 3, Live Stream Field Center.*

"Come on, Elisa! This is it!" cried Janice.

As they bolted through the lab filled with laser-light optics and disorienting frequencies, the Homing program briefly malfunctioning in all the confusion and they stopped several times and opened several doors in an attempt to locate the screaming woman and the corridor leading to the Live Stream Field.

"This place is a rat's maze!" Elisa exclaimed.

Nearly breathless, Janice checked all her programs. The combining information was attempting to lock onto a specific location. The VA program and Homing program were synching as a compass and needle—the red arrow vacillating between east and northeast. They were now between two solid steel doors. "One of these doors *must* lead to the LSF."

# J.P. Osterman

## Chapter 28 – Asa and Ruth Stein

As Elisa was about to open the door on their left, a short pale woman dressed in a flowered A-line dress ran straight toward them. She looked like someone out of the 1950s! She was panting, crying, and blowing her nose into a pink hankie. Her cheeks were running with black mascara, but when she stopped in front of them, Elisa noticed her unusual bright blue frightened eyes—like small pedals on a lilac. "Help me! Thank God you're here!" Then the black ooze under her eyes suddenly disappeared, as if the light in the lab had acted like a detergent.

Noticing the sudden change on the woman's face, but ignoring the alteration because of her dire state and urgent pleading, Elisa stepped toward the pained woman who quickly jerked backward in *a don't touch me* gesture. "Where do we go?" Elisa asked softly, trying to calm her down. Janice reached for her arm but missed it when the distraught woman jumped back in obvious terror of being touched.

"This is puzzling, and weird," Janice whispered to Elisa.

Nodding yes, Elisa asked the woman, "Doctor Ruth Stein?"

"Yes—it's me," she replied, and then panted again. "You must be Elisa Holton—and you Janice Kiplin."

"We are," Janice said. "What—"

# Astrocity Sagan

"We've been waiting for you—the experiment—it failed," Ruth interrupted.

"What experiment failed?" Elisa asked, through worried breath.

"Later—come on," Ruth turned and began waving them in the direction from where they had come. "This way!"

Running down several hallways, darting around automated monitors, kicking robotics, and dodging three popping-and-sparking processor hubs that were in states of Self-Repair, they followed Ruth into a large high-tech facility where a giant pillar had toppled, pinning down a man.

Ruth ran to him and knelt down next to his bleeding head. "He's my husband, Asa, please help him. I've done everything I can, but he's lost consciousness."

"Where did that giant pillar come from?" Elisa asked, not seeing anything resembling it anywhere in the lab, only terminals scrolling holographic codes and algorithms. Trying to lift the pillar off his waist, she heard a distracting noise.

"What's that?" Janice asked as she stopped helping her. In the distance, as if shining brightly in black space, she saw several diamond-shaped ceiling hubs in a circular formation. At the circle's center was a powerful light beam—a hot-yellow column of quantum-streaming data—flowing from top to bottom; and from there, destined for use on the astrocity. But first, the quantum information had to flow to Level-7, to Terra's Cloud Matrix for assimilation and security processing. As if feeling the magnitude of the computing power's intensity, she showed Janice. "It's the Live Stream Field," she whispered while trying to lift the pillar once more off Asa Stein. She found a long steel rod, stuck it between the pillar and his hip, and Janice and she began pushing down hard, trying with all her might to pry him free—her powerful arm pulsing with energy. The strain drained her. "This thing isn't budging," she breathed. "This pillar is a drain, depleting me," she inhaled, oxygen flushing back into her lungs, her energy level recovering.

"This pillar had to be the experiment Ruth talked about that went sideways," Janice began. "Maybe it's some kind of Roman or Greek rendering that a light-based entity touched and turned to stone." She ran to the hologram platform that appeared responsible for the rendering. The world showed a place-stamp: *Greece, 543 BC.* "What were you doing in this world, Dr. Stein?" she asked Ruth. "Was there some type of attack that happened here?"

Ruth kept shaking her head no through all her tears. She was devastated, and appeared to be on the verge of dying should her husband not survive. Elisa continued to try prying off the huge pillar while intermittently drinking water Janice had thrown to her.

"Dr. Stein," Janice began, her fingers lifting code out of several images. "I'm trying to decipher the pillar's components so we can learn how to break objects into images and then images into their composite bytes. The pillar is obviously under pressure by some type of unstable gravity. Any suggestions?"

"I tried that. It won't work," she shouted, still kneeling next to her husband and peering longingly into his face.

Then Elisa noticed Ruth's ripped dress and her bleeding arm. The blood appeared a strange glistening orange-red. Gliding over an Emergency station that had been hovering around them but now ready for activation, she grabbed a healing patch and was about to slap it on Ruth's arm.

"Don't touch her!" Asa Stein suddenly said as if snapping back to life. He was aware, but barely, and then he moaned and collapsed into unconsciousness.

"Help him…please," Ruth pleaded, again wiping her eyes. "I'm beyond help, but not him," she said softly, her voice wavering like the secrets she was obviously hiding. When tears ran down her cheeks, they were silvery streaks.

Her intuitions reaching a tipping point, Elisa stood up and tipped over the medical Emergency disc. "What the—"

A program activated, and a virtual rendering of mirrors

appeared in a large circle around them.

"We're surrounded," Janice cried, as their reflections materialized everywhere—capturing and reflecting their every move.

Ruth began clutch at the floor as if trying to hold onto a blanket. "Oh no," she screamed.

"What the hell happened here?" Elisa asked, grabbing Janice and diving behind the pillar for protection. "This entire place is half-real and half-virtual!"

"We might slide right out of reality!" Janice cried.

Ruth motioned to the column of quantum power in the distance. "The Live Stream Field is engaged in an active experiment with the processors in here," she said, and then she slid back to her husband, coaching them to stay low to the floor.

Elisa took the steel pole and pointed it at one mirror that was casting a bright light onto the pillar. She had an idea to fix two problems with one strike. "Janice, use your Homing program to narrow down all the frequencies, then we can create a target-specific plan." Janice ignited the program that synched with the room's technology. Musical chords began sounding in a cacophony, but the sounds quickly decreased as Janice's program began eliminating everything but the mirror and pillar. "Now, let's do some shattering!" she exclaimed, directing Janice's Homing program to zero-in on the mirror shining blue light on the pillar.

"Do it!" Janice shouted, her hands covering her face.

Elisa launched the steel pole into the mirror. It struck the glass and then hit the ancient pillar that looked lost in time. They could hear people shouting and screaming coming from beyond the pillar. Their words were ancient Greek, and they were obviously terrified. "The Gods are angrier than ever!"

"This place is partly in the past!" Elisa said.

"Well get us out of the past," Janice pleaded.

"What you're doing won't work," Asa said, lifting his head

and grimacing in agony. "The negative isn't antimatter." He was about at the point of death.

"Do something!" Ruth shouted. She was right up next to his lips but wouldn't touch him, and he kept ordering her to back away.

"He's more concerned about her than he is about himself," Janice said, tearing up. "I feel that way about my husband. I wish he was here." She appeared suddenly angry and vengeful. "I'm not letting this place kill us. I'm doing something!" She began crawling toward one mirror, tilted due to Elisa's powerful throw.

"Stop, Janice!"

She wouldn't listen. After managing to crawl under the tipped mirror, she ran behind a long curved hologram terminal situated in front of a tall tungsten door with a long narrow protective window. The terminal was gigantic with multiple stations, all interconnecting and capable of producing and manipulating apps, code, and electromagnetic frequencies. She was at one of *many* stations functioning with the Live Stream Field.

Through the protective window, Elisa could see her initiating holograms that began showing several scientists working on various levels throughout *Sagan*. Janice had a happy smile—a look of win and victory—as she quickly gave Elisa the thumbs-up signal and then returned to manipulating images over a hologram terminal. Elisa could see four famous *Sagan* Fixers: a software genius, an astrophysicist, Dr. Nguyen the Biomedical Specialist, and an engineer. Together, they had solved navigational puzzles and dark matter/dark energy glitches throughout the years of spacefolding to Nelta. If not for their out-of-the-box thinking and their wacky-appearing inventions, the population might not be alive, nor *Sagan* maintaining its complicated wormhole-route to Nelta. They'd all be dead; the spaceship, shrapnel that would be materializing at the fringe of Nelta's solar system in six weeks.

With platinum-blond sweat-soaked curls on her forehead, Ruth Stein suddenly cried as she told her husband: "I love you, Asa. Just hold on. I just know Doctor Holton and Doctor Kiplin can figure out a solution."

Elisa then noticed their strange way of relating to each other, and Ruth Stein's appearance and behavior. She hadn't once gotten within an inch of Asa, yet she yearned to touch him. And the rip Ruth had in her sleeve was now mended; the bleeding cut, healed; the runny mascara under her eyes and on her cheeks, gone. Did the air morph everything imperfect back into a state of perfection and Marilyn Monroe look-alike precision? She thought: if I were in *her* spot I'd be doing something, not waiting for someone else to figure out solutions. This Regent's a mess! And so is her wacky husband. What the hell kind of experiment did they conduct down here? Why didn't they just leave it when the others left?"

"I have answers to two problems!" Janice quickly cried. She lifted an image off the hologram terminal, ignited her avatar, and set the images of the scientists next to her avatar. "Hunt for a neutrino deposit in the propulsion center," she instructed the four scientists as she directed another mirror to target the pillar. White light began streaming from a ceiling processor to the mirror, then appearing on the weighty pillar. "The hologram and reality were now correlating," Janice said. She was also searching through scrolling code to activate a Separation program so she could separate the pillar from Asa. Then she said to the scientists who were busy examining neutrino compositions: "Tell Dr. Ernie Bentley that what I'm sending him is what he needs as a final ingredient to heal everyone who's been infected by the light-based creatures. It's a neutrino!" She smiled in elation. "A simple neutrino mix will cure people if you combine it with what you're now already using." The scientists began adding *her* streamed information to *their* problem solving apps, algorithms, and theoretical conundrums.

Elisa shouted Dr. Walker's information to her that appeared over Janice's wrist device. "You met him too at the

Choosing Ceremony. He's an expert on procuring technology. "He'll know how to juggle everyone's suggestions and solutions."

Janice's avatar touched hands with the thrilled scientists. Her avatar's eyes flashed green, and the scientists and her miniature Native American avatar disappeared as the five-way communication extinguished.

"Dr. Stein, give me your password now!" Janice ordered as she showed Ruth the image she could use to free Asa and return the pillar to ancient Greece. There was a yellow halo shining over the pillar, a scythe image. Janice had captured the image from the Grim Reaper and was using it to counter Ruth and Asa's bad experiment.

Meanwhile, Elisa had retrieved the pole and was holding it firmly under Asa's waist. In her left powerful hand, the pole was becoming titanium. "I'm ready! I've got strength to lift this thing off him on your command, Janice! Then send it back."

With fear-blue eyes, Ruth scooted farther away, moving as if the beam might also detect and destroy her.

Janice was calling on statistical holograms and interfacing them with unsolved equations and half-finished atomic compositions. "If I can combine a neutrino compound with anti-matter, I can use the Data Stream to resolve gravity on the pillar. I just need a few more seconds…a few more matrix grids to create the concept."

Ions began snapping and sparking high above Asa. Tiny bodies the size of gnats began popping in and out of existence. They were swirling out of control, tumbling and careening into one another.

Ruth scooted frightfully under a terminal. "Doctor Holton! Move back!"

"They *will* copy you," Asa shouted. "They'll do *anything*…become anything and anyone…to materialize into this universe!"

"Elisa, you're standing in an inter-dimensional portal!" Janice screamed, waving for her to move away from Asa. "I need it activated to eliminate the pillar, but it'll snap you up into another place, time, or dimension if you don't get out from under it!" She appeared about ready to run back into the hot zone to save Elisa.

"I have to stay," Elisa called back to her, realizing the danger. She couldn't leave. Much more than Asa's life was at stake. "I'm a stabilizing force in here...I can feel it."

Asa was now able to sit up half way. The pillar was glowing and reconfiguring to the past. It was now sputtering between two places and times. Elisa began using her left hand as a guide to fend off the eager zapping creatures from another dimension. In the interim, Asa directed Janice to another holographic stage on her right side that could interfere with the dimensional portal. After she launched the countermeasure, he shouted, "The program should now be on Assemble-mode." The circling, gnarly gnats of souls above them exploded out of sight. They all sighed in relief, but Asa and Elisa could still not separate the pillar from Asa's body. The two cell structures were intermingled, deeply.

"I'll try using your Body Double scan to extract the rest of the pillar, Dr. Stein," Janice said. A small, yellow line of flowing energy from above began beating down on the pillar. "This should take a minute...so this countdown says," Janice said. She was inspecting and integrating atomic equations so fast that her fingers looked like whips.

Ruth Stein stood up and peeked behind the partition separating the hot zone from Janice. "Dr. Kiplin, I didn't disengage one program you're working with." Janice stopped as if suddenly petrified. "I left the program on hibernate, hoping to interface it with an archival grid in Corridor-2. I tried looping two matrix grids to help him. That's what failed."

"That would have also killed you, darling," Asa said. "My Ruth, so changed, all because of me." He whimpered and then moaned in pain as the separation program Janice had launched began freeing him. He could sit up and look at Ruth; and he appeared almost healed if not for the glowing changing pillar still slightly adhering to his side. "I told you no...*no*! All this because of me—"

"No—because of me!" Ruth countered.

Janice swiped off an image of the Greek structure the pillar belonged to in the past. "Stop arguing, please! I have to send that object back into the past before we alter history."

Elisa felt the energy in her arm spread through her body, striking the pillar. As Asa slid out from beneath it, she fell down on the glowing floor. The pillar disappeared into the past, but she felt the abilities in her body now a quantum-communication conduit for the Data Stream.

After the Greek structure appeared whole over a hologram terminal, Janice began working to dissipate the Data Stream lingering around Elisa like a long hot needle extending from the ceiling. "Elisa, keep down." The stream was getting longer, its direction like a compass needle flowing toward Elisa. Janice rushed to another station and began adjusting trajectories and frequencies to the Live Stream Field. It was flowing from the circular Live Stream Field in the distance, through processor spokes along the ceiling, directly toward Elisa's body. Janice cried: "Now my friend is stuck out there as a magnet to the LSF. And the experiment *you* started looks about ready to eat her up or suck her into the matrix!"

# Astrocity Sagan

## Chapter 29 – Impulse Entity

In a state of existence between life and death, Elisa felt her mind and soul separate from her body. She watched Asa stand up, stumble to Janice behind the protective steel partition, and begin helping her stop the Live Stream Field from intensifying over her body, now lying limp on the floor. As pure spirit, she was in an exchange of information with the Live Stream Field. Seeing beautiful nano-string entities while her Neltan abilities shielded her from being detonated into the matrix, she felt drawn to the nano-string life forms delicately swirling around her. She remembered a rendering she had participated in as a teenager. Odysseus, the man who had fought against the Cyclopes and survived, encountered seven seductive Sirens who tried wooing him to death with their songs. Only by being tied to his ship's mast did he escape them.

"What you're seeing are impulses from peoples' minds, Doctor Holton," Asa Stein yelled. He obviously knew what had happened to her and knew her consciousness was still whole inside the matrix. "An entity inside the matrix has been forming for quite some time; and with you now present there, it's using your special abilities to come to life in physical form…in here."

# J.P. Osterman

"We realized that hours ago, Sir," Janice said, angrily. "But how do we stop this Frankenstein process, 'cause soon they'll accomplish their goal."

Ruth appeared shocked by that news of Elisa's biology. "But the Live Stream Field is also a particle accelerator, capability of reconfiguring space/time. Those entities *will* suck her into the matrix, body and all, if we don't stop the entity."

"Dr. Kiplin, talk her back to her body," Asa began, as he sent a Buffer program into the Live Stream Field, now crawling yellow energy hovering over Elisa.

"Elisa, think water!" yelled Janice. "Water always helps you!"

She did just that, but couldn't free her mind from the entities hypnotic grip. Then, she felt little bits of her energy lift off her body—her Nelta Encantado technology feeding the forming entity that appeared as a tall white body, right next to her. Now, *her* body was *its* conduit! The thought entities flowing out of the matrix, through her, and into the forming being appeared angelic. The burgeoning entity was now all red muscles with hollow sockets for facial features.

"I'm starting the Integration process now to bring Elisa back to her body," Asa called, interrupting the flowing entities.

Suddenly, nanytes flew out of a two ceiling hub behind Janice's terminal and began devouring the forming human being.

"The—the ssseeeaaalll! Find the Seal!" the burgeoning person cried through slimy lips. The figure was trying to complete itself, but nanytes from the terminal continued to circle around it, feeding on the androgynous being. Without skin, its body began to shrink, cave inward, and melt. It was now in state of decomposition—the abnormal process obviously torturous for it as the creature shrieked in shrill groans and moans, until its lips melted into its torso. It still had a long way to go before the creation process would end.

"*Ahhhh!*" Elisa cried, heaving in air as if breathing for the first time.

"She's released from the Live Stream Field," Janice

exclaimed.

Elisa breathed again, but felt pains in all her joints. Asa explained them as empathetic responses to the forming entity. She discerned another problem. "It wants to become human and has a mind, but then its program to create a body fails. The clone technology it linked with on Level-7 failed." Wiping away tears, she turned to Janice who appeared helpless as to what to do. "You're the expert though, Janice," she began, slowly making her way to a towering partition for safety. "I know you can help stop whatever is fueling its growth...do whatever it takes!" She felt useless now, her Neltan abilities nonexistent, but she didn't want to voice her concern to everyone when she wasn't one-hundred percent sure. "Janice, *do* something!" She wondered if Janice could even hear her. The air around her felt distorted, and she heard humming and droning. "I think this person—and me—are existing in a different reality!" She tried wetting her lips that felt like rubber. She couldn't move her arms even though she was up against a partition.

"You're both smack-dab in the center of Terra's Live Stream Field, Elisa, and we're working like heck to get you out and stop the Creation program that failed to evolve," Janice called. Lifting a holographic equation into the air, she called, "Catch!" She flung one end of a virtual tether into Elisa's hands and the other end to a ground terminal where the rope solidified into a protective net around Elisa. "I've gotcha...just hold on! This terminal has a tough photonic grip on ya!"

The entire lab became covered in rainbow arches of quantum processing, and the burgeoning being began rapidly decaying. The rope began extracting Elisa out of the Data Flow zone and toward Janice's large terminal station. Still the creature hadn't died.

As Asa Stein continued to work hard and amass more LSF capability, Janice lifted an algorithm in front of her. "This is the solution. These equations and calculations are finally combining—*whew.* "

An infinity symbol materialized in front of Janice. Then an alpha symbol attached to one curved end, and an omega symbol joined the opposite end.

"The solution is Neltan," Ruth said, joining Asa's side but also keeping a safe distance from him. "Now splice this Neltan infinity symbol and add it to the calculation you have intersecting several equations over here." She flipped two equations and then swept them to Janice.

Janice caught them and inserted the Neltan symbol into Ruth's equation. Then she flicked on her wrist device. Her tiny avatar appeared, its eyes blaring green in Wait-mode. "Initiate the Nelta language program and their *Quantum Projection Physics* program," she ordered her avatar.

The Native American avatar's eyes began projecting language symbols in front of Janice.

The Live Stream Field in Elisa's hot zone suddenly morphed into fluctuating rainbows.

Janice began linking several holograms. "I'm composing a Translation program that will interact with my avatar…then these two Neltan equations…then a new matrix grid to insert into the Live Stream Field." She whipped several calculations into a new flaring Matrix program. "It will divert into the colors, activate various electromagnetic frequencies, and then the current should melt the glue holding together the creature."

"Then the thought impulses in its mind will be free!" Ruth exclaimed.

"Let's hope so, 'cause they're really bits of other peoples' minds," Elisa added as colorful lights began intersecting around her.

"I'm altering deviation angles and enhancing dispersion quality," Janice said.

One stream of light struck Janice's avatar that acted like a prism, refracting the light into the Live Stream Field around Elisa. "Done!" Janice exclaimed and then flicked closed her wrist device after her Native American Indian avatar faded.

Elisa could hear their shouts of happy relief, but she was

still tethered inside the matrix-singularity through which enter and exit have no meaning. Even the decomposing creature was now frozen in a stasis loop. "Janice, I'm—"

"Water—I shoulda thought of that!" Janice unleashed all the wall-mounted fire extinguishers that began synching and spraying water in the hot zone. Then she grabbed hold of the tether fastened around Elisa. "Move—now!"

As water hissed and smoked off the dying entity, Janice reeled in Elisa who landed in front of the thick partition. Then Asa grabbed her, yanking her behind the wall of protection. After seconds of feeding Elisa water, Janice activated a Medical program that initiated a nurse who began examining Elisa. Janice said, "At least the entity gone, but I can't find a way to reconnect people with their lost thoughts." She continued working with Asa for a solution.

Lying down while the nurse kept scanning her, Elisa felt numbness spread over her skin. She was seeing spots, and she blinked to get rid of them, but then she realized the dark dots were really in front of her eyes, and surrounding with blue light. "Are you EJ?" No answered. "Am I dead? Are you here to take me?" She could hear whispers as she glanced at the dead entity with its white soul hovering in the hot zone over its melted body.

"You must go to Nclta," one of the glowing dots told her.

"But first remember your promise to us!" another said; and then the glowing dots streaked into the white soul.

"Connect us back to our own minds!" several exclaimed.

Suddenly, a bright yellow line of energy struck the creature's soul, lifting it high into a rotating current. The Live Stream Field had trickled into the hot zone as a network of flowing webs—feeding the main Live Stream Field in the distance. The Live Steam Field was beginning to expand everywhere …and soon, would ripple and overtake Level-9; thereafter, all of *Sagan*.

Janice said to Asa and Ruth, "If we can't reconnect these

fundamental elements to the Cloud on Level-7, this astrocity will become nanytes when the Failsafe strikes zero." They had three hours and twenty-five minutes until destruction. "We have all the elements, but not the creator of that entity and light-based creatures. We need the creator! We've got to work harder than ever to get a location on him—"

"Or her," Asa said, altering several programs and composing new code over his giant terminal.

Still trying to recover, Elisa suddenly remembered the spirits she just encountered. They were her friends! Real human thoughts! And they had access to information neither she nor anyone else could obtain. All she could do was to lie back down, recover, and hope Janice and the Steins could fix the rampant LSF.

Outside, in the hot zone, nanytes began forming an equation. Janice shouted through the sounds of zapping and hissing energy, "This powerful flow in the matrix is organizing algorithms, chemical equations, genetic information, and Neltan symbols." She walked over to the thick door with the small window and donned special glasses. Asa followed while Ruth continued uploading virtual signs and symbols into a new matrix grid. After Janice's lab glasses turned black for safety, she peeked outside into the bright powerful LSF. Terra's processor high up in the ceiling looked like a giant solar prominence interacting with the Field.

Asa stammered in obvious shock, "Terra is—is communicating to us in Neltan!"

"I need your passwords again, now," Janice called to Ruth and Asa Stein. "I can't access this one particular grid in the matrix 'cause it has a Top Secret stamp." She was lifting rows of virtual tuning forks that were responsible for generating musical notes, frequencies that had helped them before. "I can divert sound to the ceiling hubs. That should create a portal, suck up the rogue data flow in the hot zone, and help us stop the devastating expansion that'll destroy our home!"

"Astein101," Asa called.

"Rstein101," yelled Ruth.

# Astrocity Sagan

Terra's beehive processor descended from the ceiling and activated a laser-light transmission of sound from the virtual tuning forks. The reverberations interfaced with Terra's main matrix in the circular Live Stream Field in the distance. The data field in the hot zone began wavering.

"Put up more of a barrier in here or the Field could encapsulate us!" Asa yelled.

Janice returned to the terminal, doffed her lab glasses, composed a C-Major chord, and then tossed the musical notes into the ripping hot zone. "Keep repeating," she ordered the terminal.

The blaring, repeating musical notes were like cold rain beating through a hot desert air, and the hot zone began to return to normal. Still, the area had a long way to go before anyone or anything could enter it and live to tell about their experience.

Ruth raced over to several illuminating equations. "These are solutions too, Janice, so catch!" Using her hand as a directional pointer, she swooshed them over to Janice, who applied the equations to a Nelta program. "But the Failsafe countdown is still ticking," Ruth said, her shoulders slumping.

Elisa felt herself gradually slipping back to normal as she continued to watch them celebrate at least one victory. The being was gone, its body a pool of melted nanytes slurping slowly into *Sagan*'s structure for use as needed. The Live Stream Field was functioning at normal intensity, but Terra's Level-7 Cloud Matrix site was still in need of fixing. It needed a concoction, a special element only she could input to discover the creator of the light-based entities, and then deactivate the Failsafe. The time was still ticking down: 03:05...

# J.P. Osterman

## Chapter 30 – Half Way Successful

Elisa felt cold and sick. "Water, please." She breathed for relief, pushed back her hair, and tapped her cheeks and forehead. She had to regain feeling, and her senses. Sipping water Janice put against her lips, she sat up. "That person died. I—I feel like I died with her." As Janice helped her stand up, she remembered what the forming being had said. "She said something about a seal." She glanced around the laboratory now back to normal. "Is there a seal somewhere around here? I have to find it." She still felt groggy and bleary-eyed. "Janice, do you see any type of sign or symbol anywhere? Maybe the dead person left something behind." Her gut instinct fed her more information about the creature. "She was supposed to be a girl."

"Sorry, Elisa...about being able to help her," Janice said, with a choked-up expression. "And no, *she* didn't leave *anything* behind." She was still behind the giant terminal and searching for programs that had any sort of *Seal* title. "Nothing here."

Asa Stein was panting and grimacing in pain. The pillar that had interposed itself into his flesh was gone but it left residual effects. "I tried sending out another call for help," he said, "but there's still no connectivity to any of the level above us." He pointed at the door. "Right next to this lab is the

# Astrocity Sagan

Language Facility. Perhaps the creature interfaced with symbols or programs there."

"We'll go there as soon as we can open a door, Doctor Stein," Janice said. She was busy swiping and interchanging architectural designs.

As Janice explained to Elisa what she had done to terminate the rampant data flow, Elisa noticed a door materialize and open up behind the giant terminal. After showing it to everyone, she said, "It looks safe, so let's go!"

"It's the Language Facility…but it appears change," Asa said, waving for Ruth to join him.

The towering high-tech walls inside were streaming scientific data. Some were coursing with navigational coordinates, some projecting interstellar maps, and a few displaying intergalactic paths that *Sagan* had already taken to Nelta.

"Now that you opened the barrier to the Live Stream Field, Janice, these U-shaped terminals inside the Language Facility are free to communicate in ancient Neltan," Asa said.

"Because the exchange of quantum information experienced a diversion, which the creator of the light-based entities obviously exploited, we almost got killed, if not for Elisa…and her Neltan biology," Janice said, patting Elisa on the back. "You do still have some of those special abilities of yours to communicate with the light-based entities, don't you?" She appeared a bit frightened. "Don't you?"

"I don't know," Elisa replied, shuffling her feet, rubbing her left arm, and feeling a bit like in a fog. "I guess we'll have to wait and see…and hope I still have my abilities if the time comes when I have to use them."

"Me too, or we could be in for some trouble down here," Janice cautioned.

Asa continued working with codes and rendering virtual Seal worlds. "I'm hoping this ancient language has some type of Seal translation that might solve the mystery as to what element we need to interface with Terra's Cloud Matrix and find the creator of the light-based entities. I'm sure as heck pissed off...and will make sure the criminal is jailed for life...even on Nelta!"

Seeing a giant processor hub cycling around twenty hubs on the ceiling, Elisa noticed miniscule light-spokes extending everywhere. Her personal Terra suddenly appeared in front of her. "Twin!"

Janice touched Elisa's hand. "Ouch, I got shocked!"

A spoke of light struck the top of Elisa's head—a quantum connection to the matrix.

"Not again...this place is definitely trying to do something through Elisa again," Janice said, inches away from Elisa.

As Janice, Asa, and Ruth proceeded to coach Elisa away from the spoke of light, Elisa felt suddenly transported into a small kitchen inside the apartment she lived in as a child. She was like an ant-on-a-wall, watching the scene: Her mother was eating, her father washing dishes. "Where am I?" She was about to take more steps into the virtual rendering.

"No, Elisa!" Asa yelled and touched his chest in pain.

Ruth's milky cheeks paled. "Step back, Elisa! Now!"

Janice bumped her out of the spoke of light that streaked back into the ceiling processor.

Elisa woke up out of her teleportation into the past. "What happened?" she asked, watching them sigh in relief as Janice deactivate a language program. "I was home, in the past, and feeling all nice and toasty warm, but I couldn't find myself *anywhere* among my family."

The Language Facility's southwestern door unlatched, lit up, and opened up invitingly.

Asa lifted his dry bloody shirt out of his pants. "The Archives, down the hall, is connected to this Language Facility." Fatigue and loss of blood were overtaking him as he stumbled but quickly recovered. "You might not have come out of that world if you would have entered it, Elisa." He appeared about ready to give up a deep secret.

Elisa felt manipulated. "What's going on, Dr. Stein? I

think it's time you told us, don't you?"

Through an expression of fright, Ruth said: "We were halfway successful, Asa. We *almost* did it."

"Almost did what?" Janice asked, peeking back at them from the open door.

"But not all the way, Ruth. We failed." He waved apologetically at Elisa. "The space/time corridors went way out of control—*way* out of control." His blond hair was sweat soaked on his forehead and his voice raspy. Janice ran back to him and offered him a chair.

Elisa crossed her arms firmly. "You act as if I'd actually be snapped back into the past, Dr. Stein. But I wasn't in the past. Did that rendering ever even happen? Huh? Well!"

Ruth pushed back a sprig of her bleached-blond hair.

Elisa thought she saw the skin on her forehead glow. Marveling at the strange phenomenon, she gasped, "What—"

"I can explain everything, Elisa," Asa interrupted.

"I still can't break through the communications barrier that's separating us from linking with Terra's Level-7 Cloud Matrix," Janice said, trying to get a grid open over her wrist device while toying with the beads around her neck. "I'm certain people are trying to get ahold of us."

"The Regents especially," Elisa added. "This is *their* facility. They've got to be going crazy up there…jumping from rendering-to-rendering, trying to dodge the light-based entities."

Asa began sipping water, the liquid restoring his dehydrated appearance. "They know Ruth and I are here. They—they left us."

"They didn't have any choice *but* to leave you," Janice said softly with her head half-buried in a recording of the Regents' shuttle launching from Level-1's Ceremonial Platform. "No disrespect intended, but that's what I see happened here…before the imagers went dead and the entities trapped you here." Staring at them askance, she put her hands on her hip. "Elisa and I would like an explanation please. What happened here?"

Elisa stepped toward Ruth. "Dr. Stein, *something* is wrong with you. It's time to tell us, so we can move on, find the Seal element, input it into the Cloud Facility on Level-7, and wait for the language to reveal a Creator so we can stop the attacks and save *Sagan*."

"And the Neltans," Janice added. "It's clear you can't travel on any farther. You need help. After we stop the Failsafe, we'll make sure medics get down here and rescue you."

"Please—a little more time, *please*," Asa pleaded.

When an emergency medical niche suddenly freed from a stuck wall zone, Ruth ordered Janice to slide over its healing pod so it could scan Asa.

"Why doesn't she do it herself? You'd think she'd want to handle the intervention herself, not you," Elisa whispered to Janice. Ruth Stein was raking on her nerves. "And we asked important questions they're stalling to answer…so frustrating!"

Janice had an accepting expression. "That's okay, for now. It's been a hard day, and a tough time for them. Give 'em a few minutes to regain their composure, and *then* drop your grenade of answers on 'em."

Elisa whispered. "I don't trust them *one* bit though in the meantime."

When Janice initiated the body scan over Asa, a virtual physician materialized, projected a diagnosis, and administered a bio-bot injection through a mechanical arm on the pod. After the physician applied stem-cell patches to Asa's chest and torso, he exclaimed: "You are cured, Regent Stein, although I'm streaming orders to Level-2's Intensive Care Unit. I am prescribing three days' rest. I will also report this diagnosis and orders to Level-4 and the Main Medical Facility."

"Thank God!" Ruth exclaimed. "Thank you, God!" She moved her hands over her husband's head as if longing to touch him but terrified to set a finger on him.

As Asa's respiration and heart rate improved, Elisa

initialized a security program that began replaying a hologram of the afternoon when she left work to head down to Level-9 to talk to Regent Manning. But her exit into the elevator at her Corridor-15 station was as far back as the recording would display. Watching the program, she felt a bubbling intense anger. "Regent Ruth Stein, Regent Asa Stein…I have a few questions I need you to answer." Seeing Ruth's pained face, she added, "I'm missing three days out of my life and I—"

"Not now—please Elisa," Ruth shouted.

Janice stepped in front of Elisa. "I'm sorry, but I agree with Elisa. We're all on the verge of not making it to Nelta alive. If we don't…over time…who knows what will happen to humanity. We're in trouble—in real danger—and on the verge of *everyone* breaking down in chaos as people will start to do anything to save themselves—"

"*Ahhhh!*" shouted Asa.

"Don't you see that all your questions are putting too much pressure on him?" Ruth asked. "You have no idea…no knowledge of what we've been through here! We've been through hell—and—and—" She heaved in a draught of oxygen and began crying.

Elisa had to level with them. "Regent Manning almost killed me three days ago. And we almost died down here! Before I leave…well, I'd like to leave ya for the wolves—"

"Elisa!" Janice scolded.

Ruth Stein scooted into a shadow under a 3D panel. She was sitting close to Asa but still not touching him.

Still responding positively to the bio-bot healers, Asa waved her away, whispering: "There's another solution, another way, Ruth. You'll see. We'll find it."

"Strange," Elisa whispered to Janice, "these two are something else. I just don't get 'em! Maybe it's a religious thing, or some type of cultural practice?"

"Whataya mean?" Janice asked.

"Well, she cries over him, and he keeps reaching out to

touch her but never does," Elisa began. "He obviously wants to hold her, but then he swooshes her away." Listening, Janice continued searching for a program that would locate the Seal code in the Language Facility to download into her wrist device. "And what's the, *another solution*, Asa keeps talking about? Something illegal is happening with these two, Janice. This mess down here I bet was *their* fault, and that's why they keep skirting around our questions."

"I don't know...maybe," Janice began, "and perhaps other forces are involved in creating the chaos we've seen since we've been down here, such as the creator of the entities...or your female entity that just disintegrated...who really was made up of cognitive impulses from peoples' stranded minds...which we have to also return to their rightful owners—our population," Janice said. She lifted off holograms depicting theoretical equations and symbols of subatomic particles.

"Yep, we have to do that too...most likely the same time and place as on Level-7, where the creator is holed up," Elisa said.

"I'm gathering all the archival information on these two Regents right now," Janice said. "The program is interfacing with the one I launched to discover the Seal element. What a force of quantum-manifestation that woman was—my gosh!" Janice rubbed sweat off her face and a line of bangs fell on her forehead. She blew them out of her eyes.

"I agree, and what's developing now?" Elisa asked.

"My program looks for anomalies, outliers and threats to validity...anything out of the ordinary," Janice said. "We sure need a warning bell to sound before we encounter another mess."

Her tiny Native American Indian avatar began projecting all the data that the two famous Regents had in common.

"I have a hunch that what you said earlier was right. These two are still caught up in some type of failed experiment...a part of which left Asa nearly cut off at the hip!" Janice swept her avatar into a virtual rendering of where Asa and Ruth accepted their positions as Regents: The Hebrew University of Jerusalem. "And, as I said…I think something more is on the verge of happening down here. I'm trying to anticipate the abnormal, and prepare for the unpredictable, until we can find the Seal element."

Elisa flicked on her outdated wrist device, slid it into Janice's scrolling program, and a downstream activated. "I want to live so I can be part of the expedition to Nelta. Even if what you're doing is secret and illegal, at this point, I don't care. Just go and invent something to help us. You've been doing great so far."

"You too with your special abilities," Janice smiled. Then she turned serious. "I used to think I wanted to be a part of the expedition. My husband Doug encouraged me to pursue my dream. I used to think it'd be great—*exiting* to be a Chosen One. She exhaled a worn out laugh. "Not anymore—no way, *uh-uh.*" She had a dreamy expression on her face as she toyed with the silver-dollar-sized quantum-computer processor hanging around her neck beneath her colorful stands of beads. "Now, I'd give anything to be in Living Cube 404, hugging my husband and participating in a rendering with my children. I'd activate a world on Earth. I think Yellowstone, or Yosemite!" She waved in the air, obviously repulsed by a waft of disgusting stench from the dead being's disintegration. "Heck, any setting on Earth at this point!" She looked relieved as she nodded at an image of Nelta rendering on a wall monitor. "But dream's change."

"Yes they do," Elisa said. "But I signed on for this journey for the exploration. I was tired of just researching. And now, I like photography…old digital photography to be specific!"

Janice laughed, still waiting for her new program to finish. "My job inputting ratios and performing statistical computations suits me just fine, Elisa. So as far as I'm concerned, congratulations, Doctor Holton!"

"What?"

# J.P. Osterman

"*You're* going to Nelta with someone else, and I'm going home," Janice said firmly. "Send," she ordered her avatar.

The eyes of her avatar flashed green, but then blared red. The message diverted to Upload-mode. Communications were still off-matrix.

"What did you just do?" Elisa asked.

"I told the Regents I'm not going to Nelta. I don't wanna be a part of *Expedition-1*," she said. "When communications re-establish, the message *will* send."

"But Janice—"

"No more." She had tears in her eyes. "I *don't want* to be part of the expedition."

"But—"

"I've been exploring enough," she interrupted. "I've stepped on a level hardly no one's ever stepped foot on— Level-9. I've battled a Grim Reaper, nearly got sucked into a rampant electromagnetic current, and saved your butt a few times."

"Hey!" Elisa scoffed.

"And now, we're close to a ship-wide meltdown—"

"That I *will* stop!" Elisa exclaimed, showing Janice her arm. It appeared flesh-tone normal.

Janice struck the terminal over which she was processing programs. After telling Ruth and Asa she wasn't basing her decision on being fatigued, she said: "Sometimes people *think* they want to go in one direction. They take a risk and pursue that carrier path; but after a while and some hard knocks, they realize the path isn't right for them after all. That's me. I don't want this whole *exploration* thing *any* longer," she gestured magnanimously. "I want to go home."

Ruth began crying as if she could no longer hold back her secrets. "At least you have another option, Dr. Kiplin. You have a home to go to. We—"

Asa interrupted her. "We accept your verbal resignation from *Expedition-1*, Dr. Kiplin." He looked completely healed now and stretched.

"Yes, Janice, I wish you the best for you and your family,

whether you decide to stay on Nelta or return to Earth," Ruth said softly.

Janice reeled a little. "Okay—*um, ahem,* but you sound like you're saying goodbye permanently. Are you all right? Do you want us to order an emergency pod?"

"No!" she said, stepping into a shadow. The darkness made her completely disappear!

Asa began coaxing her out. "Don't go there, Ruth. Get out!"

## Chapter 31 – Ruth's Truth

The time flashed out an urgent countdown: *02:45*.

"I hope your program soon discovers the Seal element, Janice," Elisa said anxiously.

Suddenly, the program initialized a first layer of processing code, and light in the form of wheels shone brightly around all the Terra hubs high on the walls and ceiling.

Elisa could feel the power and awe of Terra's photon, Quantum-Nonlocality Information Stream—a perpetual force like Earth's magnetic field—responsible for the crew's entire survival, and *Sagan*'s structural integrity as it space folds through wormholes.

Janice increased processing power to her round neck-device. She needed both her devices functioning at maximum her new archival program.

Janice's tiny avatar popped up in front of them.

She ordered it: "I need all code sequences that initialized renderings down here between the time I arrive here and now. The only way we're going to locate the Seal element we need is to trace it through those codes."

As Asa had been flipping through renderings to help Janice, Elisa accidentally bumped into a hologram station. The station dumped a rendering onto Ruth Stein's arm and slurped through her flesh like butter, cutting it off.

"*Ahhh!*" Ruth cried, falling down. Asa ran to her with a helpless expression on his face and then stopped. The results flashed in his terror-filled eyes: he could do nothing, not even touch her.

Orange-red liquid flowed out of her forearm in a shower of nanytes that cascaded like molten plastic onto the floor.

"No—no!" He faltered as if he might lose the race against time, and then darted toward a terminal. "I have to re-create the interface—recreate the interface…" he kept repeating.

"You can't do that!" Janice countered, running to him to push him away from the terminal.

"Whata we do?" Elisa asked, dashing to Ruth as Janice called for her avatar to help them figure out an answer. Swarms of nanytes flickered like fireflies as Elisa inched closer to her. She felt her arm—powering up with Neltan power.

Ruth was sitting with hopeless downcast eyes next to her severed arm but not touching it. "Nothing can repair this…not anymore."

Janice gasped. "Whata ya mean, *can't repair this*? What are you? What's going on?!"

Elisa waved Janice out of the away and touched the edge of Ruth's severed arm.

As clouds of bright flickering nanytes streamed down around them from a ceiling processor, Janice yelled, "Here they come again…now what!?"

Asa walked back over to Ruth and leaned over her. "I'm here, Ruth, and I'll always be here for you, no matter what."

With her powerful left hand, Elisa began directing the nanytes into Ruth's arm. She noticed no bones and no muscle tissue. "Dr. Stein," she addressed her seriously, "I think you better tell us what happened and what you really are. I'm doing what I can to fix you, but the next time a piece of you slices off, it'll be much worse." Several clouds of reparative nanytes were working to escape her special Neltan current to stream back into the matrix. "I'm forcing this reconnection, like a forced feeding of the ship's energy into you. Obviously, *Sagan* doesn't like it."

"What is she then?" Janice whispered, but then she huffed out a breath of anger. "No, I'm not stuffin' my mouth with invisible cotton *anymore*, worrying about saying the right things the right way to you Regents. What *are* you, Dr. Stein?"

Sighing, Asa walked behind a terminal where Janice was accepting a Layer-2 code of the Seal element. They had two hours and thirty-five minutes to find the Seal element, stream it to the Cloud Matrix on Level-7, and discover the creator of the light-based beings so the Failsafe would stop. Two hours and thirty-four minutes before *Sagan*'s destruction. "That's what the two of us have been trying to do…to help her."

"I caused what happened down here," Ruth finally said as she sat down and slumped forward on the floor. Without her arm, she looked more like a life-sized doll than human. "Everything that happened is because of me."

"You can reattach your arm now, Ruth," Elisa said, stepping away from her after the nanytes had flown into the severed limb. She lifted up her forearm; put it next to her elbow joint, and the two affixed.

"Amazing!" Janice said.

Ruth stood up and rubbed her left arm. "Thanks, Elisa." She almost touched Elisa's left hand, but stopped an inch away from it.

"You're definitely not a virtual rendering," Janice said, her fingers over her lips in a gesture of amazement.

"No she's not," Asa agreed.

"Then, what are you, Ruth?" Elisa asked.

Ruth reached up and touched a tiny river of Terra's yellow processing stream.

"I think you should tell them the whole story, Darling," Asa said. "Sooner or later, people are going to find out anyway. Secrets," he sighed, running the back of his hand an inch away from her cheek. A blushing glow of nanytes swirled off her rosy cheek but didn't attack him.

# Astrocity Sagan

"They're sentient," Elisa said, acknowledging the connection her special biology was feeling with them. "They know her, and they know him."

Ruth laughed in self-abasement. "A ship as huge as this…and to think we couldn't just keep *me* secret—ha!" Then she moaned. "How can I continue living like *this*?" She looked down at herself, and silvery tears dripped down her cheeks until her skin absorbed them. "To think we could continue to live our lives in private …let everyone disembark on Nelta while we remain here…like this…encased in all the technology that *I* need but you don't." She shook her head no, and her whole body turned in rigid objection. A sudden breeze swept through the facility as more repair programs activated. Her A-line flowered dress rustled, and her white-blond bangs slipped on her forehead until she primed them up.

Elisa marveled at how she resembled the twentieth-century movie star. "How do you stay true to every detail of Marilyn Monroe?"

Asa pulled out a bottle of water from under a robotic station and began gulping it down as if the drink might be his last. "She looks like her because she locked onto that image from The Archives. The Archives and the matrix are in a constant state of sustaining her," he said matter-of-factly. "Come with us there and I'll show you."

"Good! We need to go there anyway to link all the code I've been accumulating in here to the Seal element," Janice said, as the Seal program displayed a download success rate of seventy percent over her wrist device.

As they finished syncing more portable technology to leave, Elisa whispered to Janice: "He's so eager to get outta here and get there. I wonder what he wants to accomplish at The Archives."

As they walked out of the Language Facility and down a long dimly-lit corridor to The Archives, Ruth and Asa took turns explaining what had happened:

# J.P. Osterman

"I brought a little piece of Marilyn back to life," Ruth said, "in me." She told Janice to activate a date and time in history that Janice, and a rendering of Ruth and Asa appeared. "Asa and I met first met in Israel, when I was healthy," she began. "But then the terrorist attacks occurred, and the fallout. Asa was unharmed because he was one of archeologists living secretly under The Temple in Jerusalem and excavating pieces of the original Temple. I was at MIT. Funny though, one of the main targets of the attack was Jerusalem! But they never did strike The Temple. Anyway, Asa emerged completely unscathed."

Laughing while rubbing the stubble on his chin, he said: "I never even knew that almost half the world's population was dead until soldiers freed us from a cave-in."

"A miracle! Thank God!" Ruth exclaimed through lovelorn eyes, her hand an inch away from touching him.

"People believed the Hand of God saved all the archeologists and Israel," Ruth said.

"But God didn't save you though, my Darling," Asa said, his voice wavering.

"Anyway," she continued as they stepped into another dimly-lit hallway toward The Archives, "Asa came out of the attacks unharmed. But me?" She motioned with her hands down her body. "A bomb exploded over Massachusetts, and radiation killed half the students at MIT. I was in an underground shelter, but still the facility wasn't completely environmentally sealed." Her chest heaved as she relived the horrible experience. "I saw most of my friends, die. And me?"

"By the time I arrived there," Asa began, "it was almost six months after the explosions. They wouldn't allow *anyone* of Middle Eastern roots back into the States until after thoroughly reviewing their background and confirming their Israeli ancestry. All computers were down. Most communications were cut off."

"If Asa hadn't discovered some of those archeological treasures to offer as proof of what he was doing at that time, I might not have ever seen him again!" Ruth exclaimed. "But by the time I did see him; doctors had already given me the bad news. I had three years to live."

"Cancer," he whispered, his head lowered at the floor. "Tumors. The pain would have been unendurable for her! But with Neltan technology streaming in after First Communication Day, I used research to help postpone her death. But now, I realize I can't keep postponing death forever." He lightly touched her finger and it passed right through her. She was light and solid matter. All nanytes working with light, the matrix, and The Archives they were near approaching.

"I don't know how he stayed with me," she said, crying. "I began breaking out into bumps all over my skin. I was so ugly, hideous and—"

"No you weren't. Not to me!" he interrupted, leaning over and kissing her—his lips never touching her. When her cheek responded with a glowing red blush, he stepped back quickly before the nanyte spot of flesh could dis-assemble and attack him. "You were always beautiful, and a caring person, Ruth," he said softly. "When global officers were executing terrorists later that year in 2057, after the last United States President approved the Torture and Execution Law, Ruth was one of the few who demonstrated against the law, and advocated for Due Process for them, even though the government threatened to imprison her for treason, and people threatened to kill her."

As he continued to speak, another rendering activated in front of them, showing a group of people trying to infiltrate Ruth's private hospital quarters where guards were keeping her under hospital arrest.

"I remember this," Janice said. "You championed the legal system…that everyone deserves to be heard in a court of law, even terrorist criminals. *Everyone* deserves to be treated with dignity."

Elisa felt the fury of that calamitous day all over again.

# J.P. Osterman

"Those insane terrorists sure didn't do the same to the people *they* captured, tortured, and executed."

Ruth replied: "I know, and you're right. That was the argument at the time—"

"And that's why I still love you, my darling," he interrupted softly, "and deeply in spite of the poisons gnawing away inside your body. But cancer *never* decimated your caring spirit...the way you keep seeing the good in everybody." He kissed the glow flowing from her lips.

Another rendering appeared in front of them as they made their way toward The Archives.

"This is how she looked when the first wormhole opened up over Earth," he said.

In the hologram, Ruth was a bubbly, brown-haired woman wearing flare jeans and an embroidered T-shirt who had tested out with one of the highest IQs of her time. In the aftermath of the terrorist attack, the after image of Ruth Stein showed her bedridden.

Elisa gasped when she saw Ruth's vital signs flat line. "You died!"

Janice reached out to touch her, but Asa shoved her hand away. "They only let *me* touch her, but only for a split second."

"And me," Elisa added, "but I don't wanna further test the nanytes' Neltan qualities," she laughed.

Asa continued: "Right after Nelta's Ambassador Shaesar transmitted the first Terra blueprints to Earth; I developed an archival program that merged Google Galactic, Terrain Site, Web Master, Cloud Computing, and every other imaging program I could get my hands on."

"You stole codes and programs then," Janice said under her breath.

He motioned for her not to label him a criminal just yet. "I combined those programs into one giant matrix program, and merged them with Neltan-based technology and Ruth's stem-cell research she had been conducting in China, Europe, and Africa. What you saw me working on in the Language Facility was our hope for a cure."

# Astrocity Sagan

"If you can call *this* a cure," Ruth said, running her right hand over her left arm. "I *am* Ruth Stein, but as you can see, I have an entirely different body…face and all."

"And there's more," Asa said sadly.

"What can be worse?" Janice asked. They were now at The Archives, and she had her hands on the door frame, obviously getting impatient to enter the facility.

Walking next to her, Asa said: "I whisked Ruth around the globe for organ transplants, stem-cell infusions, and finally cloning."

"But the old-fashioned cloning techniques failed because my body had deteriorated beyond replication," Ruth began, "so Asa had to store my consciousness until he could figure out a better solution other than cloning."

"And that's who you see standing in front of you," Asa added.

Elisa asked, "What will become of you eventually, Ruth? I mean, you can't remain light-based and function against *Sagan*'s parameters." She had another quick thought: Ruth's been inside the matrix and might have come in contact with peoples' trapped thoughts! She and Asa might have a way to free them! As she was about to bring up the revelation, Asa moved in front of a Biometric scanner and opened the sliding door to The Archives.

"In this place, and with the Seal program still trying to resolve, I hope I can find another solution to save Ruth."

# J.P. Osterman

## Chapter 32 – Last Steps

They walked into a large facility, The Archives. At the center was a rectangular fusion reactor producing a contained column of white energy stretching a mile into the dome. There, the energy broke into photons, flowing onto shiny gold plates along the curved dome. Asa said, "The plates are rare isotopes of gold we manufactured prior to leaving Earth. They're great conductors of quantum-information. The Neltans transmitted the manufacturing of the processors to us, and we use a derivative of gold to help produce plasma to power *Sagan*."

Elisa could feel the reactor's powerful force raising the hairs on her skin. Their subtle vibrations were emitting a slight green color, but there was a yellow zone, and a red zone at the center of the high-energy column. She walked over to what appeared to be an important vertical monitor, but no rendering was available. "This Display 2B seems to be in an experimental stage. What does that mean, Dr. Stein?" she asked shouting over a sudden drone.

"I think it's something to do with the Matter Stream, but Ruth and I don't know. Regents Manning and Jenkens and Navigation are in control of Display 2B," Asa shouted back.

She tried gauging his body language to discern whether he was telling the truth or lying. Deception or reality? She was at the point of total frustration and anger, and believing all of Level-9 should be made public. "People should be aware of this place, of you, and what you've been doing!" she shouted. Then the sentient monitors controlling the environment dampened the sounds, and the reactor's noises eliminated. Still, she felt as if she were standing in a giant cave with immense white walls, really LED projectors. Terra was using the walls to data mine all information throughout the astrocity. Then the matrix was simultaneously cataloging and storing every movement, sound, object and person. Since the light-based invaders had evolved to physical forms, the filtration program inside The Archives had failed, and the program progressively expanding close to becoming unstoppable as the Failsafe ticked down: *02:20*.

Janice tapped Elisa on the shoulder. "The program I'm developing to find the Seal element is almost complete; and thus far, it's indicating that *this* place *is* fueling the invaders…a type of new technology."

The Seal element now forming over the map of Level-9 was forming into a giant, glowing oval Regeneration pod.

"I can't ever remember seeing anything like this before," Elisa said. Then her head began aching, and Janice ran to her as a bolt of energy lifted off her left hand and ignited a pathway to a small level beneath them—a Core Level. "Wow! I feel energized! Fueled!" She stepped away from the map and Seal element rendering.

"I've never hear of a Core Level," Janice exclaimed, staring into the Seal element, really a gigantic glowing Regeneration pod. "The creatures also wrote that word *Core* in the sky." With anger wincing in her eyes, she turned to the two Regents. "You can stop the invaders, but you haven't. Why? Does that Core place have something to do with them? Is it their place of origin?"

"Core?" Elisa asked, her head pounding. She put her fingers on her temples and could feel strong vibrations rippling over her body.  A past event began welling into consciousness.

"I don't like what's happening to you again," Janice said after asking Asa for water.  "We've been through this before, and the outcomes weren't good…virtual monsters and now *this* place."   As Elisa drank and Asa continued manipulating holograms in a wild attempt to help Ruth, Janice whispered to Elisa: "Are you regaining more memories?"

An alarm bell resounded down the corridor, and Elisa could hear walls readjusting.  "Soon, the place in here will be converted into one giant facility—"

"Two miles wide!" Asa said, motioning for Ruth to remain near him.

A hologram suddenly activated at the center of all four of them, showing the column of energy beginning to stream faster.

The Seal element with the Regeneration-pod rendering lifted off Janice's wrist device, and a processor hub high above them sucked up the element.

"This place is now adding data to the Cloud matrix on Level-7," Janice shouted over a hissing commotion.  She pulled Elisa close.  "If you *are* regaining your memories, they better include a way out of this place when the Seal element links with the Cloud and we discover the creator of the light-based entities."  She began glancing around.  "He, or she, *has* to be around here, somewhere."

Elisa saw Ruth's shoulders slump.  She seemed to be in a state of debate.  "You're contemplating a solution, Dr. Stein, aren't you?  You know a way to stop the light-based invaders and the Failsafe."

Turning toward the crunching sounds, expanding walls in The Archives, Asa appeared terrified of something more ominous.  "She'll die though if she does stop them!"  After diverting one hologram from a mathematical equation and merging it with a rendering of a dark energy coil, he stopped cold.  "My colleagues, the other Regents, are on the verge of altering *Sagan*'s dark matter supply to make room for a more expanded version of one of their experiments."

# Astrocity Sagan

"What experiment?" Elisa asked.

"Yeah, *we* never approved of any experiment, let alone a Core level they've been keeping secret!" Janice said.

He appeared deadlocked. "They said I couldn't help Ruth anymore. They ordered me to, *put her away*. Those were their exact words." As he pushed his hands through his short sandy hair, he began shuffling his feet. "I can't—*can't* give up keeping her alive for *their* experimental forces!"

That puzzled Elisa. "Experimental forces? Oh, that's a Navigation term!"

"And it sounds frightening," Janice exclaimed. "You better explain a little more, Dr. Stein."

He was now obviously agitated, and Ruth shivering. Her blond hair, eyelashes and sagging clothes were projecting a melted quality.

The blaring alarms down the hall were intensifying as the walls in The Archives began expanding to accommodate the new force in Level-9. A hologram materialized alongside Janice.

She jumped back. "It's the Failsafe! It's initializing in two hours and fourteen minutes!"

"When it's done, *Sagan* will be gone," Elisa said. "We need to find the creator, now."

"Before another creature evolves…one more destructive than the last," Asa added as he initiated a countdown that blasted:

"*Five minutes to Action, Regent Asa Stein.*" It was *Standard Terra's* voice.

"Now there are two count downs," Janice said. "One the Failsafe, ticking down at two hours and fourteen minutes, and the other, the Action countdown, at four hours and fifty-four minutes!"

Ruth ran toward a swirling mass of contained fusion forces beginning to churn at the center of The Archives. "I have no choice, Asa!" She appeared ready to jump right inside it. "You can't keep feeding me this special mix to keep me alive—" She gestured in resignation at the walls. "I can't go on living like this no matter how much I love you."

"No Ruth!" he shouted, but Janice grabbed his arm, holding him back.

Elisa extended her left arm at the rippling, pulsing fusion forces. "I have these fusion forces under control, but I can't predict when my abilities will falter!" She felt nanytes all around her—light and light-based entities feeding her body with special energy.

Ruth stepped toward the towering torrent streaming high up on shimmering gold plates. Images were falling all around them inside gold flakes. "I have to teleport to Terra's Cloud Center, bind with the Seal element, and create an organic graft to deactivate the bio-archival program you started, Asa."

"No!" he shouted, stretching out his arms to hold her. But her nanyte skin layers, the adhesive for each cell in her body, released a lightning strike to his fingers.

"I can contain the rippling field, but I can't protect Asa!" Elisa said, a current from her left hand holding back the fusion stream at the center of The Archives.

With her wrist device, Janice showed Elisa a rendering she discovered of the exact formula Asa had developed to cure Ruth after they left Earth, and how his cure was keeping her alive. "Because they have the same blood type, he's been able to use the fusion reactor in here to create an electromagnetic sealant that every other week he infuses into Ruth."

Asa interrupted her. "Two years ago, the Regents began demanding I stop using the reactor for my personal use. They said they had to make changes to the dark matter/dark energy converters, and then they began pressuring me to put her away. I kept stalling."

"What changes to *Sagan*'s converters, Dr. Stein?" Janice asked. She whispered to Elisa: "This is serious business...propulsion business! Their meddling with the pre-programmed dark matter-dark energy mix is what *might* have set off the Failsafe, and the virtual critters."

# Astrocity Sagan

"Maybe you're right," Ruth began as she stepped toward the fusion current. "Because of me, everything's falling apart...because of *me*!" She had silvery tears in her eyes and was wiping them away with her glowing transparent hands.

"We don't' know everything's your fault, Ruth!" Janice screamed. "I don't want you believing that!"

"Still, I *know* I can make the creatures stop appearing if I'm in another form, especially since the Seal element is activating in the Cloud. I can seal them off inside the main matrix in case *you* can't locate the creator of the Failsafe. I'm a patch!" She patted her body. "I'll be the glue that'll make the Seal program functional."

"Stop Ruth!" Asa called.

The light was becoming so bright and blinding, Elisa had to cover her eyes as Janice grabbed his shirt, yanking him away from his wife. "Dr. Stein, if you try to stop her, the magnetic containment field will slip out of cycle, yank you inside, and rip you to shreds."

"Go back, Asa!" Ruth shouted, now almost blending entirely with the white-hot fusion current at the center of The Archives. Gold flakes were falling all around her—transforming her into optic impulses. "I can't have you with me when people need you here, and on Nelta." She blew him a kiss. "My darling, I love you. I always will."

# J.P. Osterman

## Chapter 33 – Within the Confines

He fell to the ground on his knees, pleading with her. "Ruth— we can find The Regents. Thornton *will* change is mind, especially if he sees you're dying."

"No he won't, Regent Stein," Elisa corrected, knowing him, "because Thornton Manning has changed. He's no longer the person I once knew at all. He tried to kill me three days ago."

"I can't imagine why though, and I wasn't there at the time, but here with Ruth. But I'm sorry, and I assure you I'll do whatever I can to get at the bottom of what happened to you," Asa said, backing away from his wife with tears in his eyes.

Elisa suddenly had a realization. "If I don't do something quick, Ruth's consciousness will be gone!" After Asa encouraged her to proceed, Janice flicked on her wrist device, and her Native American Indian avatar synched with the matrix. "Yes! I believe we can at least save Ruth's mind!" Elisa told the avatar: "Activate my regeneration hub at Station 14. Initialize a direct connection to your Storage Grid. I need a mind upload for Regent Ruth Stein, *now*."

"Access denied, Dr. Holton," Terra said.

"Damn!" Elisa watched as Ruth Stein took another step into the fusion reaction, now whipping her into a froth of nanytes. For almost a century, her consciousness had been contained within an organic hologram that Asa had managed to maintain within a special experimental mix. Not anymore.

"When I disperse into Terra's Cloud matrix on Level-7," Ruth began, "I'll seal off the program the light-based invaders have been using to access The Archives and Regeneration technology. That should stop them from manifesting and attacking people. But I can't stop the Failsafe. Only the person who is creating the entities can stop it."

Janice had located a hacking equation to circumvent Terra's access protocol. She appeared angrier than ever. "You've done something...all of you Regents. Elisa and I want to know what you've done because none of this should have happened in the first place! I picked up a Neltan warning on an electromagnetic fractal, right here, in The Archives." She gestured at the terminal responsible for the restructuring of their walls still modifying and changing. "This Failsafe is getting worse and our time is running out before Sagan leaves spacefold propulsion and stalls in dead space...where we all die."

Ruth had almost entirely dispersed into fluttering nanytes that were twirling toward the powerful fusion reactor. "Elisa, Janice—" Her words were cutting off. "Try...the Matter Stream on Nelta...locate—" Only an outline of her arms were left, and her lips moving on an invisible face. "I love you, Asa! Remember me!"

Asa activated his avatar. It immediately uploaded into the fusion reaction and formed a pathway of shining gold flakes over which Asa could walk to join her. "I'm teleporting into the matrix with you!"

"Dr. Stein—stop," Elisa called. "We can upstream Ruth's mind into a grid, and later on, figure out a way to bring her back. If you do things *your* way, you'll be with her, but you'll be stranded and trapped inside the vast expanse!"

As Ruth faded into the giant column of plasma that dispersed her body into sparkling lifting nanytes, Asa jumped onto the gold pathway leading toward her disseminated body.

"Proceed with Upstream, Dr. Asa Stein," a giant Terra hub announced.

Elisa and Janice watched his body morph into a gold light, and then his atoms teleported into the matrix.

Janice wiped her eyes and pressed down her blouse. "What a way those two have been living. They tried one experiment after another to solve their problems and have a normal life. Nothing worked. They've only been living life to manipulating life. What kind of existence is that?!" Her eyes shone a weary gleam. "Everything we've been through today makes me want to be with my family."

"What a waste for them for sure," Elisa began, "but I hope not a waste for the rest of us. Let's see." With the fusion reaction calm, a new matrix grid open, and the Action Countdown stopped because of Ruth's success at sealing off the light-based entities on Level-7, she found a way to link her wrist device with Janice's; and the guide map of Level-9 materialized. Pathways and corridors had changed because the walls and partitions continued to alter. The Failsafe had not stopped, and the countdown was still very much alive at 02:05. "We're running low on time!"

Janice was searching wildly for something. "I know, and I'm trying to locate the creator of all the chaos." She then discovered a circular terminal network, and began activating renderings of various Archival and Hardware systems. "One thing was certain...and still is certain," she chuckled, "they sure love each other." She paused, tears welling in her eyes, and Elisa walked over to help her as more terminals lit up in a fifty-foot-wide spoke network all around them. They were in a maze of transparent monitors, and under hundreds of processor hubs linking with vital sections throughout *Sagan*. "I love my husband and I know he loves me," Janice continued, "but the kind of love those two have?" She breathed, enamored. "*Whew*—I've never even *seen* that."

Suddenly, a rendering of Terra's Cloud site on Level-7 materialized alongside Elisa. The three hundred, bright-white reactors processing the quantum-computing site were all displaying normal readings.

"We've got a communications breakthrough! A real, matrix Hail Mary—yes!" Janice announced in exhilaration. "Ruth *did* succeed in sealing off the light-based invaders. We have a chance of surviving!" She turned serious. "Now, we need to find the creator of the chaos and stop the Failsafe."

"Did Asa Stein leave any message?" Elisa began watching a rendering of his disappearance. "You mentioned an alarm from Navigation, and he said he had access to Navigation, the seat of the Living Breath that's guiding *Sagan* to Nelta."

Janice hit the station when a new emergency alert launched, blaring the Failsafe countdown: *02:00*. "Damn secrets! *That's* what they've been keeping down here...secrets. People should know everything about this place, and the Core place somewhere beneath us. And if you ever remember what happened to you, you can enlighten people as to what's going on with the Regents and what they're doing, or conducting, on this ship."

Elisa felt surging anger. "You bet. We *both* can do something!"

Suddenly, images from around the astrocity began displaying on all the monitors and in renderings around them. The maze was lighting up in a multi-tiered, multi-layered networking zone. The creaking walls and partitions stopped and settled, and a few nanytes clouds struck a Terra hub high in the domed ceiling. The air where Ruth and Asa last stood was still smoking, and the circle in the distance where the fusion reaction teleported Ruth to the Cloud matrix, now dark and lonely.

But with the unraveled matrix, everyone from Enforcers to scientists could now communicate, and Dirk Hunter could broadcast to the population. Terra released the Level-9 lock down, and the Transport Crew in charge of Maglev functioning promised to rescue The Regents in fifteen minutes.

However, there is a new problem. *273* protesters had captured one of the Regent's Maglevs and were blocking all entrances into Level-9.

"Asa *did* leave something behind!" Janice said suddenly after an icon of Elisa's Regeneration Station 14 appeared inside her new program, also still working to lock onto the creator's location. "Asa succeeded in linking your station to the matrix grid that's holding impulses of peoples' minds. In just a few minutes, the illegal Mind Meddling technology will reverse and start downloading impulses back into peoples' rightful minds."

Elisa felt relief like a balm over her body. "That's great!" Then she gestured helplessly at her left arm. "Except for me."

"Why?" Janice then appeared to know the answer. "Oh, yeah."

"My abilities, that's why," she answered. "Everyone will return to normal, but I still won't remember much of what happened in those three days…except that Regents Manning, Itonovich, and Jenkens wanted me dead…jerks!"

Janice exhaled in disgust. "Well, when we receive the indication that the matrix will begin down-streaming peoples' minds, those three will have some explaining to do when we face the residents and accuse The Regents of conducting illegal activities and attempted murder!"

Then a rendering of Ruth's disappearance popped out of a string of renderings as if begging for attention. Elisa walked over to it and waved for Janice. "Look at this." She slid the rendering of Ruth's disappearance over to Janice for close perusal. "Her words though are being cut off by all the fusion noises."

Janice focused in on her lips, trying to read them. "She's implying that the answers to the Creator have something to do with Nelta." She called on a hologram showing the surface of Nelta. Enlarging a portion of green terrain, she zeroed in on a blinking spot. "Look! This *must* have come straight from Navigation—"

"From the Breath Entity, wow," Elisa said, suddenly noticing a strange ache and glow beneath the skin on her left arm. She didn't want to tell Janice about it though until she knew what was happening with the Neltan biology.

"I see someone—or something…" With her tiny avatar pointing and trying to zero-in and enlarge the bright spot, Janice added: "I'm initiating a terrain profile that should get us an exact latitude and longitude. But I—"

"But *what*, Dr. Kiplin?"

Turning around, they saw Thornton Manning standing in the sliding doorway in the distance. He was like a glowing black knight against the automated cleaning agents, robotics, and dark-and-light mazes of transparent monitors. Janice dropped her wrist device, stopping her scan of Nelta. Behind Thornton appeared two more Regents dressed in disguises.

"We have questions, Sir," Janice said as she slid behind Elisa a bit.

"I've got this covered, Janice," Elisa said firmly, her jaw clenching. "Regent Manning, we've seemed to resolve quite a few problems…but we and the population will need explanations as to what's been going on down here. Full disclosure, Sir."

"Yes, it's one of our *Guidelines for Living*," Janice agreed. She showed him several captioning imagers. "People are seeing everything that's going on in here right now, Sir." She coughed and drank some water as if she might never see another bottle of it again. Then Regent Steven Jenkens appeared alongside Thornton and they began whispering.

Thornton stepped forward, his face appearing evil red in the light. He had the same Beethoven facial features and his six-foot tall body was straight with authority. "Doctor Holton—"

"Sir, we've known each another since First Communication Day, so you can call me Elisa, that is, if you aren't going to arrest me." She folded her arms and parted her legs, her move to show him up.

"I want to know why you people wanted to kill her!" Janice

demanded, her hands shaking. The mazes of processing light were still producing holograms of people around Sagan. As their minds received the lost impulses from the Mind Meddling technology, more holograms appeared. "Healing is going on around here," Janice began, "but if we can't locate the creator of all this chaos, the Failsafe will kill us, Sir. Any ideas how to do that…to find the person responsible for the light-based entities?"

Thornton suddenly had an expression of intense pain on his face, and he gasped and grimaced as he patted his temples and moaned in anguish. Steven Jenkens dropped to the floor, groaning in agony. Their avatars activated, ordering emergency interventions.

As medics arrived to assist them and avatars began displaying their biometric-scan results, Janice whispered to Elisa: "Seems like they're regaining pieces of their minds as well. Maybe you were right, Elisa, when you told me how much he's changed. Maybe this is why. Their own illegal Mind Meddling technology backfired on 'em all, and only now are they being restored. They haven't been themselves all along."

"I don't know," Elisa said, feeling leery. "I guess we have to wait and see what happens 'cause we have more Regents arriving soon…and Enforcers and Matrix Techs."

The Archives was now fully powered up and at 85% of its normal processing, also buffering all renderings. Fifteen Matrix Techs and Engineers greeted them, synched with Janice's innovative programs and began working to restore the rest of the astrocity and locate the Creator.

"They're trying to find a permanent fix to what Asa and Ruth began," Janice said. "And they haven't said it yet," she smiled, "but we're heroes."

From what they gleaned from Dirk Hunter's live-streaming broadcast, the Regents were gradually dribbling back to their posts on Levels 1 and 9 after having spent the past few hours incognito and avoiding the destroyed invaders. An announcer suddenly appeared in The Archives, calling Regent Jenkens to the LSF facility to work on the time-ticking bomb Failsafe.

Thornton approached Elisa and Janice warily as an android medic administered him a patch of analgesic. His eyes were gray circles, his face white shock. He appeared to be waking up after years of a deep sleep. "Look, ladies, we have some intense work we have to accomplish right now, and big problems to fix—" He almost fell back but then steadied himself on a terminal. Then he looked with amazement at Elisa as if recognizing an old friend. "Elisa? Elisa Holton?" His thin Beethoven-like lips stretched into a happy grin. "My God—what are you—" He reached to touch her, but she pulled away. He had a stupefied expression and appeared lost as he glanced around at everyone working frantically in front of monitors and wildly communicating with avatars. "Where have I—" He appeared dissociated from reality, and the android scanned his head and then gave him a quick shot of medication. He was accepting of its intervention.

A brief memory of him welled up in her. Three days ago, he was mean, cold, stern, and inhumane. She thought, no way then would he let any *machine* touch him. Now, he *appears* so different.

"I think I did something to you...did I?" He closed his eyes, obviously straining to remember. "What's going on around here? What the hell has happened?!"

"You mean you don't know?" Janice scoffed.

Elisa stepped back, remembering his murdering face. "Sir, you had some pretty bad technology running rampant down here...on your *private* working level. And it filtered up to the entire population it seems."

"She's right, Sir," Janice said. "Your *illegal* Cognitive monitoring system—"

"That I call Mind Meddling technology," Elisa interrupted.

"*You* installed at some point, without our approval, and it's affected not only the population, but also all of *you*...you Regents." She waved him over to a station displaying a red hub inside Archway 1 at Level-3's Center Transport Station.

"It's blinking red 'cause it's off now," Elisa began, "and it'll be off for good, Sir, 'cause it's illegal…completely *illegal*."

After a pause wherein he turned red in the face, Janice explained: "Asa Stein managed to reverse the Mind Meddling technology by linking *this* Archive facility to several Regeneration stations. The stations are now down-streaming impulses *back* into people's minds. Now everyone should be healing…and remembering things they've forgotten."

"In other words, they'll be back to their own selves, and whole," Elisa added. She wanted to say, *except for me*, but she held it back. She wasn't going to give him information about her abilities. He might use them against her and for him. *I don't care how innocent he's acting. I don't believe a word he says*!

Appearing embarrassed, he lowered his gaze to the floor. "Oh." He splashed water on his sweat-filled face and kept repeating, "oh," and, "oh no."

"And like I said, Sir, all the residents are being informed about the technology," Janice said.

Elisa's felt a warning growl sounding off in hungry stomach, and she turned to Janice. "I don't trust him. I also want to hear his explanation to everyone, and an apology."

"Stopping the Failsafe takes priority though, or we won't *live* long enough for him to apologize," Janice said, motioning at the time stamp flashing on at the bases of all the holographic stages, monitors, and wall processors: the time: 20:15 and 08:15 p.m. The Failsafe 02:01, and ticking down.

Elisa wondered about EJ. The matrix was streaming impulses back into peoples' minds, but what about EJ? All the light-based creatures were gone, and those trapped "souls" in the matrix now free, but what about EJ? She looked high into Level-9's dome illuminating stars and Earth's half-cracked up moon. There's no EJ, and no strange large blue bird chirping.

# Astrocity Sagan

## Chapter 34 – The Return

Suddenly, a group of engineers and scientists rushed past them. They were shouting algorithms and jettisoning miniature avatars that linked with the Live Stream Field. Ruth Stein's disseminated body inside the matrix was buffering the grids responsible for producing the destructive light-based entities. The frenzied technicians were programming a permanent solution that could utilize Ruth and Asa's impulses to track and counter any future assault on *Sagan*. From their findings at Navigation, Terra had completely incorporated Asa and Ruth into the matrix, and now they transformed into irretrievable and subatomic impulses. Throughout The Archives, wavering holograms were zapping, hissing, and droning as techs and scientists worked to stabilize Navigation. As they input a code to try an experiment to stop the Failsafe, light dispersed into colors as if a prism program launched—another attempt to locate the Creator.

Elisa felt disappointed about the news. "Well, I don't see *anyone* bringing back the Steins."

An archival image of them materialized over Janice, and she touched the orange glow. "They sure loved each other, but now they're gone—*uhhh*," she sighed in a depressed expression.

# J.P. Osterman

Elisa didn't like seeing her so hopeless. "We have to remember them as being an example...and tell people the story of their ultimate sacrifice for us." She poked Janice jokingly with her elbow. "Just like you love your husband, right?" She waved her hand through a slant of blue light and watched the color disperse on its way to Navigation. "Someday, I hope to love someone at least half as much as they love each other."

"You will," Janice said.

"I don't know," said Elisa.

Navigation engineers were arriving from Level-1 to re-schedule *Expedition-1* to Nelta and help stop the Failsafe, now at 01:52. When Thornton finished consulting with them, he turned around to resume his conversation with Elisa and Janice.

Up close, Elisa could now get a deep view of his intense brown eyes. The left one looked particularly odd, and she shook with fright, careening into Janice as she noticed the tiny light gray crescent shape. Heterochromia! He had to have just undergone a Regeneration procedure. Looking closer into the dark-brown pools of his eyes, she saw anger, and all around him, a curtain of mystery. She knew his explosive and devious side, with a potential to kill. As Janice began questioning him about a Core level somewhere under them, and showing him evidence of the level on her wrist device, Elisa stood close to her. Janice could now be in danger! She had to change the subject and divert him away from his intense focus on her. "Regent Manning, you should have received several messages we sent you about this place...actually messages from Asa Stein."

"Oh? *What* messages?" he asked.

As Janice again sent them to his wrist device, Elisa noticed her bloodshot eyes and brown wispy hair, the latter static-filled from Terra's shots of pulsing electricity high above them—streaming code and formulae to Navigation in an attempt to locate the Creator and stop the Failsafe. In spite of her apparent fatigue from deviating off her routine as a statistician and programmer, and coming face-to-face with the several surprise encounters, she also looked vibrant. After all, she did manage hack a top-secret Terra grid and discover a destructive Neltan symbol that every expert technician now appeared to be working with to solve their dire situation. Janice definitely had unearthed her second wind, and looked ripe for another investigative journey. "Regent Manning, I linked you to coordinates at the Navigation Site. You'll find those useful in locating a Neltan fractal that's skipping through the matrix, trying to by-pass the Stein's Seal patch. Someone must have altered the pre-programmed software that you and the Neltan scientist, Shaesar, agreed to prior to leaving Earth.

He turned away and began talking quietly to his avatar. Then he looked up quickly and said, "Even though we were sliding through renderings to avoid detection, several Regents *did* receive all the messages you sent, Janice, and we're using the programs you invented right now. I have *every* Navigation Tech and specialty engineer trying to resolve the Failsafe. Thus far, we're stumped." He sighed and his thin lips turned down in frustration. "We can't isolate the Neltan fractal that appears to be the Failsafe. It's linking to the propulsion turrets powering *Sagan*." Manning flicked his wrist, showing them Propulsion. "In less than an hour, this astrocity will explode if we cannot delete the Neltan fractal." His tiny avatar disappeared into the matrix ether.

As Elisa fanned through each message they had sent throughout their ordeal on Level-9, something didn't feel right, and her left arm ached. Each time Thornton looked at her, she broke out in goose bumps as she tried hard to recall her lost memories. She couldn't, but she knew what he was capable of, and she had to protect Janice. They had seen so much of Level-9. No doubt The Regents would discuss what Janice and she had witnessed, and they might conspire to erase all trace of Janice's experiences, especially those of Asa and Ruth Stein, themselves an illegal experiment!

She isn't a threat though. She has her abilities, which they

# J.P. Osterman

have to be cognizant of by now. But then they'd also have to know she is impervious to any mind-altering program they might try and throw at her. Furthermore, soon, she'd be on the next expedition to Nelta. But now, she began worrying about Janice. The Regents have plenty of space *and* technology. Even when people demand The Regents dismantle everything illegal, they could still send down a Mind Meddling pulse to erase Janice's mind. She thought, I'll make the erasure extremely difficult, but how? She had a solution! She'd make the events they had experienced important and indelible renderings, and available to the *entire* population, right now.

Quickly, she called on Twin. She remembered asking Twin to link with Janice's avatar, and then to record everything they experienced throughout Level-9. "Process everything for full participation, except for our encounter with the Steins...oh, and that Grim Reaper entity...but include the Forming Woman who was trying to merge everyone's trapped thought impulses into a human being. Now that oughta shock the residents into filing charges against the Regency!" Quickly, she transmitted their location to Janice's home grid, where the Kiplin's' avatar greeter answered, "Dr. Doug Kiplin is busy fixing dinner, Dr. Holton."

"Never mind dinner, this is important! Get Dr. Doug Kiplin right now," she ordered. "I didn't have much time." Janice was busy discussing the details of her fractal discovery, and Thornton was giving orders to several Enforcers to freeze the fractal so they could isolate it once-and-for-all and locate the creator.

When Janice's husband appeared over her wrist device with his hands fully mitted up to his elbows, Elisa whispered: "Hurry, Doug. Drop everything and come to the Level-9 Regent entrance now!" That was the place she had disembarked at three days ago...but then her memory stalled. She showed him her surroundings, particularly of Janice, Thornton, and all the scurrying experts. The more faces she could record for a future rendering, the more safety she could procure for Janice, especially if the entire population would store it should something terrible happen to Janice or her family.

"Who are you?" he asked as a small boy popped his head into conversation.

"It's the other candidate for the next expedition to Nelta," the little boy answered. "She was standing by Mommy before that giant creature kidnapping those people."

"Please," Elisa began, "please listen. I don't have a lot of time!"

Even though she had never met Janice's husband, she had to come across to him as a friend and someone he could trust. "Doug, bring your children. Send the coordinates of *this* location to *Sagan*'s Home Page so as many people can meet you there too, with a big celebration, 'cause Janice is a hero." Janice's little boy gasped in excitement as Doug blinked in disbelief. Elisa continued as fast as her lips could move: "I just know Dirk Hunter will want to interview Janice and all of you when you reunite. So get down here now." She also send her location to Dirk Hunter, showing him Janice, and saying the words: "A hero saved us all, Dirk, so come to the Level-9 Entrance, meet Dr. Janice Kiplin and her family, and get the interview of a lifetime!" She closed the message to Dirk.

"Is she alright? Is she hurt?" Doug asked. "I've been worried sick. I've been tryin' to call—"

"She's fine," Elisa interrupted while looking back over her shoulder at Thornton. The second he'd notice her, she'd have to stop communicating with Doug. She did notice a Regent Maglev dock at their level, and she overheard Thornton ordering crews to rendezvous there.

A little girl peeked up into their conversation, obviously Janice's daughter. "My mom's a hero, huh?"

Nodding yes, Elisa said, "I just overheard Regent Manning order a special Maglev for Level-9. It's a private ride for media and scientists. If you go there, right now, and tell

# J.P. Osterman

the Terra conductor you're Janice's family, I'll make sure I secure you seats." She saw the time of the Maglev's departure next to the Failsafe countdown, the latter unknown to the crew for fear of mass chaos and bedlam. "It leaves your station in ten minutes.

Slapping on his Terra wrist device, Doug grabbed a jacket and said: "Thanks, Dr. Holton. Tell Janice we're on our way!"

She directed her message to transmit to Dirk Hunter. If Janice's family were to materialize suddenly *Sagan*-wide, Thornton couldn't possibly erase any of her memories and eliminate evidence because proof of everything was now with everyone, and everywhere! Janice would be safe while she would be on Nelta.

Suddenly, a message flashed over her wrist device: *Received and Stored.*

"Received and stored what?" Elisa whispered into it.

"You're in a Dea-h Tr-p! Watch—"

The garbled transmission stopped.

"What?" Elisa exclaimed. Homing in on a Pod icon from her Station 14 that Asa had reconfigured, she opened an encrypted message. Someone had hacked into that grid and intercepted her message to Janice's husband. The Regeneration-Pod icon was radiating green. *Someone outside the matrix and the Regents' influence is watching everything...and warning me!* She thought hard while keeping one eye on Thornton and his experts still working to disable the Failsafe. Who could they be? She could come to only one conclusion: *They* must be referring to those missing scientists and people like Jean Trent and Beatrice McDuff Bentley. According to Ernie, her husband, the man she met after waking up from her stupor— and more information Janice had discovered—Beatrice is a botanist who was about to release her results on research she had been conducting on plants and the Matter Stream sample Shaesar sent to Earth. Manning had told everyone that sample was completely gone, dispersed into the solar wind after it healed Earth's ozone. Something wasn't right. Obviously, he had kept some small portion of the vital force!

# Astrocity Sagan

According to what she was viewing, other prominent scientists, astrophysicists, engineers, and programmers were missing as well...kidnapped by the nanyte invaders. And Enforcers were having no luck in zeroing on their locations and apprehending the protesters. Secretly and slyly, the protesters were succeeding in outwitting Enforcers and kidnapping scientists into the transport tunnel. Then the icon transcribed the last words of the message: *Death Trap! We're working for a solution!*

It's a warning from *273*! She glanced around. The message hadn't appeared to anyone else. Thornton was still hunting *273* down, but she knew the protesters were trying to save *Sagan* and the residents. She sent a message of response—one that she knew would land her in front of a judge. She also copied the message to piggy back on Janice's Home Page icon. In the future, Janice might be the only one to help her if something terrible should happen to her—like disappearing on *Expedition-1*. She had no solid proof, but she believed without a shadow of a doubt that Thornton and his other seven colleagues were up to no good. "Nelta, all the answers are on Nelta," she whispered firmly.

# J.P. Osterman

## Chapter 35 – The Summons

Thornton Manning was conversing with several Enforcers who were asking him when they should secure Level-9 for Regent use only. Too many people were inside—so unusual with all their experiments everywhere.

As Elisa stared at him, trying to eavesdrop on his conversations while also focusing on Janice's explanation for how biologicals had fused with nanytes, light, and the matrix and then morphed into the light-based entities; she felt cold anxiety flow through her. All the commotion had triggered a flood of memories, but she didn't want the lost moments coming at her right now—right in front of the powerful leaders who could prevent her from joining the team of *Expedition-1*. As of yet, she had no idea of their identity. All she knew was that she had to be on that Expedition. Every ounce of her Neltan-human biology was drawing her to Nelta as well as the message from *273*.

Staring at Thornton's back while fending off her encroaching memories, she felt a whirlwind of terror as she observed him interacting with everyone, from Enforcers to his private Clone Techs. He had a harsh of doling out orders; and his loud voice made people immediately agree with him, cower, or leave. *Intimidating!* People were leaving his presence shaking or doe-eyed as if scolded or humiliated. She was feeling lost, except for her abilities that were powering up and energizing her to tear into him for trying to kill her.

Her pent up energy flowed out of her, igniting a spark and pop in a processor hub in the distance—her powers retaliating against him. At some point, she remembered walking extremely close to him, so close she could feel his hot breath on her face. He was angry and pointing to a sign that read: Level-10. She felt sick, gasped for air, and more processor hubs sparked in the distance like Tesla coils.

Janice left the clinging scientists and grabbed the cuff on Elisa's sleeve. "What's wrong? You see another invader? You look terrified! And I know what your abilities look like when they're set off. They interact with all the technology like your directing a fireworks display!" She handed her water. "Here, drink this; water seems to calm you down. And be sure to remember that when I'm not with you. And also try to eat…oh, and breathe deeply…that seems to help you too and—"

"*Shhh*…yes, Mother," Elisa chided as she drank then and bobbed up for breath. Her fingers felt numb and cold. She couldn't feel her toes.

"You're sweating! Something's wrong. I'm getting you outta here." Janice pulled her to the side of the hallway.

"No—we need to stay," Elisa countered, touching her aching temples. Her head was throbbing, but she inhale, and the ache stopped. "Just give me a second. I've got to think…to put things together…scenes, faces, feelings."

"You're remembering something. What?" Janice asked.

"A time, but not a place and why," she replied, hitting a terminal. It cracked in the wake of her powers and several techs raced over to investigate. She and Janice walked away and quickly escaped their discovery. "If I could *only* think of more…could only put everything together!"

Janice pulled her farther away from people. "Elisa, you're

not ready at all for *any* expedition to Nelta—not at all." She waved her to a medical niche containing a scanner. "I know a doctor—"

"No." Elisa sipped more water. "I've got to stay here, Janice. I *have* to go to Nelta."

"No way! You're powers appear uncontrollable...and the closer *Sagan*'s approach, the more you're affected." She had a stern sad expression. "You won't have me there, and who knows *what'll* happen, Elisa...and the others who will be accompanying you, that is, if we make it out of this Failsafe." The countdown blasted: 01:30. "You want to take chances you might get killed?"

"I have to be on the expedition, Janice!" She began to feel composed again as the fog of helplessness faded. "Asa said that everything I need to know I can find on Nelta. This place is a death trap for me."

"Death trap?" Janice questioned.

"Yes, death trap. I received a message," she began in a whisper with engineers and white-coated matrix techs working around them in a furry. "I have to leave here or people might lose their lives. It's a gut feeling I have. The planet's like a magnet's to me." She threw the empty water bottle into a chute.

"Maybe it is *Neltan* magnetism of some sort. You seem to be filled with it, because of your special biology." Then Janice had an expression of intense alarm. "But I don't believe you're physically *and* emotionally ready to go though, especially with people you don't know, and a job these Regents haven't told you about. Something's wrong—not right—especially since Thornton Manning hasn't acknowledged he tried to kill you and apologize." With a burrowing concern showing in her deep brown eyes, she added, "We've been able to see a few illegal activities here on their private Level-9, but I'm sure they have other technology they're hiding." She flicked on her tiny Native-American avatar that began hovering over her wrist device—the black line on its shoes flashing: *Verbal Mode*.

"I want to see the Regents' Code, the one mandating full

disclosure to everyone, please."

After her avatar made a 360° spin, it announced, "I found Law-1, Amendment 14."

"Please search, *disclosure*, Mini," Janice said.

Mini spun around quickly, and below her feet appeared the following edit in writing:

*In all decision-making processes, strategies, and interpretations; The Regency shall fully disclose to all residents any and all processes, strategies, interpretations, judgments, and decisions The Regency herewith decrees within its operational parameters.*

Janice flicked Mini twice to Hold-mode and whispered: "That's the law, Elisa. You just saw it. The Regents aren't *at all* abiding by it. I haven't seen *one* iota of information about the expedition they're sending you on. And what you showed me in the Live Stream Field facility, the landing site appears to have altered from Verba to Tractum." She shook her head no. "That's so wrong, isn't it? Isn't the landing site supposed to be the Welcome Archway at Tractum?"

"Yes, it is," Elisa replied, her body suddenly energizing. "We're supposed to greet Shaesar at Tractum."

"Well, we're not," Janice said. "The Regents are spacefolding a reconnaissance team there first, the one you're on. Why the recon? What's the purpose of *Expedition-1*? No way could the Neltans have agreed to a recon mission 'cause they're still in stasis for the next five and a half weeks! Well?"

Elisa bit her lip in confusion. Janice was right. "I don't know…maybe to survey the effects of the Matter Stream that healed Nelta?"

Janice turned to see an incoming message to the eight Regents. "It's a summons! Good. The Court of Law just ordered Thornton and his colleagues to appear before a magistrate in two days and plead their cause for the illegal use of the Mind Meddling technology. "Now they'll have to answer for what they've done, and disclose anything else they're keeping secret."

# J.P. Osterman

Elisa realized another truth. "But they can only disclose what's been discovered." She knew from the little memories she had that Thornton had other secrets, and too much empty space around Level-9. Something half empty needs filling.

Janice asked: "I'd like to know how they're managing to activate another wormhole and send a shuttle to Nelta if they don't disclose their propulsion method and show how the mission lines up with *The Pact*."

"Good questions," Elisa replied.

"This is bad, Elisa. If I were one of the chosen ones for the expedition—which I was but not anymore—I'd want answers, right after we stop this Failsafe, which I believe we're close to deactivating."

"*Hmmm*, you're right, but if I'm called as a witness—"

"Which I'm sure you *will* be, Elisa—"

"I'll still have to make a case to launch *Expedition-1*." Elisa copied Janice's concern to her outdated wrist device. "I'm sending the message of our concerns through my Station 14. I'll receive it at my Kiosk unit. That's also the place you can find me during the next few days, after we stop this Failsafe and make things right around *Sagan*." She made sure Janice had her Kiosk number and new communications' grid. "You can get in touch with me through this grid if you ever find yourself in a bind and need me to help you and your family. We're friends now." She gave her a quick hug, and memories trickled through her in a flow of sentimentality.

"Thanks, Elisa," Janice said. "You can count on me too."

Suddenly, Elisa's wrist device stopped sending and paused. She flicked her wrist several times, trying to fix the glitch.

## Chapter 36 – Navigation

"What's wrong? A quantum-stream interruption?" Janice asked, moving her avatar Mini to interface with Elisa's bulky wrist device.

"I believe someone intercepted what I sent you," Elisa replied, glancing around at the busy people who weren't looking back at them.

"Intercepted by whom?" Then a low musical chord resounded on Janice's device, and she called open the corresponding code that had helped them disperse the Forming Being in the LSF facility. "This musical chord is two octaves below C Major. The code indicates location." Then a high-C chord resonated. Everyone stopped and turned to look at her as holograms of ship-wide images continued blasting and changing in The Archives. After Janice apologized, they returned to their hunt for the Creator of the light-based entities.

Elisa had a sudden memory from when The Regents' Maglev launched. "I think the low chord represents the 273 protest group that's hiding in the transport tunnels." She told Janice she believed they were helping people, not terrorize them. "The group can't be the Creator."

# J.P. Osterman

"So what could the high-C chord be?" Janice asked, gesturing at Thornton still busily engaged with matrix techs, Enforcers, and engineers. She showed Elisa the musical note, unraveling another code over her wrist device. Elisa touched her left finger into the rendering and then quickly pulled back when Matrix Techs began noticing the code, and then approached Janice to peruse it. She also permitted them to use her Code program to interface with their programs to resolve the location of the Neltan fractal. That would give them the Creator and stop the Failsafe.

Just then, a male Regent, Regent Pervis, ran out of a white lab as sparks began popping out behind him. "Thornton!" he cried, his skinny arms waving as if frightened by a hungry light-based Dracula. "The Neltan fractal is multiplying! Scrubbers can't stop the virus!"

The high-C chord resounded in a high-pitch sound that could crack glass, and everyone covered their aching ears.

Janice's guiding map that they had used for the last several hours, suddenly illuminated Nelta, and a small light at the center of the planet. She shouted: "The fractal *is* transmitting from the surface!"

"And linking with *Sagan's* Navigation," Elisa said, showing Thornton the high and low notes interfacing in quantum-perfection. "This is *way* beyond our understanding, Sir…light and waves separating and being easily manipulated. This is a Neltan interference…and has been a Neltan interference all along!"

As people gasped, Janice whispered to her, "Elisa, you touched those two musical chords before they merged with the matrix. You *actually* affected the Neltan fractal. And because of you, they *might* be able to solve the Failsafe—wow."

Commotion and terror began spreading through The Archives. "Why would the Neltans interfere with *Sagan* though?" people asked.

"Yeah, they need us!"

"And we need *them* to return to Earth with a fix for the moon!"

# Astrocity Sagan

"They shouldn't want to stop us?"

Regent Pervis with his squinting eyes was panicking. "If we all die in this Failsafe, we can't return to Earth! Can't fix the moon! Can't—"

A medical disc rammed him and shot him with a dose of tranquilizers. The Regent scientist collapsed into the arms of two Enforcers who lifted him onto a gurney and slid him out the exit.

Regent Itonovich exclaimed in her Russian accent: "We have an impulse that's tracking the fractal Failsafe toward propulsion. But in forty-five minutes, it will morph into an explosion and shut down propulsion." The Failsafe ticked down another time: 01:45. "Oh my!" She began shouting reconnaissance and repair orders to one of the fission-fusion zones at the stern of Level-4.

Thornton said to Elisa and Janice: "Let's get to Zone-55. We don't have much time." His dark intense eyes were fully focusing on Elisa. "You resolved the two codes, Elisa, so with your special abilities, you might be able to stop the fractal when it surfaces in propulsion."

After a fast L-car ride back to the transport station through places that had been destroyed but now repaired, Elisa suddenly spotted Janice's husband and children in a crowd at the station. "There's your husband Doug; and your kids are with him, Janice," she exclaimed, feeling relieved when she saw Doug notice Janice and wave to her. As Thornton approached Dirk Hunter for a quick interview, a memory welled, and a tremble rushed through her. She noticed the location of all the exits. If they'd stop the Failsafe and live, she'd have to return to Level-9 for training for Expedition-1. She had overheard Thornton rescheduled the expedition for next week. But down here without a friend, she might need to make a quick escape, or do some investigating. Level-9 was still one giant mystery, as well as the covert Level-10 Janice had discovered.

"Doug!" Janice had tears in her eyes. "And Lucy and

Marcus are with him. But how?"

Sliding up to Janice, Elisa whispered, "I told them to come."

"You did? You're amazing!" Janice hugged her.

"*Shhh*," Elisa said. "Just keep looking at them and the shuttle. I want you outta here."

"Okay, but why?"

"Never mind, just go, and don't look back. Bye, Janice." Elisa stretched out her left arm, and Twin appeared.

"You got it working—great," Janice said shocked.

"Yep, and I'm recording your entire reunion." Twin's eyes lit up green. "I'm sending it to your home grid. And the recording will spread around *Sagan*." She whispered into Janice's ear. "You should be safe now. Go." She stepped back.

Janice reached out to hug her goodbye but caught air. "Thanks Elisa. I won't forget anything we've been through—"

"Better not—"

"Never," Janice said, wiping away tears.

Elisa spotted Dirk Hunter finishing his interview with Thornton Manning. Dirk had his entire projection crew with him, capturing everything and guaranteeing one of *Sagan*'s best programs ever! In spite of Thornton's order allowing Janice's family to enter Level-9, Regents Pervis and Itonovich had Doug and the children barricaded behind a team of Enforcers who had a long line of waist-high, yellow laser lights that if crossed, would activate as stinging jail bars. The Regents had initiated a powerful line of defense against any intruder trying to infiltrate their Level-9.

Janice threw Elisa her wrist device. It had all the programs she had spliced together throughout their journey through the corridors, Life Stream Field, and Archives. The wrist device began blaring red in her grasp. "The program activated!" she shouted to Elisa. "Use my passcode! I believe I—found— light entities…"

Her words were gibberish over the commotion of the crowds, but Elisa realized she had life in the palms of her hands: three codes all embedded in images, the Neltan language and musical notes. Quickly, she waved bye to her, rushed to Thornton's side, and whipped on Janice's wrist device. "Sir, I've discovered a solution! We have to return to the Live Stream Field facility. I'll know what to do then."

He had an astounded expression as he left Dirk Hunter, glanced at her flaring wrist device, and waved her back into the idling L-car. "What solution, Elisa?"

She hopped in the L-car, and he pushed the car to full speed with sirens whirring. Scientists jumped out of their way, androids broke apart in their wake, and robotics shattered as he floored the car to the LSF. "What's the solution, Elisa?"

When several robotics appeared stalled in their path, she stretched out her left arm, and a power invisible current flowed from her arm and exploded the robotics. "Janice's device has several programs, everything from electromagnetic-activating apps to frequency apps, to musical apps." She explained to him the various programs Janice had either composed or spliced together using Neltan-specific software, and code they had gleaned throughout their encounters with light-based entities and the Being who had formed using light-based waves, the matrix, and biogenetics. "Sir, they're all coming together in this program I have on my wrist right now...and when the programs merge, they *will* give us the Creator. We just need to follow the instructions inside the guide map that's been evolving ever since Janice and I began adding code to it."

At the Live Stream Field, engineers were dashing around in confusion and turmoil: "We're gonna blow up!" "We're about to become drifters in space!" "We'll never find home!" "I can't find a solution!"

The LSF was experiencing the same normal function as when Janice and she and had left, except the containment field was growing—destined to expand throughout *Sagan* in, *01:30*. Around the perimeter of the LSF were hologram platforms, towering transparent monitors, virtual renderings over terminals, frequency signatures, and processing icons. The Cloud facility had long ago interfaced with the LSF, and the light-based beings were being fended off by Asa and Ruth Stein, but the Neltan fractal was preventing any change to occur in the Failsafe.

Elisa hopped on top of the main hologram stage next to the entryway to the LSF. Closing her eyes, she remembered Janice's words: "Elisa, you're Neltan biology is enabling you to interface with the light-based beings."

She thought: with these programs and my biology, what if I can direct the trapped creatures to trace the Neltan fractal and stop the Creator? The Failsafe should stop!

Thornton was holding back Enforcers who had targeted Elisa, trying to take her down. "No, she can stop the Failsafe! Let her alone," he ordered.

Everyone backed away as she stretched out her arms toward the column of white-hot power. Code flowed down from all the ceiling processors, appearing in bright yellow lines around the pulsing tower of quantum-computing energy powering *Sagan*. The two wrist devices were blending code.

She shouted, "Where is the Creator of the Failsafe?"

A giant fractal appeared at the center of the white-hot LSF, and then *Sagan* materialized inside the LSF, with all its blueprints and designs.

Thousands-and-thousands of images of *Sagan*, from its conception to its current location in the wormhole appeared at the center of the white-hot LSF. At the bow of the astrocity, a flashing red light illuminated.

"It's Navigation!" someone shouted.

"That's the location of Navigation at Level-1!" another acknowledged.

In the center of the *Sagan* collage, another image illuminated with a date: *January 21, 3060, Real Time; Monday, January 21, 2166, Space-Fold Time.*

"This is two years ago…to the exact date," Elisa said, dropping her arms.

"It's the wrong trajectory!" several techs from Navigation

# Astrocity Sagan

yelled.

She felt dizzy, and someone cautiously helped her steady herself while handing her a bottle of water. "It shows an alternative spacefold course and landing site." Again, she stretched her arms and power flowed out of her, into the LSF then into Navigation.

"If we can get Sagan back on course, the Failsafe will stop," Thornton said.

She was working hard to put *Sagan* back on trajectory and re-align it with the intricate details pointing at Tractum, Nelta. "I'd like to know how Sagan got off course, Sir," she said, brushing sweat of her forehead.

Gradually, *Sagan*'s faulty trajectory corrected. "Someone altered the course. That means someone changed *The Pact*," she shouted.

"Who?" people asked.

"The Regents! That's who," several replied. Enforcers surrounded Thornton and the other seven Regents.

"I have no memory of enacting such a change," he said sternly. "I am innocent…as are my colleagues." The Enforcers backed away from him, obviously fearful of his authority and power.

When the trajectory stabilized, and a giant breath exhaled out of the LSF. The white-hot column of energy stabilized, and the yellow trails of code streaked back into the processor hubs.

Elisa unclasped the devices around her wrists. All the while, everyone appeared awestruck—from Matrix Techs to Enforcers, from engineers to medical personnel. "Wow, that was some demonstration, everybody, huh?" she laughed, not wanting them afraid of her. But she knew at that moment the power working inside of her. No longer could she or anyone else deny it. And the wrist devices? They had the power to destroy an eleven-mile-high, twenty-four-mile-wide astrocity. She couldn't keep them. And there was no way she'd hand them over to Thornton, and Enforcer, a matrix tech, or a judge! Believing they were creation power, she threw them as hard as she could into the Live Stream Field. When it received it, the LSF exhaled again—its powerful Living Breath permeating *everyone's* body on *Sagan*.

After seconds, she spotted Ernie Bentley. He was a Navigation specialist, and the one who first met her after she awoke from her stupor. Wiping tears, he waved to her and exclaimed: "The original trajectory to Nelta is resumed! The Failsafe is disarmed!"

In heaves of relief, people applauded and screamed for joy as they began streaming the news throughout the astrocity, planning parties, and celebrating. In one giant flood, the matrix dispersed the news into every grid. The date and time would turn into a yearly holiday on *Sagan*, and for humanity on Nelta.

Elisa stepped down from the platform. She felt fatigued, her strength zapped. She approached Thornton and the other Regents who had dismal expressions, especially Steve Jenkens. He looked his Jackie Gleason dour self. Standing in their shadows, she saw Enforcers ready to apprehend them. They were waiting for word from the Courts of Law. But Elisa no longer felt intimidated, although she still would demand an explanation for what happened to her, when the time was right.

"Elisa," Thornton began after he stepped toward her out of the circle of confinement. "Who *was* the Creator of the light-based entities?" People stopped to listen to her answer, their silence and avatars stilling in suspense.

"The Creator is *Sagan* itself, Regent Manning," she replied. "This place." She tapped the floor with her shoe. "Our astrocity."

He and his seven Regents appeared astounded. "We have *no* idea how this diversion from *The Pact* happened…or why…or who altered the course to Nelta," Thornton said adamantly, rubbing his temples as if fending off a piercing ache.

# Astrocity Sagan

Ernie Bentley left a terminal in the distance and ran down to her. He was panting, his eyes showing urgency and excitement. "Elisa, I received a message from Dr. Walker." He panted, catching his breath."

"Slow down, Ernie, what's wrong?" Elisa motioned for someone to give him some water, but he declined, his eyes showing secrecy.

"You know EJ?" he whispered.

"Yes, I haven't seen her for hours though…as a huge bird…but I've been looking for her everywhere."

"Well, then," Ernie began, "look at this!"

Elisa felt as if Time momentarily stopped. "Okay…"

Quickly, he hailed Dr. Walker over his wrist device, and Walker appeared from inside his quarters. There were transparent monitors in circles behind him, with avatars conversing. Way in the back, in a corner, someone was huddled down. Walker's pale-white photo-phobic face shone a shocked expression. "Elisa, I have EJ, here."

"What?" Elisa gasped.

"She's here," he began as Ernie swept Elisa off to the side where she could speak to them both without interference. "Right after the Failsafe ended and the Living Breath released its destructive code, I found a naked woman standing at the center of an eatery."

"He said she walked right up to him and began repeating her name…EJ," Ernie interjected.

"But that's all she knows," Walker added, "nothing more, not even where she's been, but just her name, EJ." He glanced back at her. She was huddled in a corner, looking at her hands and fingers as if she'd just been born.

Ernie said, "She looks like she needs to go back to school though!" He quickly answered a question someone else from Navigation had asked him. "I have to go, Elisa, 'cause I'm searching for Beatrice." Now he appeared elated. "Everyone says they're changing and remembering things they've forgotten. I just know that any second, I'm gonna find Beatrice!"

EJ...EJ—wow! Elisa said excitedly. "Walker, just keep her there until we can talk later." He had a look of fright and ignorance. "Just feed her...and give her water. She must be thirsty."

"I gave her my clone test, Elisa," Walker whispered. "She's a clone. Any idea who cloned her?"

She shrugged. "No."

"But so what," Ernie laughed. "No one needs to know but the three of us." He looked eager to quite the call.

"Just take care of her for a bit until we figure out what to do," Elisa said. "I'll be there later, Walker, but for now, just show her around, feed her, and take her places."

Walker laughed. "First, I gotta find her some clothes!" Then their three-way call extinguished.

Elisa felt tears well in her eyes. "Ernie...EJ's okay. She's going to need some intense help, but she's back. Yes!"

"That's great, Elisa," Ernie said, walking away. "I'll let you know if I find Beatrice. I'm still searching with a special program...one your friend Janice sent me." It was the Visual Comparison program Janice had developed with top-secret Level-9 software. She was supposed to turn it into The Regents, or somebody important. Elisa didn't have the heart to ask for it back and then deleted. On Nelta, she might need all the help she can get! Then Ernie returned to a group of colleagues needing more codes for input into Navigation.

When she returned to Thornton Manning, he had a contrite expression on his face and appeared shaken. I've never seen him *this* way before, she thought, not even on Earth, except maybe after Lynn died. Then, Thornton ordered his team of Matrix Techs to re-check Navigation and the Living Breath entity propelling *Sagan* to Nelta. But he couldn't fully, because ultimately, the programming was Neltan. "Still, I *will* discover who hacked Navigation and nearly killed us all," he told everyone.

A rendering of a panel of judges suddenly materialized in

front of Thornton and the other Regents. It was a summons from the Court of Law. With LSF area still settling back to normal, the techs, engineers, and medical personnel stopped what they were doing to hear Judge Harrell and her Court of Law request the Regency to defend themselves against a Charge of Attempted Murder and conspiracy. Judge Harrell said: "Appear at Level-1, Room 1, on January 23 at 09:00, Executive Regent Manning, Second-in-Command Regent Steven Jenkens, Regent Sylvia Itonovich…." Judge Harrell—a short woman with short brown hair, ocean blue eyes, and intelligent posture—finished pronouncing the names of the other seven Regents and their dates of service.

Thornton didn't appear fazed as Judge Harrell confined them to their quarters at the bow of Level-1 until she and her judicial board would release them after hearing their cases.

Quickly, Thornton responded by requesting one last word with The Regency's private Clone Techs. Then he said to Judge Harrell: "Your Honor, I have been just as negatively impacted as everyone else. We too are recovering from what happened. I need time to gather my things…research and training programs from The Archives for which we've been writing code and developing software since leaving Earth. I can't defend myself without collecting these items to prove our innocence."

I knew it, Elisa thought. "He's gonna play innocent and ignorant and plead not guilty! But he's guilty as hell."

Thornton's avatar attorney appeared next to him. "Honorable Judge Harrell, Executive Regent Manning and his colleagues are being illegally searched. You have no evidence to prove treason and murder. The Regency has spent almost one hundred years safeguarding *Sagan* and protecting the population. Is this the thanks they receive? If they intended to murder people, those people would have died long ago." The attorney continued expounding on *273*—the missing crew members. He was implicating *them* because Enforcers couldn't locate.

Judge Harrell agreed to give him and the Regents five hours to assemble the necessary proof that Thornton claimed would exonerate them, and to gather all their Level-9 personal belongings.

Elisa wanted to intervene and accuse him, in front of *everyone*, that he had tried to kill her, but she still didn't have proof. The grid that had stored everyone's thought impulses was now empty. And Terra-IV was restored when the Failsafe deactivated, thus deactivating Demon Terra. Standard Terra was already giving the population a full report on her matrix, including the status of every individual's personal grid.

As she watched Thornton prepare to gather his things, a message from him appeared over a wrist device someone had given her since her outdated one had been absorbed by the Living Breath. The message appeared as a little Beethoven icon—his avatar. "Dr. Holton, please accept my apology. I have no memory of what you say I did to you—" He coughed in an expression of bottled up emotion. "I hope the residents of *Sagan* will accept my explanation for what happened and return the Regency back to duty. I will call you as soon as we reschedule Expedition-1. Goodbye, Elisa, and I will see you in two days for the hearing." He was gone.

But not her fuming emotions!

She thought: I still have so many questions. I know I saw a Level-10, at least I believe I remember a Level-10, and there's too much empty space down here on Level-9.

Level-9's imagers were showing those previous empty spaces as housing propulsion equipment, fission/fusion machines, bioenvironmental technology, and robotics manufacturing centers. *They weren't there before. I saw emptiness even though Janice couldn't.*

The Regents passed through several Enforcers who were holding people back from questioning them at the transport station. A large L-car had arrived and its doors slid open. With lines of reporters and their devices trying to question The Regents, the eight people dashed inside the car, and it prepared

# Astrocity Sagan

for departure. The car was taking them deep inside Level-9 where they'd be holed up for at least four hours, extracting technology.

Still at the transport station and interviewing Enforcers assigned by Judge Harrell to gather more evidence, Dirk Hunter had taken center stage. He had his skinny avatar standing beside him, but Dirk had changed into a nice black suit, white shirt and tie. He still looked like a Master of Ceremonies, but he appeared changed: less dramatic, not so impulsive with his expressions, and not so aggrandizing. He appeared personable, and Elisa felt like she'd like to meet him.

Then again, people all around her appeared to be coming out of their shells, greeting one another but still shocked as they began talking to their families and discussing experiences they had forgotten but now were remembering. I wish I could remember what happened to me during the past three days, she thought. She couldn't. Are my memories gone permanently?

Dirk Hunter began speaking:

"Everyone on our astrocity has been damaged and affected by the actions of our Regents. The light-based invaders are gone, and *Sagan*'s Failsafe stopped, thanks to Dr. Elisa Holton and Dr. Janice Kiplin—" People began clapping, and Elisa ducked behind inside a kiosk niche. Now, she'd be recognized where ever she'd go. Dirk continued:

"But we're in shock as well as recovery. Everyone is in a deep state of mourning and questioning." He was pacing down the long stage with reporters, investigators and other personnel lined up in front of him. "Saganites, use your personal avatars and Terra-derived therapists to get some counseling as we move through our hurt and anger. Remember, we have only five weeks until we arrive at Nelta. And we need to be whole and back to ourselves when we meet the Neltans."

He explained more about the crux of their heightened

anger: an unapproved intrusion into peoples' minds. "Prior to accepting our positions here, we agreed to Cognitive Behavioral Relief and Repair intervention." The program was installed in inconspicuous archways. "Those CBRR programs were designed to detect criminal impulses and motivate people to seek help. But the Mind Meddling technology Elisa Holton discovered went *way* beyond detection to illegal intrusion and extraction: changing our thoughts and thus changing our personalities. We were victims!" The crowd roared in anger, but Dirk settled people down. "The Regents and a software twin of Terra inside the matrix became judge and jury of what thought were safe and what thoughts could wreak havoc on our journey to Nelta. They perfected their method of meddling with our minds during Regeneration, when our minds are uploaded into the matrix."

People screamed, "How?" and, "We should Mind Meddle with their thoughts now!"

"Some impulses in the form of memories were *not* returned, however," Dirk continued, "but lived on inside the matrix. Navigation and The Living Breath tried several ways to inform us about the deviation from *The Pact*." He showed images of several light-based beings, the Forming Entity in the LSF, and EJ. Elisa noticed her right away and became teary-eyed. But EJ was okay now. At least she believed EJ would be okay.

Dirk's avatar talked this time:

"They tried to use those impulses to create an entity, whose purpose was to tell us about the off-course trajectory." An image enlarged of the Forming Entity dissolving into the Live Stream Field. The crowd gasped in horror. "Deviating from *The Pact* we signed with Ambassador Shaesar is as good as murdering people...humans *and* Neltans...and we *must* discover who made such an illegal change that might have killed us all!"

Just then, she saw a summons appeared over her new wrist device. Judge Harrell and her board were requesting her appearance as a witness at The Regents' hearing.

She wondered: why would The Regents do such a thing in

the first place?  What could they possibly hope to gain by diverting *Sagan* from Tractum to the southernmost point on Nelta, Verba?

In two days, hopefully, she'd find out.

# J.P. Osterman

## Chapter 37 – Kiosk 193, Home

When she arrived home at Area 64, Kiosk 193 on Level-6, she lie down, staring at the LED shiny ceiling with a beehive processor hum lightly droning. She re-activated Twin, and began downloading some of her camera information in preparation to leave *Sagan*. Then she had an idea, and she launched another program to record every step of her future.

"*Everything* from this point on will be from my point of view. I want no mistakes, so these cameras shadowing me—" She patted two buttons on her blouse. "Will capture everything I do, who I talk to, and what I touch, They'll immediately stream everything to my personal grid for instant processing, photo-shopping, and rendering."

Even though she was living in a new place and Thornton Manning couldn't touch her, she couldn't trust anyone who might come to her sliding door. Sighing while eating grapes and cheese that Ernie Bentley had given her yesterday, she ordered a rendering of a Pacific Ocean sunset, and the time flashed briefly under the virtual setting sun: 10:45 p.m.

"I can't believe what I've been through, what I've become, and how people now see me," she said. "Am I a freak of nature now? Or do I have some type of permanent, Neltan nanyte infection? I feel so alienated, so alone. People are avoiding me, sending their avatars to stalk Twin, or charging me with loads of questions. Gosh, I'm never gonna be the same after today around here!" She threw a shriveled grape into a little sparkling eddy—really her sink. *Ker-plunk*. "Hopefully, when we revive those scientists from the Neltan Scientific Committee, one of them might have a solution as to how to change me back to my normal human self!"

As she thought of Janice, she could hear seagulls and people laughing at a shore-side bar with white clouds drifting over a bright full moon. "I wonder what's going on with her. I have to tell her about *Expedition-1*. But I *really* want to make sure she's okay, and find out if she's been summoned to appear before the Court of Law too." She swallowed another grape and asked the replicator to generate a hamburger with special sauce and a glass of milk.

In *standard* form, Janice materialized in a rendering next to her. She had her family with her in the background, and they were inside a large L-car on Level-2 bound for the Main Rec Center. Dirk Hunter and celebrating spectators were with her. "Elisa," Jane said, "this is turning out to be some lasting party."

"I see," Elisa said, not envious at all. "You can have all that!" she laughed, drinking some water.

"Good, continue drinking water, 'cause it helps you, like we talked about," Janice whispered adjusting her small round neck device, testing its level of connectivity to Elisa's processors.

"Will do," Elisa said, feeling finally safe, and then yawning. The next two days would go by fast, and she'd be in court, once again facing Thornton. A light anxiety made her twitch.

"From what Dirk is telling me, I'm going to be in the public eye for the next few weeks, and busy helping him preparing virtual tours of where you and I have been—"

Dirk thrust his face in front of Janice. "And game show renderings too, Dr. Holton." He had an inquisitive expression. "May I call you, Elisa? Because soon, you might be a Regent."

"What?!" Elisa exclaimed, sitting down, shutting off her comfortable beach rendering. His request sounded like Walkers when he had asked her on a date. *No way*! "No, you can't call me Elisa, but what did you say after that?" She rubbed her ear, making sure wax hadn't distorted that last word.

"Oh yeah," Janice exhaled and cleared her throat. "I forgot to tell you."

"Yeess," Elisa said hesitantly.

Janice fanned him away. "Dirk, I should tell her the news." He shuffled away.

"Okay, out with it, Janice."

She huffed and began: "Well, everyone knows about your special abilities now."

"Yeah I know. I've been ditching avatars and having Twin divert thousands of grid messages," Elisa replied. "Being famous sucks, and trying to get some privacy stinks!"

"Well get used to it," Janice continued, "because you saved people, and now they want you to be a Regent…maybe even replace Thornton Manning if Judge Harrell and her judicial panel find him guilty."

"Wow," Elisa exclaimed, but then she snickered at the idea. "He'll find a way to wheedle out of what he's done…as will the rest of them."

"Ha!" Janice scoffed. "Even if they do, the Regency is down two Regents. They need replacements, and people are nominating you." She showed her several virtual banners in a small station they just pulled up in. "I don't have much time, 'cause we have to meet some more people, but I'll be campaigning for you!" she said, giving her the thumbs up.

"No! Don't you do that, Janice. I don't want a Regency job—"

"Just think about it for a while," Janice said, moving back toward her husband. He waved to Elisa, and she returned his greeting.

"Janice…" Elisa grimaced.

# Astrocity Sagan

"Just think about being a Regent," Janice said. "People need you, Elisa. And who knows what we might encounter on Nelta."

Dirk Hunter jumped inside their communication. "You and Janice are heroes, Dr. Holton, *Sagan* heroes."

Then he gasped and stopped moving. "Wait!" A dire expression appeared on his face as if he had spotted a tornado in the little transport station. "I'm receiving some important news!"

People inside their L-car stopped to listen.

"Elisa, call on *Sagan*'s Homepage," Janice said, looking at the page now showing over her wrist device.

Dirk Hunter had a rendering in front of him. Scientists at Navigation were monitoring a large glow emanating at several terminals, and impulses spreading into a towering station connecting to the matrix.

Dirk said: "Technicians there are receiving some intense communications. They're signals, from Nelta, being directed into Navigation." After another pause with the technicians yelling in celebration, Dirk cried, "It's another Update—whew!"

Ernie Bentley was among them, and he told Dirk: "This will take a day to translate, but according to what we're receiving, big changes are about to occur as we approach Nelta."

Elisa jumped into the conversation. "Like what, Ernie?"

"An evolution in our matrix, *that's* what," Ernie said, scratching a bald spot next to his Mohawk haircut.

"Just like your abilities keep strengthening, Elisa," Janice whispered to her. Then she perked up with a look of intrigue. "Wow—this is the first time I'm hearing about *any* type of evolution in quantum-matrix processing. I thought such feat was impossible."

"So did I, but it's coming…and it's gonna be big, Dr. Kiplin," Ernie said.

# J.P. Osterman

Janice's husband and children were next to her as well as she exclaimed, "I've gotta get to work immediately." She began initiating several programs over her new wrist device, and the rim began glowing, the same colors as those emanating from the special hardware at Navigation. "I need to run tests...and figure out how I'm going to calculate...right now!" Janice's husband had an expression of resignation on his face and told her to make sure she kept on her shimmering necklace with its special strings of beads. Then she hugged him, kissed him on the lips, and then quickly kissed her children goodbye. "I'll never take them off, Doug, and I love ya...and I'll be home in a little bit!" She ran up to the Terra conductor. "Bring me another L-car, please. I have to get down to where I work, at the Math and Science Center on Level-8 right now!" She turned to a dejected Dirk Hunter and several people who appeared disappointed at her change of plans. "I'll keep you posted you all, bye!" She turned to Elisa before severing their rendering. "Call you later, pal, or should I say, Regent Elisa Holton," she giggled, and then quickly disembarked from the L-car.

Elisa continued to watch Dirk Hunter broadcast the news to the population. "You're hearing the evolution that's been taking place with Terra's matrix firsthand, folks," he began, "and Dr. Janice Kiplin is one of the pioneers who usher us all into a new era as we fulfill our *Pact* with the Neltans. And remember, you still have time to make the big decision. Will you return to Earth after we find a way to save the moon? Or will you stay on Nelta and join a human colony on their new world?"

Dirk Hunter kept talking, but she took him off Transmit-mode so she could only see him. Meanwhile, she noticed a mild ache in her left arm. An intense energy began pulsing through her as a wave of foreign images encroached into consciousness. "I'm not sure what I'm envisioning," she said into her green-lit cameras as she plopped down at her little kitchenette, "but I believe I'm actually seeing the future...or a possible future!" She saw herself, on Nelta. "It's me, and I'm stepping on black dirt…and there's a tall man with straight black hair walking toward me. Now he's calling me! Above him I see the giant Welcome Archway, and behind it, the Matter Stream…but the Matter Stream doesn't look the same, and the ground is beginning to quake!" She began coughing and then choking, until she managed to grab a bottle of water and gulp some down. "The man is Ambassador Shaesar…but I'm unable to take his hand. What the hell is happening on Nelta? Is this *bad* reality occurring right now?!" The vision ended.

She inhaled through a ripple of fright, and then guzzled down some more water. "It's like he's trying to communicate with me. But why? But I can't do anything to help anyone there until I can land there on Expedition-1."

The food replicator beeped. Her late dinner was ready, but her tongue felt dry and cottony, until a steady calmness settled her heartbeat. "Nelta," she said, remembering her special ability that had entered her through the Encantado device, really AI-nanyte entities that were modifying her mind and body. "Okay, but *you* gotta make it happen, whoever or whatever you are communicating with me inside my head, because right now, unless The Regents are exonerated, *Expedition-1* appears *highly* unlikely."

She felt a line of beads Janice had stuck into her hand before they parted ways on Level-9. The yellow beads were warm, defusing the numbness in the fingertips of her left hand. "Hope for the future is what Janice said these things will bring me. But whether I want to even *consider* being a Regent? Well, I just don't know. I'll have to give the job some deep thought, but only *after* I find out what's happening with *Expedition-1*."

### ###

# J.P. Osterman

## *Sagan*'s Specifications

**Level-1**:   At the end-most stern, there are several Garden Centers.  At center stern are the Courts of Law and Mediation Facilities.  Various religious centers are at the center of Level-1, followed by the Ceremonial Platform that has a skylight view to the outside spacefolding contrails.  After the Ceremonials Platform is The Regent's living quarters, and at the very bow is a mile-wide Navigation center.  It has special hardware that looks like bees' eyes on the hulls of the astrocity.  It's the seat of the Living Breath guiding the astrocity to Nelta.

**Level-2**:   At the stern are smart Living Cubes.  At the center is the Main Rec area where residents have the giant Lanikai Beach.  At the bow are more living cubes.  This is where Elisa's initial home is located: Living Cube Area 1, Unit 202B.

**Level-3**:   Again at the stern are living beehive cubes.  At the center is located the Arts Facilities and Children's Learning Complex.  Next to them is the Education Center; and at the bow, a large Food Manufacturing Center where workers manufacture food for residents' food replicators.

**Level-4**:   At the stern is the Engine room—Sagan's propulsion center.  At the center of Level-4 is a five-mile wide Medical Facility.  Right next to the Medical Facility is the Genetic Vault containing the DNA of all species on Earth.  At the bow, is another small Regent meeting area.

**Level-5**:   At the stern are located 20 Regeneration Corridors.  Elisa's station is 14, inside Regeneration Corridor-15.  At the center of Level-5 is the Clone Tech Center.  At the Bow are The Regents Clone Technicians and the site of Clone technology.

**Level-6**:   At the stern are quarters, and special locations where representatives from 196 world-wide countries have kiosks and booths representing their prospective countries on Earth.  This is where Elisa's secret developing unit is located: Area 64, Kiosk 193.   At the core of Level-6 are the

# Astrocity Sagan

Performance Centers where people attend cultural events and instructors offer dance, art, writing, and rendering lessons. At the bow are renderings of the Wonders of Earth—everything from the Grand Canyon to the Great Wall of China. People pour into this area to experience renderings of Earth.

**Level-7**: At the stern is *Sagan*'s Engine Room, and right next to the Engine Room is Terra's Cloud Matrix. At the heart of Level-7 are all the manufacturing centers and the Recycle Center. At the bow is the Jail and Rehabilitation Center, actually a miniature city. *237* members dispersed throughout the astrocity from here.

**Level-8**: At the stern is the Sports and Fitness Center. There are parks, tracks, and exercise equipment. At the core of Level-8 are the atriums, agricultural grounds, and grazing zones where plant life and animal life abound. At the bow is the Math and Science Center linked directly to Navigation. This is where Janice Kiplin works as a statistician.

**Level-9**: This is The Regents' private Tech Center. At the bow is their little Conference Area where they virtually greet residents who have scheduled appointments. At the very bow is a small Enforcer facility where officers train. Throughout the remainder of this level are experiments, Neltan-based technology, and AI robotics. At the center lies the Live Stream Field.

**Level-10**: Only hints of this level appear to Janice Kiplin and Elisa Holton. However, this is the area where Thornton Manning kidnaps Elisa and up-streams her consciousness to the matrix.

**Transport Stations**: There are three, gravitational tunnel passageways where Maglevs ascend and descend to the various levels. There is a stern, central, and bow transport platform for every level. Running north-and-south and east-and-west on every level are moving walkways. High up, Enforcers monitor all the traffic and congestion, and anti-gravitational L-cars follow directional sky lanes displaying colorfully lined grids to

# J.P. Osterman

transport residents to the ascending and descending Maglev stations.

***Sagan*'s shape**: Builders at *Space Station I* constructed the astrocity following blueprints from Nelta. New nano-materials at the time formed the hull. *Sagan* is comprised of nine levels, each one mile high. It is twenty-four miles in diameter, making it elliptical. From their homes on Earth, most people claimed the giant "space city" reminded them of the Island of Oahu. However, as the astrocity spacefolds through wormholes, the outside hull changes. The alteration is called, the Viscous effect, as gravity acts as oil in a water-type wormhole spaceflight.

# Astrocity Sagan

## ABOUT THE AUTHOR

**J.P. Osterman** born December 21, in East Chicago, Indiana.

**Writing Career:** As a futurist and serious Science Fiction author focused on future space travel, J.P. Osterman became an Independent Research Scientist studying the laws that govern space and issues relating to space travel, exploration, and colonization of Mars and exoplanets. In addition to the physics of long distance space travel, J.P. studied the necessary computational theories necessary to control of the physics of space travel and extreme time-space compression; optical quantum computing, quantum communication, and AI Computer intelligence reaching well beyond the "Singularity" with organic quantum level human neural interface and exchange.

J.P. Osterman was a reader and writer throughout her youth. She graduated from University of San Diego with a B.A. in English (with an emphasis in writing) and later a Master's degree from Azusa Pacific University. In the early 1990s, she met Ray Bradbury who inspired her to write science fiction. "I felt that something strange and wonderful had happened to me because of my encounter with Mr. Bradbury. He gave me a future...I began to write every day."

She has written eight novels: from exploring Mars, to spacefolding to an ancient alien world. She has won several awards, including the prestigious Rupert Hughes Award at the seminal Maui Writers Conference for her sci-fi novel, *The Matter Stream*. She won First Place for her play, *The Man Next to Me* which was published in the *San Diego Writer's* magazine.

# J.P. Osterman

**Website:** Discover these other titles by J.P. Osterman at:

Amazon.com or http://www.jposterman.com

Other Books by J.P. Osterman:

*First Communication* and *Battlefield Matrix* (Books I & II in the Nelta Series), *Cosmic Rift, Dimension Mind, The Screaming Stone, Pete's Crossroad,* and *Corporate Revenge.*

Books in the Works:  Book IV in the Nelta Series and *The Commuter Collection,* a collective work of short stories, plays and poems.